## BROTHERS IN ARMS

Below the surface of the Persian Gulf, Drew Murdock fought for control of the Trident super-submarine *Alaska* in a savage struggle of nerves, wits, and strength against the fanatically brilliant and physically giant terrorist who had taken command of the craft.

On the surface, Drew's brother, Coy Murdock, fought his own hatred of the sea as he captained the one ship that could sound the depths of the *Alaska's* underwater lair—to avenge his father's death and save his brother's life.

And around both of them, chilling ripples of intrigue and treachery spread from the dark side of the Kremlin to a shocking core of corruption in the Pentagon itself. . . .

# NEPTUNE'S LANCE

# NEPTUNE'S LANCE

## Stephen K. Forbes

A SIGNET BOOK

SIGNET
Published by the Penguin Group
Penguin Books USA Inc., 375 Hudson Street,
New York, New York 10014, U.S.A.
Penguin Books Ltd, 27 Wrights Lane,
London W8 5TZ, England
Penguin Books Australia Ltd, Ringwood,
Victoria, Australia
Penguin Books Canada Ltd, 10 Alcorn Avenue,
Toronto, Ontario, Canada M4V 3B2
Penguin Books (N.Z.) Ltd, 182-190 Wairau Road,
Auckland 10, New Zealand

Penguin Books Ltd, Registered Offices:
Harmondsworth, Middlesex, England

First published by Signet,
an imprint of New American Library,
a division of Penguin Books USA Inc.

First Printing, February, 1992
10  9  8  7  6  5  4  3  2  1

Ⓢ    REGISTERED TRADEMARK—MARCA REGISTRADA

Printed in the United States of America

PUBLISHER'S NOTE
This is a work of fiction. Names, characters, places, and incidents either are
the product of the author's imagination or are used fictitiously, and any
resemblance to actual persons, living or dead, events, or locales is entirely
coincidental.

To George Thomas Forbes
Father and Friend

PART 1

# PART I

# SUBMISS

The submarine surfaced like a bloated corpse, huge and black and stinking of death.

Her towering sail appeared first, then the dive planes. Before the sea had washed off the colossal bulk of her main deck, a hatch crashed open in the cockpit bridge atop the sail and two men scrambled out.

Sickness and disease belched out of the hatch with them.

The two men exchanged the foul stuff in their lungs for fresh air. They listened to the waves slapping the sides of their vessel. They tried to sense hope in the blue sky and sea.

It was no good. The smell impregnated their clothes. They could no more stop breathing it in than they could close their ears to the screams of the dying that now echoed only in their minds.

The officer of the deck glassed the southern horizon, swinging his binoculars in methodical steps of about five degrees, pausing at each position before moving on. At the end of each swing he raised the glasses another ten degrees off the horizon and scanned back again. Beside him, the first lieutenant was performing a similar procedure off to the north.

"There's our spotter," said the lieutenant, pointing to an E-2 Hawkeye (Airborne Early Warning) aircraft circling overhead on a wide radius. A twenty-four-foot, saucer-like radome rotating above its fuselage made the turboprop plane impossible to mistake. Less obvious was the array of cameras slung under its belly.

The OOD stopped scanning long enough to enter this in the log. "They must be wondering what happened to us," he observed without humor.

The intercom squawked: "Bridge, radar room; we have a blip bearing wun-three-zero."

The first lieutenant activated the talk switch. "Bridge, aye-aye."

"There it is," said the OOD. "Five . . . six miles off the starboard quarter, position angle twenty degrees."

The first lieutenant aimed his glasses in the direction indicated, while the OOD recorded this sighting too.

"Right. I confirm that as an SH-3 Sea King."

There was no hint of elation in either officer's voice. The medical helicopter meant salvation. But too many of the submarine's crew already had died; too many more were feared dead.

The OOD leaned toward the intercom. "Control room, bridge; about five minutes to touchdown, I suggest you have the deck crew stand by."

"Control room, aye-aye."

Before long the escape hatch below and forward of the sail came open, and six sailors wearing life vests climbed out onto the vast bow of the submarine.

The Sea King thundered overhead, settled close aboard into the lee water off the submarine's port beam, and almost immediately began disgorging cargo. Two bundles hit the sea, automatically inflated, and became rafts. Then came the passengers. They wore coveralls of bright orange plastic tied at the wrists and ankles, orange gloves and boots. Orange masks, connected by hoses to air equipment on their chests, covered their heads, except for small squares of clear plastic in front of their faces. They moved into the rafts until there were six men in each. Paddles were handed down, then black bags which contained their equipment.

As they started paddling across to the submarine the sub's deck crew tossed lines, and in seconds they had hauled both rafts aboard. The twelve orange figures clambered onto the deck.

The first to embark was half again as wide as, and a head taller than the others.

Something about these strangers dispelled any flickers of cheer. Part of this was due to their quarantine suits. Instead of inspiring confidence, the suits only underscored the vulnerability of the crew, who had no protection against the plague that had swept through their ship.

But it was more than just that. The dozen figures moved with cold precision, more like robots than men.

None of them had waved to the helicopter crewmen before rowing away, and now, as they gathered on the submarine's forward deck, they offered no greetings to the sailors who helped them aboard. They moved straight to the escape hatch.

Meanwhile the Sea King hammered at the surface until it lifted, then it flew back over the submarine.

The first lieutenant on the bridge threw up a hand to the pilot in a kind of salute. For that moment, he turned his eyes away from the men below on the deck. At the same moment the OOD was entering a note in his log. He wasn't watching them either.

Only a few of the sailors wondered why the members of the medical team were opening their equipment bags topside instead of waiting until they went below. Too late, one or two might have seen what equipment had come out of the bags.

Then the helicopter exploded.

A bright fist scorched their faces. It was a roundhouse blow that somehow blackened their eyes and boxed their ears at the same time. Blazing sea air flooded into their lungs.

Flames and hot metal rained onto the deck. Two of the

crewmen were blown over the side. The other four joined them moments later, their bodies riddled by bullets.

The OOD had thrown himself below the bridge coaming and now started crawling toward the intercom.

The lieutenant had remained on his feet. Something banged at the deck officer's consciousness: an air hammer hitting the sail. And then the lieutenant was gone.

Pulling himself up, the OOD reached for the intercom. He was half-blind and half-deaf, but an innate sense warned him to turn.

A huge orange-hooded head was glaring at him from over the coaming. One of the boarders had climbed the ladder to the bridge. There was an automatic weapon in the orange giant's hand.

The deck officer whirled to the intercom. He pushed the talk switch.

Hammering blows hurled him back off his feet. He felt as much as heard them, burning into his chest and stomach.

And then he stopped feeling.

The stink of death gathered around him stronger than ever. But he didn't smell it.

The dying screams in his mind cried out again louder even than before.

But he and his men had stopped hearing.

# Chapter One

The sunken hulk cried out in pain.

In the utter silence and near absolute darkness of one thousand feet below the surface, Glen Murdock heard the cry clearly and froze. It was a ghastly wail, a ghostly lament from the thirty crewmen who had gone with the *Batavia* to the bottom—their bodies had been consumed by the ocean depths, but their spirits had become an enduring part of the wreck.

Murdock ignited his flashlight. A murky beam of yellow light lanced outward not ten feet in front of his face mask before striking the crusted curve of steel plating.

The freighter had all but buried herself in a ravine. Only the rounded rump of her stern, bulging up from the sea floor like some massive tombstone, marked her grave. Drone cameras had spotted the stern ten days before. The drones, unmanned submarine sleds with remote controls, lights, video cameras, side-scan and bottom-profiling sonar, were towed four abreast from a surface ship by cables three miles long. They could search for months on end without tiring, without requiring a single breath of air or so much as a moment of decompression. But they could not reach out to the rusted hull as Murdock was doing. They could not feel for the lives that had been lost. Nor could the drones marvel at their good fortune in finding the *Batavia* amidst this rugged bottom in the north Hawaiian waters, where she had lain hidden from treasure hunters for more than a decade.

His light played over the faded lettering on the stern: B-A-T-A-V-I-A. Fortune, he thought, plus a lot of hard work and a good hunch, had paid off.

Murdock dove into the ravine. He followed the line of the vessel and the chilling cries until he came to a gaping hole in the ship's starboard bow just below her waterline. The beam of his flashlight explored the opening.

From this giant maw the cry rose again. Louder this time. More hellish a scream than before.

Glen Murdock didn't hesitate. Time was too precious for that. He kicked his fins and propelled himself into the hole.

Murdock knew that while the sea—particularly the deep sea—is extraordinarily quiet, its victims never are. Iron or wood, the relentless compression of the wreckage strains at every beam and plate. Added to this is the speed sound travels through water—four times that of air, which makes the wails seem to come from nowhere and everywhere at once.

More important to him now, he knew every foot of the *Batavia*'s design. He swam unerringly up vertical corridors, along ladderways lying level to the sea, and past cabins pitched onto their forward bulkheads. One by one he searched the holds. In the midships hold, the most secure on the ship, his flashlight revealed a crude heap of crates and boxes. They had been strapped down to prevent shifting even in typhoon conditions. No one had been prepared, however, for the freighter to lift her stern into the sky and dive by the bows through a hundred and seventy fathoms. Few of the crates had broken, and this said much for their original construction. Now they were inexorably approaching the limits of unrecoverable decay. They were blanketed by sea dust. They were covered by marine moss, barnacles, coral, and anemone. But below this zoological abundance was rot. The ocean would be longer consuming the cargo than it had the crew, but eventually this too would be consumed.

His stainless-steel knife tore through the planks of a wooden crate. The rusted metal screws yielded to his heavy blade. Soaked newspaper dissolved in his hands. Beneath this wrapping, bright coruscations of twenty-four-carat gold reflected against the glass of his face mask.

In all, the case contained a dozen golden goblets of intricately carved Middle Eastern designs. Emeralds and rubies were set into the bases and stems.

The cargo was here. And intact.

A king's ransom. At any rate a fortune, and a monarch's fortune at that, since a shah, by definition, is a monarch. The diver replaced eleven of the goblets. The twelfth he dropped into a fishnet bag tied at his waist. Then he did a slow turn with his flashlight among the other containers. A fortune? Murdock had no idea how much this single hold of cargo was worth. Certainly many hundreds of millions. The treasure itself, according to international law, belonged to Iran or to the shah's heirs—the world court would have to rule on that one. A healthy slice of the total, however, would become Murdock's salvage fee.

But he had no time now for further inventory. Time in the depths is a thing that no fortune can buy, that no king and no court can decree. Every minute he spent here meant hours in the decompression chamber.

He ascended through the ship's superstructure, making mental note of the last signs of the *Batavia*'s life. Few of the watertight hatches were closed. On the bridge he found the telegraph still set at full speed. Emerging onto the weather deck, he discovered that none of the six lifeboats had been turned out for service; they were still hanging from their davits at rakish angles or catching the current like jibs in the wind.

Murdock ascended on the port side, climbing the lifeline hand over hand toward the stern until he reached the top of the ravine. Once there, two powerful floodlights caught his alien figure and pinned him against the ship's fantail. What the lights revealed resembled the traditional frogman hardly at all. A yellow dry suit covered every inch of his exposed skin. The tanks on his back were slightly smaller than conventional scuba tanks and were separated by a third much larger cylinder. A number of hoses extended from its regulator assembly. Two were attached to his breathing unit and one to a curious device strapped to his left forearm. The entire apparatus was such as would have delighted the imagination of any Jules Verne fanatic. But even a casual observer might have noticed that no bubbles were being exhausted in a cloud above his head. It was a computer-driven rebreathing device that mixed a tiny amount of oxygen with his helium diluent—then, after being exhaled, the device chemically scrubbed the carbon dioxide.

The twin floodlights blinked twice in rapid succession: His time was up. He had to go back to the minisubmersible.

Murdock raised both gloved hands and clumsily signed that he wanted a few moments more. (A deaf member of the diving crew had taught them all enough sign to make this a practical method of underwater communication.) The lights blinked twice again: no. He felt like a fighter still slugging away, relishing the fight, while his trainer was throwing in the towel. He wanted to remain. One more minute. One more round. The sea, he knew, is an invincible opponent—no one goes the distance and lives. Yet to stand in the ring . . . sometimes that is enough.

He surveyed the darkness beyond the two cones of light. Somewhere out there was a Navy attack submarine. She too had gone to the bottom with her crew . . . all but half a dozen of them.

And the U.S. Navy wanted her back as much as the treasure hunters wanted the *Batavia*.

The shah's plan had been ill-fated from the beginning, but then, many plans born of panic come to the same

pass. In the final weeks of Muhammad Reza Shah Pah-
levi's reign, as the Ayatollah Khomeini's fanatical Mos-
lems closed in around him, the shah of Iran had crated
his most valuable treasures and transported the crates to
Bushire, where they were loaded on an eastbound
freighter. The wealth would one day be used to return
himself and his descendants to power. Only a handful of
confidants, most of them SAVAK agents, knew the *Batavia*'s destination. She had a schedule, all right—a long
list of ports to call—but after the freighter disappeared
no one believed she had held to this route. Certainly the
U.S. Navy had never been informed of her true course
or position. The danger of this, as well as abandoning
the trade routes and sailing without navigation lights during a storm, became clear when the American attack submarine *USS Seawind* had surfaced from routine patrol
just north of Hawaii and found a four-thousand-ton
freighter across her path where no freighter was supposed to be. It had happened before—to Soviet and British submarines as well as American. More often than
not, it was the submarine that took most of the damage.
In this case, the *Seawind*'s bow had punched right through
the hull of the *Batavia* and both ships had gone to the
bottom before either could raise an alarm or transmit a
radio call for assistance.

The *Batavia* had gone down with all hands. The *Seawind* had been only a little more fortunate. If not for the
six U.S. Navy crewmen who had fought through an
emergency hatch and thrown themselves into an inflatable life raft, no details of the collision would ever have
surfaced. The survivors—two seamen, a chief petty officer, and three officers—were picked up days later, drifting south toward Hawaii.

Both vessels simply vanished, defying for more than a
decade all attempts by the Navy and salvage firms, Murdock's included, to find them. Murdock himself had been
searching for almost three years. One hunter, a troll of a

15

man named Archibald Wick, had been looking four times as long, almost from the very beginning. Others had tried and gone broke or just given up. All their efforts had been fruitless, until eight months before when Murdock had decided to play a hunch. Ten days before, that hunch had paid off.

Now the Navy would assemble here in force—a few Navy ships had already arrived—for one of their own remained to be found. She would be close by, and at this depth she probably had not imploded. But that wouldn't have saved the men who had drowned or suffocated within her steel walls.

The twin floodlights flashed twice in his face, stayed on a moment, then flashed twice again. Marie Delamer, his second-in-command, was insistent. No more delaying.

Murdock slipped under the submersible's undercarriage and turned the hatch on the aftermost of her three spheres. This was *DORiS*'s lockout chamber, the access compartment pressurized to their depth. He emerged into the small chamber, closed the lower hatch behind him, and removed his tanks, preparing for the hours of waiting that were a necessary part of decompression.

A speaker crackled over his head: "Well?"

Murdock merely tapped the talk button with his finger to tell her he was ready to go, for he would be breathing heliox for almost an hour—he couldn't sign from the chamber, and the helium-oxygen mixture made his voice squeak.

"Oh no you don't, Glen. Not this time," the young woman's voice said. "Talk, dammit. What did you find in there?"

Murdock tapped the button twice more, showing the same insistence she had with the floodlights and smiling at the thought of her becoming infuriated.

Almost at once the Deep Ocean Recovery Submersible, affectionately referred to by members of the diving crew as *DORiS*, began moving.

Murdock leaned back and closed his eyes.

Meanwhile Marie Delamer began the routine of salvage. Using *DORiS*'s hydraulic arm she laid marker beacons around the wreck so it could be located again. These replaced the transponder, which had been set ten days earlier and whose battery would soon give out. Marie performed a complete inspection of the wreck to determine how deeply the *Batavia* was embedded and what means might be used to refloat her. The hull and superstructure could be sealed and air pumped into her belly until she rose. Special floation devices called "camels" could be strapped under her keel. The ship herself might need to be ionized to break her free of the muck. If all of these failed to raise the *Batavia*, her cargo would have to be removed in place. In the end, this might be the fastest and cheapest procedure. Everything Marie saw was recorded on videotape from the minisub's four external cameras.

After an hour, Murdock switched to a nitrogen mixture and then activated the intercom: "How's it going?"

"Just fine, Glen. About finished. Now don't leave me in suspense any longer. What did you find?"

"I'll tell you all about it. As soon as you agree to that date."

"What is it with you? When are you going to give up?"

"You act as though I'm setting you up with a goon. The guy is a Navy commander. He's upright, like me; reasonably handsome, like me; and a great conversationalist, as long as the conversation concerns submarines. Like me. What the hell, this is my son I'm trying to set you up with, not some dockyard creep."

"Granting he takes after you, why should I settle for a close copy when I've already got the original?"

"Because the original is more than thirty years your senior. I'm nearly twice Drew's age."

"And twice any man I've ever known."

"Not Drew. He's a better officer than I ever was; a better submariner or hydronaut than I'll ever be."

"If he's half as secretive, no woman could stand him. All right, a dinner date. But understand, I look upon him as a future stepson, not as a future husband. Now tell me about that cargo before I burst."

By the time Murdock had finished describing his exploration of the *Batavia*'s hold he had reduced pressure in the access chamber to fifteen pounds per square inch. At that point he opened the two hatches that led to the central compartment, passed through this to the smaller forward control sphere, and took the copilot's seat beside Marie Delamer.

Once there he handed her the golden goblet and watched her eyes widen in appreciation.

"There's good times ahead for us, honey," he told her. "But getting you and Drew together will make me every bit as happy as bringing up this treasure. I mean it. You'll like Drew. He has everything going for him except a woman like you."

Unmistakably French, with arresting dark features, Marie looked as good out of the water as in, but Murdock never tired of seeing her soaked to the bone. He loved to watch her free-diving, long black hair flowing over her back as she swam. Her credentials as an aquanaut were impeccable. She had dived in all the world's oceans and most of its seas, fresh as well as salt-water. Marie was smart. She had guts. But the slick Parisian packaging was nothing to sneeze at.

"Did you find where she'd been hulled?" Marie asked, forcing him back to business.

"Yes. Starboard bow, just below the waterline. You could almost have sailed *DORiS* inside the hole. If you could get her into the ravine."

"I couldn't. I tried."

"I'll see the replays once we surface. Now if you've finished your inspection, what do you say we make a swing of the area? Admiral Reinholt would dearly love to find that submarine of his. After a collision like that the *Seawind* couldn't have gotten very far."

For the next couple of hours, the submersible circled the *Batavia* in ever-increasing radii. They found the sub less than two hundred yards to the south, lying at the foot of an undersea cliff. This vessel, too, had all but buried herself, and if Murdock had not known the sub was close he probably never would have found her. She was sitting upright, but only her sail was visible. Evidently the *Seawind*'s death dive had sent her crashing into the cliff wall, striking it again and again on her way to the bottom and setting off an avalanche of sand and debris. Once she had bottomed, this sandslide had covered her from bow to screw.

"Well," said Murdock, "Admiral Reinholt will be happy to hear she's been located. If they can get her cleaned off, it looks as though they may be able to raise her intact."

"Did she carry ICBMs?"

"No, she was an attack submarine. Torpedoes is all. Still, the Navy will be glad to have her back, if only to study her and determine what went wrong. They don't like to have their inventory strewn over the sea floor."

"Is there a salvage fee for her, Glen?"

"Mercenary twit! The admiral did us a favor cutting some red tape and getting us a great deal of information on the *Batavia*. Giving him the location on this submarine is the least we can do. Set a magnetic transponder, why don't you?"

Marie maneuvered near the submarine and activated the utility arm in order to place the last of their transponders on the *Seawind*'s sail. A radio signal of the correct code and frequency to the transponder would activate its ELF transmitter to send another signal in return. Having the right equipment and knowing the correct frequency, the Navy could send down the Deep Submergence Rescue Vehicles, or DSRVs, and board the *Seawind*.

After this chore, it was time to surface. Murdock released the descent weights and *DORiS* began a steady rise. Their ascent continually accelerated as they left below the pressures that compressed her hull and decreased her buoyancy.

At six hundred feet they entered the zone of photosynthesis and found the first traces of sunlight.

"Another two or three weeks here, Marie," said Murdock, "and we can head back to San Diego. You know Drew is due for some leave, too. Maybe I could have him meet us there. What do you say?"

"You damn matchmaker. Do I have any choice?"

"Not anymore. You made a deal."

By the time the sea had paled from sheerest black to purest blue, Marie was calling *Nomad*, their support ship, in order to verify that *DORiS* was not rising under the *Nomad*'s hull or under one of the Navy vessels around her. *DORiS*'s sonar, like that of the *Seawind* and most other submarines, looked only ahead and below, and therefore could not detect silent danger above.

"*Nomad*, this is *DORiS*. Hello, *Nomad*, over."

"*DORiS*, this is *Nomad*. We have your position. You're clear to surface."

Marie turned to Murdock. "Captain Duggan must have posted himself in the radio room. Apparently he couldn't wait to hear what we found. Let's refuse to tell him anything until he agrees to a date with my mother."

"Very funny. I'm surprised he hasn't asked us already. Maybe Duggan is not a curious man."

"That's like saying maybe the sea isn't wet. Unless we're talking about two different Captain Duggans."

The radio broke in: "*Nomad* calling *DORiS*."

"Here it comes," said Marie. Then, to the microphone, she said, "This is *DORiS;* go ahead, *Nomad.*"

"I'm sending the outboard to tow you in. We're going to haul you aboard rather than ready you for a second dive. Over."

"What's the problem, *Nomad,* that's not—"

"Just do as you're told, Marie. I thought you damned Germans knew how to follow orders."

Murdock snatched the mike from her hands, depressed the transmit button, and then stopped. He and Marie exchanged puzzled glances.

"Germans?"

Marie nodded. "That's what he said."

"Something's wrong. Go ahead and acknowledge."

She did so.

Soon waves were splashing across their acrylic viewports, and they saw the big twin-hulled support ship in the distance. Two other boats were also on the water. One, a small outboard, was streaking out from the *Nomad* toward the minisub.

A second vessel, a private sub-tender much smaller than Murdock's support ship but considerably faster, was tied up alongside the *Nomad.* Murdock recognized this ship at once and scowled.

"What the hell? That looks like Archie Wick's rig."

Marie craned her neck to see through the downward-looking viewport. "What's he doing here? He knows how you feel about him."

"Nothing good. He couldn't beat us to the *Batavia.* So he may be trying to beat us out of it."

As he spoke, the outboard spun to a stop in front of them. The two crewmen began attaching lines to *DORiS's* framework. Instead of hauling her alongside the *Nomad,* where she could be fitted for another dive, the outboard would tow her to the subwell between the *Nomad's* twin hulls, and there a crane would raise *DORiS* onto the deck. Despite the gathering darkness, this was contrary to plan.

Dives were supposed to continue through the night. After all, there was no sunlight at a thousand feet, night or day.

Normally neither Murdock nor Marie would have paid much attention to this towing operation. They were paying close attention now. One of the men attached a towline while the other remained in the stern. This first man was having difficulty keeping his balance, owing in part to the pitch and roll of the little outboard but also to his failure to watch what he was doing. He was looking directly into their viewport, speaking, with exaggerated use of his lips. His words, however, couldn't penetrate the thick acrylic.

"What's he saying?" cried Marie.

"I can't make it out," replied Murdock. "He must be talking to the other—" But when Murdock looked at the second man he knew the deckhand was not talking to him. It was Emmott, the deaf diver, sitting ramrod-straight against the transom. You can't talk to a deaf man, even one who reads lips as well as Emmott, when your back is turned to him. Emmott was supposed to be handling the outboard controls, but actually he was doing so with an elbow. This more than anything else was responsible for the outboard's gyrations. But Emmott's hands were otherwise engaged. His series of fierce but concise gestures were carefully hidden from the view of those aboard the *Nomad*.

Murdock repeated the words as Emmott signed:

"Crew . . . attacked . . . *Nomad* . . ." He turned to Marie. "I can't get that last part. What does that last sign mean?"

"I don't know either. I've never seen it." Marie placed both hands against the viewport and signed for a repeat.

By this time the deckhand had the first tow secured and moved to the other side.

Emmott was making a pistol with his right hand—a fist with his first two fingers extended.

"He's spelling it now," Marie said. "That's an H."

Another fist with the small finger aloft.

"I."

He hooked the little finger.

"J," said Marie. Then: "A . . . C . . . K . . ." She whirled. "Good God, Glen, someone has hijacked the *Nomad.*"

# Chapter Two

It didn't make sense. Captain Pad Duggan was a two-fisted veteran. He and Murdock had fought their way into and out of more scrapes than either could remember. The deck crew were good seamen, graduates of many a dockside brawl but well paid and fiercely loyal; the divers were tough, seasoned professionals. The possibility that such a ship's company could be surprised by the likes of Archibald Wick simply didn't exist. But beyond that, what group of hijackers would dare move against them? Three U.S. Navy vessels were already nested within signaling distance of the *Nomad*. A shot fired, even a blast of the ship's horn, and the game would be lost. No, it just didn't make sense.

Not until the crane had raised *DORiS* out of the sub-well and lowered her to the deck did either Glen Murdock or Marie Delamer get a look at what had happened aboard the *Nomad*. Murdock helped Marie from the hatchway and then climbed out beside her and stood looking around.

He saw not three but four U.S. Navy vessels on the horizon—sometime during the dive another rescue ship had arrived on the site. But they were no longer within signaling distance. All four were steaming at full speed to the east. Very soon they would be gone.

So much for reinforcements. Somehow—Murdock couldn't understand the way of it—the Navy had been diverted. He and his men were now on their own.

Meanwhile, the *Nomad* crew was scattered over the ship, clustered in small groups at duty stations but performing no duties. With grim faces they were watching Murdock, waiting for him to signal his intentions. Within every group was at least one new face that watched the crewmen in the same way the crew watched their employer. These new men were easily identifiable, for they carried side arms and wore the insignia of the U.S. Navy Shore Patrol.

So that's it, thought Murdock.

A youngish man dressed in Navy whites and wearing the aiguillettes of a vice-admiral's aide coiled on his left shoulder stepped up to the diver. Another SP walked just behind this officer, holster flap open and thumbs hooked over the gun belt.

"Glen Murdock?" the officer asked.

Murdock narrowed his eyes. "I'm Murdock. What the hell's going on here?"

The young man's appearance was flawless: service cap precisely arranged, hair neatly cropped at the sides, uniform correct in every detail. Captain Pad Duggan couldn't be faulted for having allowed these men on board. Murdock himself might have been fooled. Only the superstructure of Archibald Wick's salvor, visible over the *Nomad*'s starboard side, gave the lie to this carefully contrived piece of fiction. Navy uniforms are more easily arranged for than real naval vessels.

"My name is Commander Stout."

Murdock smiled arrogantly. "I can read name tags, *Lieutenant* Commander, as well as insignia. What kind of piracy is this?"

"By now your captain will have returned to the bridge. Shall we join him there?"

"Do I have any choice?"

"No."

"In that case, after you."

Even before Commander Stout started for a port ladder, Murdock had called to his maintenance chief standing in a small huddle farther back in the stern. "Gandy, get these batteries recharged and the ballasts replaced!" As though concerned his words would not carry half the length of the ship, Murdock gestured with his hands while he spoke, making rough slashes across his body.

The maintenance chief got an okay from the SP beside him and began this operation.

As Murdock followed Stout toward the bridge, though, he saw Emmott repeating these same signs to one of the divers positioned forward. The message was soon passing furtively from diver to diver and group to group until it had silently made the rounds of the *Nomad* crew.

Captain Duggan and Archie Wick were waiting when Stout and Murdock, then Marie and the SP, came in.

"My fault, Murdock," growled Duggan. "I let these damn hijackers aboard. U.S. Navy, my sainted ass!"

Duggan and Wick, who stood with his arms folded, were opposites in character. Some fifteen years before they must have been about the same size, but where Duggan tended to weight Wick had shrunk with the passage of time. Captain Duggan's face was an open book—he was frankly pissed off and it showed. Wick's features had always been sly—year by year they withdrew farther into his skin. He had begun life as a man, but he would end it as a shrunken, troll-like creature.

Murdock held up a hand. "It's all right, Pad. They look genuine enough. I'd have believed it myself if not for our friend Archie here. What would the real Navy be doing in cahoots with a skunk like him?"

"Not nice, Murdock." Wick's surprisingly deep voice was a sneer. "We're both in the same line of work, aren't we? Course treasure hunting makes for some stiff competition. Maybe you don't like that."

"You're no hunter. Looter is more like it."

"Not at all nice."

Murdock challenged Stout: "What about it, Commander. What is going on?"

"We're taking over your vessel and your submersible."

"By what authority?"

"I have all the authority I need."

"Just like that?"

"That's right."

"Suppose I say no?"

"Say what you please. I've got enough men to ensure your cooperation. Here's a statement for you to read to your men." Stout produced a paper from a jacket pocket. "Captain Duggan, turn on the PA."

Duggan glanced at Murdock.

Murdock nodded. He held out his hand for the paper. Stout passed it over as the diver stepped to the microphone.

Events at that point became a blur of motion.

Glen Murdock shouted into the transmitter, but nobody later recalled what he said. Murdock himself was too busy to care. He grabbed Stout's wrist, spun him around, and wrapped his neck in a hammerlock. An eighteen-inch stainless-steel blade appeared from under Murdock's dry suit and suddenly pressed edgewise against the commander's white collar.

Archibald Wick stepped forward. But Captain Duggan, moving even faster, drove a ham-sized fist into Wick's face. The little man flew back off his feet, through the bridge door and out onto the wing.

The SP had simultaneously reached for the butt of his service pistol. The holster was empty.

"Hey, sailor."

He whirled and found Marie, smiling as only a French girl can smile, but aiming the business end of the semiautomatic at his belly. The SP instantly raised his hands over his head.

"That's a good boy," she told him.

The entire sequence of events had lasted not more than a heartbeat or two.

"It won't work," growled Stout. Murdock threw the man against the chart table, and the officer stood there leaning over it and massaging his throat. "I've got a dozen men scattered over this ship," he said.

"Look around you, Commander."

Slowly Stout came erect. He looked out the forward screens and saw that his SPs on the bow had been relieved of their weapons. Stout stumbled onto the wing, nearly tripping over Wick's still prostrate body, and surveyed the last of the scuffles. His men had been badly outnumbered; only their weapons had given them the advantage, and that had been lost when every deckhand and diver on the *Nomad* had bolted into action at precisely the same instant.

Everywhere he looked his men were picking themselves up off the deck, while the crew of the *Nomad* were holding them at bay with their own pistols.

"I was warned about you, Murdock," said the commander. "They told me you were tough. Now I see they were right."

"Never mind that. Dump your pockets, Stout. And you, too," Murdock said to the SP. "I already know about Wick, but I'm gonna find out who you guys are. Just pile it all right here on the chart table."

Marie kept a watchful eye while Duggan and Murdock went through the wallets and papers. Both men had what appeared to be bona fide military ID cards.

"So what do you make of it?" Duggan asked the diver.

Murdock tossed Stout's ID on the pile. "It seems that they are who they claim to be."

"Navy!"

"I guess so. Okay, give them back their papers. Put the commander and his men back on their ship and then give them back their weapons, too." Murdock pushed a finger into Stout's chest. "The Navy will hear about this,

Commander, and I'll let a military court decide what to do with you. Just don't try coming back here, or next time my men and I may have our own little court-martial.''

"I'll be back. Or someone else will. This thing is too important to forget about just because I made an error in judgment.''

"What's too important? Three times I've asked you what this was all about.''

"I was sent here to commandeer your ship and your minisub.''

"You tried to hijack us.''

"I've admitted I made a mistake.''

"You admitted underestimating me and my crew; that's not the same thing as saying you're sorry. Who sent you?''

"Admiral Reinholt.''

"Dan Reinholt! Why didn't you say so?''

"I was ordered to get you and your vessels, not submit to an interview. Everything else is classified information.''

Murdock shook his head slowly. "Mister, you have a lot to learn. Are you going to tell me what's going on or not?''

"I've told you, it's classified.''

Murdock turned away in disgust. "Captain, put Stout and his men back on their ship. Wick, too. Then we'll call up Reinholt at Pearl Harbor and find out for ourselves what's going on.''

"He's not at Pearl Harbor.''

The diver again squared off with Stout.

"I know. He's in Washington. But we'll get to him eventually if—''

"No. He's not in Washington either. He was at Pearl this morning, but by now he's on his way to the location.''

"What location?''

"The downsite."

"What went down?"

Commander Stout inhaled deeply and strode to the chart table. He then pointed to an expanse of sea some three hundred miles north of the Hawaiian Islands and about the same distance east by northeast of the *Nomad*. According to the charts, its depth varied from less than eighteen hundred feet to more than twenty thousand. It is called the Murray Deep. Treasure hunters and salvage operators who know its reputation for swallowing up ships or who have searched its ragged, treacherous bottom have another name for the region: the Subpacific Lost.

"That's where we think she went down."

"She?"

"One of our vessels. It's missing. Presumed sunk."

The *Nomad* captain was shaking his head. "It will take us twelve hours to reach that point from here," Duggan said, "even if we leave at once and proceed at full speed through the night."

And then Marie was standing at the table, too. "Any ship that goes down in water that deep isn't going to have survivors after twelve minutes, and certainly not after twelve hours," she said.

"It wasn't a ship."

Murdock glared at the commander.

"It was a submarine. Performing sea trials when—"

"*DORiS* isn't designed to dock with a Navy submarine," Marie interrupted. "What about your rescue vehicles? The DSRVs? What about your *Pigeon*-class recovery ships?"

"Not available. In addition to those, the Navy has two deep-sea exploration submersibles. Also not available. We went to Archibald Wick first." Stout looked toward the port bridge wing, where the SP was just then bringing Wick around. "He was nearby and we knew he had a minisub. But it turned out to be down for repairs. Admiral Reinholt told us where you were diving. Wick volunteered to bring us in his vessel, because it's fast and because he thought he could help talk you into the job. Being as you're both in the salvage trade. The admiral is on his way out to the downsite, and we hoped to meet him there with whatever you could loan to us.''

"All right, all right," said Murdock. "Which submarine was it?''

"One of the Trident-class subs." Stout was going on but Murdock wasn't hearing him. A Trident. The Navy's largest submarine. Two football fields long, it displaces more weight than most cruisers. The Trident II submarine-launched ballistic missiles (SLBMs) it carries are bigger than many submersibles and can travel a quarter of the way around the world.

"She was on the surface," Stout hastened to explain. "The observation planes recorded an explosion. And then she just disappeared." The commander's story rushed on. Once security had been breached the words poured from his mouth like water gushing through a crack in a dam, the force and speed of them washing away at their own barriers.

Murdock held up a hand and stopped him.

"Which Trident?" he demanded.

Stout glared. "The *USS Alaska.* What difference does it make?''

Murdock started to reply but the words jammed in his throat. He couldn't speak or hear or even think straight. And then, inexplicably, he heard himself giving orders. He was telling Marie to lash down the minisub. He was telling Captain Duggan to make *Nomad* ready to sail.

Stranger still, when Archibald Wick offered to let him go ahead to the location in Wick's faster craft, Murdock nodded his head in agreement. That way he could be fully apprised of the situation before the *Nomad* arrived all ready to dive. Then he was shaking Wick's hand and rushing to his cabin to gather what few things he needed to take.

Sometime that evening, Murdock's sense of reality came back. It occurred to him that getting to the site of the accident long before the *Nomad* and *DORiS* meant a lot of time waiting in a place where waiting was unlikely to be easy. By then Archie Wick's salvor, the *Enchantress,* had already passed the four naval vessels that were also making full speed to the *Trident*'s last known position. The SPs were on board as well, for Duggan had wanted them off his ship. Only Commander Stout had remained with the *Nomad.*

"So what do you think, Murdock? She's fast, don't you agree?"

"Huh? What's that?"

"The *Enchantress.* Does she fly, or what?"

"Yeah, Wick, she really flies."

"What would you guess?"

"I don't know. Maybe forty knots?"

Wick's little troll eyes almost bulged from their folds in delight. "I know you don't like me much. And maybe I don't like you too much either. But you say she's fast. That's good. And you have to admit that sometimes a treasure hunter has to get to a place fast."

"And if you don't plan to report what you salvage, you may have to leave a place even faster, huh, Archie?"

Wick's withered mouth curved into a smile. "Is that like a joke? I don't think it's too funny."

"I'm not feeling too funny."

Murdock kept his own company. Wick's crew was a sinister lot, not tougher than Murdock's men but meaner. There was little they hadn't done for money. He noticed that they, too, for the most part kept to themselves, rarely even looking at one another directly. There seemed to be no camaraderie. Men who cannot be trusted are loath to trust.

As they neared the coordinates, Murdock stood on the

bow and peered into the darkness. When he could hear and feel the engines begin to idle down, the first of several silhouettes outlined in running lights appeared on the horizon. A single brooding black bulk, showing no running lights whatsoever, slipped by to starboard. For a moment Murdock thought it must be a Navy submarine-hunter, a floating electronic laboratory forever trolling the waters with sonar in search of enemy subs and today, maybe for the first time, looking for one of its own. When it passed close enough for the salvor's searchlight to illuminate the Cyrillic letters on her bow, he knew he was almost correct. It was a Russian trawler, fishing for anything in or out of the water. Radio messages. Information of any kind. Did they know what had happened? Did they know even more than the Navy? And then the dark shapes of the Navy vessels were on all sides. The diver could make out fully a dozen vessels lying with quiet menace on an innocent circle of sea. Wick made straight for a battleship showing a distinguishing toplight of the flag officer.

How like Admiral Reinholt, he thought, to have picked an old dreadnought like this one for his flagship. The ship and the old man had much in common. Built before World War II, only four battleships still retained their commissions; no more had been built, and it wasn't likely any ever would be. These days a ship had to be small and fast and carry her own air support. Barring the giant aircraft carriers, these battleships are the biggest warships afloat; they are the most powerful, hard-hitting warships bar none. Their sixteen-inch guns can hurl a one-and-a-half ton explosive projectile twenty-five miles with amazing accuracy. Her armor plating—the heaviest on any vessel ever built—can withstand a virtual broadside bombardment from any cannon in the world. But these ships are dinosaurs doomed to extinction. And in a sad way, so was Admiral Reinholt. There were few of his type left from the war as well, but the ones who still survived were fighters. Battle-tough. It would be a shame, Murdock thought, to see them all gone.

A motor whale boat shot from the side of the flagship and intersected the *Enchantress* before Wick had even cut his engines. Minutes later, Murdock was climbing the flagship's accommodation ladder. He had faced the stern, and his salute was halfway to his brow when he froze. Old habits die hard. He turned to the officer of the deck and requested permission to come aboard.

He had supposed a stiff seaman or petty officer third-class would escort him to Admiral Reinholt, but the man who met him was no less than a captain.

He was a little taller than Murdock, a little younger. He was thin, too, and had an office complexion that made Murdock doubt he commanded this or any battleship.

"Captain Cassidy," the officer introduced himself. When they had shaken hands he gestured for Murdock to follow him. "Admiral Reinholt is anxious to see you. At the moment he's in a meeting with his SubDisPrep staff, but he asked to be informed as soon as you came aboard."

"I'm out of the Navy now, Captain. SubDisPrep staff? Can you put that into civilianspeak?"

Cassidy adopted a stern tone. "Submarine disaster preparedness." Then his face broke and he smiled. "Admiral Reinholt doesn't like Pentagonese too much either. He calls it his SubLost team."

"That, I would have understood."

The two men left the quarterdeck and passed the three aft-facing sixteen-inch guns, as well as some more modern weapons and electronics that had failed to clutter the battleship's graceful lines. Tomahawk-launchers looking like railroad boxcars sidetracked about the ship's after-stack were new; so were the Harpoon missile canisters and SATCOMM antennas. Phalanx automatic fire-control systems perched above her tried-and-true five-inch guns.

The *New Jersey* was an old fighter with a battery of new weapons.

"I suppose," said Cassidy, "I should offer the Navy's appreciation for your coming, Mr. Murdock. I hope it doesn't foul you up any on your *Batavia* business."

Murdock turned in surprise.

"Oh, I know all about it," Cassidy reassured him. "I'm Admiral Reinholt's chief of staff. I was the one who dug up most of the information you requested on the *Batavia* as well as the *Seawind*. That's how we knew where to find you."

"It'll still be there when this is over," Murdock told him.

"Quite a coup. Finding what no one else could find. I hope you're as lucky here."

"Let's hope so."

Leading the diver up a ladder to the bridge deck, Cassidy asked, "Any sign of the *Seawind* herself?"

"Yes. We located her earlier today just west of the *Batavia* wreck about two hundred yards."

The captain turned around and blocked the ladder by grabbing the two rails. "What's her condition?"

"She's got a light cover of bottom but she seems to be pretty much intact. If she's not holed too badly you can probably wrestle her off the bottom with the trim tanks."

"That's great news! You'll tell the admiral?"

"Yeah, I imagine he could use some good news," Murdock said drily.

Cassidy started down a short corridor with cards on the doors indicating that these were visiting officers' cabins; he selected a door at random and knocked three times. This should have been a clue to Murdock that something was wrong, but he missed it.

They could hear a toilet flushing and a voice calling: "Just a minute, O.K."

Cassidy said, "I did a lot of work for you, Murdock—

at the admiral's request, naturally—and I'd appreciate knowing. How did you find the *Batavia?*"

Murdock shrugged. "It's no secret. Not anymore. I made an assumption that no one else had been willing to act upon."

"What was that?"

"I assumed, out of frustration more than anything else, that the *Batavia* was holding to the route she had laid from the beginning. That she was on course and on time."

Captain Cassidy had gone rigid. "But that route wouldn't have intersected with—"

When he broke off, Murdock continued. "With the *Seawind's* course? No, it wouldn't have, you're right. I assumed it was the Navy's submarine—infallible inertial navigation system notwithstanding—that had wandered off course."

Cassidy was shaking his head. "I don't think the admiral will like that at all."

"Right about now," said Murdock," I'd say that was the least of his worries."

# Chapter Three

Once inside the cabin Murdock stopped dead. He about-faced. His brows came up in silent inquiry, demanding an answer to the obvious question.

"Admiral Reinholt will be waiting for you in the ready room as soon as you're finished here," said Captain Cassidy, who then eased the door closed at Murdock's back.

The man who sat on the side of the bunk removing his shoes and socks was—except for his bare feet—dressed in civilian clothes. A conservative gray jacket hung alone in a tiny closet. His conservative blue tie was loose and his shirt collar was open, revealing clumps of white hair on his chest and an Adam's apple that stuck out farther than most people's chins. The man would have been tall had he been standing up straight, but he was sitting hunched over and probably stood the same way. Skin sagged from his cheeks and his chin, which were stubbled with white. What hair he could claim on his head was white, too, confined to a narrow patch in back of his ears working lower and lower each year as though it were, like the rest of the man, slowly losing a battle with gravity.

Murdock didn't like him.

"Sit down, Mr. Murdock."

The diver found a chair under a small writing table and spun it around.

"I'm Eliot Packman. From the office of the Secretary of Defense. I wanted to meet you, sir, and assure you of the Defense Department's cooperation in this sad tragedy.''

"Okay. Thanks."

Murdock started to rise. Packman's hand came up and patted the air until Murdock settled back into his chair.

"In a little while you'll be briefed by the admiral and I want you to feel that afterwards, or at any time, you can come to me with any problems or information."

"Why?"

"I want to work with you."

"I work alone; and I'll report to the admiral."

"Of course. When you have, I'd like to know how it goes. I've already talked with some of the other officers and I'm convinced that the admiral may attempt to . . . Well, let's just say that I'd like to keep on top of this thing. I'll make it a formal request if I have to. Do I?"

"No."

"You'll do it then?"

"No."

Packman rolled up his dirty socks and threw them into the small head. "I don't understand you."

"I'm not in the Navy. Formal or not, your request means nothing to me."

"Look, you probably know that the admiral is past his retirement age. He has been extended in the service because of some very powerful friends. He's popular, and don't get me wrong, he's earned the admiration of us all." Packman began massaging one of his feet. "However, some of us feel that it is time to give younger men an opportunity to prove what they can do in his place."

"So Reinholt's getting old." Murdock stood. "Well you're no spring chicken, Packman. Hell, I'm only a few years younger than Dan."

"Perhaps, but you and I aren't experiencing the early symptoms of senility. We're not suffering from delusions of persecution or—"

Murdock stopped him by raising his voice.

"I don't want this information."

He started for the door.

"Hear me out," said Packman. "In recent years Reinholt has become increasingly . . . well, paranoid is the only word for it. He has fanciful, almost ludicrous fears about the Soviet ability to make off with military secrets. He has taken expensive precautions that have been far and away more than required. He trusts no one. Don't get me wrong, we know the Soviets have spies. But not at the levels that Reinholt's apocryphal fears place them. We regard the Soviets as political opposition, naturally, but in these times of sweeping political change we've got to look at the big picture. We're seeing it happen: the disintegration and collapse of the Communist system. We can take advantage of this global rebirth or we can cling to the Cold War days of the past. The admiral's pathological suspicions do not fit in with recent events. He sees Red conspiracy behind every mutual technical advance that the United States and the USSR coincidentally achieve. It's gotten so that we at Defense are having our long-range plans hampered, and we feel that he would be happier without the constant anxiety his duties seem to provoke."

"In other words, you want him out."

"All I want is to see that, until Dan Reinholt can be eased of his tremendous work load, he won't suffer any major stresses. Whatever he tells you or whatever he arranges for you to do, I'd like to know about it. This is for his good as well as for the good of the service. I'd like to think that I can count on your support. Can I?"

"You can think it."

"You'll help me then?"

"No."

Packman's sagging face furrowed in disapproval. "I just don't understand you at all, Murdock."

"I'm just a diver who's going down to look for a submarine. If I find it, my job is done and I'm out of the picture.''

"But if you don't find it?''

"I won't be done then, will I?''

"But don't you see, I can help you.''

"How?''

"I have powerful friends, too.''

The diver laughed. ''Packman . . . at two thousand feet below the surface your friends aren't worth shit. Now get this: I don't want your help. I don't know you; I have no reason to trust you; quite frankly, I don't even like you. Reinholt I know. I trust him and I like him. If I didn't have my own reasons for being here, I'd come as a favor to him. He'd do the same for me. Reinholt might be a little eccentric. Hell, he may be certifiable for all I know. I don't care.''

Packman came slowly erect. ''You are without any doubt the most ill-mannered, undisciplined man it has ever been my displeasure to meet.''

"There, you see,'' Murdock said, smiling fiercely again, ''you do understand me after all.''

Cassidy was waiting for Murdock in the corridor. Once they were headed toward the ready room he apologized for the detour. ''Packman's D.o.D. He's on the sidelines watching us move the ball. But that doesn't keep him from calling the plays, does it?''

"Packman's a jackal,'' said Murdock. ''And he's sniffing around behind Reinholt's back because he knows if he hit him head-on he wouldn't be D.o.D. any longer. He'd be D.O.A.''

"Here we are, Mr. Murdock.''

This time Cassidy knocked twice, a traditional signal for a junior officer visiting a senior one. He opened the door without waiting for permission, showed Murdock through, and then disappeared.

The battleship's ready room was a small but efficient affair. Two dozen comfortable folding chairs and a podium filled the front half of the room, while a bank of filing cabinets and a lighted map table occupied the back. Several officers with sticks in their hands stood around the table; they took turns pushing little ship-shaped toys about the tabletop with the points of their sticks.

Admiral Dan Reinholt was a reminder that the early submariners had been picked for their small size. He was neatly compact, with economical gestures and habits and a crisp appearance—the starched creases on his shirt collar and jacket were sharp enough to slice bread. As he shook hands with Murdock, the diver could see that Reinholt's hard features, the firm set of the jaw, and the blue-green eyes like chips of glacier ice, had not softened with time.

"I'm damn glad to see you, Glen. And sorry as I can be that it has to happen under these circumstances."

"It's no fault of yours," said Murdock.

"Well, I really meant the way we went about getting you here. I should have gone myself or called you on the radio, but of course it was out of the question to let any hint of this get out on the marine bands. The best I could do was to send my aide. Anyway, you certainly made good time."

"I got a lift. The *Nomad* probably won't arrive for another three hours."

Reinholt nodded. "That's about right. Commander Stout radioed in their position just a few minutes ago and briefed me on his encounter with you. You made quite an impression on him, I'm afraid."

"He made one on me—what's the status here, Dan?"

"We're holding in a SubMiss condition at the moment. We've no evidence at all the *Alaska* went down; she's simply not where she's supposed to be and hasn't surfaced to radio in her situation. She was here—then she vanished. Leaving no traces."

"You have no clues? No debris?"

"We've got debris, which naturally we hope is not the

*Alaska.* One of our sub-hunters picked up a concentration of metal on the sea floor at a depth of over two thousand feet. She can't submerge deep enough to confirm these readings.''

"What kind of a signal is it?"

"Scattered. Low density. Spread out over a good piece of bottom."

"The Trident is already pretty spread out."

"You could be right. It's more likely some natural iron content in the floor, though." The two men stepped to the map table and Admiral Reinholt made introductions. The officers were cordial, despite the emergency, and eager to cooperate with Murdock perhaps because of this. "There's a marker signal on the bottom just about here," said Reinholt. "It's a three-second ping. That will be your starting point."

"How close to where she went down do you figure the bottom marker was dropped?"

'Right on it.''

"How can you be so positive? I understood you had only some planes in the air at the time."

"Correct. That's where we got lucky. We'd dropped the marker three days before. This morning—yesterday morning, that is—the *Alaska* came here for a test firing of one of her Trident missiles. Captain West, commanding the *Alaska,* notified Pearl Harbor that he was right over the site."

"A missile test? What was the target?"

"We have a reef several hundred miles southwest of Hawaii that we use for testing. An uninhabited stretch of shoals in the Johnston Island chain. I can see what you're thinking. There was an explosion all right, but we've ruled out launch accident as the cause."

"I wasn't thinking that, Dan. Had there been a nuclear accident, you would have had to do more to keep it quiet than employ a little radio silence."

Reinholt smiled ruefully. "A launch accident wouldn't

have been nuclear. The Nuclear Test Ban Treaty with the Soviet Union requires us to use conventional warheads for this kind of a test. Anyway, launch depth is a hundred feet, and the *Alaska* was photographed on the surface just before the explosion.'' Reinholt reached for a folder and produced an eight-by-ten photograph showing a Sea King helicopter nestled in the water beside the massive bow of the Trident. A true monster. Her conning tower, or "sail," right forward of amidships, looked small, and yet it was the size of a three-story building. Any number of large planes could have landed and taken off on the *Alaska*'s deck, she was so big. The fifteen-passenger Sea King was positively dwarfed.

Right aft of the sail were the twenty-four launch tube hatches, in two rows of twelve extending nearly two hundred feet along the submarine's spine. All of them seemed to be secured.

"How much can you tell me, Dan?" asked Murdock.

"Very little, because very little is all we know. Four hours before the launch was scheduled, Captain West surfaced and radioed to Pearl Harbor that he had a medical emergency. His medical officer was requesting immediate assistance from a research facility at Pearl. The SH-3 chopper flew out with a team of emergency personnel and made an amphibious landing, as you can see there. That photograph was taken by a Navy spotter plane which was circling, waiting for the launch. The pilot saw but did not photograph a life raft crossing to the sub. An explosion came as the spotter plane was making a second pass." Reinholt handed Murdock a second photograph showing a cloud of smoke, below which the *Alaska*'s sail was just slipping under the surface.

"What about the helicopter?"

"Destroyed. We found debris from that, as well as some aviation fuel on the surface. Some light material. And the body of the pilot, who was wearing a life preserver. Nothing else. I was already at Pearl to oversee the test when the word came in. We mobilized at once. Photographic overflights have been continuous. Two other submarines are in the area now and others are coming but, as you know, they hunt hit-and-miss. No less than a dozen SH-3s and H-2 sub-hunters have been airborne since the SubMiss was declared, covering a hundred square miles of ocean.''

Murdock knew about these antisubmarine helicopters. They could take off from the deck of a destroyer, fly six-hundred-mile sorties at speeds of one hundred and fifty miles per hour. They could lower a sonar buoy into the water that was capable of detecting the presence of submarines for miles in any direction. And unlike the attack submarines or sub-hunter ships the helicopters' presence was never detected by the sub they were chasing, since the sonar of the submerged vessel could not extend out of the water. But all the helicopters, surface ships, and attack submarines in the Navy's inventory would not get Admiral Reinholt a look at what was right down below them.

Murdock led the admiral away from the other officers and spoke in hushed tones. "What about your DSRVs?"

Reinholt wagged his head. "The worst kind of luck. DSRV II was loaned to the South Africans a week ago. One of their submarines went down back in 1988 beyond the Cape of Good Hope. They just located it a month or so ago and began petitioning the Navy for the use of a rescue vehicle so they could get inside the sub without bringing it to the surface. I finally decided to let them use one. Meanwhile, DSRV I should have been kept operational but some asshole scheduled it for a special refitting at Groton. Guess who the asshole was? Honestly, I don't remember signing the order. We sent a transport plane to pick up DSRV II the day before yesterday, but by the time they get the submersible to Cape Town and we fly it to Pearl Harbor, put it on a nuclear submarine, and bring it out here, we could lose a week. And what happened to the *Alvin* and *Trieste,* our deep-sea submersibles, was every bit as frustrating . . ."

"Never mind all that, Dan. You're telling me *DORiS* is the best we can do for the next few days?"

"I'm afraid so."

"You tried to get the DSRV back a day before the test firing? Why?"

"When we got word you'd located the *Batavia,* I thought the discovery of the *Seawind* would surely follow."

"Then why loan it out? I sent word about the *Batavia* more like ten days ago."

"It didn't reach me until the day before I came down here."

Murdock thought this over. Finally, with a shrug, he changed course entirely. "Could the metal concentration you're reading on the sea floor be the wreckage of the Sea King helicopter?"

"I doubt it. Too much of it and too scattered."

"I don't understand how a helicopter explosion could have sent the *Alaska* to the bottom. Even if she went under with the hatch open, she should have had enough buoyancy to compensate for a flooded sail."

Reinholt agreed and Murdock continued. "Is it possible the explosion of the helicopter somehow triggered the *Alaska*'s missile inside a closed launch tube? Or that the explosion occurred on the *Alaska* and caught the helicopter before it could get clear?"

Reinholt waved the suggestion away. "The missiles can't fire until they're near the surface, well clear of the submarine. And examination of the debris makes it pretty certain that the explosion occurred aboard the helicopter. No, Glen, I think the answer lies somewhere else."

"What are you getting at?"

"The helicopter could have been shot down."

"Why?"

"Because of something she saw. Something the spotter planes were too high to see."

"That doesn't explain the *Alaska* disappearing."

"Glen, you were a hydronaut in the Navy. A deep-sea diver and submersible pilot. You didn't concern yourself with missiles and attack submarines. What I'm going to tell you now isn't classified, but there aren't very many people who know it."

"Go ahead."

"The *Alaska* isn't just any submarine. It's a Trident, the end of a generation. The single most lethal weapon on the face of the earth and, God help us, nothing will ever surpass it in death-dealing destruction. Lethality is the word for it. For ICBM submarines that means the ability to move quickly and quietly, to remain submerged for years at a time without surfacing. Despite its size the Trident can do this better than any class of submarine ever built. But the Soviet Union has already stolen the technology for this, or purchased it openly from countries like Japan or Sweden who only care about making a buck while we patrol their shores for them. The missile technology is something else again. A missile's lethality is calculated as a product of its range and its accuracy as well as its explosive potential. The Soviet Union has always led us in megatonnage, because it was easier for them to build a bigger missile than a better one. You hear megatonnage every time the Pentagon goes before Congress because that gets them the appropriations, but our generals know and the Soviet generals know that what really counts is accuracy. Our missiles are so much more accurate than theirs it's difficult to draw a comparison."

"I know all that, Dan."

"You may not know this. The Soviet SS-N-18 was a single-warhead missile with a lethality rating of 2 compared to our early Poseidon missiles of the same era which introduced MIRV technology. Multiple Independent Re-entry Vehicles. The Poseidon was rated at 13 on the same scale. We built a Trident I missile with a lethality of 28, but still small enough to replace the Poseidons in the launch tubes of those Poseidon submarines. When we put these same missiles into the Trident submarine tubes they looked like twenty-two caliber shells in the chamber of a forty-four magnum—if, that is, you can extend that analogy by a factor of several thousand. But we knew what we were doing. The Soviets had already stolen this technology and produced a larger three-MIRVed warhead on the SS-NX-18 missile for their Typhoon-class submarine, which was itself a copy of the Trident. The accuracy of those missiles is close to the Trident I and the megatonnage is greater; its lethality is rated at 31.''

"Sounds like the arms race is neck and neck."

"Not for long."

"Go on, Dan."

"By this time we were leapfrogging. The *Alaska* and other Trident submarines were being fitted with the Trident IIs. Forty-two feet high, not coincidentally the height of the *Alaska* less her sail, and seven feet in diameter. Each missile carries seven three-hundred-kiloton warheads or fourteen one-hundred-and-fifty-kiloton warheads and has a range of more than six thousand nautical miles. This means the Trident submarines can hide in most of the world's oceans and still be within striking distance of her targets in the Soviet Union. Not Moscow maybe, but at least the Soviet Union. And they'll miss their targets by no more than the length of a football field. The lethality rating of these Trident IIs is calculated at 1,500. But even that is not the bottom line. The next development in Trident technology was a concept called MARV. Maneuvering Reentry Vehicles. Each of the fourteen warheads in a MARVed Trident II carries its own power supply and guidance system. Their accuracy is not to be believed. We pessimistically calculate their radius of miss at ninety feet. The lethality of each missile is figured at 14,000. That's what we've been arming our Trident submarines with for the past two years. Let me do some quick arithmetic for you. The *Alaska* carries twenty-two Trident II missiles. That means she can target three hundred and eight objectives simultaneously, striking each one with seventy-five times the explosive force of that which devastated Hiroshima.''

Murdock found his mouth and throat had gone dry. ''There are twenty-four launch tubes on the *Alaska,*'' he said.

Reinholt nodded his head slowly. ''Right. None of what I've just told you is classified. What I'm going to tell you now is classified so high I'm surprised the President himself has been told. We were test-firing a Trident III.''

''I didn't know there was a third-generation Trident.''

''Not many people do. I'll tell you this much. It has a range of twelve thousand nautical miles. You know what that means. Anywhere on the globe, from anywhere on the globe. Off the coast of Tasmania, rounding the Strait of Magellan, or just lounging in their home docks in Puget Sound, the Tridents are still within range of their targets, no matter what the targets might be. Twenty-six separate warheads, each with four times the destructive potential of the Soviet SS-NX-18, the Soviet's most powerful missile. A calculated radius of miss or . . . well, it calculated out to three and a half inches, but when you're dealing with a million megatons of explosive you ignore inches. A new type of fuel was the real advance. Allows us more range on smaller tanks, which means more room for warheads. Trident III has a lethality of 150,000. That missile, my friend, is a goddamned nightmare.''

''There were—are—two of these on the *Alaska?*''

''Yes. Tubes one and two. The rest are Trident IIs.''

''And you'd like them back.''

''I'll put it this way. A submarine like the *Alaska,* armed with twenty-four Trident III missiles, would carry more destructive potential than the combined nuclear arsenal of the Soviet Union. Remember what they used to say about economic powers? The United States is first, then Japan and a couple of European states, and Exxon is fifth. Or was it General Motors? In military strength, the United States is first. The Soviet Union is running second. The *Alaska* is third . . . as she is now, with just two Trident IIIs. If someone ever managed to duplicate the technology and load all her tubes with the same kind of missile, that someone would immediately become the second greatest military power on earth.''

Murdock took a deep breath. ''You're saying the Soviets would like to get their hands on her.''

''They want it so badly it hurts.''

''But with what's going on in Eastern Europe these days, the Soviet Union especially . . . their economic problems and moves toward democracy . . . it just doesn't make sense they'd try anything on the scale—''

''Don't be fooled by that, Glen. It wasn't so long ago the KGB created a special department, Agency Four, just for the purpose of stealing Trident technology. Their military is bigger than ours. Navy, too. Its political clout is a damn sight greater. I don't know what's going on over there, but I do know that their military machine is driven by a very conservative, powerful group of officers who may or may not approve of this *glasnost* crap. And don't make any mistake that they know about Trident III. They do . . . and they're out there right now.''

''That much I do know. We passed a Russian trawler on the way in.''

''That trawler was waiting right there when the *Alaska* arrived. The spotter planes photographed it long before the explosion. Now while we're searching for the *Alaska* we find two Kilo-class Soviet subs sitting quietly at three hundred feet. God only knows how long they've been around. Or what they're doing here. But don't you get it?

The Kilo class are attack submarines. SSBN hunter-killers.''

''You think they torpedoed the *Alaska?*''

''They'll do anything, *anything* to get a Trident III. They're not innovators. They're not even good imitators. They're thieves.''

''Don't let Eliot Packman hear you talking like that.''

''Packman!''

''Yeah. You don't know him?''

''I know he's here on the ship. How do you know about him?''

''He waylaid me on my way to see you.''

''What did he say?''

''Just that you're paranoid and seeing spies under your bed and until he can manage to stab you in the back he'd like me to keep my eyes and ears open and report everything you do or say.''

''You think it's funny?''

''It is, in a way . . . but I'm not laughing.''

''No, of course not. I'm turning to you for help here, Glen. The Navy people are good, very good, but we know that the Soviets have infiltrated every level of the service. You and my own personal staff are all I'm trusting on this one. You've already met O.K.''

''Okay?''

''Captain O.K. Cassidy. I've called him O.K. for so long I don't even remember his first name—Orville or something equally horrible—but he's my chief of staff and a very fine administrator.''

''What's his connection to Packman?''

''None whatsoever. I doubt if they've spoken a dozen words to each other. Cassidy feels the same way you and I do about bonehead bureaucrats like that. What'd you think of the captain?''

''He seems like a good enough man. Maybe more interested in my discovering the *Seawind* than the *Alaska.*''

''Did you?''

"Yes, this afternoon . . . yesterday afternoon, anyway."

"Well, that's something to cheer about. Damned if I feel like cheering. But don't let his reaction throw you. Cassidy has his reasons. Twelve years ago he must have been just about the same age that your boy is now. And he was holding down the same job: executive officer. His vessel went down, too. It was the *USS Seawind*. He and five other men barely got clear with the life raft before she sank. He never accepted another undersea assignment. I don't think you could force him into a sub. Damned fine staff officer, though. Doesn't matter. My other man is eager to go. He's never been down, and I promised him he could tag along with you tomorrow."

"Why?"

"I want to have one of my men on the trip before somebody else gets the idea."

"Who is this officer?"

"You met him. Commander Stout. He's a good man."

Murdock laughed humorlessly. "I met him, all right. Your good man tried to hijack me and my vessels earlier today."

"What!"

" 'Commandeer' was his word for it, but he didn't use that until we'd calmed him down. He tried to take my crew and ships by force. I tell you frankly, Dan, it was almost as though he didn't want me to come. That he had to try, but did it in such a way that he would alienate me and my men. On the way in here I kept wondering if he'd intentionally pushed us too far, that he let us turn the tables on him and hoped to report that I'd turned him down. If that's true there may be something down on the bottom somebody doesn't want us to find."

"I can hardly believe that. Of course he wanted you to come. I impressed upon him how vital it was. It must have been a case of over-zealousness."

"If he'd really wanted my help, all he had to do was

introduce himself and politely inform me that the submarine, on which my only son is executive officer, had disappeared.''

The admiral's thoughts seemed to be far away.

''He may not have known it. I did. I'd helped Drew get the assignment. But I didn't tell anyone else. Anyway, you old liar, you have two sons.''

Murdock shook his head.

''I did once. I lost one. Now it looks like I may have lost them both.''

# Chapter Four

First light revealed an ocean of battleship gray. A fleet of U.S. Navy vessels that must have beggared Pearl Harbor surrounded the *Nomad.* Cruisers, destroyers, subtenders, and tankers. There was even an aircraft carrier and the hulking sails of two nuclear attack submarines. None of them moved. They lay off waiting and watching. Activity centered on the deck of the *Nomad,* where a traveling crane slowly brought the ship's minisubmersible over the subwell. Once there she was gently lowered into the Pacific.

The search for the Trident had begun.

If the submersible looked ugly and awkward when perched on her pontoon undercarriage, or hanging from the crane cable like a deep-sea angler fish dangling from a quayside scale, she looked ugly no more. With her three steel spheres bolted together, her array of propellers and fins projecting from every side, the robot arm projecting from her control sphere, and the two pontoon-like legs of her undercarriage, the minisub looked no more outlandish than any other alien creature from the ocean depths. In the pilot's seat of the forward-most sphere, Glen Murdock grew increasingly uneasy. To be sure, this dive possessed an urgency beyond any he had ever made, but it wasn't just that—Murdock was always uneasy before a dive. People said he looked more at home in the water than out, but Murdock knew better. His dives were carefully planned and of limited duration. When the time came to leave, he returned to the surface. Like everyone else, he was only a visitor.

The crane halted when the yellow vehicle was half-in, half-out of the water. Two wet-suited divers jumped in behind her. While Murdock and Marie Delamer watched on video monitors, these divers pulled the red-flagged pins holding the iron descent weights in place. Murdock acknowledged an "Okay to dive," which came over the speaker. Small waves lapped at the blisters of six-inch-thick clear acrylic that served as the submersible's windows. Then the sunlit world vanished and a dimension of blue took its place. A mad swirl of bubbles scrambling for the surface gave Murdock and his crew a last look at the world they were leaving behind. Gone was the world of light and air, of warmth and safety, of physical laws fitting and forgiving to man. None of these applied anymore.

Their descent was halted a second time just yards below the surface, while Murdock and Marie in the copilot's seat went through their pre-dive procedures. Commander Alan Stout, the dive's only passenger, stuck his head through the connecting hatchway. This was not the arrogant, self-assured officer who had boarded the *Nomad* at gunpoint sixteen hours before. Flickering his eyes nervously, Stout watched Murdock's and Marie's every movement from over their shoulders.

Murdock tested the yoke for control of the planes and rudders. "Okay. Stern props?"

Marie began throwing toggle switches. "Check."

"Heliprops?"

"Check."

"Batteries, pumps, and ventilators?"

"Check, check, and check," she said.

"What's sonar say?"

"Bottom sounding at eighteen hundred feet."

"And you have a marker signal?"

"Couldn't be clearer—a three-second ping on the edge of my scope. We shouldn't have any trouble finding it."

"There's no consolation prize for finding a position marker," Murdock reminded her. "Let's just pray the Trident, if she's down there, is close to the marker."

Suddenly Murdock faced Commander Stout, whose chin practically rested on his shoulder.

"Commander, have you ever taken the express elevators down from the roof of the Empire State Building?" Stout, puffing himself up, announced that as a matter of fact he had done just that. "Well, what we're about to do now," Murdock told him, "is to drop twice that distance . . . after the elevator cables have snapped. I advise you to strap yourself in." Stout blanched and his mouth came open. Then, without uttering a sound, he snaked back to his seat in the central compartment. Murdock turned to Marie with a face devoid of expression.

"You're such a comfort," she teased him.

Murdock didn't smile back. Marie had never seen him so grim. His sense of humor under any circumstance was the thing about him she had always loved most. Usually he would reply to a comment like that with something rather salty and even a bit disrespectful, considering their passenger's rank. But all he said now was, "Cut us loose."

She transmitted the order.

There was a banging of metal, then a sensation of falling free. Stout, with his back to the starboard viewport, gripped the straps at his sides and closed his eyes. The submersible fell by the bow. She shot downward like a rocket launched into a nether universe. In only seconds the outside world had altered from skylit blue to purple and then to deepest violet.

"One-third power ahead," ordered Murdock. This was done and, once forward speed was added to their descent, flow over the rudders and diving planes gave the submersible minimal control, she began maneuvering downward instead of plummeting in an uncontrollable dive. When the sonar blip disappeared off the scope astern, Murdock steered the craft in a half circle. Soon the blip reappeared right ahead. Second by second the needle on the depth gauge swirled around the bezel, showing their depth at one hundred feet, two hundred feet, three hundred, and then four and five. Minute by minute the marker blip edged closer to the center of their scope.

The minisub was plunged into darkness. Murdock turned on the instrument lights, which bathed the control panel and the interior of both forward spheres in soft green fluorescence. When Murdock activated the exterior floodlights the darkness outside retreated, but not very far. On the surface these floods would have lit a city block, yet a mere two hundred yards below clear morning skies the blackness mocked their pitiful efforts from a few feet away. A myriad of tiny creatures—mollusks, crustaceans, and coelenterates, as well as the microscopic versions of these and a billion more like them—clouded the water, making the bright floods as useless as automobile headlights in the thickest of fogs.

At eight hundred feet, Marie swiveled to the low-frequency transceiver and issued the call sign for their support ship. *"Nomad,* this is *DORiS. Nomad,* this is *DORiS."* A few moments passed in silence. *"Nomad,* this is *DORiS.* Come in, *Nomad,* over."

Another short silence followed.

"Doris?" asked Stout.

"That's us," said Murdock.

"Why Doris?"

No answer came back from the forward sphere.

"Named after your wife, I'll wager," Stout said, doing his best to sound calm.

"No," said Murdock flatly.

Marie frowned at his abruptness. "His wife's name was Sally," she answered for him. Then Marie turned back to the radio. *"Nomad, this is DORiS.* Come in please, *Nomad."* She released the transmit button, swept across her instruments, and spoke to Murdock in the same even tone. "Passing through a thousand feet, Glen."

Stout's voice came again. "A daughter, then? Or a sweetheart?"

Murdock ignored him.

"He's got two sons," said Marie. With a cynical smile, she went on, "Any woman who thinks Murdock loves her is all wet." She thought about what she'd just said, then added, "Of course, if she *wasn't* all wet he wouldn't give her a second glance." There was no indication her remark had even registered with Murdock. "Deep Ocean Recovery Submersible, D-O-R-S, that's where the name *DORiS* comes from," Marie explained, giving up and going back to her radio to adjust the frequency settings. *"DORiS* calling *Nomad,* come in, *Nomad.* Come in, *Nomad,* over."

"What's the trouble?" asked Murdock.

"I don't know. It was working fine yesterday."

Commander Stout began struggling out of his straps. "I heard you use that radio just before we began our descent."

"That was the phone line," Marie told him. "We cut free of it when we released the cable. Once we're submerged, the only communication we have is by means of very low-frequency transmission. That's the only way you can transmit through water."

"You mean we're cut off from the surface?" asked Stout. A yellow glare from the sodium lamps outside his viewport caught the right side of his face; a green glow from the instrument panel caught the left. The result was to make him look unnaturally pale and gaunt. Murdock could see the stirrings of doubt in the other man's eyes. Doubt is the first symptom of fear; fear, the first sign of pressure, the kind of extreme pressure that exists only in the extreme ocean depths. A somber heaviness surrounded them. The hundreds of pounds of pressure on every square inch of the sub's outer surface somehow was able to work its way right through the hull. The deeper they dove, the greater the pressure became. The steel hull actually compressed. Just knowing this created a compensating tension within it. Though Commander Stout didn't know this, he was suffering the effects all the same. Pressure is the most compelling of the physical laws that challenge man's intrusion in the sea. He can ascend the fifty-mile height of earth's atmosphere without ill effects, but at twelve hundred feet deep they had already passed through forty times this atmospheric equivalent.

"We'll try again once we reach bottom," said Murdock. "Anything else on the fritz?"

"She's doing just fine," Marie reported.

They descended through thirteen hundred feet, and then fourteen. The depth gauge continued to spin downward, gathering angular momentum with each revolution. The bright blip of light on the sonar scope settled into the center. After that, Murdock steered the sub into a right-hand bank and trimmed it there. The constant clockwise turn held the marker off their starboard side. The gyro compass began to whirl in its cage while the submersible and depth needle spiraled together into the blackest of voids.

At fifteen hundred feet Marie announced that the bottom echoed three hundred feet down.

Murdock eased back the yoke and leveled the sub.

Two downward-thrusting propellers, one on each side of the central compartment, whirled into motion. The stern screw idled to a halt. Gradually, as the fathoms passed them by, *DORiS*'s descent slowed, until the depth-gauge needle moved around its bezel at only a fraction of its earlier speed.

"Seventeen-fifty, Glen. And I'm showing a fairly flat stretch of bottom off our starboard beam."

"And the marker?"

"Starboard quarter. About a hundred and forty degrees relative."

"Good enough."

Murdock steadily increased forward speed. Marie called off bottom soundings at five-foot intervals and gave him heading corrections to the flat section of sea floor.

When the bottom appeared, it did not come hazily into view from a distance and become clearer and clearer as they neared. It simply appeared all at once only feet away, clear and bright in the floods' myopic field of vision.

*DORiS* hovered a moment above the floor and then settled, helicopter-fashion, onto a sandy bank sprinkled with rock and long-dead coral skeletons. Clouds of sea dust billowed out from all sides under the propellers' disturbance and rolled in miniature avalanches away from the sub.

For several seconds no one spoke or moved.

Their eyes bore through the concave viewports searching for signs of life . . . or death. Stout was at his window now too. To him it seemed that they had landed on a distant planet—a desert planet of sand and rocks—a sunless planet eternally dark, eternally cold. A colony of sea urchins with foot-long spines bristled near their undercarriage. Jellyfish the size of small parachutes swam through the floodlights, filling and collapsing their canopies with rhythmic undulations. It was not a lifeless planet, but its inhabitants were extraterrestrial in every sense of the word.

Marie announced abruptly but quietly, "Eighteen hundred and twenty feet. Can the Trident submarines survive a dive to this depth?"

"Her maximum free-dive capabilities are a carefully kept secret," replied Stout. He, too, spoke in undertones, though not for fear of breaching security. He'd been gazing out the viewport with horror and awe. Now he seemed glad of the chance to turn his eyes and his thoughts in another direction. "The engineers tell us she can operate safely down to a thousand feet," he told Marie. "That's what? Thirty atmospheres?"

"About that," she whispered back.

"That may be a conservative figure, I don't really know."

Murdock wondered, what is it about the deep that makes visitors behave as though they are inside a church? It is humbling, this ocean. Powerful beyond our imaginations. Perhaps, he thought, this was the answer. Men can love the sea as a god, even worship it; but mostly, Murdock knew, the sea is a thing to be feared. Because the sea doesn't love back. And it never forgives.

"The *Alaska*'s not built for really deep dives," Murdock said, "not like a research submersible. A fleet submarine's crush depth is usually estimated as half again her operating depth. But that's still only fifteen hundred feet. Most of this bottom is closer to two thousand. If the *Alaska*'s down here, her crew is in the worst kind of trouble."

"Shall we try to raise *Nomad* again?"

"No. Let's wait until we have something to tell them. Where's that marker?"

"Eighty, maybe ninety yards, thirty degrees relative."

"Okay, that'll be our starting point."

The overhead and stern propellers were activated. Slowly *DORiS* rose from the sandy flat and moved reluctantly ahead before veering off to the right. Within minutes the floodlights revealed a bright orange cone nestled among a collection of rocks thrusting up from the sand.

Again they settled onto the bottom.

"Try the call-up again," ordered Murdock. "Let them know we've located the marker."

Marie went through the call-up once more without any result. After several tries Murdock told her to give it up.

They were, he reminded her, at the extreme edge of the low-frequency transmitter's range.

He outlined a search pattern by which *DORiS* would circle the marker, holding its signal off the starboard beam. Whenever their gyro compasses indicated they'd come fully around they would turn to the left, extend their search distance by fifty yards, and circle clockwise again.

"Fifty yards is a very wide pattern, Glen," said Marie. "You don't think we might miss it? As it is our headlights don't show twenty yards head, and not even half that to the sides."

"We won't miss it. The *Alaska* is two football fields long. Practically fifty yards wide. It's almost the size of a battleship, for chrissake."

Murdock took the first shift, while Stout and Marie moved back to the central compartment to watch out each of the side viewports, from which lateral floodlights were directed. They tried to keep a record of the bottom features by sketching notes onto the depth lines of their nautical charts. Generally the seabed to the north rose very slightly, with a bottom of rippled white sand only occasionally broken by slabs of rock thrust up from the floor. To the south the terrain became more and more rugged, with deep ravines and mammoth outcroppings appearing more and more regularly. At the same time this southern seascape fell off more and more steeply with each wider swing.

By early afternoon their circle had reached half a mile in circumference; the marker signal would soon be off the scope altogether. They had found nothing.

Marie's turn at the controls had twice come and gone. Now Murdock called for her to relieve him again.

Once Murdock had crawled into the central sphere, he grabbed a sandwich from the food hamper and moved to the starboard viewport. Across from him, Commander Stout spoke to his back. "The admiral told me you were part of the crew that located the *USS Mako* when it went down off the coast of Nova Scotia.''

''The admiral was right.''

''He usually is. Was the searching this slow on that mission?''

Murdock grunted. ''The *Mako* went down in eight thousand feet of ocean. We spent weeks locating the wreckage, and we never had fewer than four submersibles on the bottom at any one time.''

''But it was your sub that found her.''

''Yeah.''

Murdock would never forget the scene. The ocean had been clearer there. When his working lights revealed the site of the destruction, he couldn't believe it. At some point between the *Mako*'s maximum design depth and the sea floor, extreme pressures had simply crushed the attack submarine's hull. She had imploded. But there must have been explosions as well, for she lay in a thousand pieces of bizarre, twisted wreckage, scattered over a dozen square miles of bottom.

One particular fragment stuck in his mind. It had been a sobering glimpse of the kind of forces the *USS Mako* had foolishly defied. A roughly circular section of pressure hull—like a big satellite dish but four inches of solid steel—lay on the sand. Rising from it was a length of ballast tubing. The tube was forked at one end and the three narrow lengths of the fork were impaled through the steel. The hull had collapsed so quickly and with such power that the thin tubing had pierced the steel plating in the same way a tornado drives a straw through an oak tree. But what had struck Murdock most was the image of a trident, the three-pronged lance of the sea god, thrust through the shield of the sub, as though Neptune himself had destroyed the *Mako* in a warning to all submariners.

''You resigned your commission right after that?'' Stout asked him.

"No. Not after the *Mako*. It was after the *Vilinov* recovery, the Victor-class Soviet sub that went down in the Celebes a couple of years later."

"Sure, I remember. Admiral Reinholt commanded the operation."

"It was Captain Reinholt back then. And he was only a nominal commander. It was a Central Intelligence Agency operation. They were calling the shots."

"There was an accident. We lost a submersible."

"That's not all we lost. We were ordered to recover some of the *Vilinov* wreckage before the Soviets could get to the scene—for intelligence purposes. There was no question of saving lives. Well, we got what we wanted all right, but not before two good submariners and friends of mine had died trying to attach a towline to a scrap of the *Vilinov*'s shattered hull."

Stout turned around. "So that was it, then. The admiral never fully explained. There were three of you in the submersible. You alone made it back to the surface." Murdock remained silent, and soon Stout returned to his observation duties. "No wonder you feel the way you do about S&R."

"I approve of Search and Rescue. Of saving downed subs and ships—by which I mean saving their crews—whenever possible. I approve of risking life to save life. I don't approve of trading lives for a dozen kilobytes of data in the CIA's computer banks."

"Still, you don't blame Admiral Reinholt."

"He was in charge of the Navy end of it, all right, but he didn't like it any more than I did. Dan tried to talk me out of resigning, even though he understood." Murdock stared through his plastic bubble and found himself looking not at the alien landscape beyond but at his own reflection: an aging face worn by wind and sea and pressure and now twisted in torment. "No, I don't blame Dan Reinholt. Dan is a friend. He's done more for me than I can ever repay. My first salvage job out of the service I owe to him. Financial help, a couple times. When my son Drew wanted to try for Annapolis, Dan Reinholt pulled the strings. Dan helped Drew get his undersea service assignment.''

''What's your boy's rank?''

''Commander. He's an executive officer.''

''He must make you proud,'' offered Stout.

''He does indeed.''

''But Miss Delamer said you had two sons.''

Murdock shoved the last of the sandwich into his mouth. Stout waited for him to swallow, but either the food or the topic was a difficult thing to get down. At last Murdock merely grunted, ''Coy takes after his mother. Poor Sally never could stand the sea.''

There was something in the way he said it that put an end to the conversation.

Deep undersea vistas are an incredible combination of shapes and shadows under a powerful light, particularly as the bottom grows rugged. Rocks, coral, and plants, and the creatures that inhabit this sheltered environment, all have their own way of avoiding detection. Murdock, Marie, and even Stout felt that something was out there. But it seemed to remain just outside of their floods. Sharks occasionally sliced through the water at the edge of the sub's field of light. Other alien forms moved into investigate too, blocking their view of the sea floor for seconds on end. Once Marie investigated a dark line across the sand bottom, a line that extended as far as they could see on both sides of the sub. It turned out to be a caravan of lobsters, hundreds of them, marching along head to tail. One moment the depths would be a vacant undersea wasteland, devoid of any hint of life, and the next these same depths would be a veritable zoo of activity.

''Hold it!'' cried Stout. ''What's that?''

Stout's plastic bubble revealed a rapidly steepening incline, descending far beyond and below the circle of light thrown by the lateral floods.

But when Murdock joined him and Marie had eased off the power, Stout was pointing to a rough furrow gouged out of the sand and continuing out of sight down the slope.

Marie directed the more powerful forward floods on the furrow while Murdock consulted the charts.

"It doesn't look like a natural formation," she said.

At first Murdock was silent. He knew only too well the routine of a search. A pattern should never be broken. If anything was down that abyss they would find it on the next swing around. On the other hand he was remembering a report on the search for the American H-Bomb that had dropped in the ocean off Spain. Apparently the currents had billowed the parachute and dragged the bomb several dozen yards along the bottom before pitching it into a ravine. Had the search team not followed the rut they never would have found the device.

Here the nautical charts showed a submarine canyon that was both wide and deep. Certainly a dangerous place to go snooping. But the chart showed something more. A crude circle that completely encompassed the canyon had been penciled in by Admiral Reinholt just hours before the dive had begun. Down there was the iron concentration the Navy had detected on the sea floor. Murdock hated the thought of going down—and knew he had no other choice.

"Let's take a look," he said.

Murdock wormed through the hatch to the control sphere and took over the copilot's chair. *DORiS* turned and faced darkness until they pushed her nose down and the floods revealed the furrow's path running down the incline. They followed both until the incline and furrow ended. Blackness yawned beneath this brim. "Another three hundred feet to the bottom," said Murdock. "A little more than two thousand. Maybe deeper. These charts aren't even close to accurate at this depth.''

"Well?" Marie asked.

"Try backing down. I'll watch your ass on the sonar."

Using the overhead propellers again to slow their descent, and with Murdock monitoring the sonar screen, Marie spun the craft one hundred and eighty degrees about. The floods played down the cliff wall as they descended.

For a quarter of an hour the sheer rock wall of the submarine cliff passed in front of their viewport. Murdock called bottom a few fathoms off, and almost at once a loose rocky talus reached out for their undercarriage. Marie turned the sub back around and let the forward floods sweep the floor of the canyon. But the floor was still hidden from view.

"Oh, God!" cried Murdock.

A smashed hunk of metal the size of a Sherman tank blocked their path. The metal itself was nearly three inches thick, and yet the object looked as though it had been crushed like a wad of aluminum foil.

"Maybe not," Marie answered uncertainly. "You can't say for sure what that thing used to be."

She brought power to the overhead props and slowly *DORiS* rose, sending her floodlights streaking over the top of the twisted hulk and at last onto the canyon floor.

Two other misshapen scraps of black metal fell under their floods.

"No," said Murdock with conviction. "No, it's the *Mako* all over again."

Everywhere they looked they saw more of the same.

Everywhere their floods shone it was the same story. Chunks of black metal. Ruptured, twisted sheets of steel. Bent and crushed iron plating. Electrical and mechanical hardware of every description. No piece was recognizable. And no two were quite the same. There was only one thing they all had in common: Collected, hammered out, repaired, and reassembled, they would be a nuclear submarine. But that wouldn't happen. For the rest of time these tortured metallic hunks—like grotesque tombstones—would serve only to mark this seabed as a giant graveyard.

Murdock ordered Marie to halt the submersible over a particularly gruesome display. A ragged round fragment of hull had been pierced during the implosion by a length of forked iron tubing. It looked for all the world like a Goliath's shield impaled by an even more powerful three-pronged lance.

"Jee-sus!" said Murdock, "It really is the *Mako* all over again."

Commander Stout was shaking his head in dismay.

"No one could have survived this," he muttered to himself. He turned to Murdock for confirmation. "Nobody could have survived an implosion like this, could they?"

"No," said Murdock slowly. "Nobody did."

# Chapter Five

They had crossed through a graveyard and come upon that one nameless tombstone. But even to Stout and Marie who had never witnessed such things before, it meant something more: an open grave yet to be filled. The two of them shared a premonition of doom; in some odd way they knew that the sea had not claimed its last victim.

"That's it, then," said the commander. "We've found what we came for. It's a tragedy—a terrible blow to the Navy. But it's over. There's nothing more we can do. Let's get the hell out of here."

"It's just gotten started," said Murdock.

Stout retired to the central chamber, leaned back in his seat, and closed his eyes.

"He's right, though," Marie said softly, "we should go back and report."

"We're going back. But I'm taking that damn thing with us." Murdock pointed to the grim metal debris outside their viewport. He ordered Marie to maneuver the sub right beside it. Then Murdock deployed *DORiS*'s utility arm, got a grip on the circular base with the hydraulic pincer, and dragged it onto the forward skids of their undercarriage. He didn't stop pulling until the thick shaft of pipe thrust up right in front of the viewport.

Only then did they prepare for ascent.

Marie opened a cover on two rows of six toggle switches and twelve corresponding indicator lights. She threw the switches in pairs from bow to stern, cutting power to the electromagnets that held the descent weights in place. As the last of the indicators went out, Marie watched the video monitor to see the undercarriage lift off the bottom. But the undercarriage remained where it was.

"Uh-oh," she said.

"Too heavy?"

"It sure looks that way."

"I wouldn't have thought so. Try giving us a bit of a boost."

Marie engaged the overhead props and steadily increased power until the two electric motors were running at maximum speed. A storm of sand raged all around them; waterborne silt and debris swirled aloft. But even after some minutes at full power the minisub remained on the sea floor. Marie eased off the throttles before the motors could overheat. Slowly the sand storm abated.

"It's no use," she said.

"I hate to go back empty-handed," grumbled Murdock. "Have you got this on videotape?"

"Every bit of it, Glen. I've been recording since we descended into the canyon."

Reluctantly, Murdock used the utility arm again to push the debris off the undercarriage. This took even more time than the loading. In the end Marie had to drive the stern screws at maximum reverse and drag the minisub out from under it. And then *DORiS* was free.

"Okay, that's that. Shut off the magnets again, Marie."

"But Glen, they're already off."

For the first time, there was real concern in Marie's voice. Murdock sensed it clearly. So did Commander Stout. He moved up behind them.

"What's wrong?"

"Get back in your seat, Stout. Let me try, Marie."

Murdock was already reaching across her. He activated and then deactivated the two rows of switches in rapid succession. One by one the lights showed, then winked out.

"It's damn queer," he murmured. "Maybe we're mucked into the bottom. Hold on, I'll take a look."

In the central compartment, Murdock craned his head through the concave viewports and finally spotted a length of what appeared to be heavy-duty electrical cable snagged on the after undercarriage assembly. "You've backed into some wiring," he called to her. "It may be holding us down. Try the props again."

Once again Marie activated the propellers. As the power in the overhead motors neared maximum she could tell it was going to work. *DORiS* rose heavily but rose nonetheless, and hovered a few seconds. Murdock could see that the cable was well entangled on the rear skids, but despite this it didn't seem to be holding them down. If it had been, they were now free. He informed the others of this. Marie replied with an exclamation of relief. But when she cut power the minisub, instead of rising, fell back to the sea floor with a solid crunch.

Marie's face showed a mixture of fear and frustration as Murdock came forward. No one, he mused, was immune to this kind of pressure. "Dammit," she snapped, "I don't think the magnets have shut down." Together they directed the video camera onto the undisturbed patch of sand below the submersible and verified the fact at once.

"Why don't you just blow ballast tanks?" cried Stout, his voice breaking under the strain. "Or whatever it is you do to go up." If he didn't sound as worried as Marie, it was only because he didn't know as much as she did.

Murdock tried to explain: "We don't blow ballast, we jettison it. Our ballast is twelve detachable iron weights on our undercarriage. *DORiS*'s bouyancy tanks don't take her up—we use them only for trim, shifting her weight fore and aft to keep her from pitching. When the iron ballasts are attached, the sub sinks. When the iron ballasts are released, the sub rises—it's that simple. But for some reason the weights won't release. They should be lying there on the bottom, but they're not.''

"Can't you just use the props?''

"You mean a power ascent all the way to the surface?''

"Why not?''

"Because I'm not stupid, that's why. The motors aren't up to it; neither are the batteries. And when we failed to make it to the top, we'd need both to get back down here in one piece.'' Murdock turned to Marie. "It must be a short in the electrical system. Nothing to worry about.''

"Can you fix it?'' asked Stout.

"Not from inside the sub; but I may be able to bypass the problem.'' Murdock crawled out of his seat, pushed Stout aside, and pulled a panel on the central sphere bulkhead. Inside was a series of breakers. He went right for the uppermost lever, the main, and threw it.

Instantly the interior was engulfed in utter darkness. Every light inside and outside the minisub was extinguished. The silence was every bit as profound. All the motors and pump had shut down. The compressors, even the tiny drives that kept the gyroscopic instruments of the control panel spinning, had gone quiet. This was the still of the grave.

Then came the sound of the same switch thrown again and light filled their eyes.

The three of them bent to the viewports, where the exterior floods again illuminated their few yards of bottom. *DORiS* hadn't budged.

"I can't figure it,'' Murdock murmured. "The short must be between the main bus and the breakers. But that doesn't make sense.''

Stout sank into his seat. "Are you going to be able to fix it or not?''

"Only from outside the sub. Unfortunately we can't get outside the sub—the access sphere only pressurizes to four hundred fifty pounds—which translates to about a thousand feet of depth. Anyway, our scuba equipment isn't worth a damn below twelve hundred feet."

"We're below two thousand feet!"

"I'm well aware of that, Commander."

"So what are you saying?"

"That we may just have to sit back and wait."

"How long before they can send someone down to help us?"

Murdock grunted. "Three or four days. A week."

"Good Lord, do we have enough food to last a week?"

"We don't have enough air to last another twelve hours. I meant we may have to wait for the batteries to die."

"What happens then?"

"We go up. The lights, heaters, motors, pumps, and air compressors—everything in the minisub is powered by three hundred and twenty-four batteries under the main compartment flooring. More than two thousand amp hours of juice. Those batteries also power the electromagnets that hold the iron weights in place once the pins have been removed. That's what makes the system foolproof. The last result of a power problem is that the weights drop off and the sub rises to the surface."

"But how long will that take?"

"It depends on how much power we use. Several more hours at least."

Marie cut in with an idea. "We could help it along. Turn on the heater strips and all of the external and internal lights. Everything. Even the props."

Murdock nodded in halfhearted agreement. "But if we're going to run the props, we might just as well go somewhere. Let's try to find a way out of this hole."

They made a slow circuit of the canyon floor, but found no ascent more accommodating than the route by which they'd come down. After returning to their starting point, Murdock announced they would try a power ascent from the canyon and traded places with Marie. He brought the overhead propellers to full power and slowly the cliff fell before them. They saw a replay of the sheer wall of rock in their floodlights, only this time played in reverse and at nothing like the same speed.

Still short of the top, the starboard motor showed signs of overheating. When Murdock brought both motors to two-thirds power, their ascent slowed to a crawl.

It was a climb that *DORiS* should never have been able to make. The minisub was designed to plane. Once the overhead props lifted her free of the bottom, the two stern propellers carried much of her negative bouyancy. She could hover for short periods with the overhead props alone. And she could climb, but only long enough to top small obstacles in her path. *DORiS* had not been designed to ascend with her ballasts attached, for anything more than a few minutes at a time. She should have failed to reach the top of the cliff. And a failure of her motors near the top would have sent her plummeting back into the canyon.

Murdock was holding the stern props in reserve for just such an emergency. If the overhead motors failed, he would come about and power-glide down.

But the tiny submersible did top the cliff.

"We made it!" cried Stout, as the floods revealed the brim of the cliff and the furrow that had led them into the canyon. He sat back, expelling a dry liter of air.

Ten minutes later the sub was resting on the sandy bank up the slope, well away from the cliff. Murdock allowed all four motors to run idle, so they could cool at the same time as the batteries continued to drain.

"If we could just get in touch with the *Nomad*," said Murdock.

Marie raised tired eyes to him. The ascent had been a strain for them all. "What could you do?"

"Report what we've located, for starters. But if we could talk to them we could arrange for a tow."

"How?"

"Have them lower a cable with a sounder and hook at the base. We could locate the cable by means of the sounder and use the utility arm to attach the hook to our forward frame. It'd be an uncomfortable trip up, but I think we could make it."

"What a terrible coincidence," said Marie, "the radio and the magnets both malfunctioning on the same dive."

"I wonder." After saying this, Murdock fell silent. Then he seemed to resolve something in his own mind. "Marie, I'm going to pull up the floor boards. Why don't you do what you can with the radio?"

When Murdock had the floor boards removed and he had exposed the network of batteries underneath, he realized there would be no way to disconnect the hundreds of batteries from the busbar without specialized tools. The connections for the magnets themselves could be gotten at only from below.

"You said in time the batteries would die," said Stout, crouched in the access chamber watching him. "What's wrong with just waiting?"

"I don't know, Commander. And that's what's wrong with it. What you don't know down here can kill you."

By the time Murdock had replaced the flooring and returned to the control sphere, Marie had the radio in a dozen small pieces. "I can't find anything the matter with it," she announced in exasperation. "The trouble must be with the *Nomad*'s radios."

"No. I've decided you're right. This is no accident."

"What are you saying?"

"Could someone have come in the minisub while it was standing on the afterdeck? Did you see anyone in or around her?"

"There were lots of people. Do you think it was sabotage?"

"Yes. But not the *Nomad* crew—how about someone from Admiral Reinholt's party?"

Stout sat up in alarm. "Now hold on!"

"Any one of them could have," said Marie. "They all looked it over, I guess."

"But if someone slipped inside to knock out the radio he didn't have enough time to dismantle the damn thing, like you've done. He would have had only seconds. A minute or two at best before a member of the crew spotted him."

On a hunch, Murdock scooped up Marie's screwdriver and removed the cover plate on the radio loudspeaker. They both stared at the torn remnants of the speaker diaphragm in open-mouthed amazement. Then Murdock attacked the screws of the handset cover and found the same kind of destruction to the microphone. A screwdriver like his, jabbed and twisted through the circuits, would have done the job nicely.

Murdock acknowledged the handiwork with a grim smile. "Quick and effective. Without a speaker or microphone, any radio is just so many spare parts."

"I can't believe it!" cried Stout.

"There's your proof."

"But all he's done is delay your report. When the batteries die . . ."

"You're right. It wouldn't do any good to destroy the radio unless they could keep us from ever surfacing to tell what we've seen. But if they had seconds to sabotage this, they had no more time to sabotage the electromagnets."

"How could they do that?" asked Marie.

Murdock dropped into the pilot's seat and directed the video camera at the sub's undercarriage. Clouds of silt and sand rose off the bottom until he shut down the overhead props. After that, the lower framework of the sub slowly became visible. He panned the camera down each skid.

"Jee-sus Christ!"

"What is it?" Stout demanded. He and Marie were craning their necks for a look at the monitor.

Murdock was almost too stunned to speak. "The weights are still pinned in place."

"Wha . . ." Stout fought for words. "But we all saw your men pull the pins. The flags . . ."

Murdock reached for the controls and shut down the stern motors. In rapid succession he shut off all the lights and ventilators, leaving the three spheres in soft green surrounded by blackness and cold. Only his voice broke the silence of night.

"The weights are pinned and flagged from the outside of each skid so they can't possibly be missed. Someone—at this point we should say 'the saboteur'—inserted another set of pins, without flags, from the inside. When the batteries die we'll be dead, too. They're the only thing keeping us alive. And we've been doing everything in our power to exhaust them."

Without the heating strips the spheres would begin to cool. Without heat the baralyme crystals in the ventilation system wouldn't be able to scrub carbon dioxide. Though both of these would take many minutes to have any noticeable effect, the air seemed to grow cold and stale almost at once.

"Let's discuss our options," said Murdock.

"What about banging a message?" suggested Stout. "There must be someone listening up there on sonar. We could tap out a distress signal on the hull."

"It's a thought," agreed Murdock. "Do you know Morse?"

"Heavens no! I thought you—"

Marie spoke up at once. "I for one," she said, "am not going to sit here and wait to die."

"That's the spirit. Why don't you and the commander cannibalize the telephone/intercom speaker and see if you can wire it into the radio. The mike isn't transferable, but maybe the speaker is. If we can't call for help, we can at least listen. It's possible someone on the *Nomad* has an idea they're trying to tell us about. In the meantime I'm going to test *DORiS*'s dexterity.''

Murdock turned to the control panel, activated the underbelly floodlights again, and worked the controls for the utility arm. Using the video monitors, he maneuvered the arm under the forward sphere and delicately grabbed the forward-most pin on the port side with the pincer. It took three times to extract it. After he had done so the heavy weight fell to the sand in a small explosion of waterborne silt. ''One down!'' Murdock called out, and for a moment their spirits soared—until he informed them that at least eight of the weights would have to be released for a free ascent, a forlorn hope. By then Murdock had turned the arm and the video camera around and was trying to repeat his success with the forward weight on the opposite side of the undercarriage.

''I've got an idea,'' offered Marie.

''Let's have it.'' Murdock didn't bother to turn.

''The two end spheres are held to the central sphere with explosive bolts, right? In case of flooding, either one can be detached. But aren't these smaller spheres buoyant under normal conditions?''

''Sure they are. By a hundred pounds or so.''

''Put me in one and send me to the top.''

''Forget it.''

''Glen, I weigh hardly more than a hundred pounds!''

''They're a hundred pounds buoyant at the surface. At depth, they're compressed—you know that. Their density is increased. Everything is. That's why bodies, wooden ships, anything that falls into the great depths of the ocean never ascends. You'd roll around out there for the rest of time.''

''I'm the only one small enough.''

''That's final, Marie. I won't let you try it.''

''We could put a message in the sphere then.''

''That might work. But it'd be an expensive message.

If you send up the forward sphere we lose the controls and the utility arm; send up the after sphere and we lose the thrusters and rudders. We couldn't do anything after that but sit here and wait. If they lowered a cable and sounder we couldn't get to it. We couldn't attach to it even if we could reach it. They'd know we were in trouble, all right, but they'll know that much in another few hours anyway.''

Marie nodded her head and turned away.

Murdock went back to his work. Shortly he managed to pull the forwardmost starboard pin. But try as he would, he couldn't get *DORiS*'s mechanical arm to reach any farther under the minisub. Another five pins on each side of the undercarriage still held their ballasts in place.

"I don't like it either," Stout announced. "But in the absence of any better idea I support Miss Delamer's plan."

Murdock shut him off with a glare. "You know better than that, Stout. I'm in command here and what I say goes."

"Well, what do you propose to do?"

"Is that speaker working?"

Marie nodded. "It's wired in. Nothing's coming over. Whether *Nomad*'s not sending or this speaker is the wrong impedance, I just don't know."

The diver quickly made up his mind. "We don't have much choice. We're going to try a full-power ascent."

Marie's eyes widened.

"We'll never make it to the surface. You said so yourself."

"We won't have to. If we can get five or six hundred feet up, I can force my way out the access chamber and pull the damn pins."

"We'll never make that—we almost burned out the motors coming up three hundred feet."

"We're a little lighter now. I released two of the ballasts."

Taking the pilot seat, Marie brought the overhead propellers to full power. Slowly they rose off the bottom. In seconds the sea floor vanished and blackness surrounded them again.

Stout helped Murdock climb into the waterproof rubber dry suit complete with hood, boots, and gloves. The diver slipped on fins and then spat onto the glass of his full-face mask before cradling it on the top of his head.

"Fifteen hundred!" called Marie.

"Keep me posted." Murdock called back. "I'll be in the pressure chamber." He slid the electrolung into the chamber ahead of him and then crawled in behind it. He first closed and latched the main sphere hatch. After that he closed the pressure hatch. He activated the depth settings for maximum pressure at maximum rate of pressurization. Almost at once came the hum of the pumps and the hiss of air being driven into the chamber at high speed. Murdock yawned and cranked his jaw as the pressure worked throughout his body.

There was no viewport in this afterchamber. All he could do was listen to the incoming air and the occasional reports coming over the speaker from Marie.

Murdock felt the sub heeling to starboard and guessed that the starboard motor was overheating again.

He watched the pressure gauge under his small overhead light move to two hundred pounds per square inch. At this point pure air itself becomes toxic, poisoned by the high volume of oxygen, and Murdock slipped the electrolung device on his back and began breathing from the three-percent oxygen mixture. Even at this low percentage, it was the equivalent of breathing pure oxygen at sea level.

The speaker blared: "Thirteen hundred feet, Glen. But we're slowing down drastically. The starboard motor's about gone and I've had to slow down the port motor, too, in order to keep us from heeling too badly to rise. I don't think we can make another three hundred feet.''

Murdock pressed the talk button and said merely: "Keep going.''

He winced at the squeak of his voice from the helium gas in his lungs.

The pressure gauge slowed almost to a stop at the four-hundred-pound mark and then edged on toward the red line with incredible sluggishness. From this Murdock knew that the batteries, which powered the compressors as well as the props, were running down. They hadn't much time.

The voice that came over the speaker was filled with alarm. "Twelve-fifty, Glen! But it's not going to work! The starboard motor has about had it. The batteries are reading nearly dead. We're just barely holding our own!''

Murdock's fist hammered the intercom panel, driving in the talk button and most of the surrounding faceplate as well: "Trim 'er bow down! Throw both stern props on full-power reverse!''

Marie didn't answer. And in the next horrifying moment Murdock remembered they'd cannibalized the intercom speaker. He couldn't tell Marie what to do. It was all up to her now, for he couldn't get out of the pressurized chamber any more than they could get in. Murdock felt the sub pitch. Were they diving? No. He sensed the vibrations of the stern propellers just aft his chamber and knew she had figured it out for herself.

"Good girl," he thought.

The pressure had red-lined at four hundred fifty pounds per square inch. Murdock's ears ached and his chest had grown ungodly heavy. He'd never before pressurized so quickly.

"We're moving again, Glen. I've got the stern props dragging us up in reverse. Passing through twelve hundred feet. It's slow going, but I think I can get us to eleven hundred feet before the stern motors give out, too. If only the batteries last.''

The numbers whirled through Murdock's brain: twelve hundred feet deep, more than thirty-six times sea level pressure. Five hundred thirty pounds per square inch. His eyes flashed onto his pressure gauge. Four hundred seventy pounds inside the chamber. A difference of sixty pounds per square inch. Still twelve tons pressing against the outside of his hatch.

"Eleven-fifty, Glen. But the batteries are about gone. Another thirty or forty feet if we're lucky!" Her voice was strained, almost panicky. He'd never known her so scared.

Chamber pressure had now reached nearly five hundred pounds.

His head pounded horribly; even his eyes ached.

The two pressures were coming together, but not fast enough. Perhaps not at all.

"That's it! We've stopped, Glen. I'm holding for the moment, but the batteries are showing dead and we'll start to fall any second.''

Murdock slammed the hatch lever open and pushed down as hard as he could with both hands. The hatch wouldn't budge.

"Glen, it's right now or never!"

Murdock squatted over the hatch, placed his feet on either side of the handle, and braced the heavy tanks on his back against the overhead. With all of his strength he shoved downward.

The tiniest jet of seawater found its way through a crack of the hatch. This crack was almost microscopic; the pressure behind it, intense. The water hit his ankle in a razor-thin sheet with such speed and power it sliced through the rubber dry suit like a scalpel. It sliced through his skin and bone. It sprayed the chamber with blood and salt.

Murdock screamed.

He tried to keep pushing, but it was no good. The light in the chamber faded to black—his mind, not the batteries, going. His last sensation was one of collapsing, of falling down and down.

Water entering the chamber almost instantly equalized the difference in pressure. The metal hatch simply fell open.

Murdock, dazed and delirious, came to in the sea. The insufferable pain in his leg was numbed somewhat by the freezing waters, but the combination of these numbed his mind, too. Through blurred eyes he was seeing above him the belly of the submersible in the feeble glow of a once powerful floodlight.

With torpid, dreamlike strokes he swam upward.

He kicked, but his legs didn't have the power to propel him. Or if they had the power, they lacked the will.

Something came drifting down.

One of his fins.

No wonder he could make no speed. As it passed by him Murdock made a grab for the fin and missed. He saw a yellow rubber boot inside the foot pocket. Inside the rubber was his foot.

Nausea turned him away. He spotted the first of the pins just beyond his reach. Kicking didn't seem to get him any closer. Then, strangely, the pin was right in his hand. He hadn't swum up to the sub; the sub and the pin had come down to him.

He pulled it out, dodged the falling weight, and grabbed for the second pin in the same movement, pulling and dodging again. He reached for the third. But the pin was no longer there; the submersible was no longer there.

It was falling away.

He grasped at the skid . . . and missed.

Murdock had a clouded picture of the undercarriage and the two after-spheres growing more distant. He saw a green glow from a viewport, where Commander Stout watched him fall farther and farther behind. Stout's face, frozen in terror, slowly faded out of sight as the sub made a fatal plunge for the bottom of the sea.

# Chapter Six

Murdock floated in a frigid, starless oblivion that sapped his senses in the same way it had drained the strength from his body.

The sub was doomed—that much he knew. Marie and Stout had no hope of survival. Murdock himself had one small chance to live. He had to start up. Now. If he were lucky and the loss of blood didn't kill him . . . if sharks drawn by the blood didn't eat him . . . if he could swim with one leg the quarter of a mile to the surface . . . and if he surfaced within hailing distance of the *Nomad* or one of the other vessels, he might live. He might live for an hour or perhaps even two before the mind-racking agony of "the bends" overcame him. Once the rapid ascent boiled the gases in his body, folded him up like a fist and he died screaming in a nightmare of anguish, luck would no longer be a factor. Of course there was always the chance they might get him to a recompression chamber in time, but the closest he knew of was five hundred miles away in Hawaii and this would stretch his good luck past the limit. A few seconds thought would have given Murdock little reason to hope he'd survive an ascent—and that was his only sane course of action. But men bereft of their senses do not spend time in thought. Insane men do not reason.

Murdock inverted his body and lashed downward in a mad pursuit of the sub.

The last blush of light from *DORiS*'s exterior floods

was just disappearing. She was diving much faster than Murdock could swim. He couldn't find her. He couldn't catch her.

His legs kicked frantically. But with only one fin he was making half his normal speed and leaving a bloody wake in the process—a vertical column of blood now a hundred feet deep. His hands clawed at the distant darkness. But there was only more darkness below him.

The sub had vanished completely.

Murdock swam on like a madman.

When something long and tough snaked over his body he didn't even stop thrashing. He could feel it right through the dry suit, coiling around his calf, dragging across his back and along his arm. He could see nothing; he didn't even slow down. Whether this was a sea snake, the hundred-foot tentacles of a jelly fish, or a deep-sea squid, it didn't matter. He couldn't waste the seconds it would take to find out.

In the same instant the tentacle pulled free, Murdock knew what it was: the electrical cable still entangled on the sub's undercarriage.

He grabbed blindly. His fingers curled around the end of the cable. It nearly jerked out of his hand but somehow he held on. Suddenly he was barreling down.

To his death.

There was no doubting that. Even now it was all he could do to draw air into his lungs, for the pressure surrounding him was almost more than the pressure inside his tanks.

He started pulling himself down hand over hand.

A faint greenish glow appeared below him—a circle of green from one of *DORiS*'s viewports. Marie had extinguished the floodlights, saving what minimal battery power remained until just before impact.

Little by little, the sub came into view. She was still slightly bow-down, but losing her pitch as the access chamber continued to take on more water. As Murdock hauled himself closer the sub seemed to hover below him, but the rush of water against his dry suit and mask, and the increasing pressure with every foot they dove, gave the lie to this tranquil notion. At the speed she was falling, the impact would break her apart. The acrylic viewports, the gaskets between the spheres, the hatches—all of them would go; not even the hull itself could withstand a crash of that kind.

He knew the dilemma Marie faced. The hatch on the access chamber was still open to the sea. The deeper they dove the more water flooded the chamber, thus increasing the negative buoyancy of the sub and making them dive all the faster. She couldn't close the hatch from the forward unpressurized spheres. All she could do was activate the explosive bolts, jettison the access sphere, and hope for the best. This would momentarily control their downward acceleration but it would cause them to lose all control once they got to the bottom, because *DORiS*'s diving planes and rudders were welded to the outside of that sphere.

A dilemma like this could end in only one way: a violent collision with the sea floor.

Finally the diver succeeded in crawling down to the minisub's belly. He gripped the undercarriage framework with weak, lifeless hands. His vision was gone. Murdock had been holding his breath for the last thirty yards, while the increase in pressure was squeezing his chest in the same vise that had crumpled the nuclear submarine's hull. Any moment oxygen depletion would snuff out the last flicker of consciousness. The access chamber was just over his head, the eight iron ballasts much farther forward. Before he could climb down and release the remaining pins, he would be dead.

Murdock pulled himself through the access hatchway and brought the hatch closed behind him. Water half filled the chamber. He inhaled several times. The pressure on his chest eased at once and life returned to his limbs, but at that point the pain in his leg became almost unendurable. His stump of a foot was mercifully still hidden in water. He didn't lift it up. He didn't explore the damage with his hands, for he didn't want to know. There was no time. Murdock spun the valves that bled air pressure from the chamber directly into the sea—using the pumps to draw out the pressure would waste power they couldn't afford, and time they didn't have. The decrease in pressure was so rapid he scarcely needed to inhale at all, since the air in his lungs expanded as quickly as he could exhale it.

Then Murdock threw open the connecting hatches. Water spilled into the central sphere as he clambered over the hatch coaming on hands and knees and turned to close the hatch at his back.

Standing above him, Commander Stout was clenching the sides of the chamber for support and staring at Murdock in awe. Had Davy Jones himself staggered into the sub the commander could not have been more astonished.

"Damn, man!" he exclaimed. "I thought you were gone!"

Marie, in the pilot's seat, whirled.

The horror on her face was swept away in a flood of relief. "We're at fifteen hundred feet and falling fast," she called back, running the words together. Murdock was already working through the forward hatchway and into the copilot's position. "Oh, Glen! Your foot! God, what . . . ?"

"Forget it. You're coming down like a pancake. You've got to get your bow down."

"I'd just sent the commander back to jettison the access sphere."

"We can't do that!" cried Murdock. "Not yet. We're going to need the diving planes before we hit bottom. Have you got 'er trimmed all the way forward?"

"Every bit of the weight is forward."

Murdock looked back into the central compartment, where Stout was hurriedly strapping himself into his seat. "Come up here, Commander." He turned quickly to Marie. "Whatever happens here, honey, you've got to promise that you'll do something for me."

"Anything, Glen."

"You'll go after my son. Promise me that. You'll get him. . . ."

Stout had come up behind them. "What can I do, Murdock?"

Murdock ignored him. "Promise me, Marie!"

"My word on it, Glen."

Murdock faced Stout.

"You've been practically sitting in our laps the whole trip. Now when we need all our weight forward you're being a good boy in your seat. Stick around and"—Murdock's face twisted into a smile—"try to be heavy, huh?"

Marie gathered her strength. Murdock's humor had come back. His iron-gray eyes were bright. He was his old self again, and everything would work out all right.

Murdock swept his eyes across the instrument panels— the low power made their accuracy doubtful. "The marker signal is just to the west, Marie; turn forty-five degrees to port. We'll try for that stretch of sand north of the marker. If we land in the canyon, or on those rocks . . . we're finished."

The darkness rushed at them at a hellish speed. Plankton and protozoa bombarded their viewport faster than the onrush of seawater could wash them aside.

"Another two hundred feet!" shouted Murdock. "You're doing fine. We've got some forward speed. Maybe enough. Get ready to rotate on my signal. If we do it just right, we'll lose a lot of our momentum before falling back down. Commander, when I give Marie the signal, I want you to jump back to your seat and hold onto something."

"Right!"

The sub burrowed on through the black depths.

A hundred feet from the bottom Marie activated the bow floodlights, but the glow from those once powerful beams barely illuminated the forward part of the undercarriage. Beyond, it illuminated nothing at all.

Without warning a huge bulbous mass appeared right in front of their eyes. It looked like a half ton of boulder. Marie instinctively rotated the planes while Murdock shouted for her to bank. It was too late for either maneuver. The mass exploded against their viewport.

Marie screamed. When it was over she stared at the unmarked acrylic in awe.

"A goddamned jellyfish!" Murdock was pushing the controls back down. "We're still a hundred feet off the bottom!"

Stout, who had fallen back into the central chamber, climbed up the steep slope of the deck and threw himself back into the control sphere. The rotation had cut their descent speed, but it had come too soon. They were now falling by the stern—out of control and gathering speed. Slowly the trim and their body weight brought the bow down again, but not soon enough to rotate a second time.

"Twenty feet!" Murdock shouted. "Get back, Stout. You too, Marie. Get through the hatch!"

Murdock pulled back the useless controls. As Stout and Marie climbed through the hatch, the forward viewport was swallowed up in the sand. The sub plowed into the bottom. A spray of seawater caught Marie's back and slammed her head against the steel of the hatchway. Commander Stout grabbed her arms and pulled her through as the control sphere began flooding. When the commander looked back Murdock was coming through, too, pulling the hatch closed behind him and closing the lever soundly.

*DORiS* settled down onto her supports, balanced by both of the end spheres now flooded or half-filled with water. Only the central chamber was still intact.

Murdock lay back against one of the seats, looking down at Marie. In his eyes was exhaustion and sadness. And a pain that went far beyond his desperate physical condition.

"That leg of yours," Stout gasped, catching his breath. "It has to be stanched. Bandaged or something. You'll lose too much blood."

The diver almost smiled, but his teeth were ground solidly together and his jaw remained a hard line. "I've already lost too much blood. But don't let it worry you—blood loss won't kill me."

"It will if you lose enough. And you're losing a lot."

Murdock shook his head. "I mean it won't kill me in time, and that's too bad. The way I've got planned to go is much more unpleasant. I didn't decompress before coming out of the access chamber."

Stout's eyes grew wide. He watched Murdock's hands alternately squeezing and hammering his thighs. He saw the diver's stomach and chest muscles tensing right through the dry suit. Even a Pentagon sailor knows the effects of the bends.

"Bad?" he asked.

"It's bad enough," Murdock admitted, "but it's going to get worse." He crawled to Marie and lifted her eyelids one at a time. He examined the wound on her head. "She may be a while coming around, Commander. I want to tell you some things—for her and for you."

Stout swallowed hard. "All right, what is it?"

"Somebody up there—one of my people or one of Dan Reinholt's—will have monitored our ascent and free dive on sonar. As it turned out, we gave them a better signal than any SOS. banged on the hull. They know now we're in trouble. They'll be trying to figure out some way to help. But it will take time. You may have to get by for a few hours on your own."

Murdock told him how to drain the buoyancy tanks into the sphere for emergency air; how to extend the life of the baralyme crystals by warming the containers against their bodies; How to bleed the electrolung cylinders when the other air had gone too stale to breathe. What he didn't tell Commander Stout was that the Navy wouldn't be able to get another submersible into the area for days, and no measure he could take would keep them alive for that long.

"Just do me one thing, Commander," he said. "When Marie comes to, remind her of the promise she made me. That's all, just remind her she made me a promise."

"I'll do it, Murdock."

"She told you how to jettison the spheres?"

"Yes. Sort of . . ."

"Watch me closely. They'll both have to be done."

Murdock moved to the forward end of the compartment and pulled open a cover plate set into the deck near the control sphere hatchway. Inside were two roundish knobs. Before Murdock could activate these dials he cried out. Stout watched helplessly as the diver threw himself to the deck and rolled into a ball. He writhed as though every muscle in his body was simultaneously suffering from the most severe cramps. In a moment the spasm eased.

"Are you all right, Murdock?"

The diver fought for breath until his face purpled, and then he lay on the deck only slightly unbending, taking in air in huge gulps.

After a while he rolled over, so that he was again at the knobs. He began grunting, and it took Stout a while to understand he was talking. The words came out in bursts, as though disgorged from his lungs by body blows. "It arms the explosive bolts," he was saying. "Then, when this other knob glows as it's doing now, shove it all the way in."

As Murdock did this, the forty-eight charges exploded in the same instant. The noise was so shocking and the chamber shook so violently that the two men fell to the deck with their hands over their ears. Almost at once came the crash of the heavy control sphere landing on the bottom.

When the silence returned Murdock grunted, "It works. I had my doubts the sub could withstand the strain. Okay," he said, getting to his knees and crawling aft. "Now you blow the access chamber."

"Why can't you do it yourself?"

"I'll be inside."

"But that's crazy! You told Miss Delamer it wouldn't take her up. It sure as hell won't take you. You're twice her weight and the sphere is half-filled with seawater."

Murdock pulled himself up with a superhuman effort. "I'm not going up alone again, Commander. Once was enough." He opened the hatch and started through, but abruptly turned back. His whole body was shaking, and the muscles of his face were contorted in pain. He was enduring intolerable torture for the moment, but it was clear he could not last for long.

"If you're a bit superstitious like me, Commander, like most seamen, you may care to know this: Marie told you that *DORiS* stands for Deep Ocean Recovery Submersible." Murdock stopped to cough blood. He wiped his mouth with a forearm. When the arm fell to his side the rubber dry suit was an ugly smear of orange. "The truth is, the name 'Doris' is Greek. It means 'Out of the sea.' This damn sub is gonna rise. When I bang on the hatch, blow the sphere."

Stout remained speechless as the diver closed the hatch between them. He waited for the sound of the access chamber hatch closing, too. Several seconds passed and the sound didn't come. Then he heard the pumps starting up.

All at once Stout understood.

Every pound of pressure that came into the chamber was like the wheel of Murdock's rack being backed off another turn. With half its regular volume, the chamber should pressurize quickly. Regrettably the batteries wouldn't drive the pumps long. One way or another, Murdock hadn't much time.

Murdock could not fall asleep, must not lose consciousness, but as his mind drifted through the memories of a long and full life, he tried to focus on one single memory that could see him through the next several minutes:

*Coy Murdock clutched a stanchion with both hands. He stood on the gunwale of his father's salvor and looked down into the sea. Three-foot swells tugged the boat against its anchor cables. If he timed his dive right, hit the swell when the boat was still in the trough, he would be no more than four or five feet above the water. If he missed and didn't get off until a swell plucked the ship high into the air, it would be more like ten. Still, it wasn't those ten feet that bothered him—it was the fifty feet to the bottom.*

*"Dad, I'm scared."*

*"I know you are, Coy. But you can do it."*

*"I don't want to do it."*

*Glen Murdock swallowed his pity. "You have to, boy. Dive in, get to the bottom, bring me up a handful of sand. It's that simple. You saw Drew do it, didn't you? I did it twice."*

*That was true, Coy had watched. But his older brother loved the ocean, and his father practically qualified as a marine animal. To them it was fun. Not to Coy.*

*Drew spoke for the first time. "Don't make him do it, Dad."*

*"You stay out of this, Drew. This is Coy's problem."*

*Murdock strode across to his younger son. "If you don't do it now, boy, you'll never be able to face yourself."*

*"I'll do it sometime, Dad. But not now."*

*In a rage of frustration, Murdock reached over and snatched the U.S. Navy dog tags from the chain around the boy's neck and held them out of his reach. Drew had worn tags just like them for more than five years. A present from Murdock on his son's twelfth birthday. Coy had gotten his on the same birthday two weeks before. It was a medal of honor for Coy; for Glen, a medal of bravery that now had to be earned.*

*Murdock hurled the tags over the side. "Forget the sand!" he challenged. "If you want to wear those again, you'll dive now while there's still enough light to see."*

*The metal tags hit the sea with a hint of a splash and twinkled down out of sight.*

*Coy's face was a grimace of confusion, of fear.*

*He climbed over the lifeline. He stood on the gunwale, with his hands clutching the wire at his back. Seconds passed while his small body balanced on the edge, shifting in awkward, jerking movements between horror and dishonor. Suddenly he turned away. He climbed back over the lifeline, sat down on the deck, and shook his head.*

*His big brother stepped forward.*

*"I'll go down and get them for you, Coy."*

*Murdock whirled. "No you won't, Drew! If Coy wants them back, he can go get them himself." And then he had turned his back on his son and walked away.*

*An hour before sunset, while his family was below-decks at dinner, Coy had gone in to get them. He had dived not once but fourteen times to the bottom, searching the bright coral reef for the tags. By the time he reached the bottom his breath had been exhausted, and he could search only for seconds before scurrying back to the surface. Then he would inhale dangerously deep for several breaths and dive down again.*

*When he dragged himself over the transom more dead than alive, Glen and Sally Murdock carried him below to his cabin and put him to bed. In the process of stripping him down and checking him over, they discovered the dog tags and chain clenched in Coy's fist. They weren't able to unlock his fingers to put the chain back around his neck.*

*This incident was not mentioned when Sally petitioned for divorce three weeks after they docked. She belonged to the land, wanted the land, as much as Glen Murdock wanted to belong to the sea. Nevertheless, when Sally moved to the midwest she took Coy along. Murdock had gotten custody of Drew. Six years after that Sally died. Coy never saw his father again.*

Glen Murdock winced.

The pain had largely subsided. But he had spent his final minutes thinking not of his proudest moment but of his most galling. Not of Drew but of Coy. Perhaps this was his mind's way of telling him that Drew Murdock was dead.

It was too late to live up to the one—there was still time to live down the other.

Murdock reached through the open hatch of the access chamber and grabbed the outside of the central sphere hatch. The gasket between the two spheres and the forty-eight bolts holding them together encircled his body. He banged on the steel with his fist.

And then he died.

He died in unimaginable horror. The blast ruptured his eardrums and catapulted his body against the steel hull with the force of forty-eight sticks of TNT. His consciousness teetered on the brink of a canyon from which no mind emerges. But that explosion was nothing, nothing compared to the pressure that rushed in upon him. When the sphere fell away and Glen Murdock hung from the central compartment, a thousand tons of seawater squeezed him in its giant's fist. Murdock was dead before he had released his hold on the hatch. He was dead when he fell to the sea floor. The pressure surged through his eardrums and stabbed into his brain like two frozen icepicks; it crushed his chest with such speed and power that broken bits of his ribs slashed through his heart and lungs.

He couldn't possibly have dragged himself to the descent weights or begun pulling pins. And yet Murdock must have done this. For less than a minute after the access sphere hit the bottom, *DORiS* started to rise. And when she bobbed on the surface and was hauled aboard the *Nomad* half an hour later, the recovery crew found two dazed people inside, and only two ballast pins still in place.

# Part II

# SUBSUNK

He wore no uniform. His guise as the skipper of an innocent Russian fishing trawler was transparent enough without that. Nevertheless, Semen Pudkov was a captain in the Soviet Navy, an officer of the KGB, and one of the newest recruits of the KGB department known as Agency Four. None of these facts was lost on the members of Pudkov's crew.

His men didn't know very much more.

Even Pudkov's junior officers didn't know, for example, the name of the admiral who'd assigned them to monitor this operation. Soviet AGIs (intelligence gathering vessels) habitually shadow U.S. Navy formations. Even as the walls separating East and West have begun to crumble, at sea American and Russian ships still pass like dogs with their shoulder hairs high. Sailing too close aboard, cutting in front of larger ships, running without lights—Pudkov had played all these games. But he wasn't playing them now. This mission had nothing to do with any Soviet government policy of harassing the U.S. Navy.

He wasn't here to harass.

And he wasn't here on orders of the Soviet government.

Pudkov didn't think much of *glasnost* or of President Mikhail Gorbachev. Democratization meant only one thing to him: an eventual end to the military dominance of power, prestige, and privilege.

Unfortunately he wasn't alone. Many military men of

high rank in the Soviet Union feel much the same way, and some of these men command units of the Soviet Navy. One of these was a certain admiral.

Pudkov was working for him.

The holds of his trawler had never held so much as a single fish. Banks of electronic apparatus lined the bulkheads and created narrow labyrinthine passages which, when his technicians occupied their stations, were all but impassable. Every vessel the Soviets build is larger and more imposing than its Western counterpart. They have to be. Unfortunately for the Soviet soldier who must fit himself inside these vessels, all the electronic and mechanical hardware that must travel with him is accordingly outsized, because the Soviets have never really gotten the hang of miniaturization.

From the companionway Captain Pudkov could see all the important stations: the radar boards which monitered air and sea activity; sonar, for subsurface activity; radio monitors which recorded military aircraft transmissions, ship-to-ship and ship-to-shore, and submarine traffic. The trawler was also equipped with jamming devices and communications equipment linking them to the Kremlin via satellite, as well as several computers for deciphering encrypted U.S. Navy transmissions. However, the message that Pudkov received once darkness had fallen over the site of the *Alaska* disaster came from none of these high-tech electromagnetic eavesdropping devices but from a seaman posted in the masts with a pair of binoculars.

"Signal from Petr, comrade captain."

Tarasov raced to the weather deck, grabbed his own pair of binoculars, and panned the black bulk of the *New Jersey*'s superstructure.

Amid the array of riding and deck lights that illuminated the big battleship like a Christmas tree, there was a faint and winking red light where no red light should have been.

"What does Petr say?" Pudkov demanded.

"He's telling us to prepare for an extraction, Captain. He fears he may be uncovered, and wants us to be ready to pick him up if he has to make a run for it."

"And just how does he expect us to manage that?"

Pudkov's question was rhetorical; he knew the Soviet's agent-in-place, code-named Petr, would come up with something.

Admiral Reinholt gazed over the ranks of ship's captains, task force commanders, intelligence officers, and various staff advisers seated in the ready room. There were engineers and experts on every aspect of submarine science, who understood the physics of an underwater implosion in a way Reinholt never could. There were public information officers who could describe the tragedy much better than he. But no one in the room except Reinholt himself could speak the words that had to be spoken.

"As of 1700 hours yesterday," he announced, "when the accident investigation team and I completed a debriefing of Lieutenant Commander Alan Stout, the status of SSBN 732, the Trident submarine *Alaska*, officially advanced from a SubMiss to a SubSunk condition."

A buzz of alarm filled the room.

"We expect no, I repeat, no survivors in the *Alaska* sinking. I have so informed the Pentagon." Reinholt's tone was flat but it showed the strain of thirty hours without sleep. "We'll debrief the civilian diver who survived the submersible accident, Marie Delamer, later this afternoon, but I have no reason to believe that her testimony will alter this condition."

A bald captain in the front row raised a hand and spoke without waiting for recognition. "Sir, there's a lot of scuttlebutt going around that the civilian minisubmersible was sabotaged. If that's true, it raises the question of whether the *Alaska* herself may have been deliberately sunk by . . . by unfriendly forces in the vicinity.''

"Do you listen to scuttlebutt, Captain?''

Admiral Reinholt's small frame and firm but kindly face belied his occupation as Deputy Chief of Naval Operations in administrative command of Submarine Warfare. He was not a man to cross. Yet such was Admiral Reinholt's reputation for fair play that the captain dared to reply as he did.

"Officially, no sir,'' he said. "Unofficially, I often get better intelligence from my messman than from I do from higher headquarters. I'd be a damn fool not to listen.''

There was some uneasy laughter.

"Well,'' said Reinholt, "I'll submit your messman's name and qualifications to Washington. After today they'll likely be assigning me to a galley and might want to consider him as my replacement at DCNO.''

No one laughed at this.

"Two hours ago,'' Reinholt continued, "a side-cleaner on one of the tenders found a ship's log floating in the water. It was from the *Alaska.* Pure chance. The OOD's last entries confirm what the photographs from the spotter plane suggest, that the disaster struck very soon after the SH-3 helicopter landed. But now we get one additional piece of information: the twelve members of the medical unit were logged aboard.''

"Sir, was the helicopter's departure logged?''

"The OOD was in the process of making that entry when the explosion came. His writing is interrupted there. I don't need to add,'' Reinholt added, "that all of this is confidential.

"I'm circulating an assignment sheet that will outline the various phases of the investigation and delegate areas of responsibility. The logistics people will be expediting the arrival of the DSRV. In the meantime, investigation into the cause of the accident will continue along routine lines, primarily in Pearl Harbor, where an analysis of all radio traffic with the *Alaska* is being conducted. I want a full ocean sweep made to determine the extent of possible radioactive leakage and to locate, if possible, the missiles from the submarine. Pearl Harbor should expect the salvor *Nomad* to dock within forty-eight hours and be prepared for a complete examination of the minisubmersible. You public information people will clear all news releases through me, but I'll tell you this as a guideline: Don't bother writing up anything that even hints the Navy may have lost a Trident-class submarine. Until we can positively establish that we have lost the *Alaska,* our official position is that we haven't.''

The same officer, Captain Louis Krosmeyer, interrupted again. Captain Krosmeyer commanded the *New Jersey;* this was his ship. But he would have spoken out anyway. One of the things Reinholt liked about Krosmeyer was the man's habit of speaking his mind.

''What's the reaction in Washington, Admiral?''

Reinholt didn't blink. ''Needless to say, Captain, they're not any happier about it than we are. We'll probably be hearing from them, through Eliot Packman, very shortly. But that's my concern, not yours. This was my show. And my responsibility. Any other questions?''

There were none.

''One last item: There will be a memorial service at dawn tomorrow, here on the *New Jersey,* for the civilian diver who died during the minisub accident. Some of you may have known him. His name was Glen Murdock. He was a former U.S. Navy commander and a World War II veteran. He was also a good friend and a good sailor. I'll expect everyone here, as well as all your senior officers, to attend.''

''What about a service for the *Alaska* crew?''

Reinholt glowered at the speaker. ''I shouldn't have to explain that a service for the men of the *Alaska* is out of the question at this point. SubSunk is an action condition, not a post mortem, and it's classified 'Confidential.'

If any of you have any doubts about what that means, please talk to your immediate superiors." He looked over his audience. "Anything else? No? Thank you, gentlemen."

Someone called the assembly to attention.

Admiral Reinholt stalked out of the ready room without a backward glance.

Krosmeyer turned to his executive officer. "It'll be ironic," he said softly, "and terribly sad, if that burial service is the admiral's last official act. Unfortunately, if Packman has anything to say about it, Reinholt won't even last that long."

"This will finish Reinholt," said Eliot Packman. "A Trident submarine lost. A hundred thirty-two dead. What a tragedy!" Packman wrung his hands—not in despair, but with glee.

"Thirty-three."

"What's that?"

"It's a hundred thirty-three dead," Captain Cassidy said. "Don't forget Glen Murdock."

"How could I forget him? It's certain, then?"

"There doesn't seem to be any doubt about it. He left the submersible without air tanks at two thousand feet down. He never came up. He's dead all right. They're planning a memorial service for him tomorrow morning."

"Without question the most unpleasant man I ever met."

"Yes, sir. And then there's the twelve members of the medical team who flew out to the *Alaska*, and the helicopter pilot. A hundred and forty-six dead . . ."

Packman waved it away. "I know, I know, it's too bad. But as bad as it is, it's just the thing I've been waiting for. This mess is going to end up on Dan Reinholt's doorstep, and he's going to take the fall for it. The Trident submarine program was his project from the beginning, and the Trident III missiles. A missile test was his idea. He picked the crew. He's responsible for not having one of the DSVRs on active status. Am I right?''

"It's DSRV, Mr. Packman.''

"What?''

"DSRV—not DSVR, Deep Submergence Rescue Vehicles.''

"What the hell difference does that make?''

"None, sir.''

"I'll see to it that someone else takes over Reinholt's job commanding the recovery operation. Once we've cleaned up his mess, that'll be the end of him. He'll be out of it. Completely isolated. Who can he possibly turn to? Murdock is dead. I control you, and you, my friend, control Commander Stout.''

"What about the rest of the *Nomad* crew. Duggan and the Delamer woman?''

"What can they do? Murdock himself was no more than a minor annoyance. The others are nothing without him. They don't know Daniel Reinholt and they don't care what happens to him. Technically, they're not even employed anymore. No, Murdock Salvage is out of the picture.''

"Just the same, Mr. Packman, I think you ought to have their ship impounded. At least for a few days.''

Packman frowned. "What would be the point?''

"It would keep them out of our hair.''

"Huh. Let Reinholt do that for us. He'll impound the *Nomad* just to examine what's left of Murdock's submersible. I would in his place.''

"He may not have the authority. But you could arrange it. And you could have your own people give it a good going over. That way, if there are any discoveries to be made, the credit will go to you, not to the admiral.''

"I'll think it over, O.K.''

Cassidy rose, on the point of leaving, and then

stopped. "Will you be recommending me to take Reinholt's place?"

"You? Deputy CNO, Submarine Warfare? That's a three-star position."

"Not Deputy CNO. But you could recommend me to take over the investigation of the *Alaska* sinking while you're looking for a permanent replacement. It would look good in my folder."

"It would be a dangerous move. As Admiral Reinholt's chief of staff you could claim you have the experience, but you're only a captain. I would look foolish."

"I'm due a promotion to admiral. You could arrange for that, too."

"You'd still be junior to half a dozen men in the submarine service."

"Orders of command signed by the President would see to that, and you know it."

"I won't jeopardize my career for you, Cassidy."

Anger suffused the captain's face. "Haven't I jeopardized mine, for you?"

Packman shrugged. "We're both ambitious men. Ambition requires certain risks. Don't try to kid me that you're doing any of this purely for my benefit. You realized Reinholt was on his way out and decided to tie up with me rather than go out with him. We're both after immense rewards. We're both using each other. I just happen to be a little better at it than you are."

"My rewards may not be worth my risks."

"Don't start with that. Now go on back and keep your eyes and ears open."


"Homicide."

The fat sergeant pressed the telephone receiver to his ear and frowned as one might at a poor connection.

"You're who? Are you sure you got the right number? This is the Wichita Police Department, homicide division." The fat man strained to hear. He held the phone at arm's length and glared at it. A crank call. But he brought it back to his ear and determined to go along just a bit more. "What's that? Did you say 'admiral'?"

At the next desk, another detective showed interest.

"Murdock?" The fat face moved up and down. "Yes sir, we have a Detective Sergeant Murdock on the force. Do you want to talk to him?"

Both men looked toward the far wall.

A wall of glass separated the open arena of desks used by the homicide detectives from their division captain. Under normal circumstances the detectives could see but not hear what was going on in the captain's office. But these were not normal circumstances.

"I'm sorry, but Sergeant Murdock is not available right now. He's uh . . . conferring with the captain on an important policy matter." The fat man guarded the receiver with a palm until the other detective's laughter had subsided. "Can I have him return the call, mister . . . er, Admiral? What? Oh, yeah . . . over."

Typewriters had stopped clacking.

"You're on a battleship in the middle of the Pacific Ocean, huh? What's that area code? Over. Mmmm. Yeah, I can see how that would be a problem. Maybe you should hold on a minute. I'll see if I can find out how much longer this conference is expected to continue."

Two other detectives closed in on the fat officer's desk while yet another headed toward the water fountain, which Providence had located near the glass wall. When Murdock and the division captain "conferred" the plate glass was hardly an obstruction. After filling his cup with water the detective turned and faced the arena, keeping an ear cocked to the glass.

"They're just getting to the 'Murdock,-you're-a-damn-good-investigator-but-you-don't-know-how-to-follow-orders' stage of the chewing out," he said. "Another two minutes should do it."

He leaned closer.

"The captain wants Murdock to write a letter of apo—"

He turned away with his face screwed up in pain.

"What now, Denkle?"

"Murdock just bought himself a ninety-day suspension."

The sound of a fist banging onto a desk top needed no explanation.

"That's all, folks."

Sergeant Denkle quickly swallowed the last of his water and sauntered back to his desk. Meanwhile the fat officer uncupped his hand from the telephone.

"Yes, sir. That conference is breaking up now. Murdock will be right here."

The glass door in the glass wall came open. It banged shut behind Murdock with a force that established once and for all that its tempered panes were more shatterproof than they were soundproof. Murdock walked through a gauntlet of smiles to his desk.

"Hey, Murdock! Phone call for you. Some Navy bigshot. He says it's important."

Murdock didn't even slow down. "Oh, yeah? Tell him to fuck himself."

"You can't say that to an admiral."

Murdock stopped. "An admiral?"

"So he says."

"An admiral outranks a captain, doesn't he? Here, let me take that. I'll tell the son of a bitch myself. If he's as dumb as a captain I'll not only have to give him directions, I'll have to spell any words over four letters."

The fat man relinquished the phone and rested his chin in his palms. And smiled.

"I didn't know you used any words over four letters," he said.

# Chapter Seven

Nothing about the service seemed real. Marie's first burial at sea came off too ceremonial, too grand to have anything to do with Glen Murdock. An "All hands bury the dead" had brought out more than a thousand off-duty seamen, whose ranks filled the *New Jersey*'s fantail from her aft-facing sixteen-inch guns to her helipad. Officers from every ship in the fleet turned out in dress whites and stood at attention to hear Admiral Reinholt deliver a solemn eulogy. It was Glen Murdock's name the admiral spoke, but the turnout as well as the solemnity made it apparent that all one hundred thirty-two members of the *Alaska*'s crew were being eulogized. On Reinholt's signal, a canvas-shrouded bundle slipped out from under the Stars and Stripes and plunged into the ocean. Everyone knew this bundle contained nothing but ballast, because Murdock's body had not been recovered. They presented the folded flag to Marie. She felt as though this, too, had been weighted, for it was almost too heavy for her to bear.

Two days had passed since *DORiS* had risen from the sea. Not once during those forty-eight hours had Marie stepped outside her cabin. A Navy physician treated her head wound and pronounced her fit for outpatient care. A stroll around the ship two or three times a day and some fresh dialogue with her crewmates, he said, would do her a world of good. Marie remained in her bunk. She saw no one except Captain Duggan. She ate from a tray the captain brought to her bedside and turned callers away by pretending to be asleep. There were two exceptions. The second of these was Admiral Reinholt, who showed up with two representatives of the Navy's Accident Investigation Team to debrief her.

When Marie had recorded her statement and the two investigators had left, Reinholt hesitated at the door, unsure how to continue.

"What's the trouble, Admiral?"

"There is one other thing, Miss Delamer," he said. "Have you seen or spoken to Commander Stout since . . . since you've regained consciousness?"

Marie admitted that she had; Stout had been the first of the two exceptions to her self-imposed isolation. "He came late last night," she told Reinholt. "He wanted me to go with him to the funeral service tomorrow. I explained that I would go with the members of the *Nomad* crew and he said he understood."

"That was all he wanted?"

"Well . . . he also wanted to remind me of something."

"May I ask what it was?"

"It was personal."

"Something personal between you and the commander?"

"No, no. It had to do with Murdock."

Reinholt persisted. "Is there some reason you can't tell me?"

"Is there some reason I should?"

"It's important."

"Why don't you just ask him, Admiral? You could order Stout to tell you. You can't order me."

"I can ask you, Miss Delamer. I can't even ask him. Commander Stout is missing. He had a seaman bring him to the *Nomad* around 2100 hours yesterday and return him to the *New Jersey* thirty minutes later. You say he was talking to you. The officer of the deck checked him back aboard the *New Jersey*, but he hasn't been seen since. I'd like to know what brought him here.''

Marie considered this. ''Well, it can't have anything to do with his disappearance. Glen asked him to remind me I'd made him a promise. But Glen didn't even tell Commander Stout what the promise was, and as it happens it wasn't necessary to remind me because I hadn't forgotten.''

''Did you tell the commander what the promise was?''

''Yes. There didn't seem to be any reason . . . All right, you've made your point. Glen made me promise to notify his son of the accident.''

''That was it?''

''Yes.''

It was Reinholt's turn to consider. At one point he seemed on the verge of making an announcement, but then he changed his mind and said instead: ''You don't need to worry about making good on that promise, Miss Delamer. I got the information on Murdock's next of kin from his naval records.''

''There's a younger son named Coy. . . .''

''I've already taken care of it. I only wish he'd given us more to do.''

''I wish,'' Marie said half to herself, ''that he'd given me less. I'm not sure I can face him.'' Even to herself she could not admit that it was the reality of Murdock's death she could not face. When Marie finally came out to face it she had found something else in its place. The service had not been surreal, only unreal.

The tilt board was raised.

The canvas bundle pitched over the side and fell with a barely noticeable splash into the sea.

Admiral Reinholt opened his prayer book. When his voice broke, he paused a moment before going on: ''Unto Almighty God we commend the soul of our brother departed, and we commit his body to the deep. . . .''

How Glen Murdock would have laughed at this religious pageantry, thought Marie. As much as Glen had loved the sea, as much as he had loved his country, he had never had a Navy way about him. A quick cremation and a quiet dumping of his ashes in the *Nomad*'s wake would have been more to his taste. And look at the *Nomad* crewmen around her! Captain Duggan had shaved for the first time in days. Gandy and Emmott and the others from Murdock's ship—civilians one and all—stood rigid as posts, with their hands clasped against the seams of their trousers. It wasn't real.

". . . in sure and certain hope of the Resurrection unto eternal life, through our Lord Jesus Christ; at whose coming in glorious majesty to judge the world, the sea shall give up her dead . . ."

These words moved her only because she knew that Daniel Reinholt, an orthodox Jew, had insisted on delivering them personally. Like most mariners, Marie had her own kind of beliefs which transcended religion. Call it superstition. She looked out to sea and searched the skies for sign of a seagull. The first bird to appear after the body has been committed—as any sailor knows and many still believe—would carry the soul of the departed. This is why sailors never kill gulls. But there were no birds in the sky.

Anyway, she told herself, that was nonsense, too.

". . . and the corruptible bodies of those who sleep in him shall be changed and made like unto his glorious body; according to the mighty working whereby he is able to subdue all things unto himself."

Reinholt closed his prayer book.

Seven seamen raised bolt-action rifles into the air and began firing volleys.

The flag was presented to Marie. Sailors and officers alike began drifting off to their assigned duty stations or to the launches that would return them to their ships.

Captain Cassidy said something comforting that Marie didn't really hear and then wandered away.

Captain Duggan's arm encircled her shoulder.

But Marie was looking to the southeast.

A small black dot rose off the water where the sea and the sky became one. In only seconds she saw and heard the rotors of a large Navy helicopter chopping straight for the flagship. Closer yet she identified it as a Sea Knight. The big Sikorski was capable of carrying twenty-six combat marines or, in antisubmarine work, a variety of Search and Destroy weaponry that included homing torpedoes. The whirlybird hovered over the pad until all the mourners had cleared and then it settled onto the gently rolling deck.

While the two pilots remained with the craft, shutting down the engines, a young man in a Navy jacket, apparently the only passenger, disembarked from a side loading door. He moved away from the chopper in a defensive crouch, until he was well beyond the blades a full two feet over his head. He was not tall, only slightly above medium height, with a slender build and brown hair blowing wildly in the downwash of air. There was nothing remarkable about his physical features, until the idling, rotors whined to a stop and the hair fell back off his face; then Marie knew who it was. The face bore a certain likeness to a photograph she'd been shown, but it was the startlingly clear gray-green eyes that dispelled any doubt. Once she had believed that eyes like those could belong to no other man.

"Come on," said Duggan. "The boys are waiting with the launch to take you back to the *Nomad*."

"No, wait. That's Murdock," she said, and then added quickly to avoid confusion even in her own mind, "Glen's son."

She met him at the tilt board, which still protruded between two stanchions pointing down into the water where the weighted bundle had fallen. The young man was leaning over the lifeline as though he were looking for traces of his father on the water's surface. A set of

Navy dog tags had fallen from inside his shirt and dangled from a chain around his neck.

"This should be for you," said Marie, holding out the folded triangle of flag.

He stood up and turned toward her slowly. His face was haggard, his eyes filled with suffering. Obviously he had not eaten for more than a day. He hadn't shaved since being informed of the tragedy. That as much as anything told her how completely his father's death must have stunned him.

"Get lost, huh?"

Marie started. "I don't want to intrude on your grief, Commander Murdock, believe me I don't, but I have to talk to you."

The young man was stuffing the dog tags back inside his shirt. "How do you know my name?"

"I know practically everything about you. Your father talked about you all the time. He always wanted us to meet. Only a few days ago he arranged for a dinner date between us." Marie found herself staring. She had thought herself unable to face Murdock's son. Instead, she could not turn away. "My name is Marie. I worked for your father. This is Captain Padraig Duggan; he commands your father's ship, the *Nomad*." She pointed off the battleship's starboard quarter. "All the men would like to meet you, I'm sure."

He accepted the flag but didn't turn in the direction she was pointing. "Okay, darlin', I'm glad to know you. You too, Captain. Now at the risk of sounding unfriendly, why don't you blow? I'm so damned upset I'm about ready to chuck myself over the side, and I don't need an audience."

The voice was a coarse baritone like Glen Murdock's, but it was not of the older man's timbre. And closer, his features resembled the photograph of Murdock's son less than she had thought. Subconsciously Marie stopped contrasting this man with the picture and began comparing him to Murdock himself. This man was taller and thinner. But then, men thicken with age. This face was certainly good-looking, but Murdock's had been ruggedly handsome. Marie suddenly realized she was trying to see something in this young man that might not be there.

"You're right, it was thoughtless of me. You and your father were very close, I know, and it's too bad you didn't get here in time for the ceremony. Admiral Reinholt said some beautiful things. If you want some time alone . . ."

"What I want is some time in a bathroom that doesn't roll back and forth."

This threw her for an instant. "If we'd known you were coming I suppose we could have postponed the service. I had Admiral Reinholt inform your brother, too. I didn't have his address, but the admiral said he could check the next-of-kin listings in your personnel file. Somewhere in Oklahoma, isn't it? But don't expect him to show up. Glen told me he hated open water so much he moved as far as he could get from the ocean."

A pained smile twisted the young man's features. "You've got it all wrong, darlin'."

"What do you mean?"

"I mean, it's my brother Drew who was so close to dear old dad, not me."

"You mean you're not . . ."

"I mean it's Drew who's not coming. He was executive officer aboard the *Alaska* and went down with the rest of the crew."

Marie's expression froze.

"And you've got it wrong about me, too. I moved to Kansas. Oklahoma has too damn many lakes."

She forced the words out. "Drew's dead?"

"That's what they tell me."

"Then you must be . . ."

Coy Murdock nodded wanly. "That's right, darlin'. I'm seasick."

Now Marie saw what she'd seen before but her mind had refused to acknowledge. The collar of the borrowed jacket had hidden hair too long for Navy standards. The stubble on his jaw was more like four days' growth than one or even two. The smell of sickness was on him. He'd been sick just now. He'd eaten all right, but he hadn't been able to keep it down.

She brushed by Captain Duggan suddenly and ran toward the officer of the deck, who was just then exchanging salutes with one of the helicopter pilots.

Duggan glared at Coy Murdock. "You were pretty hard on her, weren't you?"

Murdock grunted. "I'm like that when I'm retching my guts out and some skirt tries to pick me up."

"She was very good friends with your father."

"Oh, yeah?" Murdock looked sideways, following the girl across the deck. "Well, there was sure nothing wrong with the old man's eyes, huh?" A wave of nausea swept over him and he turned and spat over the rail. Then he straightened up again, wiping his mouth with the back of a hand. "Look, maybe I was outa line. I'll try to take it a little easier on her next time, okay?"

"Why are you here, Mr. Murdock?"

"Reinholt sent for me."

"Why?"

"Ask Reinholt."

"I'm asking you."

For only an instant the gray in his verdigris eyes flashed a brightness reserved for newly forged steel. "Don't push it, Captain!"

Marie reappeared and stepped between them. "Captain Cassidy is on his way down. He's going to take us to see Admiral Reinholt."

"He can only give you a few minutes," Cassidy told them on the way to Reinholt's cabin. "As ranking staff officer of OpNav he's representing the CNO as well as the SeCNaV." Cassidy turned to the three with a smile.

"Secretary of the Navy," he said by way of explanation. "And trying to keep peace between the CinCPacFlt and the ComSubPac at the same time—it's no easy matter."

Marie nodded without understanding.

Duggan glared.

"A few minutes of Navspeak is all I can take," said Murdock.

Shortly afterward they were outside Reinholt's cabin. "Would you two mind waiting out here?" Cassidy asked Marie and Duggan. "The admiral would like to talk to Mr. Murdock for a minute or two alone." He led Murdock inside, then returned to the corridor and remained with them for what turned out to be more like thirty minutes than one or two.

"Captain," said Marie at last, "I wish you'd tell Admiral Reinholt that it's very important I see him."

"I think he'll be ready soon, miss," replied Cassidy, leading her and Duggan to gather he acquired his information by a kind of clairvoyance, because no sounds had come from the admiral's cabin during that entire half hour.

Without warning Cassidy rapped twice on the door, opened it without waiting for permission, showed the captain and Marie inside, and then closed it at their backs.

Reinholt's quarters were quite spacious. The bunk was actually a double bed. There was a dresser, a walk-in closet, and a small writing desk. Coy Murdock was standing near one of three windows, which could be opened but were now closed. Reinholt had been sitting at a swivel chair that he had turned away from the desk so that it was facing the room. Immediately when Marie and Duggan entered, he came to his feet. Though it must have been years since he had had to perform this duty at the sound of two knocks on his door, he did so now in deference to Marie and made a good job of it.

"Drew Murdock is on the *Alaska,*" Marie blurted,

without waiting for any niceties. "You already knew that when you talked with me?"

"Yes, I knew it," said Reinholt, waving her and Duggan to chairs. "I thought you knew it, too."

"I didn't. Glen never told me." Marie glanced toward the windows, toward the man standing there. "So you sent for Coy instead."

"He told you to notify his son. Drew was already dead. Murdock knew that when he exacted the promise. I learned Coy's address in Wichita from Drew's personnel file and sent a Navy fighter to pick him up and take him to San Diego. From there to Pearl. That's the whole story."

"Glen told me to go after his son. I think he said, 'go get' his son."

Reinholt's shrug was answer enough.

"But, Admiral, don't you see what this means?"

"I'm afraid not."

"You'd have to understand how Glen felt about Drew and Coy. Commander Stout interrupted him before he could say any more, but whenever Glen used the word 'son' like that—" again Marie looked uncomfortably at Coy Murdock—"well, he'd only use those words when referring to Drew. He didn't speak of Coy that way. In fact, he never spoke of Coy that I remember."

"What's your point?"

"Why would he have told me to go after Drew if he knew that Drew had been killed when the *Alaska* went down?"

"You tell me."

"It's obvious, isn't it? He knew that Drew hadn't been killed. He knew that the *Alaska* hadn't gone down. Not down here anyway. Someone sabotaged the minsub to keep us from reporting that the wreckage we found is not the *Alaska.*"

"Or to keep you from reporting that it is."

"But it's not. Glen recognized something about it. He

knew that it wasn't the *Alaska*. I didn't understand what he was saying at the time. I don't think he completely trusted Commander Stout, and there wasn't time to explain."

This much at least Reinhold knew was true. Murdock had expressed reservations about Stout.

"What could he have recognized?" he asked.

"There was one hunk of debris in particular. He wanted to bring it to the surface. I told you about that. When it was too heavy, he asked me specifically if we had that hunk on videotape. Of course we lost all the videotapes when we jettisoned the control sphere."

Admiral Reinholt was momentarily thoughtful. "Murdock had seen only two downed submarines before," he said after a pause. "Both had imploded. The Victor-class Soviet sub he helped to recover, and the *Mako*."

"But that's it! That's what he said. He said it was the *Mako* all over again."

"But, Miss Delamer, the *Mako* went down twenty years ago in the Atlantic, south of Nova Scotia."

"I don't understand it, Admiral. I'm only telling you what he said."

Reinholt looked to Captain Duggan for further argument. The big Irishman returned the glance in baleful silence. At length he pointed a meaty finger at Murdock. "Where's he fit into all of this?"

"I should think that would be obvious. Coy Murdock is your new employer."

"What?" asked Marie.

Duggan was on his feet. "Is that his idea?"

"It's nobody's 'idea,' Captain. It's the law. Murdock was the sole owner of the *Nomad*, the minisub, and all of the support equipment. He's dead. His wife is dead. His only living son is standing right here. Of course, I imagine the ship and most of the equipment are heavily mortgaged, but the business itself and whatever it owns in the way of property or rights belong to this man. Or will very soon.''

Marie said, ''Drew isn't dead.''

Duggan's position was more to the point. ''I'm damned,'' he growled, ''if I'll take orders from that pup. Look at him! He's no sailor. He's no diver. For the love of Mike, the man is seasick.''

''That's hardly relevant.''

''What's your part in this?'' asked Marie.

''I admit to a small interest. I want the *Nomad* to take the minisub to Pearl Harbor where it can undergo a complete investigation by a team of Navy technicians. Who should I deal with on this matter? I could ask you, Captain. You're in command of the ship herself, but you have no proprietary authority over the minisub. You can't even guarantee your crew would stick around once you're in port, and I may need to question them. You, Marie, may have been Murdock's second-in-command, but your position means nothing now. I wanted to have an understanding with the owner. Now that Coy Murdock is here, these problems no longer exist. He has agreed to do this.''

''And once we get there,'' said Duggan, '' how does he keep the crew from quitting?''

''Why would they do something like that? Murdock Salvage has just located the largest treasure in its history. Possibly the largest treasure in salvage history. It's a prize. You and your men are due generous bonuses, and Glen Murdock no doubt promised you'd have them. But without Murdock to claim it, what have you got? Coy here needs you, more than his father did. And you need him. Because the rights to the *Batavia* salvage also belong to Coy. When our investigation on the minisub is finished, you can return to the *Batavia,* raise her treasure, pay off the mortgages, and still have money enough to make you all rich for the rest of your lives. Who would want to walk away from that?''

Once Duggan's eyes had latched on to Murdock they remained there; now they narrowed to mere slits.

"So that's why you came," he said.

Coy Murdock spoke for the first time. "Isn't that what brought *you* out here, Captain?"

"Goddammit!" Marie was on her feet, shaking her fists in the air. "Stop this bickering. What's important is the *Alaska*. And Drew Murdock. If that wreckage down there is not the *Alaska*, then where is she? And what is she doing?"

Two raps sounded on the door. The door came open.

Clairvoyance had apparently summoned Cassidy yet again, for no one had called him and he had nothing to say. He stood waiting. However, the admiral's next statement made it at least a good guess that the captain's entrances were all well timed, according to the strictest instructions.

"O.K., will you show Mr. Murdock to the PX, where he can buy some Dramamine and fresh clothes?" To Murdock he said, "When you have what you need, I'll see that a launch transports you, Captain Duggan, Miss Delamer, and Captain Cassidy to the *Nomad*."

"Me, sir?"

"Sorry, O.K., I had intended to have Commander Stout accompany the *Nomad* to Pearl Harbor, but it's been twenty-four hours and he continues to elude us. I'm sending you instead." Reinholt's casual tone failed to mask his concern over Stout's disappearance. "How long will it take you to pack?"

"My footlocker is ready to go, Admiral. As soon as I can round up a couple of men to carry it down."

"Don't overdo it. You'll only be gone for a few days. Mr. Murdock, again please accept my condolences on the death of your father. We shall all miss him greatly." Marie and Duggan watched in tight-lipped silence as Coy Murdock stalked out, with the folded flag under his arm and the captain at his back.

"Miss Delamer," the admiral began again once the door had closed behind them, "let me reassure you that I am keenly aware of the situation here, and that the questions you asked concern me greatly. I have already taken steps to answer them. One of those steps, as I've explained, involves getting Coy Murdock here to take charge of his father's business and continue to cooperate with the Navy. You and the captain can make my job a lot easier if for the next few days you'll simply do as you're told."

"If that includes doing as that insolent pup tells me to do . . ."

"It does, Captain. Of course I can't order you to do anything, but I can ask you to be reasonable."

"Reasonable!"

"That's right. I don't think you're being fair."

"Fair to whom?"

"To Coy Murdock. Or to his father. You berate young Coy. Okay, so he's brash. Glen Murdock was as cocky as they come. Maybe Coy's a little green, but he just needs some experience and a little guidance."

"He's not just green, he's liverish."

Admiral Reinholt stood. "Marie, you knew Glen Murdock for five years. You, Captain, knew him for fifteen. I knew him for forty-five. I met Murdock a few months before the end of World War II." Reinholt dipped into a briefcase that was on his bed. "I had his entire file faxed to me this morning so I could write that inadequate speech of mine. I enjoyed very much reading through it. Ah! Here's the one . . . Listen to this and see if it sounds familiar. It's Murdock's Officer Fitness Report:

'Murdock is a poor sailor who comes ill equipped to command. He gets low marks for seamanship. Has no feel for the ship or his duties. Shows talent only for ungentlemanly behavior, having more than once been accused of conduct unbecoming an officer. In spite of this Murdock has a knack for getting a job done, seeming to accomplish with audacity and raw nerve what his limited nautical talents fail to achieve. I have assigned him to engineering, where his shortcomings will be less likely to jeopardize the crew and where he can keep out of trouble.' "

Captain Duggan leapt to his feet. As Reinholt read, anger had slowly darkened Duggan's face like a black squall. Now the storm blew up with gale force.

"I'm damned," he shouted, "if I'll sit here and listen to this! You gave the sermon, Admiral. 'Inadequate.' That's what you said your words were. And now you stand there and spew this kind of bilge."

"I'm only trying to demonstrate . . ."

Duggan wasn't having it.

"Come on, Marie," he said, "We're going."

She looked at Reinholt, who merely shrugged gently and then nodded.

"Go," he told her. "There are things you must know. Things I must tell you. But Captain Duggan makes a point. Now is not the right time."

# Chapter Eight

Somewhere between the site of the *Alaska* disappearance and Pearl Harbor, sometime during those twenty-seven hours of pitching, rolling, and corkscrewing madness, somehow or other Coy Murdock fought his way out of his cabin and met the *Nomad* crew. His address to them, made at Marie's insistence, was criminally terse. It left divers and deckhands alike with the impression that Murdock didn't really care whether they hung around once the ship docked in Hawaii or not . . . if they went over the side and drowned in the Kaulakahi Channel right then and there. To tread solid ground once again, that was the only thing he cared about.

In any case Coy had no way with people. Only with the young Japanese diver, a powerful little tug of a man named Katsushi Kato, did Coy's hardboiled shell crack even a bit. "Sushi" had muscular legs and arms, two black, daggerlike eyes, and a grin so infectious Coy all but forgot the pitching, rolling, and corkscrewing gyrations of his stomach. He congratulated Emmott Nichols on having foiled the attempt to hijack the *Nomad,* spoke with Gandy Henderson about getting the minisub operational once the Navy had completed its inspection, and then dashed back to his father's cabin, which because of its midships location enjoyed a stability rare on the tender craft. He threw himself into a chair.

"You'll get used to it after a while," Marie said, following him inside the cabin. "If you stick around long enough. Does the Dramamine help?"

"A little. I've already taken half the bottle."

Captain Duggan, who had entered with Cassidy, shook his head in despair.

"If you need some more," said Marie, "there should be a bottle or two in the medicine cabinet."

Murdock looked around "In my father's bathroom!"

"Please, Mr. Murdock!" exclaimed Duggan. Horror screwed up his face almost beyond recognition. "It's called 'the head,' and I'll thank you to refer to it as such on this vessel."

Marie hastened to get the subject back on an even keel. "I've seen Glen use Dramamine more than once," she said. "What about you, Captain?"

"Heaven forbid!" he snapped.

"Not you. I mean, did you ever see Glen take it?"

"Maybe once or twice."

"Come on now. Be honest. Glen told me he practically lived on Dramamine through his first enlistment. And when he came back to the Navy after college, he had to get used to the sea all over again. In any kind of heavy weather he would come down here and gulp dimenhydrinate tablets like they were candy."

At last somebody had said something to make Coy Murdock smile.

"I'll be damned," he muttered. "Aquaman himself."

Marie laughed lightly.

But her eyes were suddenly far away.

"Maybe he did," said Duggan, springing to his long-time friend's defense. "But no man ever loved the sea more than Glen."

Cassidy glanced down at Murdock with a wry grin. He had found something amusing in the circumstances that had eluded the others. "The admiral told me that you don't share your father's enthusiasm for the sea," he said. "I can see he wasn't kidding."

Coy returned the glance sidelong. "Neither am I."

"What's your problem?"

"Let me put it this way: I drink my liquor neat, I stay indoors when it rains, I get queasy watching Jacques Cousteau, and I shower instead of bathe—to me, a tub is just a small body of water. You're the staff adviser, you figure it out."

"You don't like water."

"Bingo."

"But the ocean—"

"Is just a big body of water. Ask Funk and Wagnalls."

This effectively silenced Cassidy.

Pad Duggan shook his head. He had found himself doing this more and more often since Coy Murdock had joined them. "Can you believe," he asked Marie, "that a son of Glen Murdock could say something like that?"

"I don't know, Pad," she replied. "I'm not so sure you were right about Glen. I don't think he loved the sea as much as he loved being on it. Or under it."

"It's the same thing."

"No, it's not. You love a friend. Or a god, if you believe in one. For Glen the sea was neither a god nor a friend. It was a foe. He respected it as an unconquerable enemy. And he fought it. But I don't think he loved it. It was the fighting he loved."

Captain Cassidy's wry grin disappeared. They had lost him. He blinked once or twice and inhaled deeply. "Well. I'm going topside."

"Don't go, Captain."

It was Murdock's tone more than his words that brought the staff officer up short. There was no trace of humor in his voice now whatsoever. "We've time," he continued, "for you to tell us a few things before we arrive."

"What sort of things?"

"The sort of things that happened to the *Alaska*."

"That's all highly classified information, Mr. Murdock. In fact, everything you and your men have seen and heard at the downsite is classified, and I have to give them a warning about their being subject to federal criminal prosecution if they so much as breathe a word.''

"Prosecution? For what?''

"Espionage.''

Murdock's brows soared. "You're going to be about as popular as I am before you get through with that speech, Captain. I thought the admiral asked you to come along so you could give us some help.''

"That's right.''

"With what, plea bargaining?''

"In return for your cooperation with the Navy in its investigation, I'm to assist you in every way possible once we get to Pearl Harbor.''

"Fine. It would be a great assistance if you would tell me everything you know about the *Alaska*'s disappearance.''

"I can't do that.''

Murdock, Marie, and Duggan all regarded the captain with a less than kindly gaze. After a long pause, Murdock said: "All right. I'll start out by telling Miss Delamer and the captain here what I know—what Admiral Reinholt told me. You can fill in the gaps. How's that?''

Once again Cassidy was startled into silence.

"Good,'' said Marie.

Murdock settled back in his chair.

"The *Alaska* was holding at launch depth for a missile test when the engine room crew came down sick. The men were vomiting, throwing themselves on the floor, and writhing in agony. Before long the crew on the reactor deck got sick, too. Then those in the missile room. In one section after another the crew started dropping like flies. And for all the medical officer could do, they were dying. Some kind of highly contagious and incapacitating virus was working its way through the sub.''

Coy was speaking to Marie and Duggan, but he regarded

Cassidy with watchful eyes. "The captain ordered all the communicating hatches closed. All personnel were restricted to their stations or to their own quarters. They even shut down the air-conditioning system to prevent the spread of the virus through recirculation of the air. But the virus, whatever it was, continued to spread, until only the control room area was left unaffected. In less than an hour the submarine was effectively immobilized. Captain West surfaced and radioed Pearl Harbor for help. The Navy has a bacteriological warfare lab where—"

"It's not a bacteriological warfare lab!" snapped Cassidy. "It's an epidemiological research center. They study prevention and control of contagious diseases."

"Uh-huh. Anyway, all that the Navy really knows is based on Captain West's radio call to the research center. West was told to hold his position. A Navy medical team flew by helicopter to the site. The helicopter landed on the water and the medical technicians, wearing full quarantine suits, crossed to the sub in rubber rafts. They boarded the sub. Meanwhile the helicopter lifted off and apparently exploded right over the *Alaska,* which then disappeared. Reinholt has photographs of the helicopter setting down and the subsequent explosion, but no explanation of what really happened." Murdock turned full on Cassidy. "Now does that version square with your understanding of the facts, Captain? Is there anything you'd like to add?"

Cassidy, drawing himself up, glared at Murdock with terrifying dignity. "I have nothing to contribute, Mr. Murdock, other than to express how astonished I am that Admiral Reinholt would disclose sensitive information like this to you." Cassidy didn't add "of all people!" but his tone managed to convey the impression that he had.

He turned and made for his own quarters, and wasn't seen on deck again until the *Nomad* steamed into the great harbor west of Honolulu. At that point he materialized and, taking a position on the ship's bow, began a nonstop monologue that could have been culled from any Hawaiian handbook. This, he explained, is the headquarters of the U.S. Pacific Fleet, the world's largest naval command. The harbor itself—named after the pearls once found in its coral beds—is a large, roughly circular shelter formed as the double estuary of the Pearl River. Ford Island sits in the middle of the harbor, creating a kind of lagoon. Murdock could see for himself that the Navy Yard occupies mostly the southeast quarter of the lagoon as well as Ford Island, which is the headquarters of the Third Fleet and has a landing field and hangars. *Nomad* had just steamed north of Hickam Air Field and turned into the lagoon between Pearl Harbor and Ford Island when a Navy launch with security markings intercepted them. Cassidy interrupted his tour-conducting long enough to expedite their entry. With the security boat leading the way they made for a concrete wharf on the southern side of the harbor.

"The white concrete markers forming a line off Ford Island," Cassidy continued, "is Battleship Row. The large memorial in the center actually sits astride the wreck of the battleship *Arizona,* which was sunk during the Japanese raid. Of all the Navy vessels sunk or damaged here that day, the *Arizona* is the only one that wasn't raised, repaired, and returned to duty during World War II; her eleven hundred and two crewmen are still entombed inside her sunken hull. Today, the memorial is the most frequently visited place in all of Hawaii."

As they approached their assigned dock, Captain Cassidy began swinging his arms like a signalman. Duggan waved back from the bridge. Crewmen not involved in the process of docking could see the scowl on Duggan's face, but the Irish captain's shouts for Cassidy to "clear the goddamn bow" went unheard and unheeded.

Once they had docked, a dozen Navy technicians piled aboard the *Nomad* and converged on the minisub. When the docking lines were secured, a delegation of *Nomad* crewmen rounded up Murdock and Cassidy. "What about us?" asked Sushi, speaking for the rest of the divers and deckhands clustered behind him.

"If they insist on leaving," said Cassidy, "they may do so. I have orders to provide them transportation into town. But anyone who stays will be confined to the ship. This is a United States military establishment; no one is allowed to wander around without authorization. Try it, and you'll be arrested and prosecuted."

Murdock, looking at the men's faces, sensed a mutiny in the making. After three weeks at sea, Honolulu had to beat hanging around the dock.

"I'll stay," said Emmott.

Sushi nodded quickly. "I'd like to go into town for a while," he said, "but I could come back."

The others hesitated a moment too long. "You'll all have to stick around," said Murdock. "I may need you."

A rumble of discontent worked its way through the crew.

"What I said about being arrested if you're caught off the ship," Cassidy reminded him, "goes for you, too, Murdock."

"I'm coming with you."

"Oh no you're not. I'm going to the research center." Cassidy pointed across an arm of the lagoon to the eastern side, where a two-story concrete cube of a building squatted on the end of a long, narrow jetty, like a medieval fortress overlooking the harbor. The concrete walls were without any openings. Entry could be made only along the jetty, which led back to a forest of more modernistic structures on the harbor's edge.

"That's where I'd like to go, too."

"Forget it, Murdock, the center is strictly off-limits. What do you think you're up to, anyway? Playing detective? This is a Navy investigation and the Navy will handle it."

"Then I'll go to Ford Island and talk to somebody who saw the helicopter take off."

"How did you know the helicopter took off from Ford Island?"

"Didn't it?"

"Yes, but how did you know?"

"I didn't know. I guessed. When they flew me out to the site, I first had to take a launch over to the island to pick up a chopper."

"What do you expect to learn over there?"

Murdock shrugged. "I dunno. It beats sitting around here."

"Look, I know you mean well. Admiral Reinholt and I appreciate your cooperation. But why don't you just let us handle it? We don't encourage visitors to the island. If you're just bored, I can arrange some magazines and movies to be brought around here for you. Maybe some blue stuff, huh?"

"Blue stuff?" Murdock deadpanned.

"You know, blue movies." Cassidy stirred uncomfortably inside his jacket. "Skin flicks."

Murdock feigned distaste. "Oh, you mean oceanography pictures! With skin divers and like that." His expression was a mask of mock horror. "Didn't I tell you I hate Jacques Cousteau?"

With his face flushed a bright crimson Captain Cassidy whirled, crossed a plank to the dock, stepped into a waiting jeep, and sped off in a cloud of exhaust and a grinding of gears. Not until he was long out of sight had the howls of laughter quieted from the *Nomad*'s foredeck.

Even Marie was smiling. "It was funny," she told him. "But I'm not sure it did us any good."

"Sure it did, if it got him out of here two seconds sooner. He's obviously not going to do anything to help, so there's no point in letting him look over our shoulders." Murdock addressed the crew. "Let's see how fast we can get the minisub off-loaded. Attach her to the crane and help the Navy people move her onto their trailer. The sooner we get them out of here, too, the sooner we can get down to work.''

No one knew what Murdock had in mind, but less than an hour later the minisub was inside a nearby warehouse and the Navy investigators—after informing Murdock they might want to interview certain crew members—had left the *Nomad.* Only one marine paced wearily back and forth on the dock. The ship's company had gathered in the mess decks, out of sight of prying eyes.

"How are we fixed for scuba tanks?" was the first thing Murdock wanted to know.

Marie informed him that there were plenty of tanks.

"Enough for several dives?"

"We have our own compressor on board, Coy. We can fill the bottles as fast as we use them.''

"All right, then. Here's what we're going to do. From now until nightfall the deck crew is going to give the *Nomad* one helluva cleaning. Decks, brass, windows . . . everything. Break out the paint buckets and the brushes. Rig some scaffolding over the sides and scrape off the hull."

"For this we didn't go into town?"

Murdock looked his men over, but the speaker had retreated into silence.

"No. This is just a cover. I want the deck crew to generate enough activity that the guard out there, as well as anybody else who's watching, won't spot the divers coming and going.''

"Coming and going where?" asked Gandy.

"Into the subwell, under the hull, and then out into the harbor.''

Murdock's announcement was met with murmurs and frowns. Suddenly one of the men spoke up. Murdock remembered he was a diver and had been introduced as "Mac" something or other.

"We've been ordered to stay on the ship," said the man.

Others among the divers nodded.

"It's Mac, isn't it?" asked Murdock. The man nodded just once. "Does the idea of disobeying an order bother you that much, Mac?"

"I can live with it," he growled. "What really bothers me, mister, is you."

"Keep talking."

"I guess we'd like to know what you're up to. The word we got was that you're after money. That you showed up here to grab the *Batavia* treasure, sell off your father's vessels, and scoot back to Oklahoma. We could understand that, all right. We don't like it much, but we can understand it. But now we find ourselves smack in the middle of Pearl Harbor about to take on the United States Navy, and we have to ask ourselves *why?* What the hell are you up to?"

Silence consumed the galley.

"Would you have dared to ask my father that question?" asked Murdock.

The man grunted. "I wouldn't have *had* to ask your father that question."

Marie was watching Murdock's face when his gray-green eyes flashed like molten steel. His voice was hard enough to chip a tooth.

"If you ever ask me again," Murdock growled, "I'll personally throw you over the side!"

Murdock looked from one to another of these weathered, sea-toughened men. He didn't want to fight them, but they couldn't be allowed to question his authority. It was all right if they didn't trust him or like him. Murdock didn't even care if the men talked about him behind his back. But those same words spoken to his face became a challenge. Better to lose a fight than to lose face. He felt the muscles tightening in his shoulders and arms. He sensed his fingers clench into fists. Then Murdock looked into the men's eyes. Mac was no different than any of the others. These men weren't really against him. They just needed a reason to be with him. He stopped when he noticed Marie nodding her head slightly and saying without words: *Give them something.*

"I'll tell you this much," he said, looking around him again. "I'm here to claim my inheritance, all right. But I don't give a damn about the money."

Nobody spoke.

"Any of you who don't care to be a part of this," he continued, "call the guard and get transportation to town. It's still not too late. Anybody who stays takes orders from me the same way he would from my father, and he keeps his mouth shut."

Mac cleared his throat. "If we thought there was any chance we were going after Glen Murdock's killer," he said, "we wouldn't care what kind of trouble you got us into."

There it was.

Murdock's fists fell open. "Well, don't worry. There's no trouble I can get you into here that Admiral Reinholt can't get us out of. He's behind us in this little project. I don't guess any of you know Reinholt any better than I do, but my father knew him and trusted him and that's good enough for me. Now shall we get down to business? We're going to carry out the underwater end of this investigation. That's what you guys do, right? All right. You can slip into the water through the subwell and swim out deep enough that you won't be seen from the surface. I suggest we work you six divers in three two-man teams." Murdock spread out a rough drawing of the harbor on the table in front of them.

"There are seven divers," Marie pointed out.

"Yes, but you're staying back here on the ship with me. Sushi, you and Mac cover the west side of the jetty where the research center is located. And you—isn't your name William? Willy. You and Emmott take the docks

here on Ford Island across the harbor from the center.''
Murdock pointed to the eastern side of the island. ''I've
seen it from the air. There are three docks the medical
launch could have come to. None of them very large.
The two here are just south of Battleship Row. This other
to the northeast of the row looks like a private dock, but
you'd better check it out. The *Arizona* memorial is right
here in the middle of the row and it's heavily visited.
Stay away from it or someone will spot you. Stay out of
the shallow water, too.''

''What about us?''

''Your names are. . . ? Reed and Findlay. You two take
the offshore waters on a direct line between the docks
and the jetty on the mainland side. You'll have the most
bottom to cover, so the others will give you a hand once
they've finished checking their areas.''

''How deep is the bottom?'' asked Reed.

''Not too deep. According to Captain Cassidy's little
spiel it had to be dredged, so how deep can it be? Are
you worried about decompression?''

''Not if it had to be dredged, I'm not.''

Sushi raised his hand. ''What are we looking for?''

''Anything that seems suspicious. Firearms, clothes,
maybe a small boat intentionally sunk.''

Someone from the back murmured, ''Scuttled.''

''Whatever. Or even some bodies.''

''What's on your mind, Mr. Murdock?''

''It's what's on Admiral Reinholt's mind. He's got it
figured that somehow the Soviets are behind all this. Personally, I think he's got us screwing around here in Pearl
Harbor so we'll think we're helping and still be out of
his hair. Find something, anything, out there in the water
and I'll get us some good explanations.''

Never did any seagoing vessel receive finer treatment
than the *Nomad* received that warm afternoon. The crew
did a job cleaning her that put the United States Navy to
shame. They actually drew, rather than avoided, atten-

tion. But it was all put down to boredom, and no one noticed the steady traffic of men going down into the subwell and remaining away for hours at a time, any more than they might have noticed a few errant bees from a busy hive. Murdock waited until the three teams had departed and then dropped into the water with Marie. He had worn diving gear before he had worn shoes and socks, but everything it was possible to forget Murdock had forgotten. Everything else he only remembered with dread.

The water was mercifully clear and comfortably warm—Hawaiian water never varies far from seventy-five degrees—and this made his initial plunge endurable. When the bubbles cleared he found Marie dropping beside him and gesturing with her fingers on her left wrist. What the hell did that mean? Had she told him? Everything they had reviewed before the dive somehow was swept from his memory. When she made a circular motion with a hand, pointed to the north, and then swam away, Murdock nearly panicked. What did she want him to do? He clawed after her, working his hands and legs like a turtle. But when he pulled up beside her she was smiling at him through her face mask, and he knew she would not let him drown.

Together they explored the bottom of the harbor. Marie showed him brain coral in convoluted boulders the size of basketballs, brown sea fans like defoliated winter trees, and everywhere red-castle structures of stone coral, living and dead. She held starfish up for inspection, turned some pincushion urchins onto their bellies with the tip of her knife, performed an underwater ballet among the striped angel fish, and poked at the flowerlike tube worms so that they sucked themselves back into their tunnels faster than the eye could follow.

Finally Murdock knew it must be time to go up. His single tank could hold only about an hour's supply of air, and he felt that his time and his air must have long since expired. This realization struck him like a blow. He had to rise right away. He should hold his breath until he was sure his air supply would even get him to the surface. But the next thing he knew, Marie had a hold on his leg and was pulling him back to the bottom. She signed something he couldn't begin to grasp and pushed him off ahead of her in a direction he couldn't have named. Minutes later they burst out of the water into the *Nomad*'s subwell.

Murdock removed his gear, scrambled up the ladder to the deck, and collapsed on a beach towel.

Marie lay down beside him. "Don't bend your knees so much when you kick," she was saying. "Let the fins do the work. And try to breathe more smoothly. You're gulping air. Take it easy—enjoy yourself and try to have fun."

He glared at her. "Have fun! That's easy for you to say. You're swimming. I'm drowning. Drowning takes all the fun out of swimming."

She shook his humor aside with a wag of her head. "And never, never hold your breath while you're coming up! The air expanding in your lungs will blow you up like a balloon."

"Yes, Mother."

"We'll rest for a while and then try it again."

"Won't we have to refill our tanks?"

"We've plenty of air left. We were only down twenty minutes."

Twenty minutes!

When they surfaced the next time, they met the first of the search teams just coming back. Sushi and Mac had found nothing unusual on either side of the research center building. They had checked all around the jetty, concentrating on a small landing on the west side but going as far out as their air supply would take them. Fifteen minutes after filling up they were back in the water with a new area to cover. Willy and Emmott checked in from Ford Island. The two lower docks were clear. It had taken them as long as it had only because some Navy investigators hanging around the larger dock had kept them from swimming in close until their air supplies were running low. The two divers planned to return to Ford Island and search the northern dock before moving into the lagoon with the other four. By mid-afternoon they were all working the deeper water, swimming six abreast at intervals of twenty feet, back and forth across the one-mile width of the lagoon. Each leg covered a hundred-foot swath and took a half hour to clear. Between training dives of his own, Murdock checked off their discoveries—or lack of them—on his map, assigning new territories while their bottles were being refilled.

When they returned for the last time the sun was just setting behind the hangars of Ford Island. A corresponding darkness settled over the *Nomad* crew—a disheartening darkness. Murdock felt it more than any of them because success was his responsibility.

Captain Cassidy stopped by one last time before nightfall. He had brought no movies or magazines of any color, and he had brought no news. Whatever he had learned at the research center the captain kept to himself. His assistance in this case amounted to an offer to escort the *Nomad*'s cook to the PX for supplies if theirs were short. His offer was not accepted. He wasn't invited to stay for dinner. No one proffered him a drink. After informing Murdock that Admiral Reinholt would likely arrive at Pearl Harbor some time the following day, Captain Cassidy made a couple of complimentary remarks about the *Nomad*'s appearance, crossed back over the brow, and sped off in his jeep.

Murdock never saw him again. He remained on the deck long after the others had gathered in the galley, watching the incandescent bonfires of the harbor—dock lights, buoy lights, running lights of passing ships, and riding lights of ships at anchor—mock the stellar sky.

"What are you thinking about out here, Coy?"

He looked around.

Marie was standing not a yard away, forearms resting on the rail, her gaze following his across the harbor. She had performed some miracle with her hair and thrown a terrycloth coverup over her swimsuit. In the water that day Murdock had been fascinated by her sleek, stream-lined figure; she was almost like a creature of the sea, fast, exotic, and unapproachable.

"I was wondering," he said, "how many men have drowned right out there in that harbor."

She shrugged. "Perhaps thousands. Captain Cassidy said eleven hundred men went down with the *Arizona*. He said the bodies are still inside, though I can't believe they would be . . . not after so much time."

It struck Murdock suddenly, a notion so vivid it was like a supernova blazing among stars. He looked across the lagoon to the electric fires that outlined the oblong bulk of the *Arizona* memorial. Of course. It had to be. He shook his head in the sudden realization of what this knowledge meant.

"Now what are you thinking about?"

"It's a lot of water for drowning," he said half to himself.

"I don't think it's a question of how much water. A man can be afraid of the sea and drown in his own bath-tub."

He turned back to her. "What's that supposed to mean?"

"Coy, I don't think it's the ocean that frightens you. I think you are afraid of facing what hides in the ocean."

"And what is hiding in the ocean?"

"In France we say of a certain kind of a man: *Il noye dans un verre d'eau*. This means: 'He drowns in a glass of water'."

"Me, huh?"

"No. No, Coy, I don't think that describes you at all.

137

But of another kind of man we say: *Il peut avaler la mer.* 'He can swallow the sea.' ''

"Like my father."

"Yes. He was that kind."

"I suppose you think he was quite a guy?"

Marie moved her head sadly. "He was, as you say, quite a guy. But he was not perfect. Glen had many fears and many failures. It is not my place to say what they were, but he was far from perfect."

"Oh, go ahead. He was my father, and I grant you leave. I'd love to know. Tell me one of his fears. Or a failure. It would make me feel better to know."

Marie smiled a French kind of a smile.

"I think he was afraid of something that was hiding on the land. Something that lurked beyond the water's edge."

"This is fascinating. Tell me more. What was hiding on the land?"

"His failure."

Murdock had worn a sort of half smile. As the moments passed in silence the smile slowly dissolved.

"So?"

"And so," Marie continued, "Glen Murdock went into the ocean to hide. He is there still. Lurking in the depths. He will be there until the day when you go out to face him." Marie straightened abruptly, smiled again, and said, "Come. It is time for you to eat."

At ten o'clock, while Marie was in the galley helping with the dinner dishes, while the men were breaking out the cold beer, while the moon was still obscured by clouds and the marine who patrolled the docks was grabbing a cigarette, Murdock donned his scuba tank, mask, and fins and slipped down into the subwell.

# Chapter Nine

Had Murdock dived into a tank of crude oil it couldn't have been any darker. The harbor lights, dock lights, even the lights from the *Nomad* a few feet over his head vanished completely. Murdock held the mask against his face as he descended, and even then couldn't see his hands on the glass.

He knew he was going down. Pressure squeezed his eardrums harder and his face mask tighter with each downward foot. Cool and then colder water swept upward over his body. But only when his swim fins brushed over a coral formation and his knees crunched into sand did he know he was on the bottom. He risked the flashlight long enough to check the bezel on his diving watch before aiming it out into the lagoon. The light burrowed a narrow tunnel of dingy yellow through the darkness.

When he turned off the flashlight the darkness redoubled, and Murdock regretted having used it at all. The flashlight would be essential once he got to the other side, but the trip across the lagoon could take a half hour and the batteries wouldn't last if he used it all the way. Using it only now and then would destroy what night vision he had.

He pushed away from the shore.

Murdock swam in the style Marie had taught him, arms hanging loosely at his sides, leg muscles driving from the thighs, knees slightly flexed, head up. Almost at once his fins slapped at something hard and his chest smashed against the bottom. A clump of stone coral had missed his head by a hair's breadth. He shoved off again, and swam for a dozen yards before he wound up right back on the sand. This didn't make any sense. If he had been swimming toward the shore and a rising bottom, perhaps he could understand it. But the harbor was supposed to be getting deeper.

Once more Murdock launched himself off, more upward than forward this time. He kicked harder and faster, trying to keep himself up. Seconds later he plowed into the bottom again. His mask buried itself in the sand. Water poured into the mask before Murdock could wrestle it back onto his face.

A minor emergency, but one that ground his journey to a halt. In this darkness he didn't need the mask for seeing, and yet as long as it was filled with water he couldn't go on.

Marie must have told him how to purge a flooded mask, but Murdock had forgotten. His only solution was to race for the surface, exhaling all the way up to keep his lungs from bursting. The first thing that struck him when he threw his head out of the water and ripped the mask from his face was the sight of a wild, chopping sea. The calm harbor he'd entered only minutes before had utterly disappeared. Two-foot swells rolled past his head. Then he saw the stern lights of a powerful patrol boat moving into the harbor and realized he'd come up in its wake. He'd have to be more careful. Before he could shake the mask free of seawater and clamp it back on his face, a wave buried his efforts and sent him back under. The water level in the mask was down across the bridge of his nose, but having the water wash into and out of his eyes was somehow even worse than having the mask flooded.

Murdock reached for the surface but grasped only water. The surface had pulled far away. He was gripped by a sense of frustration that turned into anger when he felt his fins touch solid bottom.

He was too heavy. Murdock pushed off, kicking and clawing his way to the top and showing none of the caution he'd promised himself. Once on the surface he had to pump his legs furiously just to stay afloat long enough to empty his mask. He pinned the top of it against his forehead and pulled out the lower edge so the water could drain. And then he was under. It had been a rush job, only partially emptying the mask. And yet it had shown him the way. Hovering there below the surface he performed the same maneuver again, only this time blowing air from his nose. Air filled the top of the mask and forced all the water out a small crack above his lip.

So pleased was Murdock with his success that he didn't realize he was sinking again until he had plunked back onto the bottom. The knowledge came to him in a sharp, stinging pain in the leg. He'd been stabbed. Or bitten, one or the other. A scream burst from his mouthpiece in a muted explosion of bubbles. He twisted around, shone the light down through the swirling sand onto a black sea urchin. He had landed right on top of the creature and rammed several spines into his leg. It was only a minor nuisance and yet it hurt.

Enough was enough. He must get things together. This project was getting on his nerves. He was virtually blind; there was nothing to feel down here that didn't cause pain, and as for hearing, the inrush of air to his mouthpiece and the exhaustion of bubbles made a mockery of any notions about undersea silence. On top of that he could smell and taste nothing but rubber. None of his senses was worth a damn and Murdock didn't like it. He had no business here, no business even in having come when Reinholt called.

He used the flashlight to verify that a small piece of sea floor below him was free of marine horrors and then let himself settle heavily down.

The first thing to do was lighten his load. He was too heavy to make it across the harbor. After only a few minutes swimming and a few more treading water he was nearly exhausted.

It was the weight belt.

He couldn't take it off—then he would be too light. The wet suit top that he had worn because it was black acted like a thin life preserver. The life vest, even uninflated, had some buoyancy, too; and so would the air tank once his air supply began running low. If he didn't have the weight belt on when that happened, he wouldn't be able to stay underwater. No, he couldn't take off the belt.

Certainly he couldn't take off the wet suit or life vest without first taking off the scuba equipment. That was a real problem. It had taken him twenty minutes to put them on while standing on the *Nomad*'s deck with light enough to see by. Here, in darkness, under water, he'd be lucky if he didn't lose half the gear. Marie could have helped him to put the right amount of weight on the belt but Murdock had sneaked away without telling anyone what he was planning.

But Marie had showed him how to inflate the life vest. The emergency lanyard would blow the thing up in a heartbeat by puncturing a $CO_2$ capsule. However, he could also inflate it manually by blowing into a valve. Just a little air would compensate for the excess weight on the belt.

He tried it. It didn't work well at all. He was light on the chest, heavy on his waist and shoulders, and when he swam it took most of his energy to keep himself from rolling onto his back. At last Murdock gave up, loosening the valve of the vest and expelling all the air. When he had settled to the bottom he took off the belt and removed several of the lead weights, while holding the flashlight between his teeth.

This did the trick.

Murdock checked his watch and then began swimming. He felt for the first time that everything was under control. Ten minutes had passed, much of it wasted. But he could make up for that. After another five minutes of determined swimming he would surface to check his progress. By then he should be almost halfway across.

Things seemed to go well. He stayed off the bottom, made good time, and came up to a surface almost mirror-flat. And when he surveyed the shorelines it did look as though he were about in the middle between the two shores. The only problem was, Murdock didn't recognize either of the shores. He couldn't locate the slip where the *Nomad* was tied, and he couldn't make out the lights of the *Arizona* memorial. That far shore there, that had to be Ford Island. But where was Battleship Row? And where was the *Nomad?* It took several minutes of treading water, sculling his arms at his sides, before Murdock realized his heading had come ninety degrees off course. He had all but left the harbor. If he hadn't come up when he had, he'd have swum right out to the Pacific Ocean. Next stop, Tahiti.

It was no problem, he told himself. Don't worry. He should still have enough air to reach the *Arizona* Memorial and return, and ten minutes of reserve air after that when he threw the reserve lever on the regulator. All he had to do was swim nearer the surface and check his position more often. It had been foolish to go so long without verifying he hadn't strayed from his course. He wouldn't make that same mistake again.

No, he heard himself answer, there are plenty of other mistakes to keep you busy.

He was the worst kind of rank amateur, and he was up against hardened professionals. Murdock was sure of that. Everything Reinholt had told him convinced him of that.

Reinholt was convinced of it, too.

These men, Coy Murdock thought as he pushed through the darkness, could have arranged for a small epidemic aboard the *Alaska* knowing that the sub's captain would request assistance from the epidemiological research center. They could have had some men waiting. Intercepting the helicopter after it took off from Ford Island would have been tricky with naval radar tracking it all the way out to the sub, but inside the Navy Yard itself no one would have suspected a thing. They could have waylaid the medical team here on the water and taken their place. Wearing those full-body quarantine suits and helmets, they could have climbed right into the helicopter that was waiting off the tarmac on Ford Island. The pilot never would have known the difference.

Murdock surfaced to check his position and progress.

Up ahead were the lights of Battleship Row and the *Arizona* memorial. Another fifteen minutes and he would be there. He'd learn if his vivid notion was correct.

It helped him to think about what waited at the end of his swim. He had to think about something to keep his mind off the swimming. But even this was better than thinking about the swimming. His feet hurt. The mask had given him a headache, because he hadn't learned how to exhale a little air through his nose to offset the pressure of the dive and keep it from squeezing his face. His jaw muscles ached from clamping his teeth on the mouthpiece. And the endless whoosh and sputter of air coming into and out of his demand regulator system was driving him crazy. Murdock was tired. He was also sore and scared—a dangerous combination for any man who is out of his element. When that element is the sea, the combination can be fatal.

Murdock half imagined a dark shape following him from a distance. A shark? That seaweed which brushed across his leg was an octopus tentacle exploring his naked flesh. And between his inhalations and exhalations came a low-throated gurgle . . . a rumble that could only be the awakening of some prehistoric sea creature . . . a churning like that of a thousand piranha boiling the water behind him.

Murdock ignited his flashlight. Bright flashes of fish

darted into the safety of darkness. He turned, swinging the beam like a saber. The churning was growing louder by the second but there was nothing around him. What the hell could it be? His light slashed across something off to his right and he swung the beam back in that direction. It was gone. No, there it was. His light played over a solitary fish that glided through the darkness with hardly an observable movement. A sleek, silver torpedo, six feet long with black fins and black tail fin. But it was the head that froze Murdock's blood in his veins. The long, low-slung jaw with its vicious underbite, the needle-sharp, piranha-like teeth . . . were attached to the body of a fifty-pound barracuda.

Fear lent him the kind of strength he didn't know he still possessed. He struck out like a madman, kicking and paddling with his arms, too. After nearly a minute of this he shone the light to the side: It was still a few yards away. The vicious-looking streamlined monster could keep pace with a casual wag of its tail or strike with blinding speed.

Murdock knew he couldn't outswim it. If he headed for the shore or the surface he would only make an easy target of his back or his feet. And he mustn't panic. That was the worst thing he could do. He knew sharks sense panic in their victims. Surely barracuda sense it, too.

He dove to the bottom. The rumbling and churning grew louder each second. Murdock threw his back against a large outcrop of coral and drew his diving knife. Then, holding the knife in his right hand, the flashlight in his left, he squared off against the manhunter.

Unlike a shark, a barracuda isn't drawn by the scent of fresh blood. It goes after whatever looks interesting, and the stainless-steel knife, bright and sparkling in the beam of his flashlight, was more than any ordinary barracuda can resist. It attacked.

Straight in. Not a torpedo, a silver lance. A thrust, and then straight back again to wait.

Murdock swung with the knife, but the fish was too fast. When it came in again, Murdock severed a wide sweep of water and that was all.

This time the barracuda had backed out of range of his flashlight. Murdock waved the light in circles. In vain.

The barracuda had vanished.

Now it was Murdock's turn to wait.

Seconds passed. Seconds became a minute. His heart raced, knowing that what he couldn't see or hear or—

A fifty-pound sledgehammer with teeth slammed into his back. At first Murdock thought it had hit his neck but in fact, the silver plating of his regulator had been just too tempting a target for the barracuda to pass up.

The effect on Coy Murdock was no less terrible because of this.

When he whirled, the mouthpiece was torn from between his teeth. His flashlight illuminated a shower of bubbles and nothing more. His knife slashed through the bubbles again and again. He scrambled for the mouthpiece, but with both hands full he couldn't begin to find it. And he wasn't willing to give up either light or knife until his need for air was so great that nothing else mattered. When this moment came, it was too late to act.

The barracuda struck a final time at his back, nearly throwing Murdock onto the bottom. Out of breath, he did what Marie had told him to do: He blew up his life vest by pulling the emergency lanyard.

When the $CO_2$ capsule blew, the vest fully inflated in a fraction of a second. In a flash, Murdock was going up like a missile launched from a submarine. He couldn't have slowed if he'd wanted to.

He shot up to forty feet. And then thirty.

The low-throated rumble became a roar. And now it grew louder, not with each second that passed, but with each upward foot.

He sped through the twenty-foot depth without slowing.

Exhale, he told himself. Don't forget to exhale. You can breathe again on the surface.

Ten feet.

He never reached the surface.

His body collided with a roof of iron so encrusted with ship barnacles it could have passed for a coral reef; the collision staggered his senses, his sense of direction, even his sense of up and down. He decided that for some nightmarish reason he'd come back to the bottom. He pushed away from the reef, only to fall back. Struggle as he did he couldn't break free.

The reef was moving. And then suddenly it wasn't even a reef anymore, but the hull of a huge vessel moving through the harbor.

And washing Murdock back toward the stern!

He tried to crawl up the side, but the momentum of the ship rolled him onto his back, onto his head. And then he was back on his chest. His swim fins were useless. His hands were both full. In sudden panic he let go of the flashlight. He didn't need it to see what was happening: He was being sucked into the propeller! He could see that clearly enough, a ten-foot circle of boiling phosphorescence.

He couldn't swim away from it. He couldn't even look away. Murdock stabbed the life vest and then let go the knife, too, as the air poured from his chest and was carried in a frenzied cloud into the propeller's blades. Murdock's hands clawed at the hull until the barnacles had torn the flesh from his palms and fingers. And then his vest was empty of air and he catapulted himself downward, oblivious to the screaming of his lungs and the hammering of his heart, both of which pleaded that to go down was to die.

The screw banged against his scuba tank. Murdock felt his fins being whacked and torn. He didn't stop kicking. The darkness of depth closed in around him. Delirium and death moved nearer, too. Murdock didn't swim up until the roar of the ship's engines and the churning of her propellers had faded. At that point he was almost too weak to rise. And too heavy. Had he not unbuckled and abandoned his weight belt he never would have made it to the surface.

The destroyer was well up the harbor. Murdock treaded water, inhaling in loud, whooping gasps.

When he found his mouthpiece dangling off the side of his backpack he put it back in his mouth. Some time passed before his demand regulator could meet his demands.

At this rate he would soon hyperventilate and pass out, or just exhaust his air supply. Either way, he'd be lucky to have any air left by the time he got to the *Arizona*.

Murdock didn't care. Getting there was all he cared about now. And the lights of the memorial were not more than a hundred yards away.

For a moment his hopes soared. Then he remembered the flashlight. What good would it do to reach the memorial if he didn't have the light?

Murdock turned and swam back until he was over the area where he guessed the flashlight must have fallen. In his mind was another dive altogether. "It's only fifty feet down," his father had once told him. On that occasion he had gone after some dog tags instead of a flashlight. He had dived then without tanks or snorkel.

Even though this was a night dive it should be easier. After all, the flashlight was still on; that would make it simple to find. And he could stay down as long as he needed to until he found it.

Of course, on this occasion a six-foot barracuda was waiting for him to come down.

Murdock wished his father was here to explain how easy it would be. Perhaps if Drew had been with him, his older brother would have offered to dive in his place. Then he remembered what had happened to his father and Drew.

Murdock threw his legs over his head and tunneled down, scooping out huge handfuls of water and sweeping them behind him with his feet. When his hands grabbed the bottom he started to search.

It took forever to find the flashlight. It had landed on its face, and the light was so dim that he didn't see it until he swam right over the spot. The glass had cracked. The battery was pathetically weak. He made a half-hearted try at locating his knife and then sped away.

Maybe the destroyer coming through had scared off the barracuda. Maybe it just didn't like the taste of steel. Whatever the reason, Murdock never caught another glimpse of the manhunter.

Ten minutes later he was scrambling onto the memorial dock. He lay there for a long time, gripping the wood with bleeding hands before crawling inside the white concrete structure. He'd never swim back, he told himself. No power on earth could every make him swim back across that harbor. He'd wait right here on the memorial until the sightseeing boats started running in the morning or until one of the Navy patrol boats came by. He'd risk whatever punishment they wanted to give him. Anything was preferable to going back in the water.

How much better it would go for him, though, if he had something to show them. A body. A spent casing. Or even just a few drops of blood.

He had no hope of finding anything useful inside. With the tourist boats coming and going at all hours of the day, any evidence of villainy would have been discovered and turned over to the Navy long before. Certainly the men he was after wouldn't have left any bodies where they could easily be found. Or spent casings. In the first place, no shots had been fired; if they had been, the whole Navy Yard would have been alerted. There would be blood.

Murdock looked down. Plenty of blood. But it was his. From his hands and his shoulder. Apparently the barracuda had gotten a small piece of him after all. He wouldn't know how bad it was until the next day, when the shock had worn off and the adrenaline had left his system. He could hardly think now, let alone feel.

All he knew was that he would find nothing in here.

And yet here was the logical place to begin looking. The memorial was just north of a line between the research center and the Ford Island docks. It was well out in the harbor, where no one would be likely to witness an ambush. A dozen bodies, properly weighted, could be thrown over the side and not be discovered for weeks or even months.

Without warning the memorial interior was washed in a shower of moonlight. The moon had risen above the cover of clouds and Murdock could see without using the flashlight.

Pictures and plaques filled the walls. There were information boards and photographs.

Murdock got to his feet and clumsily walked farther inside. The memorial was a long white corridor, straddling the battleship's deck just forward of amidships like a futuristic bridge wing. Halfway down the corridor the ceiling and the two walls were open to the weather. And because the ship's superstructure had been removed, it was possible for Murdock to see the red can that marked her sunken stern. He could turn one hundred and eighty degrees and see another red can over her bow, too, because the *Arizona*'s sixteen-inch forward cannons also had been removed. The deck itself was under several inches of water. Only a little structural metal aft was still visible, and the incoming tide would soon see to that. Forward, the first of the two forty-foot-diameter gun turrets was almost completely submerged, while the one behind and superimposed over it projected several feet out of the water like a huge fish tank.

Murdock returned to the dock. He took off his scuba

and then his life vest and wet suit. After that he put the air tank on again.

There was no way around it. He slipped reluctantly into the harbor. He dove until he reached the bottom. Once there he used the waning light from his flash to search every square foot of the sand under the docks. When this produced no results he began a patient search around the *Arizona* itself, circumnavigating the battleship, checking the bottom for twenty feet out on all sides, but he came back to the dock without having found a single suspicious item.

Murdock couldn't believe he had come all this way for nothing. He had been so sure. When he climbed onto the dock again and walked back into the memorial he was still sure. The ship was the obvious place to hide bodies. But how could they have been put inside? He had found no openings in the *Arizona*'s hull where torpedoes had struck her. But there must be a hole somewhere, for she had certainly sunk.

In the feeble beam of the flashlight he studied the posted battle summary and learned that the Japanese had sunk the *Arizona* with an aerial torpedo. It had landed behind the guns, just forward of amidships, igniting a powder magazine and sending a fireball several hundred feet in the air. The memorial itself was sitting right over the hole.

He stepped through the arched openings into the knee-deep water on the afterdeck. Very little was now showing above the surface.

What he found was a small cavity where a hatchway had once led to the lower decks. He crawled through the hole. The water that slowly came over his head was surprisingly warm. Yet the degree of darkness inside the hulk came as no surprise. No light found its way here, night or day. Once completely submerged he ignited the flashlight, but the beam it threw was so heartbreakingly dim. Foot by foot he played his weak light over the corridor immediately below the stairs. One by one he swam into the compartments that gave off the corridor. He descended a ladder and found himself surrounded by boilers and plumbing. The next room, the engine room, was too cluttered with machinery to offer a prayer of finding anything else.

By this time his light had become so faint it could hardly project a beam onto his hand.

It was madness to go on.

Anyway, it slowly dawned on Murdock that only a madman would have dragged twelve bodies this far inside the wreck. They wouldn't have had to. They could have waded across to the hatchway and stuffed the bodies below; there would have been no need to do more. That much they could accomplish without even getting wet, if they took off their shoes and socks and rolled up their pants.

He had continued to search deeper and deeper into the battleship, only because he could not accept the idea that he was wrong. His light and his hopes seemed to extinguish at the same moment, and a blackness reserved for the tomb swallowed him up.

Murdock felt the first stirrings of panic.

He shook the flashlight. Banged it against the walls. But it was no use. He let it fall to the deck.

Keep calm, he warned himself. No reason to be afraid. All you have to do is retrace your route. The search may be finished, but you can still find your way out.

He returned to the boiler room by swimming with both hands extended in front of his body. He found a ladder and pulled himself up. There was a corridor. He was following this to the hatchway when a solid wall of rusted iron blocked his way. Perhaps he had come too far. He went back to the ladder. It continued upward through another deck and Murdock decided he'd not climbed far enough. The walls he encountered did not seem familiar, but then he was feeling his way along them. Looking for the slightest traces of light coming from above.

By the time Murdock knew he was lost he'd lost all sense of direction, too. He didn't know if he was moving toward the stern or the bow. Consequently left and right had become meaningless. In the end, only up and down retained any clear definition in his mind.

The stirrings of panic became a genuine clamor when his scuba tank gave up its last breath of air. Murdock, remembering the reserve supply of oxygen built right into the regulator, reached behind his back and twisted the lever. But the lever was already in the reserve position.

The barracuda must have knocked the lever when it attacked him.

His air was finished.

He inhaled until his lungs ached, and then he thrashed upward. He hammered his fists against the deck head. He searched frantically for any crack, any hole, no matter how small. There was nothing. No openings. No hatches. No way out.

Murdock decided to die. A single inhalation of seawater was better than choking to death. He sucked the last ounce of air from the mouthpiece and then spat the thing from his mouth. He leaned against a bulkhead and closed his eyes.

But something in him wouldn't let him quit.

He peeled the air tank off his back, unscrewed the regulator assembly, and put the valve stem of the bottle right to his lips. A whisper of air swept into his mouth.

Air! stinking of steel, and as delicious as anything he had ever tasted.

So. He was not quite dead yet.

He forced himself to remain still for a moment. To think. And to sense.

There had to be a way.

What could he see? Not a damn thing. Did he hear water lapping against the structure higher up? Maybe.

But any sound coming through the hull or reflecting down these corridors would never show him a way out. How about *feel?* A stupid question. His head was splitting open. His shoulder was stiff and ached like the devil. Now wait, Murdock! he thought. What do you feel all around you? Water. Nothing but warm water.

He took another sip of air. Perhaps one more remained; two, if he was very lucky.

Think again, go back. Was the water so warm? Most of it was, and yet there was a slightly cooler current sweeping past his legs.

Where did the difference come from, and how could it help him?

It had been low tide up until a few hours ago, he knew that much. The upper deck of the ship had been baking all day in the sun. The water inside had been warmed. He had felt it when he'd first entered. But by then the high tide was covering the deck. The warmer water inside would have poured out the top. And cooler water from the bottom of the harbor . . . might have come in through the ship's hull.

It was a crazy idea.

The worst of it was that it would take him down when he knew that the way in, and maybe the only way in or out, was up.

Murdock tucked the bottle under his arm and pushed down into the bowels of the battleship. In another minute he had sucked out the last ounce of air and let the bottle go. Seconds later his lungs were pleading for more.

At first it was all but impossible to follow the faint thermal current. But as he descended lower and lower in the ship and farther and farther forward there was no mistaking its course. If only he could last long enough to find its source. When Murdock's lungs could stand no more he slipped off his mask and, holding it up over his mouth, drew out the few cubic inches of air from inside with puckered lips. And then it too was gone. He swam on. His arms and his legs grew numb. His chest threatened to explode. He felt his consciousness drifting away. Then his head crashed right into the ship's side with such force it should have split his skull. But it didn't. His head had hit something soft.

His fingers clawed at the barrier. Sand. Water gushing in through a gash in the hull had deposited a small dune on the inner plating. By scooping enough of this sand aside he was able to fashion a hole large enough to squeeze through.

Seconds later he was coming up the side of the ship and climbing onto the bow near the forward turrets. Never had salt air smelled so sweet.

He sat down against the turret, with the water up to his chest, and smiled. He had made a muck of the entire night, but at least he was still alive. Tomorrow he could start again with another idea. Despite his failure Murdock felt strangely good. He had found no bodies. But he had found something. He had also come out here to face his father, and perhaps he had caught a glimpse of the man.

There was still the swim back to the *Nomad*. But even without his scuba and mask, Murdock knew he could do it. If a patrol boat caught him paddling along on the surface he wouldn't even care.

Murdock grabbed the top edge of the turret and pulled himself up. The lights across the lagoon where the *Nomad* was docked didn't seem quite so distant. Wasn't the road back always shorter?

Something pulled his eyes down into the turret. It was half-full of water and a lumpish mass, like an overstuffed garbage bag, was just visible above the surface.

Murdock scrambled over the turret wall, lowered himself down, waded out, and grabbed hold of the bag. He ripped it open. A stench belched into his face and whipped his head around with the force of a roundhouse right; it emptied his stomach before he could throw his head over the edge of the turret. And then he was cling-ing to the turret wall. There were more soft piles just under the surface. More yet across the turret. Quite some time passed before he slogged back into the water and located ten other bags just like the first.

# Chapter Ten

"So who's the missing man?" asked Murdock.

Admiral Reinholt merely glared. "Lots of people have turned up missing lately," he snarled.

"You know who I mean: the one from the medical team. Twelve men boarded the launch from the research center but there were only eleven bodies in that gun turret. You've had your guys on the job for three hours now; they should have been able to identify the twelfth man by a process of elimination."

The glare on Reinholt's face intensified, but Murdock did not cringe. The admiral had brought this face with him to the *Nomad;* the glare had waxed and waned according to what he had heard; in all probability he would leave with the glare still intact. But now, as he aimed an accusatory finger at Murdock, his expression seemed especially fierce.

"It's true, then," he charged. "You actually climbed in and disturbed the evidence!"

"Evidence! These were corpses. Dead people aren't so easily disturbed. After getting their necks broken, crammed into garbage bags, and kept under two feet of water for four or five days, I'm sure they regarded me as no more than a minor annoyance. Come on, dammit! That twelfth man is the answer to a whole lot of questions. He provided the virus that swept through the *Alaska.* He timed the trip across the harbor for a moment when he knew the hijackers would be waiting. And he directed the launch over to the memorial instead of the Ford Island dock.''

"You're right about the three hours," said Reinholt. He glared at Marie and Captain Duggan in turn and then he turned back on Murdock. "But you've known about those bodies since yesterday evening. You trampled all over a crime scene, then waited twelve hours before notifying the proper authorities. I should think a detective sergeant would know better.''

The silence in the room assumed a density so real it could be felt.

Duggan recovered first. "He's a policeman?"

"Oh, you didn't tell them about *that*, eh?" Reinholt snapped at Murdock. "Apparently you're not as free with your own secrets as you are with the Navy's.''

"It's not a secret; I don't talk it around, that's all. And just because I take them into your confidence doesn't mean I have to take them into mine. I don't take anybody into mine.''

When Marie found her voice, she directed her anger not at Murdock but at Admiral Reinholt. "You told us you sent for Coy only because you wanted to deal with the owner of Murdock Salvage," she said. "And to see that *DORiS* was properly turned over to your people for inspection. Now you tell us he's a policeman. Is he investigating for you?''

"What I told you was true. He's no longer a policeman. I didn't tell you he used to be a policeman, just as I didn't tell you that he's been suspended from the police force. Which he has. Nevertheless he's an experienced investigator. And I figured that as long as he was coming to Pearl Harbor anyway, he could keep his eyes and ears open. Of course Mr. Murdock is long on initiative and short on discipline. His eyes and ears are not his problem. His problem is his mouth. Keeping it closed.''

"What happened?"

"What I said: suspended for three months without pay.

There are a number of insubordination charges pending against Mr. Murdock. Departmental reprimands too numerous to count. The powers that be in the Wichita Police Department don't think very much of our friend here. Mr. Murdock has taken no pains to conceal from them that the feeling is mutual. On the contrary, he goes into detail. It seems Mr. Murdock not only advises his superiors where they may go but he also supplies quite specific directions.''

"Where's all this getting us?" asked Murdock. "This is no concern to anyone but me."

"It concerns me greatly. I brought you out here and I take responsibility for what you do. And when you screw up I'll take the fall."

Duggan could stand no more. "All this really doesn't matter a damn!" he bellowed. "What he said or didn't say in Kansas. What he did or didn't do when the bodies were found. He found them. He reported it to you, late or not, and what more could the Navy have done during the night anyway?"

"I don't know, Captain Duggan. Tell me what Murdock managed to do last night after he got back to the *Nomad* and I may have some idea."

Murdock treated himself to a smile. "I managed to get back here," he replied. "That was the big thing. Then I had Gandy patch up my shoulder and I got some sleep."

"Sleep!"

"That's right."

"Why didn't you inform my people here at Pearl what you'd found?"

"Because then I wouldn't have gotten any sleep. First thing this morning I started the boys working. They spent an hour or two catching up with the Navy by finding out how civilians, in this case eleven civilians, get in the harbor; specifically, how they get onto the memorial."

"I don't even know the answer to that. I understand the Navy runs some kind of service."

"They do. A shuttle from Halawa Gate. There are also a couple of civilian sightseeing boats that come in regularly from downtown Honolulu. We decided that was a more likely route for our friendly ambushers, and so I took the Navy boat into town and had a talk with the operators."

"What did you find out?"

"A trimaran named the *Ala Moana Kai* is missing. And so is the owner and operator. Ceased operations the day of the *Alaska* disappearance. I've got the boys out poking around on the downtown docks."

"You see what I mean about people disappearing? There seems to be an epidemic of disappearances. My man is missing, too."

"Tell us about the Navy medical technician. The one who's not folded up in a garbage bag. We already know about Stout."

"I'm not talking about Commander Alan Stout, damn his hide. He's turned up. I'm talking about Captain Cassidy, my chief of staff. Now *he's* gone. And in another two or three days you won't find me around, either."

"Oh, yeah? Where are you going?"

Reinholt shook his head in resignation. "Washington will send me somewhere out of the way. Any place where I can't participate in recovering the *Alaska*. I have very little time left. I'm just trying to accomplish what I can until the orders come in. Or to keep idiots like Packman and his bunch from giving away the store. As soon as I'm gone he'll march right across the street to the Soviet embassy. He'll hand them all the specifications for a Trident-class submarine. He'll tell them all he knows like a good little boy and a dues-paying, card-carrying member of the world community, then he'll ask their help in locating the *Alaska*. And he'll be the most surprised fool on earth when they use that information to home in on every Trident submarine we've got everywhere in the world."

"It sounds like you're acknowledging the *Alaska* is on the loose?"

"We haven't any choice. Yesterday afternoon the team going over your father's submersible—*your* submersible now—discovered that the length of electrical cable entangled on its undercarriage is not from a Trident-class submarine but from a Sturgeon-class. The only Sturgeon-class sub that's ever gone down is the *Mako.*"

"The *Mako!*" cried Marie.

"That's right. They also discovered some particles of paint on the forward undercarriage of the submersible. Those came from a Sturgeon-class submarine, too. We have a DSRV in the water now, and its initial reports confirm that this wreckage is that of a somewhat older U.S. submarine. Most likely it is the *Mako* debris."

"You told me the *Mako* went down in the Atlantic Ocean south of Nova Scotia," she argued.

"It did. And I can't understand how it got to Hawaii—but I can at least get it into the Pacific."

Duggan bolted upright. "Maybe the Russians recovered it. Glen Murdock helped recover some of their submarine debris for study. Who would want some of our wrecked subs if not the Russians?"

"That would have been my thinking exactly, Captain, except for one thing—we recovered the *Mako* ourselves."

"What!"

"Yes. To keep the Soviets from bringing her up just as you suggested. We were first on the scene. Coy's father was part of the recovery crew. We got every piece of debris of any real size."

"Then how did it get to the downsite?" asked Murdock.

"That I can't say. It's been sitting in a warehouse in San Diego for the past twenty years. Oh, the Navy studied it for a while, stress lines in the metal, hull failure points, and fatigue signs. The engineers had a ball. And we learned some things we didn't want the Soviets to learn. But for the past few years it's just been sitting there. I don't know who moved it out.''

"That's for you and your men to look into," said Murdock. "I still want to know about the twelfth man on the medical team."

"I see you do. In for a penny, eh? His name is Kester. He's no technician. Captain Laurence Kester. Number three man at the research center. He commanded the medical team. An excellent biochemist, they tell me; that, and the fact that he was the only staff member with any submarine experience, made him the logical choice to head the team. You think he's the one responsible for the *Alaska*'s epidemic, and that he murdered the eleven members of his own medical team so others could be substituted? Don't expect much help from the Navy in proving it. His record is a model of dedication and service. The feeling among my investigators is that he was taken at gunpoint."

"Your investigators are wrong."

"I know."

"You do?"

"Yes, I'm satisfied that Kester is a Soviet agent."

Murdock grunted. "Then you're wrong, too."

Reinholt slammed his fist down on the table between them. "Are you really that good of a detective, Murdock, or is arrogance just your style?"

"Cute, but it doesn't fit; try it on somebody else. Haven't you read the papers, Admiral? Don't you know that the Cold War is over? The Iron Curtain is coming down and Communism is on the run. They're not launching an attack, they're fighting for economic survival."

"I had this same discussion with your father. How do you know the Soviet military is willing to yield to economic forces so quickly? They may have different ideas than the Politburo. Some of them, a cadre of extremist conservatives in the Soviet Navy or Army, may not like the idea of running without making a fight of it. They may feel that a confrontation like this is exactly the thing to consolidate their authority.''

Murdock smiled. ''Well, I have to grant your superior knowledge of the extremist conservative military viewpoint.''

''Smart aleck.''

''If the Soviet military is capable of launching a rogue operation to steal the Trident, isn't it possible that some of your own Navy people have done precisely the same thing? The Soviets didn't intercept that medical team in the middle of Pearl Harbor. They didn't sail into San Diego and steal several thousand tons of submarine debris from a Naval warehouse. And they didn't sabotage our submersible's radio or its ballast pins. The only people who came close to it were members of the United States Navy. You can't connect the Soviets with any of this.''

''Can't I?''

''Not with anything I've seen.''

Admiral Reinholt stood up and produced a five-by-seven photograph from an inside jacket pocket. He laid the snapshot on the table where Murdock could see. Captain Duggan and Marie moved in as well.

It showed the Russian trawler that had remained for so long just outside the task force perimeter. Beside it was a surfaced Soviet submarine. A plank had been laid across the few yards that separated the two vessels, and three men were crossing in single file to the submarine deck while a Soviet officer looked down from the bridge atop the sail. The two on each end of the plank wore Soviet submariners' uniforms. The middle of the three men wore the white uniform of a U.S. Navy officer. He was raising a hand toward the camera with his index finger and thumb forming a circle in the classic gesture.

''That's Stout?'' asked Murdock.

Before Reinholt could reply, Captain Duggan and

Marie were nodding in acknowledgment. "That's him, all right," said Duggan.

"How did you get this picture?"

"We have camera equipment directed at the Russian trawler twenty-four hours a day."

"And is there a feeling among your investigators that Stout may have boarded the Soviet sub at gunpoint?"

"Very funny!" said the admiral. "You think they ordered him to signal that he's okay? To thumb his nose at us?"

"No, I don't."

"I wish I could believe they did. I liked Alan Stout. I trusted him and relied on him. But I've always known that the Soviets have completely infiltrated the Navy with their agents. It all fits. Stout is the one I sent to get your father when we needed his help. He tried to commandeer this ship and the submersible. To seize them by force. As a result of that your father almost didn't come. He wouldn't have if Stout hadn't mentioned the name of the downed sub. But Glen felt that Stout wanted him to refuse, that there was something on the bottom we weren't supposed to discover. Not yet, anyway. On the trip back, Stout had twelve hours or more to sabotage the submersible. He was the only Navy man on the ship the whole time. He killed your father. Who else had the opportunity? Stout knew all the plans for the missile test—where the test site was to be and when the launch would take place—and he knew all that long before even the *Alaska* officers knew about it. If anyone arranged for the hijacking of the sub it was Stout. That picture proves he's an agent for the Soviet government. Is it any wonder I don't want to cooperate with the damn bastards?"

"I'm not so sure that picture proves what you think it does."

"My god, you're as bad as Eliot Packman."

Murdock crossed the small cabin and stared out his porthole. Then he wheeled. "I'd sure like to know what

Stout did after he talked to Marie that night and before he disappeared.''

"That's what my investigators wanted to know, too. Now that we've identified him as a traitor, every move he's made takes on an added importance. My men searched his cabin and found a unidirectional signaling device. Very clever. It's basically a flashlight with a red lens. There's a tube fitted over the end so that it can be aimed like a gun. Only someone in its direct line of sight could possibly see the signal, even at night. And of course the trawler had laid off the starboard side of the *New Jersey* since the task force arrived. Stout's cabin was on the starboard side.''

"So you think he signaled to the trawler. But they couldn't signal him back?''

"Not without one of our watches seeing it.''

"What else did he do?''

"Returned to the *New Jersey* after seeing Miss Delamer, that much we know. The officer of the deck checked him aboard. It was dark at that time. He must have signaled the trawler he was going to make a run for it. That's all we knew until this morning, when a radio operator remembered Stout sent a message to Washington. We have a copy of the transmission and the reply.''

"Who to in Washington?''

"Deputy CNO, Manpower and Personnel.''

"What was it?''

"A request for the *Alaska*'s crew list.''

"When did he send that?''

"Zero three hundred hours.''

Murdock performed some quick calculations in his head. "Nine o'clock in Washington, D.C.?''

"That's right. The radio operator thought he'd come back to the message center later and made another call, but there is no copy of another message sent or received.''

"It sounds like Marie said something that night that

got him thinking. Maybe he suspected my brother was aboard the *Alaska*. He must have waited until someone he knew at the personnel office would be at his office in Washington and then called for the crew list. Then, something he saw on that list made him feel it was time to skedaddle. How does that sound to you?''

"It could be.''

"Admiral, I want to see that crew list.''

"I'll try to arrange it.''

"Get in touch with Stout's contact in Washington. It's just a hunch, but Stout may have sent the second message, if there was one, to the same guy again. We need to know what that was all about.''

"It's worth checking.''

"Check something else while you're at it. The captain who headed the medical team. Laurence Kester.''

"What about him?''

"You said he had submarine experience. Find out what submarine he served on.''

"You think it might have been the *Alaska?*''

"I'm not saying what I'm thinking right now, just what I want to know.''

Reinholt, too, had little more to say. He gave a brief report on the eleven murdered medical men that was anything but pleasant. Marie and Duggan listened in stunned silence. Only four of the men had had their necks broken. The other seven had been shot in the heads at close range with small-caliber automatic weapons, most likely silenced. The Navy investigators had found shell cases on the *Arizona*'s forward deck under two feet of water, and tissue spatters along the white concrete exterior of the memorial; these clues allowed them to reconstruct the murders with probable accuracy.

The medical team's launch had tied up to the memorial dock, and the team members were herded into the memorial itself at gunpoint. They were ordered to take off their quarantine suits. They were pushed through the arched openings to the forward deck, lined up with their backs to the memorial, and there, all at once, they had been shot to death. Pistols had been placed against their foreheads and, at a signal, their brains had been blown out the backs of their heads. Except four. Perhaps these four had resisted or tried to escape. Their heads had all but been wrenched from their bodies by a brute of a man who enjoyed killing with his bare hands. The technique and strength necessary for those bestial murders made it certain that one man had committed them all.

On this note Reinholt departed. His glare was undiminished. Duggan went to the bridge moments later, leaving Murdock alone with Marie.

She attacked without warning. "So!" she screamed. "You don't take anyone into your confidence! You don't tell anybody what you plan to do, is that right?"

"Sorry, darlin'."

"I'm not your darling, don't be offensive!"

"Well, there you are. Seems like you get offended when I don't talk to you, and when I do."

"I'm not offended! I'm angry! Dammit, Coy, you almost got yourself killed. Gandy told me what happened to you last night; no wonder you went to him for first aid instead of coming to me. I'd have given you hell for going out alone like that, and you know it."

"You're giving me hell now."

Marie had stepped close enough to push a finger into his chest. "Nobody goes diving alone. Nobody! Haven't you ever heard of the buddy system? Even professional divers always take a buddy along and, mister," she said, poking him with the finger three times to emphasize each word, "you're . . . no . . . professional."

Rather than backing off, Murdock stepped in. Too close for poking.

"Yes, Mother."

"Don't call me that!" she snapped.

"You were going to marry my father, weren't you?"

167

"No."

"You wanted to. At least that's what they tell me."

"Who told you that?"

"Somebody."

"Well, I didn't marry him."

"No, because he wanted you to marry my brother. Somebody told me that, too. A little gossip goes a long way on a small ship like this one, huh, sis?"

"I'm not your sister. I would never have married your brother either—and don't change the subject. The next time you even think about going in the water you'd better have somebody with you."

Murdock's eyes were fastened on hers; curiosity sent his brows soaring. "Any buddy in particular?" he asked.

When Marie tried to back away she ran up against a wall, and then he was pressing against her again.

"Any of the divers would be glad to buddy up with you." There was hesitation in her voice now.

"What about you, Frenchy?"

"Don't call me that, either."

"You're French, aren't you?"

"I'm American now."

"What shall I call you?"

"My name is Marie."

"Yes, but that's what everyone around here calls you. Our relationship is going to be different." He leaned on the wall with both hands, trapping her between his arms. "We need something more friendly for us. Something that defines our new and close association."

She didn't resist. "Like what?" she asked.

"How about . . ." His lips stopped an inch above hers and whispered: ". . . buddy."

How Marie extracted herself from between his arms Coy Murdock didn't know, but suddenly she was across the cabin, smiling at him from the door. "Okay," she said. " 'darling' it will have to be. I like you, Coy; I like you very much. But I made a promise to your father to go after Drew. And I can't think about anything else until it's finished."

She left him.

When Murdock's men returned to the ship they brought with them the last of the news they were likely to get from the docks. Navy investigators had taken over the downtown harbor and sent them packing.

"Did you learn anything?" Murdock asked Mac, whom he'd placed in charge of the dock detail.

"We found somebody who saw eleven men board the *Ala Moana Kai*," Mac related. "A shell trader. He's got a small shack not far from the trimaran's slip. The guy is a Jap; for some reason he didn't want to talk to us. Doesn't speak much English anyway. Sushi here yakked awhile, and the next thing we knew this guy was dumping the whole story."

There was little to tell. The trader had been gathering shells on Sand Island, across from the downtown area, when the *Ala Moana Kai* had left her slip and sailed out of the harbor as she did twice each day. But on this occasion she anchored near Sand Island and eleven men, each carrying a bulky duffle bag or satchel, waded out to her. The trader recognized one of these men, the largest of them, as one who had come by the slip near his shack a day before. He was not the sort of man one forgets. Huge, like a sumo wrestler, he'd said, but not so big-waisted. Though he'd gotten only a quick look at the others the next day as they boarded the trimaran, he had observed that they were all of a common stripe. They were not black, but dark-skinned and dark-haired with dark features. They were lean-looking and angry. The trader had said they were Iranian terrorists. Sushi questioned him on this and the man relented only to the extent that they might be Iraqis, but certainly they were one or the other. And they were terrorists.

Murdock turned to Sushi. "How can he say Iranians or Iraqis?" he asked. "Why not Saudis or Egyptians? Or even Kuwaitis? And if he thought they were terrorists, why didn't he inform the Hawaiian police?''

"The trader is an alien resident," Sushi replied. "He is new to Hawaii, very patriotic. He reads the papers every day. He knows who are the enemies of America and he regards these enemies as his enemies, too. In order to get him to talk I told him we were looking for some men who had killed several Navy officers. His mind jumped to the logical conclusion.''

"But they were Arabs?''

"That much is certain. All but two.''

"What were these two?''

"One, a smaller man. Heavier and gray. Perhaps fifty years old. The trader thought he was foreign but apparently the man never spoke. The big man was American. The trader had heard him speak—according to him everyone at the beach heard this man speak, he had a voice like a megaphone. He passed right by the shell shack on his way to the *Ala Moana Kai* wharf. He was a giant of a man, maybe six feet eight and two hundred seventy-five pounds.''

"Him I know," said Murdock.

"Who is he?''

"A man who enjoys breaking necks.''

Before the divers could learn any more from the old trader a wave of Navy investigators swooped onto the docks. Murdock's men were ordered to leave.

Murdock tried to give this information to Reinholt when the admiral returned to the ship that evening, but it became clear that Reinholt already knew.

His service cap was perched precariously on the back of his head and gray hair straggled out from under the visor. He stepped onto the *Nomad* deck, unbuttoned his jacket, pushed his hands into his pockets, and dropped unceremoniously into a deck chair.

Duggan and Marie stared at him in disbelief.

"I'm out," he announced. "The Navy officially gave

me the boot two hours ago. Eliot Packman called me personally to tell me the news. Effective immediately, I'm ordered to have no further contact with any of the recovery team. I'm to return to Washington at the first opportunity and await reassignment. Of course the reassignment part is pure crap. In another week or two I'll be quietly retired." Reinholt looked up at Murdock in an almost fatherly fashion. "You're on your own now, Coy."

"Did they give any reasons?"

"All they needed. Once the *Alaska* was missing I had my last chance at bat. And I struck out."

"Give it to us, Admiral."

"Strike One: I'm accused of breaching naval security. Captain Cassidy has reappeared in Washington, working hand-in-glove with Eliot Packman. Cassidy has testified that I gave confidential information to a civilian that compromised the recovery investigation. Meanwhile Stout's defection is being blamed on me, too. He was my man, and everything he passed on to the Soviets he got from my office."

"Look, if I—"

"Wait, you haven't heard the best part. Strike Two is a real belly laugh. The *Mako* wreckage was taken out of San Diego at my direction. My signature is on a transfer paper ordering the wreckage moved to Seattle. It never arrived. And I never gave such an order. But the paper is there, and it's my signature all right. Another memento from Stout. He could have arranged it easily enough. Lord knows, I signed enough papers that he brought to my desk."

"Like orders transferring the two DSRVs and the Pigeon-class recovery ships, huh?"

"Oh, that's old news. The latest has to do with the men who took over the *Alaska*. Thanks to your finding those bodies and the witness at the downtown docks, they've been definitely identified as Arabs. So Strike

Three is on you. Now, in addition to being criticized for letting the Soviets get too much classified data out of the Navy, I'm being held to blame for failing to cooperate with the Soviets in finding that sub. The bureaucrats feel if we'd cooperated sooner the Soviets might have gotten a line on the *Alaska* in time to stop her. Strike Three, I'm out.''

"What do you plan to do?"

"I've got only one move left." Reinholt removed a folded slip of paper from his jacket and handed it to Murdock unopened. "Now that I've done that," he growled, "I'm finished."

Murdock read in silence while Captain Duggan and Marie, scarcely able to restrain their curiosity, probed his face for any hint of what the document contained. Murdock blinked and then squinted his eyes. His chin sagged. Based on his expression, not a word on the page could be believed.

Murdock looked up. For a moment speech utterly failed him. When he did speak, his voice was pitched at least an octave too high. "Does Packman know about this?"

"He does. Captain Cassidy helped me draft it before he disappeared. I must assume he told the assistant secretary. Packman informed me today that those orders have since been rescinded. Of course their value to you is undiminished."

"Their value to me is shit! What do you expect me to do with this?"

"Hold on to it. Keep it with you every minute. When the time comes to use it, you'll know what to do."

"That's ludicrous. No wonder the Navy kicked you out; they must think you're insane."

"Probably." Reinholt levered himself upright. "Anyway, it's your problem now. Do what you want, Murdock. Say what you want, go where you want, break any rules you want."

"I intend to, but—"

"Go get that *Batavia* treasure, if that's what you want to do. It's all on you from now on."

"Oh no, you don't. You've got information and I need it."

"The general crew list? I have it for you. But I hope it means more to you than it does to me."

"Not just that. I need it all. Everything you know. Why do you think I waited twelve hours to report all those bodies? Any fool could see what was happening. The debris on the bottom, the DSRVs you failed to keep in readiness, Stout's defection, and then the butchered medical team. It was all working against you. All of it. I wanted to know about that twelfth man so badly I could taste it, but you needed more time. When I blew the whistle it would be over for you. So I gave you twelve hours. And everything you learned in those twelve hours belongs to me."

"How . . . ?"

"You're coming with us."

"Where?"

"You tell me."

Reinholt took a moment to consider. "Stout did make a second call to the Pentagon. To the same friend as before. He requested a copy of another crew list."

"For another submarine?"

"That's right. The *USS Seawind.*"

Murdock turned to Marie. "The sub that collided with the *Batavia?*" She acknowledged it and Murdock turned back. "And the biologist, Captain Laurence Kester," he asked, "what submarine did he serve on?"

"The *Seawind.*"

Murdock smiled.

"You knew that, didn't you?" asked Reinholt.

"I suspected." Certainly Murdock's face gave no hint that this information had caught him by surprise. Now he became businesslike. "Captain Duggan, how long will it take you to get the *Nomad* ready to sail?"

"She's been ready for twenty-four hours."

"Crank 'er up and let's go."

"What's our heading?"

"The *Batavia*. Wherever the hell that is."

"And the admiral?"

"He's coming along. He's got a whole lot to tell us."

"That's fine by me," said Duggan, "He can stay just as long as he remembers who runs things around here. He may be an admiral, but you own the business and I'm captain of this ship."

Murdock's smile held its first hint of humor. "Now now, Captain," he said. "On this ship we're all just buddies."

# Chapter Eleven

The sea floor had parted like a giant maw and devoured all but the rump of the freighter in a single gulp. Only the rusty, barnacle-encrusted stern bulged up from the bottom. Murdock's helmet light threw a murky beam over the letters across her escutcheon: B-A-T-A-V-I-A.

As if sensing his presence, the half-consumed ship let loose a shriek of agony, a gut-wrenching scream of pain and terror that chilled Murdock's bones. He literally shivered inside his suit. Had the wreck thrashed in its basalt pit, like a creature snagged in some colossal jaws, it could not have startled him any more.

"Noisy bitch, isn't she?" said Marie, her voice coming over the speaker in his iron helmet. The words came to him through an electrical cable that stretched from her helmet up to the *Nomad* and down another cable to his.

When Murdock turned by taking a series of awkward steps, his light found the unfamiliar form of Marie Delamer perched on the edge of the submarine canyon into which the freighter had plunged. She was directing her light on the canyon wall, trying to find a way down. They couldn't swim down, not the way they were dressed, and they sure as the world couldn't climb. Just walking the thirty yards across a relatively flat bottom to reach the wreck had been an ordeal. Murdock watched Marie's outlandish figure lumber about in his light. She was streamlined no more. The trunk of her one-atmosphere suit—like his—was a bulky steel barrel with a dome-

175

shaped hatch for a helmet. Articulated steel tubes protruded from the barrel at the appropriate spots for her arms and legs. Pincers on the end of the arm tubes served as hands. Heavy iron boots kept her feet on the bottom.

When Marie walked over to him, he could barely make out her features through the three feet of sea that separated them, and through the thick Plexiglas of their faceplates.

"The hole is down there," Marie said, pointing not with her pincer but with her hand, drawn into the trunk in front of the Plexiglas.

Murdock looked down. His helmet light wasn't powerful enough to find a bottom to the canyon. All he could see was more of the same dark void that surrounded them. He remembered thinking how dark the bay waters of Pearl Harbor were. They were nothing compared to this. Here was the infinite black velvet of the deep as he'd never imagined.

The *Alaska* could be out there right now and he'd never know it, quietly generating its own power, manufacturing its own air from the sea, moving invisibly through the depths—faster below the surface than above it—navigating by means of a computer-driven inertial guidance system so sensitive it could circle the globe without once coming up for a peek at the stars.

Reinholt had spent many hours describing a sub's hunted existence; it had all seemed rather technical and impersonal until Murdock entered this private world in a submarine suit of his own. Military satellites can find any submarine that comes near the surface. Land-based or sea-launched missiles can destroy them. Attack submarines can outrun their bigger, ICBM-launching cousins; outmaneuver, out-dive, and outfight them. The threat of a retaliatory strike by SSBNs remains real only so long as the other side doesn't know where they are. They survive by stealth.

They skulk through the night of the deep sea, waiting

for the signal they hope never comes. Then they rise to a hundred feet below the surface and unleash their nightmare arsenal.

The more Reinholt talked, the more Murdock realized the utter hopelessness of his plans to locate the *Alaska*. "Detection is the game," Reinholt had told him. "American sonar systems are superior to the Soviets'. Our submarines are quieter. Not only can we hear their subs better than they can hear ours, we can hear theirs better than they can hear theirs. Nobody," the admiral boasted, "hears ours."

Of course, he went on, any machine with moving parts has to make noise. It's difficult to build a nuclear plant small enough to fit instead a submarine, even a sub the size of the Trident. But the major obstacle is to balance the power takeoffs, the reduction gears, and the propeller shaft. The propellers themselves are computer-designed for maximum propulsion with minimum vibration. Vibration will give away a submarine's position as quickly as noise. The Trident is a masterpiece of this technology. Compared to her, Russian submarines sound like cement-mixers.

But if the United States Navy couldn't find the *Alaska*, what chance did he have? A hydrophobic cop with a talent for trouble. The Navy—specifically, the Ocean Surveillance Information System—has underwater listening devices called hydrophones planted on the edge of the continental shelf in all the world's oceans. They have static buoys that float on the surface but listen to sonar traffic for miles in every direction, fixed long-range sonar arrays, and other listening equipment. Data from all of these sources are picked up by satellite and beamed to Navy command headquarters for OSIS.

Even before a SUBMISS was declared, OSIS had gone to full alert and begun an extensive undersea search for the *Alaska*. At first they were concentrating on the waters of the upper Hawaiian ridge, but as the hours became days their search necessarily extended throughout the Pacific Basin. "Looking for a needle in a haystack" hardly described it. They were looking for a specific needle, an invisible one, in a haystack that harbored a hundred or more invisible needles at any one time, a haystack larger than the combined land mass of the planet. Several dozen American submarines were currently cruising the Pacific. Even more Soviet submarines patrolled this same area, not to mention those of the British and French. They didn't get even a hint of it.

Once the condition went to SUBSUNK the alert automatically ended, but Reinholt privately had requested OSIS to maintain the search. This news would have surprised Marie, who had argued in vain with Reinholt that the *Alaska* had not really gone down. But it didn't matter. Nothing was heard or seen.

Then came Murdock's discovery of the eleven bodies. This seemed to trigger a volley of possible soundings. Reinholt had described it like this:

"Imagine an airport control tower with a dozen or more men at radar screens; each person has thirty or forty blips which are aircraft flying in regular air corridors at prescribed altitudes. Each aircraft is in constant radio contact with the ground. Each pilot, upon request, can press a button to identify himself on the radar operator's screen.

"It's not that way under the sea. There are no vectors to sail in underwater, no regular traffic routes. Submarines can't communicate with their bases, because high-frequency radio waves don't propagate under the water. The subs can be signaled from shore only with extremely low-frequency transmissions, but these, to carry any distance, require literally hundreds of square miles of land mass to generate; subs can't radio back without surfacing. The signals OSIS does receive come in a bewildering mishmash of sounds.

"Those blips on the radar screens that we were imagining? You'd have to add in all the birds in the sky and all the clouds to make it a decent comparison. Put them all on the screen without identifying anything and see if the operators could handle the traffic. That's what they do at OSIS. A gray whale trumpeting five miles away sounds like the wrenching of steel. A large school of fish can churn the water like a seven-foot screw. Even the sea floor can rumble and shake like a whole fleet of submarines going by. The operators don't receive a few signals now and then, they receive thousands every hour of every day. Only computers could possibly sort if all out. What you have in the end is a best guess made by machines.

"Our first move was to try to identify all of our own submarines on patrol, so these could be eliminated from the confusion. At a special naval facility in South Dakota, the granite bedrock of thousands of badland acres was shaken in what amounts to a minature earthquake. The tremors were felt round the world. Our submarine fleet picked up these signals on receivers more or less like little seismographs. The message was a simple one: Check in. All the captains had to do was to sail near a hydrophone. The OSIS computers would automatically identify their submarines' nationality and class and in many cases even the acoustic signatures of individual vessels."

Once the American subs were accounted for and the subs of the Soviet Union, England, and France were discounted, a number of unidentified signals remained. At that point it was up to the human operators to figure out which was most likely the *Alaska*. For example, a possible Trident-class submarine was detected south of Wake Island heading west for the Philippines. But the signal was poor, and it could just as easily have been a Soviet Typhoon-class sub traveling at reduced speed. A probable American sub, class unknown, was picked up south of the French Frigate Shoals moving toward the southwest. This was determined to be a British or French submarine because all American vessels except the *Alaska* had been identified by that time, and this submarine didn't echo anything close to the size of a "boomer."

Murdock had stopped him.

"What's a 'boomer'?"

Reinholt blinked once or twice in amazement. For the first time it struck him how ill prepared Murdock was for this or any other marine operation. Murdock knew nothing. Nothing. Yet he was hunting a rampaging Trident submarine. Maybe Reinholt's superiors were right. Maybe he was crazy, after all, to send such a man on a mission like this one. But what did that make Coy Murdock for going?

"It's a submarine carrying large ICBMs," he explained. "Which means a very large submarine."

"Okay, go on."

Reinholt did so.

With those echoes eliminated, the Navy was left with an unidentified signal on a west-northwest course a few hundred miles away from Japan. OSIS believed it was the Soviet SSK. Reinholt thought it was the Trident racing for the Soviet port of Vladivostok. He had been on the point of ordering a blockade of the Soya Strait when word came of his dismissal. More timid heads had prevailed. The Soviets were informed of the emergency. They immediately volunteered the *Alaska*'s location. Soviet hydrophones had caught her coming through the Sunda Strait between Sumatra and Java just hours before Reinholt had left Pearl Harbor's Naval Command Center for the last time. Eliot Packman delivered the news personally. Had the Soviets been informed sooner of the emergency, they would have tried to intercept it themselves. Now the *Alaska* had the whole Indian Ocean to prowl. No chance to contain her.

"Could the *Alaska* have crossed the Pacific without OSIS picking her up?" Murdock asked him.

"It's possible, but not likely. My guess is a couple of

Soviet SSKs took her in tow. With all the racket those two subs would make, no hydrophone or sonar would ever hear the *Alaska.*"

"There's one other possibility."

"And what's that?"

"If Captain West knows where those OSIS hydrophones are, he could simply avoid them."

"We're back to this naval conspiracy theory of yours, huh? And West is in on it, too?"

"It's a thought. But I'm not the only one thinking it. Packman must have considered it, too. Why else bring in the Soviets? West knows where you've planted your hydrophones; he doesn't know where the Soviet Union put theirs."

This argument ended abruptly when a vessel appeared on the horizon. It looked like a salvor. They were near enough to the *Batavia* coordinates that any salvage vessel had to be viewed with suspicion. As the *Nomad* approached, the men saw she was listing badly to port and making no way. Closer yet they identified her as the *Enchantress,* Archie Wick's speedy little salvor.

They hove to beside the smaller ship. Grapnels were thrown across, and when the *Enchantress* scraped the *Nomad*'s fenders several crewmen held them together with handspikes. Murdock crossed over with Mac, Emmott, and Gandy. There was evidence everywhere of violence: blood spatters on the deck and gunwales, even bullet holes through some windows, but no sign of the crew alive or dead.

Mac, armed with a big revolver, crept through the cabin door. Gandy followed him below. Moments later, Mac reappeared.

"There's nobody aboard," he reported, shoving the gun back into his trousers. "Clean as a whistle down there."

Murdock was rolling a smear of dried blood between his fingertip and thumb. "It looks like they were lined up here on the deck and machine-gunned. Plenty of nine-millimeter cases around.'' He pointed forward. ''Some of them tried to leap overboard and got it there . . . and there. Is there any way of knowing where the ship came from?''

Mac signed this question to Emmott.

''Yes,'' the deaf diver replied. ''The current runs south here; wind is out of the west. She's been drifting southeast about three to five knots.''

Murdock held out his hand; the ball of blood rolled freely in his palm. ''Six hours,'' he said. ''Maybe eight. Call it twenty to forty nautical miles.''

''And the *Batavia* site is about thirty-five knots to the northwest,'' offered Mac.

By that time Gandy had emerged from below with news of the *Enchantress*'s condition. ''Somebody,'' he said, ''has done a very poor job of trying to scuttle this boat. The engines are all right. There's water coming in through the sea cocks, but the bilge pumps are damn near keeping up with it.''

''Can you fix it?''

''It'll take time to make her seaworthy. Two or three hours at least.''

''No time, Gandy. In two hours we'll be at the site. But if you're sure it won't sink on you we'll leave you here and let you catch up with you. What will you need?''

''She has everything except a crew. Can you let me have a couple of men? Preferably someone who can navigate.''

''Take Emmott and Mac. And I'll send Admiral Reinholt over to do the driving. We'll meet you at the *Batavia* site as soon as you can make it.''

''Won't be long,'' Gandy assured him. ''Hell, I've seen this thing go. We can reach the site in an hour.''

No sooner were they back on their way to the *Batavia* than Sushi and Marie had brought out the two metal suits with A1A written in bright white letters across the orange breastplates. Murdock stared in amazement.

"I recognize Robbie the Robot," he said, "but who's his pal?"

Marie laughed while Murdock circled around them. Back in front he pointed to the bold lettering.

"A1A?"

"American One-Atmosphere suits. They're also known as Jim suits. In France we used to call them *complet d'acier*—suits of steel."

"Keep talking."

"They're called one-atmosphere suits," Marie explained, "because they're not pressurized. The air inside the steel hull is air at surface pressure. There's no decompression, so no danger of the bends. We'll be breathing pure recycled oxygen, so there's no danger of nitrogen narcosis. And since it won't be pressurized oxygen, there's no danger of oxygen poisoning either. They're a little awkward, naturally—they're really just small submersibles molded in human form with flexible limbs. But you can stay down as long as you want—as long as your air supply lasts, that is—and at surface pressure it lasts an awful lot longer than scuba. And that means no danger of getting into trouble you don't have time to get out of."

"How do I get into the damn thing?"

Marie drew back in surprise. "You're not going!"

"Why not?"

"It's too dangerous."

For a moment or two Murdock eyed her in silence. Then: "Who do these suits belong to?"

"To Murdock Sal— Dammit, Coy, why do you want to go?"

"*Want* to? The very idea appalls my sense of survival, which is keen but not easily appalled. I'm going to, that's all." He turned to the Japanese diver. "Sushi, how do you walk around in this thing, assuming I figure out how to get in?"

"The upper part is slightly buoyant. The boots are weighted. That helps to keep you from falling over. But you will sink. We use cables to lower you down and bring you back up. Usually I just run one of the davits. Marie is the expert."

Murdock turned back to Marie. "I tell you what: If you ask me nice and call me 'buddy,' I'll let you use the other one."

Her mouth had compressed into a thin line. "I won't call you 'buddy,' " she managed to say without easing the tension on her lips.

"I'll settle for Robbie."


Darkness surrounded Coy Murdock like a blanket.

He stood alone on the edge of the canyon and looked all around. Marie was gone. The light from her helmet was gone, too. When his own light lanced across the canyon, he spotted her steel suit descending into the void. Seconds later, she had vanished below the brim.

Submarine volcanoes had spewed molten lava across the sea floor a million years before. As the millennia passed the lava cooled. Fissures appeared in the basalt bed. Centuries ago, tectonic pressures had widened the fissures. This canyon had formed. Ten years ago a freighter had sunk. It plunged bow-first into the canyon and all but disappeared. Today Marie and Murdock had to follow.

"Are you ready, Coy?"

Sushi's voice was only inches away, though he himself was safely ensconced on the *Nomad* a quarter of a mile above, operating the number two davit.

Murdock closed and then opened his eyes. He was still in the dark. And it was darker down there. But if any light was to be found, it would be found down there, too. "Okay," he said.

He felt his weight leave the sea floor. His body swung out over the emptiness of the canyon. "Easy, easy," he heard himself say as he started down. Sushi heard it, too, and the descent slowed a bit.

The wall of the canyon rose past his faceplate. Into and then out of the beam from his light. His outstretched arms and his feet kept the rock wall away. Murdock called up his directions to Sushi. The davit was swung fore and aft to keep him clear of the walls; *Nomad,* holding into the wind, would be eased ahead or idled a bit when this became necessary to lower him safely. Several times Murdock swung into the middle of the canyon. The walls moved beyond his vision. When that happened the only thing he could see was the other cable about seven yards away, hanging off the opposite side of the ship from davit number one. Once or twice he caught a glimpse of the freighter's silt-shrouded hull in the background. And then he saw the light of Marie's suit below him. She was standing underneath an ugly gash in the *Batavia*'s side. Seconds later Murdock's boots gently struck bottom, and as the cable continued to slacken he walked stiffly over beside her to inspect this wound in the carcass of the beast. It was at least eight feet across, and high enough over their heads to make climbing up unthinkable.

The wails of pain, the wrenching of iron plates, seemed to gush from this gaping hole. Louder now than before. The cries more plaintive. Coy had heard his father describe them as the sad songs of the spirits who haunted the wreck.

"Is that the only way in?" Murdock asked her.

"This is how Glen got in."

Marie went first. Murdock listened to her directions. Then it was his turn. "Up ten feet," he said. He rose off the bottom, hovered in open sea, and then moved against the ship's side as he called out the distances. The next thing he knew, Marie's pincer was reaching out and pulling him inside the hole. He stood beside her on a forward bulkhead.

"I think it will be easier going, inside the ship, if I

cut loose from the cable,'' he said, retracting a hand from its arm tube and reaching up into the top of his helmet for the release lever.

Marie exploded. ''You never, never cut free of the cable! It's the only thing that can bring you back up. Once it's loose you may never get it back on again. And no one can help you down here.''

''Okay, darlin','' he said. ''You pull my cable through the hole and I'll see how far I can get. Did you get all that, Sushi?''

''Every word, brother. Here comes your slack.''

Murdock started pulling himself up the deck.

The pincers on the end of his arms, activated by levers inside, were useless for this kind of work. Murdock found that the only way to climb any distance at all was to push up with his legs and find something to grab on to before his suit brought him back down. Fortunately there were no long corridors to pass through, for they were all standing on end like chimneys. Going down ladders was easier, for these were horizontal. Murdock could just walk along them, making sure his feet caught the rungs.

The hold was right where Coy's father had told Marie it was. Coy followed her directions and the shrill songs of the spirits, until his helmet light shone through the watertight door.

His light panned over the contents of the hold. The crates and boxes piled against the forward bulkhead were gone. In their place was human lagan. They floated about the confines of the hold like astronauts working in zero-gravity conditions. Decomposition was far enough advanced that gases had begun to form in their bodies. It bloated them up like inflatable caricatures, distorting their features and making them more and more buoyant as the hours passed. One, two, three . . . Murdock counted seven bodies. Without a doubt it was the crew of the *Enchantress*. He had heard them described. Sinister men with untrusting faces and shifting eyes. Those characteristics were still remarkable even as the bodies ballooned. Apparently they had been right not to trust. Someone had unloaded a clip of nine-millimeter shells into the lot. Bundled them all up in a net, winched them down to the bottom, and stuffed them in the *Batavia*'s prize cargo hold. Murdock knew they wouldn't last long down here. If the Navy didn't get to them within a few days there would be little evidence left.

"What are you doing, Coy?"

Murdock had whirled in a panic. Marie's voice coming over the cable sounded as though she were right beside him. But he was alone with the dead.

"Coy? What have you found?"

Now he saw one corpse dressed differently than the rest; the *Enchantress* crewmen wore jeans and sweatshirts, while this other sported Navy whites. Murdock inspected the death mask of a face. He had never seen the man alive, but he had seen a photograph. In life, the man had been smiling and flashing an "okay" sign as he crossed to a Soviet sub. But Commander Alan Stout had been wrong. He was not okay. Not anymore.

Turning his back on the grisly debris and the ghastly laments, Coy Murdock followed his cable through the network of passageways to the outside, where Marie was waiting.

# Chapter Twelve

If the notion that bad news travels fast has any basis in fact, then the rate at which word of the *Batavia* treasure's disappearance raced through the ship's company could only be described as a breakneck speed. Every member of the crew knew the details before Murdock and Marie had even been hauled to the surface. When crewmen swung the two of them onto the deck, opened their helmets, and hefted them out of their steel suits, Murdock could read the disbelief and defeat on their faces. For a little while his men had forgotten why they had come—that they were hunting a doomsday submarine, not sunken treasure. At the same time Murdock could see alarm in their eyes, and he realized they also were afraid. But of what? And then he knew. They were afraid for him. Finding two mass graves in the same number of days has had its effect. Murdock was close to the edge, and his men knew it.

He suggested there was still one place left to search, and was busying the crew getting the equipment ready when the *Enchantress* came alongside. Gandy, Emmott, and Mac were soon back aboard the *Nomad,* and Reinholt took charge of lashing the two ships together.

"Did you get lost?" Murdock asked Gandy.

"Repairs took longer than I'd figured. But we didn't get lost, not with that Reinholt at the wheel. For a man who's spent his time in submarines or behind a desk he does know the ropes. And I think he's having a ball—say, did somebody die? Why all so glum?''

Murdock explained.

Their faces went through the same sequence of disbelief, disappointment, and defeat as the others' had.

''Who?'' demanded Gandy. ''How?''

Marie answered for Murdock.

''It looks like Wick and his men came here to grab the treasure while we were at Pearl Harbor,'' she replied. ''And found something or someone they weren't supposed to see.''

''And you say Stout was there, too?'' asked Reinholt. ''Dead?''

Murdock nodded.

''Serves him right, I suppose,'' the admiral replied, but he turned and strode to the side of the ship, where he spent several minutes looking out over the ocean in silence.

''What's our next move?'' growled Mac.

''Yeah,'' said another, ''where do we go from here?''

Murdock replied that the answers to all of their questions and perhaps even the *Batavia* treasure itself would be found on the *USS Seawind*. Unfortunately, when they activated the transponder Marie and Glen Murdock had placed on the sunken submarine's hull, it failed to give them a locator signal. Gandy, pressing the transmitter button again and again without result, surmised that the batteries must have given out, and Murdock said that he hoped Gandy was right. Privately, he didn't believe it.

They attached one of the drone cameras to a winch and lowered it into the water. The winch unreeled hundreds of fathoms of cable while the *Nomad* moved slowly off to the south. Soon the remote-controlled camera sled was trailing two miles behind and below the ship. It took several passes to find what they were looking for—or more correctly, to find where; what they were looking for was no longer there.

Marie stood in front of the television monitor while a dozen of the crew crowded around her, and Murdock paced the stern with his head bent to the deck.

The rugged nature of the sea floor made it difficult to keep the bottom in constant view. The controls operator was alternately climbing and diving the drone, banking right and left to avoid minor hillocks and outcrops of volcanic stone. The bottom had been deepening steadily but irregularly until the cameras sailed out over an abyss and the picture shifted to black.

"That's it," said Marie. "It's at the base of that cliff right there, I'm sure of it."

Murdock stopped pacing to watch the knot of men tighten around the television screen. "Try that transponder signal again," Marie was saying. The operator indicated there was still no return signal; he phoned Captain Duggan on the bridge for another pass of the cliff base while Murdock lowered his head and resumed pacing.

After two more passes, the drone glided along the base where the talus of sand and gravel had collected. Marie recognized the location almost immediately. Again Murdock broke off his pacing, but this time he weaved through the knot of spectators to stand right in front of the monitor.

"It was right there," she insisted.

The camera revealed nothing but a trench in the loose bottom, wide but still longer, where sand had piled to each side. One could almost calculate to the foot the length and width of a Sturgeon-class submarine by the depression that remained.

"Gone!" muttered Reinholt. He was too stunned to form words of more than one syllable. "But . . . how?"

Murdock's fist slammed onto the control table. "Because I waited twelve hours!"

He started forward, stopped, then turned on a sudden impulse and ordered the drone brought aboard and the ship made ready to sail. Then he leapt up a ladder toward the bridge, taking the rungs in pairs.

Reinholt and Marie found Murdock and the captain bent over the chart table, looking at nautical charts that showed the waters to the south and west of Oahu. "These are the Johnston Islands, here," Duggan was saying. "At least five hundred miles from our present position."

"How soon can we get there?"

Duggan pursed his lips. "Twenty-four hours; twenty if we really push. But we oughtn't strike out blind."

"No," said Murdock, "twenty hours isn't good enough."

Admiral Reinholt's interjection brought them both up and around; it was almost electric with authority. "What's this about the Johnston Islands? You can't go there!"

"Who says?" asked Murdock.

"The Navy. They use the islands for target practice."

"I know that," said Murdock. "For the Trident missile test."

"That's right. And may I remind you that missile has not yet been launched. It could be at any moment. Anyway, no one lives there. It's just a pair of small islets and a reef. Only the guano made them of any value, and even that isn't worked anymore. What do you hope to find?"

"The *Seawind*."

The admiral's mouth came open. Before he could utter a word it closed again.

"Your OSIS people caught what they called 'a probable American sub' south of the French Frigate Shoals," Murdock reminded him. "That's not far from here. It was heading southwest, in the direction of the Johnston Islands. Even though all their other subs were accounted for, OSIS didn't believe it was the *Alaska* because it didn't echo big enough. But we know something they don't—that one of their subs isn't accounted for. A Sturgeon-class sub that was crossed off their list twelve years ago is out there somewhere. I think it's heading for the Johnston Islands. The Navy made sure the islands would be evacuated. And the *Alaska* is making sure they stay that way. If the *Seawind* is going to surface, to be abandoned or to rendezvous with some other vessel, that's the perfect spot for it."

Reinholt didn't hesitate again. "The *Enchantress* can make it there in fifteen hours," he said.

Murdock seized the words like a drowning man clutching at a single strand of rope.

"Have you got enough fuel?"

"To get there. Perhaps not to get back."

"To hell with getting back. Can you find it?"

"Don't talk foolishness."

"Good. We'll take off in twenty minutes. Captain Duggan, follow at your best speed. We'll leave you three or four of the crew and take the rest with us. What about weapons? Do any of the men have their own guns? Mac was flashing a big Blackhawk, and a few of the others must have something." The captain acknowledged this with a quick nod. "Collect every weapon on the ship. Put them on the *Enchantress*. Marie, have some scuba equipment and one of the drone camera sleds loaded, too. Gas up the two A1A suits and throw them in."

"I've got a pistol that Glen gave me."

"You can give it to me."

"I know how to use it."

"You're not going to get a chance. I wouldn't let you, even if you were coming with us. But since you're not coming you won't."

"What!" Marie exploded. "What do you mean I'm not coming?"

"It's too dangerous."

"Is this more of your humor? Do you want me to call you 'buddy', is that it?"

Murdock looked uncomfortably at Duggan and Reinholt, who had simultaneously leaned over the chart table

in a woefully transparent attempt to consume themselves
in navigation. Murdock shook his head. "I don't care
what you call me, you're not coming."

"Then I call you a fool. I'm going whether you like it
or not," she declared.

Murdock grabbed her by the arm, pulled her out onto
the port bridge wing, and closed the door behind them.
Having done this, he proceeded to yell so loudly that
even the wind and sea and the racket from the *Nomad*'s
twin diesel engines couldn't keep his words from coming
right through the glass. Duggan and Reinholt observed
by means of careful sidelong glances. Murdock's position—put baldly—was that Marie, having already taught
him everything he needed to know about deep-sea diving, would hereafter be an annoyance. She'd be under-
foot, a nuisance, a hindrance. In short, a female.

"In other words, he likes her," said Reinholt in a
undertone. "And he wouldn't have a moment's peace
worrying about her."

Marie countered by shouting that she had made a
promise to Coy's father which she intended to keep. She
was going to be involved in any operation having to do
with the *Seawind*, the Trident, or getting Drew Murdock
back.

Duggan quietly clucked his tongue and shook his head.
"She's scared sick he'll do something crazy if she's not
along," he whispered.

Who was she doing this for, Murdock wanted to know:
his father or his brother?

"For you, you damn fool," muttered Duggan.

For herself, she replied clumsily.

If she did come . . .

"She's coming," said Reinholt.

"No question," Duggan agreed.

. . . would she stay out of his way and stay out of sight
if any shooting started? No, she'd do her job, that's what
she'd do, whether Murdock liked it or not. Fine, but if

he even caught a glimpse of her on deck once they encountered the *Seawind* he would personally boot her ass into the sea.

"They've got it bad," mused the admiral.

Duggan nodded. "You can always tell."

Twelve hours later the *Enchantress* was raising a wide wake through calm seas. Reinholt stood at the helm himself. His glacial gaze was fixed unwaveringly upon the sea. His jaw was set. And yet something about him, for the moment at least, had softened. "Don't think I don't know and appreciate why you've brought me along rather than Captain Duggan," he told Murdock, who had come into the wheelhouse to coax another knot or two of speed from the helmsman—even though the salvor was virtually airborne already.

Morning was minutes away. Upon the still black sea their white backtrail traced a line that didn't vary by a point of the compass for five hundred miles. They had seen no other vessels.

Admiral Reinholt hadn't spent more than one of those hours away from the wheel. He had eaten and then returned, refusing offers to be relieved. Not once in those twelve hours had Coy Murdock closed his eyes.

"I don't think you do know why I brought you," Murdock replied. "In the first place, Admiral, you couldn't pry Captain Duggan off his precious *Nomad,* and in the second, Duggan couldn't do what I need you to do."

Reinholt was instantly wary. "And what's that?"

"You know the location of some of those OSIS hydrophones, don't you?"

"Of course I do. Why?"

"I need to borrow a couple of 'em."

The admiral leveled a glacial stare at Murdock but the younger man missed it; he was grinding the heels of his palms into his eyes sockets and running his fingers back through his hair. When Coy looked up, Reinholt saw the strain he was under. Exhaustion marred his features.

Seasickness and worry had reddened the verdigris eyes to the color of rust.

"Nobody's rules but your own, right, Murdock?"

"Whatever you say, Admiral."

"This is what I say: I'm not doing it until you let me in on what you've got. I want to know what you know and how you figured it out."

"And then you'll do it?"

"No promises. Except that I won't play along if you don't open up. You're just like your father: playing them close to the vest. Never trusting anyone. Well, you have to trust me now. You've figured something out that the Navy hasn't and I want to know what it is."

"I could lie."

"Then lie. But tell me something."

So Murdock told him some things.

Reinholt knew about two hydrophones in and around the Johnston reefs. The first, off to the east and about a hundred feet deep, eluded them for hours. They trolled back and forth with the drone camera while Murdock paced the deck in a fury, staring off the side of the ship as though he could better see the damn thing with his unaided eyes than by monitoring the television screen. Crewmen avoided him. His nerves were strung tight as piano wire, and as likely to lash out when they snapped. Finally the hydrophone's yellow housing appeared and Marie went down with her scuba to attach a cable. A winch brought the hundred-pound device to the surface. Miraculously, the second hydrophone on the west side of the island appeared in the camera lights almost at once and this one, too, was hoisted aboard.

They looked a bit like small satellites with legs.

Gandy picked up a wrench and a screwdriver and attacked one of the devices. Babbit Cook, the radio expert, assisted in the operation. They talked in the language of ohms and amps, transistors and transducers, frequencies and flux, while the rest of the crew stood around them sporting blank faces.

At last they approached Murdock.

The hydrophones, they explained, are essentially energy transformers which convert the acoustic energy they "hear" underwater to electromagnetic energy that they transmit into space. Could the hydrophones be retuned to transmit on the marine channels instead? Yes. But the signals couldn't be properly interpreted, because the *Nomad*'s radios didn't have the circuitry to do this. They would know when a submarine moved into the vicinity, but until it surfaced they wouldn't know how fast it was moving or which way it was going.

Murdock said he would settle for that.

Emmott and Mac replanted the first hydrophone below the southern rim of the coral reef instead of the eastern shore; they staked down its legs and ran a test of its transmitter. If someone on the *Seawind* knew where the Navy had originally placed these hydrophones, he could use the islands themselves as a cover to sneak into the lagoon without being detected. Moving them to different sites, Murdock felt, was a minimal precaution.

He and Marie climbed into the A1A suits when it came their turn to plant the second device in the deeper north channel. The cranes lowered them over the sides.

The reefs surrounding the Johnston Islands are shaped like a giant donut several miles wide. Both islands are nestled within the central lagoon, which is deep and joined to the sea by a channel on the northern side. This channel deepens from about a hundred feet in the lagoon to nearly three hundred feet by the time it reaches the sea. They decided to place the second hydrophone here, where it was sure to detect any submarine passing to the north of the reefs or trying to enter the lagoon.

"One hundred feet," came Sushi's voice over their speakers.

Marie and Murdock hung in mid-water, like lifeless puppets waiting for the puppeteer to pull on their strings.

Murdock clutched the hydrophone in his left pincer; its yellow housing clashed with the orange metal of his A1A suit just as Marie's and Murdock's suits clashed with the jeweled green of the sea. The surface was a hundred feet over their helmets, a dazzling sky of diamonds scattered across a green baize; on every side emerald, flawless and semitransparent; two hundred feet beneath their feet lay a bed of black jade.

The puppets descended. But they knew they were going down only by the numbers that came over their speakers and by a subtle deepening of the sea. As the fathoms passed, the diamond-lit sky ceased to sparkle. The emerald gradually merged into the blackness of the jade.

From the *Nomad,* Sushi called off the depth marks on their cables. "One hundred twenty feet, boys and girls."

A single large fish moved out of the distance, wagging its tail with aimless ease. As it swam nearer, Murdock could make out the large dorsal fin, the wide wound of a mouth, and its multiple rows of wicked teeth. The gills fluttered like sails close-hauled to the wind.

"Look out!" Murdock called.

"Problem?" asked Sushi.

"No. I was talking to Marie. There's a shark."

"It's only a lemon," she replied in a bored French way.

Lemon sharks, her tone seemed to imply, were something one saw everyday. Murdock didn't share her composure. A shark was a shark. He watched it paddle between the cables just over their heads, and had to admit it didn't show any more interest in them than Marie had in it.

"One hundred thirty-five feet," said Sushi, "Coy, have you bumped the 'test' transmit switch? Babbit says that he's getting a signal."

"It must be picking up the shark," he replied. "That's the only thing moving down here."

"Is it still around?"

Murdock cranked his head to look out the side of the helmet. "No. Thank god."

"We're still getting a signal."

Murdock held the hydrophone out in front of his helmet. The transmit switch was clearly in the "on" rather than the "test" position. "A school of fish went by a little while ago," he said. "Must have been about a million or so."

Sushi acknowledged this information but he didn't sound really convinced.

An idea occurred to Murdock, but he let a few moments and a few fathoms go by while he thought the thing over.

"Sushi?"

"Yeah, Coy?"

"Still getting that signal?"

"Hold on." And then. "Apparently so."

"Maybe it's picking up Marie."

Pause. "I'll mention it to Babbit."

By shades the emerald sea deepened. By degrees the cold waters turned colder. And the silence became something profound.

"Coy?"

"I'm still here."

"Babbit says no. He gets a burp every time one of you talks. Gandy thinks it may be picking up the sound of your breathing. I mean if one of you is really winded . . ."

What a nice way to put it, thought Murdock. Meaning, "if one of you is gulping air like a panic-stricken amateur." That would have been much more to the point. Yes, by God, he was breathing hard! Had he been before? Murdock tried to make himself breathe slow and deep. Slow and deep.

Darkness slowly rose to embrace them.

For some reason he couldn't explain, Murdock's heart began pounding. He tried to force a calm. This dive was neither so deep nor so dark as the *Batavia* dive, he told himself. It should be an easy operation.

Then why the hyperventilating? Why the hypertension?

He needed rest, that was it. More than thirty-six hours without sleep will make any man nervous.

"One hundred and fifty feet, you two. We're holding you here for a minute."

Their descent slowed at once.

"What's the trouble up there, Sushi?"

"Coy? Babbit says your hydrophone's going crazy! He wants to bring you back up and check it again."

"What's it doing?"

"It's banging like a five-alarm fire. We can hear it all over the ship."

My God, thought Murdock. His chest was banging the same way. Could it pick up the beating of his heart right through the steel suit, for crissake? How embarrassing it would be if his men ever found out.

"Let's take it on down, Sushi."

"But if—"

"Down, dammit!"

The two divers continued their descent.

Murdock could feel it in his head now, behind his eyes. In his hands and feet as well as his chest. Blood was hammering through his veins with pneumatic force and speed.

"Getting louder, Coy!"

Murdock was looking at Marie when a huge zone of utter darkness behind and below her separated itself from the jade and slid with swift, silent menace into the semi-transparency of the green. Black consumed the emerald sea beneath their feet in a single pounding of his heart.

Murdock gasped. "Whoa! Whoa!" he cried. "We're about to hit the bottom!"

His suit snatched suddenly like a hanged man reaching the end of his rope. It jerked Murdock's body down and knocked his chin against the helmet frame.

Marie had stopped descending, too. But the blackness still rushed upward.

"What the hell, Coy? The bottom is another hundred eighty feet down."

Marie's voice followed Sushi's. "What is it, Coy? What's wrong?"

"Something behind you! Something big!"

He saw her head twisting in the steel helmet. But there was no glass in the back for her to see out. He watched her steel arms whirl like awkward paddles trying in vain to turn herself around.

And then the blackness took on form. A blunt, black iron bow, followed by a long round iron body that disappeared into the farthest reaches of the emerald depths.

Murdock stared in awe as the submarine rose like a rocket from out of the blackness. It was coming up—not straight up, but straight at them.

"It's the *Seawind!*" he cried.

No sooner had he uttered the words than he knew they were wrong—absurdly, stupidly wrong.

This wasn't the *Seawind*. It was no submarine Murdock had ever imagined. Not this big. When the sail swept in behind Marie it looked like a skyscraper. The sailplanes that projected outward halfway up its sides were the size of aircraft wings.

The sail was going to hit them. Murdock was convinced of that until it passed, and then he could see it was thirty feet farther down. Even so he could read the bow numbers across the top of the sail as though they were written on the glass of his faceplate.

"Seven, three, two," said Murdock, half to himself.

He could see the white cross hairs and bull's-eye of the escape hatch right forward of the sail. How could paint buried twelve years under an avalanche be so bright? The hull flattened out just behind the sail, and he could make out the twenty-four interlaced rings that extended a third of the length of the sub. Hatches? Launch tubes? But the *Seawind* had not carried missiles!

"Coy! Did you say seven, three, two?"

Excited voices came over the speaker. Sushi's. Then another voice interrupted his. Finally Reinholt broke in. But Murdock wasn't listening to any of them. He already knew.

It was too big to be anything but a Trident submarine.

It was a Trident!

And it was where no Trident should be.

It was the *Alaska!*

Murdock's blood raced faster than ever. He thrashed on the end of his cable like a puppet tangled in its strings. He shouted at the top of his lungs for Sushi to lower him down.

"What're you gonna do, Coy?"

"Get me down, dammit!"

He felt himself starting to go down, but it wasn't far or fast enough. Once the sail moved out from underneath him the submarine's main deck would be sixty, seventy feet down, and moving quickly away.

In another few seconds it would be gone.

"Down! Down! Down!" Murdock cried.

His descent accelerated, but still not fast enough. Voices were yelling at him. Marie's. Sushi's and others' from above. They were telling him what to look for. What to do. He couldn't hear them. Every move he had made up till now had been wrong. Everything he had tried had failed. Chasing the Trident had only seemed to put it farther and farther away. Then, without warning, it was right at his feet. Ten small steps away—a single short leap. And he was trapped in an iron shell, dangling from a steel cable that kept him from advancing an inch under his own power.

Murdock screamed.

He had stood on the edge for too long.

Marie saw his hands scrambling inside his suit, tugging at the cable release in his helmet. And she knew.

"No, Coy!" she cried. "God, no, don't do it! Don't—"

When his suit broke free of the cable Marie's words ended abruptly, and Murdock was alone with his own screams.

He fell in a kind of slow motion.

Marie watched in terrified silence as he dropped faster and faster. At first she thought he would miss the submarine altogether. She prayed that he would miss. But he didn't. He struck the port sailplane with a bone-jarring concussion of steel against steel that sent shock waves for miles in every direction. The hydrophone was knocked out of his metallic grip. He was swept off the trailing edge of the plane. He plunged twenty feet more and struck again on the flat surface of the upper launch deck. Another crash of steel even louder than the first shook the sea.

Murdock rolled down the submarine's hull with unchecked and ungovernable speed. Marie couldn't believe he'd survived. But he had. His pincers, clacking like castanets and clawing uselessly at the aerodynamic plating of the hull, were proof of that. But he wouldn't survive long. The launch hatches were set perfectly flush with the deck, and not so much as a rivet projected high enough for him to hold on to. Suddenly, inexplicably, Murdock was on his feet. Then the sea wash and the sub's climbing angle threw him onto his back, and he slid down the black hull, his arms and legs flailing like an overturned turtle. Nothing would stop him. The clacking and clawing of his pincers were replaced by a genuine cacophony of steel grating against steel, a screech of terror reserved for the doomed.

The last of the Trident passed under Marie. It was an eighteen-foot circle of whirling destruction.

She rocked back and forth on the cable as the currents caught her. When she looked back down, the black monster had vanished—disappeared as though it had only existed at all in her worst nightmare—and then the sea was once again flawlessly green.

# PART III

# SubRage

The Assistant Secretary of Defense had been sitting hunched over, and when he stood to address the Joint Chiefs of Staff he stood up hunched over, too.

"I've just come from the office of the secretary," he began. "The secretary himself had just left a meeting with the National Security Council, a meeting—I'm authorized to report—that dealt solely with the Trident matter."

Packman swept the faces of the four men. The four-star chiefs of staff of the Army and Air Force, and the commandant of the Marine Corps, would play no part in this. If and when trouble came it would come from the fourth man, Admiral John "Helms" A. Lee, the Chief of Naval Operations and Chairman of the Joint Chiefs.

He continued:

"There seems to be some question about whether this is an administrative or an operational matter. It began as an administrative concern, when the Deputy CNO Submarine Warfare authorized a test-firing of a new Trident missile. He then proceeded to take charge of the investigation after the test submarine was hijacked. Admiral Dan Reinholt has since been relieved of his duties for gross incompetence and misconduct, and his replacement has been named. Any decision as to what steps should be taken once the *Alaska* has been located will be made by the President, but accomplishing the mission might be construed as an operational activity, which should therefore require the attention of the commanders in chief of the unified commands before—"

"Can't we cut through this crap, Packman?" snapped the CNO.

"Please, Admiral. This is a pertinent—"

"It may be pertinent but it isn't getting us anywhere. Has the President declared a SubRage condition or not?"

"Yes. He has."

"What's your next move, Mr. Assistant Secretary?"

"We're going to find the *Alaska.*"

"And then?"

"Neutralize it by any means necessary."

"You mean blow it up."

"If necessary."

"Kiss a hundred thirty-two lives and a billion dollars good-bye. Is that the idea?"

"I repeat. We'll do what's necessary to ensure that the *Alaska* will not drag us into a nuclear exchange."

When Packman paused, the Air Force chief of staff stepped into the fray.

"What is this 'SubRage' all about?" he wanted to know. His question was put—rather pointedly—to the admiral instead of the assistant secretary.

Admiral Lee obliged him. "Essentially it indicates a rogue SSBN. One of theirs or one of ours. A captain gone round the bend. A mutiny. Even a breakdown in communications associated with a false Strike Order. The cause isn't important. It means there's a sub out there with shitload of SLBMs aimed at us or the Russians, with somebody's finger on the button."

Packman nodded. "That's the idea. SubRage allows the President to implement weapons and procedures he otherwise wouldn't be allowed to use. The *Alaska* has to be stopped at all costs."

"Okay, fine," said Admiral Lee. "We got through that. Now, how about this Soviet story that the *Alaska* has entered the Indian Ocean? My people haven't been able to validate that information, and we've got a lot of ASW hardware in the East Indian area.''

"Now, as to that . . ." Packman shifted his feet and cleared his throat. "The President had a frank telephone conversation with the Soviet General Secretary earlier today. Mr. Gorbachev was very helpful."

"Helpful! Those twenty-two Trident missiles on the *Alaska* are aimed at him, not at us."

"He appreciates that fact. Apparently the information concerning the *Alaska*'s arrival into the Indian Ocean was a bit premature.''

"What you're really saying is, the Russians gave us a bum steer.''

"It begins to look that way. Mr. Gorbachev hinted that there is an element within his military establishment, Navy as well as Army, that remains at odds with the politburo over recent political developments that would include scaling down of their armed forces and expenditures in response to relaxed tensions vis-à-vis the West. The Indian Ocean lead seems to have come from one of these . . . military hardliners.''

"In other words he's got some screwball commanders who may be loose cannons.''

"We can't rule out that possibility. Of course, we have no evidence the Russians actually abetted in the hijacking itself. All the evidence points to this being strictly an Iranian operation. We've found several witnesses now who saw all of the hijackers and their testimony clinches that. The big leader is a probable American and another man is a possible European, but the rank and file are Iranian or Arab types. A few of them were overheard in Honolulu conversing in fluent Farsi. No, this is an Iranian extremist operation. But these Russian military hardliners might have foreseen in the situation an opportunity to regain some of their clout. A confrontation with our Navy might suit their interests if it checked their government's unilateral shifting of appropriations from the military to the civilian sectors and spotlighted an ongoing need for a vigorous defense posture.''

The CNO took a deep breath. ''You mean they're trying to scare their own government into another arms race.''

Packman leaned over his podium. ''Admiral Lee, must you rephrase every statement of mine?''

''I'm just trying to translate your Washingtonese so the rest of us can understand.''

''What don't you understand?''

Admiral Lee came forward in his chair.

''Well, sir, a number of things. But they boil down to these: I don't understand how you can get rid of a man like Dan Reinholt for refusing to play patty-cake with the goddamn Russians when it turns out all they're doing is jerking you off. I don't understand how a bunch of Iranian camel jockeys get the know-how to snatch a Trident submarine and sail it around for a week undetected across the Pacific Ocean unless they're getting some help. I don't understand how you can stand there with your patty-cake hands out when you've been caught with your pants down. And I don't understand what the 'B' stands for.''

Packman was all set to explode. But this threw him.

''What 'B'?'' he demanded.

''The one on your ass. When those guys pat it and prick it, and mark it with a B. What does the B stand for, Mr. Packman, 'Bolshevik'?''

The assistant secretary controlled himself. ''Anything else, Admiral?''

''Yes, sir, now that you mention it. I also don't understand why the investigation has been turned over to Admiral Reinholt's chief of staff instead of a regular investigative officer of flag rank.''

''Captain Cassidy—I guess I should say Admiral Cassidy; his promotion became effective today—was working closely with Dan Reinholt before his dismissal. He was the logical choice to take over. He left for Pearl

Harbor this morning, and I think you'll find that he's completely on top of the situation. Now if there are no more questions, I think this fact sheet I've prepared will give you all the particulars. Gentlemen. You'll have to excuse me.''

Packman bustled from the room, nearly tripping over his feet before the door slammed behind him.

Marie Delamer was fighting back tears.

"We combed the bottom for hours," she told Duggan, "and found no trace of Coy or the A1A suit. But that doesn't mean anything. At the speed the submarine was traveling he could have held on for a minute or two and been hauled half a mile out to sea. If he held on for even five minutes we have no hope of finding his body. None at all.''

"Crazy fool," snapped Duggan. "I didn't think much of him at first, but he . . .'' The *Nomad* captain was having a hard time accepting this outcome. ". . . well, he had something. I don't know what to call it.''

"Just like his father.''

Marie and Duggan stared at Admiral Reinholt, not with animosity but with curiosity. He wasn't taking this nearly as badly as they were. Unlike them he wasn't having a hard time accepting Coy Murdock's demise—he just flatly refused to accept it.

"We've got to consider the possibility," he said, "that the man may be holding on still.''

Marie's mouth fell open. "When I saw him last," she managed to get out, "he was just seconds from being sucked into the propeller; that was four hours ago. There's no way.''

"Then how do you explain that?''

Reinholt aimed a finger at the *Nomad*'s wheelhouse radio, which was adjusted to the marine emergency frequency and was emitting a steady intermittent tone. It was the same signal they'd heard from the *Enchantress*, and it was coming over the same channel. Whenever it grew weaker, Duggan ordered a course change until the signal grew louder again. He'd picked up the signal thirty miles north of the Johnston Islands on his way south to join up with the others. When he called and informed them of the emergency signal, they came north to join him instead. Now the *Enchantress* and the *Nomad*, working together, were following the signal farther and farther out into the Pacific.

"There's only one explanation," Marie replied. "Coy must have snagged the hydrophone on the *Alaska* somehow."

"And himself, too?"

Marie tried to believe it. But she couldn't. "It's funny what you said about him being just like his father. I only know of one other time when a diver wearing one of those A1A suits became disconnected from his cable." She wiped her eyes—they hadn't been running, but they were welling up. "Wouldn't you know," she said, "it was Glen."

"He did it on purpose?"

"No, it was an accident in Glen's case."

"How long could a man last?"

"Glen was down for most of a day. That was two years ago. We were searching for the *Batavia* in some deep canyons off the Gardner Pinnacles when his surface cable snapped. He fell down a loose slide and then lost his helmet light. By the time his dive buddy—Mac, I think—got to the base of the cliff, Glen was gone. We hunted him for almost eight hours using the drone cameras and sonar sleds. Some of the boys had given him up for lost, and I was getting a little worried myself, when one of the camera cables almost yanked off the crane. Glen had managed to grab a towline with his pincer and hang on, even though the drone had to be making five knots. We hadn't found him so much as he had found us. We reeled him in like an eight-hundred-pound marlin. Now I ask you, who but Glen Murdock could have pulled off something like that?''

"That's what I'm asking myself, Miss Delamer. A few days ago I tried to explain some things to you and to the captain here. You weren't ready to listen. I think perhaps you might be ready now."

Marie nodded. Duggan glanced at the steersman, observed that his own presence was not immediately needed, and said to Reinholt: "I'm not ready to hear any unkindnesses about Glen Murdock, if that's what you mean."

"Nothing could be farther from my mind, Captain. In the first place I don't know any unkindnesses about Glen. It's true he didn't do so well as a husband, and I guess he wasn't much of a father to Coy, but I think he simply fell short."

"His personal life was none of my business."

"Nor mine. And that aside, I think he did pretty well. Before you conclude I was thinking of speaking unkindly of Glen you may want to hear the rest of my little story. I read you some of Murdock's Officer Fitness Report and it did sound rather bad. He was counted a poor sailor, ill equipped to command. Low marks for seamanship. Shiphandling abilities next to none. Ungentlemanly behavior was his only remarkable skill, except for a suggestive note that he had a knack for getting a job done and often succeeded in achieving with raw nerve what his nautical talents failed to achieve. I think that's how his commander put it. Anyway, his CO put him into the engine room to keep him out of trouble."

"When you first read us that report," Marie broke in, "there was something that bothered me. . . ."

"It bothered me, too," said Duggan.

"No, wait," she raced on, "hear me out. I didn't figure it out until just now. Officer Fitness Report, you said."

"That's right."

"But when was it written?"

Reinholt smiled. "That report was written on December 3, 1941. Murdock's ship, the destroyer *USS Harvey*, was one of eighty-six naval vessels moored at Pearl Harbor four days later when the Japanese launched their attack. Japanese torpedoes and bombs had already sunk or severely damaged twenty ships. The *Harvey* had been heading out to sea when she was hit several times and collided with a cruiser just coming in. The two ships became entangled in a hellish cauldron of flames and began sinking together, inevitably blocking the harbor entrance and preventing any other ships from escaping to sea. Orders were given for both crews to abandon ship. Murdock, as was his habit, disobeyed those orders. Remarkably, his engine room crew remained, too. He raced to the wheelhouse, which by that time would have been nothing less than an incinerator. He took the wheel. They literally rammed the larger cruiser to one side of the channel and then made a spectacular run out of the harbor. I've heard it was quite a sight. Like one of Hawaii's volcanos belching black clouds and boiling magma a hundred feet into the air, and all the time making flank speed for the Pacific where the Jap subs were waiting. A lot of ships followed them out."

Duggan nodded his head in appreciation of a nautical tale well told; beside him, Marie was shaking hers—she wasn't buying it.

"Glen Murdock wasn't old enough to have fought in that battle," Marie objected. "He was just a kid when he joined, and that was in 1945. Not only that, I always thought Glen was one of your frogmen. He never served on a destroyer. When the war was over he went back and got his commission, but he spent all of his time on submarines after that."

With another smile, a knowing smile but not a happy one, Reinholt continued.

"You're right. That was George Murdock, Glen Murdock's father. He was cremated alive before the Harvey went down. The day Glen turned eighteen he joined the Navy. The ocean scared him silly, but he was going after the people who'd killed his father. He got more sick, and got sicker more often, than any sailor I ever saw. He practically drowned the first time I threw him into the water. But he learned to swim. His part in the fighting was brief, because even before Glen was out of training the Japanese were already losing the war and knew it. But I never saw the like of the man. There was something in him. I can't explain it. A kind of iron. He was obstinate. He was unruly. At times he was criminally insubordinate, but he got things done. We sent four divers into Tokyo harbor with limpet mines to try and sink the carrier *Yoshio* in the summer of 1945. One man's oxygen rebreather gave out and he turned back after dropping his mine. Sharks got another of the four. And then they hit some unexpected crosscurrents. Murdock was the only one left. Somehow—I've read his report a hundred times, and I still don't know how he did it—Glen Murdock carried his own and two other mines into the harbor. They weighed thirty pounds each. He dropped his weight belt and blew up his life vest, but even so . . . His rebreather quit, too, still a quarter of a mile out, and he swam on the surface to the carrier—the man wasn't yet a decent swimmer, and his best stroke resembled nothing so much as a dog paddle, but he made it. He placed the three mines on her hull. You see, the *Yoshio* was one of the carriers from which Zeros had been launched in the Pearl Harbor strike. It sank. And with the Tokyo harbor ablaze and gunships steaming around in circles, Murdock dogpaddled five miles out to sea where a waiting submarine picked him up.''

"I've never heard that story," said Marie, staring at the admiral in disbelief.

Duggan agreed.

"He never mentioned it to me, either."

Reinholt folded his arms and sighed. ''There are many more stories I could tell, but Glen was not one for talking and I'm only trying to make a point. I knew him for twenty years before he even mentioned his father. When he did I went to the trouble to look up the record. George Murdock had something—call it 'iron' or 'chutzpah' or whatever you want—and he gave what he had to his son. I know that because Glen had it too, in spades, and it's not a thing you can teach. Now then, I'm going to tell you something else you may not know: Glen always took pride in Drew for what his eldest son has. Drew is a fine officer, I'm told. Better than Glen ever thought about being. Drew's got an aptitude for naval duty; submarine work comes easy for him. He's at home on the ocean, a natural sailor, which you must admit, Glen never was. The Navy is lucky to have Drew. But Drew isn't Glen Murdock. And Drew didn't get what he's got from Glen. I'm betting that Coy Murdock did.''

Duggan and Marie spoke together.

''Coy?''

''That's what I'm betting. I'm betting everything I stand for. And I'm throwing the *Alaska* in, too.''

''But how can you know?''

''I know that man—I've known him for forty-five years. Coy Murdock's father has been murdered, just as Glen's was. Coy's brother has been killed or . . . or worse. And he's after the men that have done it. I don't think Coy's still alive, I damn well *know* he is. Because I know him. He's arrogant; he's defiant; he's insubordinate. You can't tell him what to do because he won't listen. You can't make him do what you want him to do because he doesn't care. And you can't stop him from doing what he's come here to do. You can slow him down, you can hurt him . . . you can even kill him. But you can't stop him. He's down there right now, hanging onto the tail of that Trident sub. I don't know how he could do that, but he's done it. I don't know how he plans on bringing the damn thing up. There's no way he can. It's not possible. But I'm going to keep following that signal, helping however and whenever I can, because I want to be there when he does.''

# Chapter Thirteen

Musa al-Kaseem stalked the *Alaska*'s command center with the fury of a restless and brooding beast.

And fear.

Fear and Musa al-Kaseem stalked the *Alaska*.

One had slipped in unseen and unheard, to poison the air like a deadly gas or a radiation leak. And while submarines have meters to detect a buildup of carbon dioxide, hydrogen, or chlorine gas before their concentrations become toxic, and rem badges and Geiger counters to meter radioactivity, there are no such meters for fear. It flows from a frightened man like sweat. It stinks, but the smell of it doesn't wash off. When a whole crew is running scared the stench of fear fills the ship.

SSBN 732 stank of fear.

Musa al-Kaseem had seized the *Alaska* by storm. He held it by sheer intimidation. Even setting aside his well-armed and demonstrably ruthless companions, Kaseem himself was intimidating beyond belief.

He was also immense. An aberration of size and proportion that defied description. His thick stump of a head had been thatched with steel wool. His black button eyes were pasted too close together, and his black stubbled jaw thrust out like an icebreaker's prow.

Manning the command center while he lumbered about was tantamount to working in the cage of a tiger.

Sometimes his huge arms were folded. More often they hung at his sides while he made and unmade his great fists. He would stretch his fingers like claws, and then tighten them into knots with such force that the thick slabs of muscle ballooned on his forearms and the swollen veins rippled his burnt-umber skin. Sometimes he stood in the center of the control room, screaming in red-faced rage and hammering his fists at the air.

He prowled from station to station, pausing to glower over the shoulders of the crew, checking their instruments, grunting approval or barking corrections before passing on.

It had been going on this way for hours.

The crewmen kept their eyes on the instruments and the controls. They never saw Kaseem move in behind them. They never needed to see him to know he was there. Man has a primeval instinct that warns him when the beast is nearby: a shiver at the base of the spine, a tingling of the small hairs on the back of the neck. Kaseem generated this kind of instinct.

They never turned to watch him move on. Only one man, a valve operator, had made that mistake, and once was enough. Kaseem had pounced on the man in a rage, thrown him against a bulkhead, and all but bludgeoned him to death with his fists.

It had taken three of his own men to pry him away.

When the operator had been carried below, Kaseem did a slow turn from the center of the room, picked out the spot where his circuit had broken off, and continued as though nothing had happened.

Kaseem used to tramp through the ship, inspect the missile, reactor, and engineering compartments and check on the rest of his men. But for hours now he had not left the conn. He circled. He growled. He knotted and unknotted his fists.

The man never tired.

If anything, he'd grown even more restless. The closer the *Alaska* got to the Johnston Islands the worse he became. He bounded from one station to the next like a madman. The least unexpected event threw him into a fit. If navigation reports didn't come in on time he stormed into that section and pounded his fists on the chart table. When a planesman took his hand off the wheel to scratch the back of his head, Kaseem blew his top and threatened to kill him. He ranted. He raged.

Like everyone else, he was scared.

His men—they were scared, too.

The crew—something frightened them now even more than Kaseem. They stared at their gauges, monitors, and screens like creatures possessed. Nothing, not even Kaseem, could make them turn away.

They listened for the first staggering crunch of the *Alaska*'s eighteen thousand tons slamming into the reefs at full speed and power.

They waited for the crash of rupturing steel and the sickening surge of millions of gallons of seawater pouring in through the hull.

The *Alaska* was now churning through rapidly shallowing waters, waters that were poorly charted and hazardous in the extreme. She was burrowing a hole the size of the Holland Tunnel, sweeping it over her hull and propelling it behind her at better than thirty knots. The coral reefs closed in around her. The sea bed slipped under her keel by a matter of yards. Massive outcrops of rock and coral passed by to each side. If they hit the reefs at this speed, not even the reinforced bow of the *Alaska* could withstand the collision.

Like everyone else, Kaseem knew this.

Fear ran down his face and back. The sides of his pants were stained by the fear he had wiped from his hands. His clothes were sodden with fear.

He knows what I'm going to do, thought Drew Murdock.

With the same single-mindedness with which the crew watched their instruments and Kaseem and his men watched the crew, Drew Murdock was watching Kaseem.

Here was the completely primitive man.

He was a predator that could smell the fear of its prey and enjoyed it. An animal that could sense the hunters who came after him as well. Kaseem was sensing it now: a shiver at the base of his spine, a tingling of small hairs standing up on the back of his neck.

He knew.

But he didn't know what or where. It could be an attack submarine on their tail, with wire-guided homing torpedoes, or a Navy submarine chaser waiting for them in the channel with hedgehog depth charges and Sea Lance nuclear depth-missiles. Antisubmarine helicopters could be following every move the sub made from beyond the range of her sonar. Even the reefs themselves. In a way the reefs were hunting them, too. Any of these might be the hunter.

But it wasn't any of these. The hunter was Commander Drew Murdock.

Kaseem stopped at the forward end of the command center, where a passage connected to the radio and sonar rooms. He bellowed: *"Sonar!"*

Sonarman First-Class Fencil's tenor came back to them over the squawk box: "Sonar."

*"No contacts. Nothing at all?"*

"I'm reading bottom three hundred feet and rising fast. Fifty feet under our keel. We have to slow down or surface."

*"Goddammit! Are there any vessels up there or not?"*

"I'm getting something. But it's weak. No engines. It could just be a large buoy. But if we don't go up or slow down pretty soon it won't matter."

They should rise, thought Murdock, to periscope depth at least. It was the only sane thing to do. At this speed, in these shallow waters, they'd ram the reefs sure as hell.

Kaseem turned to Murdock. *"Bring power to two-thirds."*

He's afraid to go up, Murdock said to himself, and he fought back the ghost of a smile. *Got you, you bastard!*

Drew Murdock spoke into his headset, a sound-powered telephone tied in to vital stations in other compartments and decks. Even Kaseem's booming bullhorn of a voice couldn't penetrate the ship's length to the engine room.

"Engineering, conn. Ahead two-thirds."

"This is engineering; aye-aye, skipper, ahead two-thirds."

Murdock breathed a sigh of relief. He was more afraid than anyone. He didn't want to die any more than he wanted all the members of his crew to die. Nevertheless, he was going to run the *Alaska* onto the reefs. Fear wouldn't stop him. Only Musa al-Kaseem could do that, and Kaseem had decided to remain submerged until his rendezvous made an appearance and signaled him it was safe to surface.

From the passage forward to the radio room and sonar, Kaseem lumbered by the diving stand and the trim manifold. He scowled aft into the navigation center. He moved past the hydraulic manifold and the hull-integrity board toward the helm. Two men sat on comfortable chairs with pedestals between their legs. Atop the pedestals were aircraft-type steering columns which controlled the diving planes and rudders. The wheels were pushed forward or backward to dive or rise and swung side to side to make the submarine turn. An instrument panel in front of them was as complex as any jet aircraft's.

"This is sonar. Obstructions ahead. Bottom formation off starboard bow, one thousand yards. We'll have to climb to one hundred and fifty feet or come left to course two-eight-zero to avoid."

*"We'll stay down!"* shouted Kaseem. He told the planesman to make the course correction.

"This is sonar again. The bottom's still coming up."

Lt. (j.g.) William Fletcher came into the conn on the jump. He was carrying a section of nautical chart, which he held out for Kaseem to read.

"This channel is no channel at all," he said. "It's a damned maze of tideways. Maybe we can find our way through it, but not at this speed. There are crosscurrents and tide rips in these reefs. You've got to slow down."

The intercom squawked: "This is sonar. We've got another obstruction coming up fast. Nine hundred yards. Recommend we rise now or come left to one-six-seven."

*"Left to one-six-seven!"* Kaseem bellowed, and then glared at Murdock. *"Bring power to one-third!"*

"One-six-seven, aye-aye."

"You'll lose steerageway at one-third power," Murdock told him. "If you can't maneuver quickly, it doesn't matter how slow you're going."

*"I said one-third power!"*

"We're still too deep," said Fletcher.

The deck swayed under their feet as the rudders came hard to port.

"Engineering," said Murdock into his headphone. "Bring power to one-third but be prepared to move fast. Things are happening quickly up here."

"Engineering, aye-aye; ahead one-third."

"Sonar. Obstruction dead ahead. Clear broad off both bows. A Y formation. It's a labyrinth to the right. We may not get through at all. To the left we may have enough water to squeak through if we rise to periscope depth."

Fletcher thrust the chart under Kaseem's nose. "Here's what sonar's picking up. Eventually we're going to have to surface. . . ."

*"Get away from me!"*

Kaseem swung an arm that knocked the navigator across the command center. Fletcher landed on his back next to the helm. Then the terrorist made slow circles, looking at every man in his turn.

*"I know what you want. What all of you want. You want me to surface so the Navy can find us."* Kaseem stopped his slow rotation when his eyes locked on Drew Murdock. Now for the first time his voice lowered to something just slightly above conversational level. "I know there are hydrophones to the east and west of these islands, you brass bastard! I also know that the only way to get into the lagoon without setting them off is to stay in these canyons until we reach the channel. Now tell your men—"

"This is sonar. We have to make a decision. Recommend we turn to left one-one-four and rise to periscope depth."

Murdock swung to the intercom. "What's the other course, sonar?"

"One-nine-zero degrees. Do something fast, skipper."

He turned quickly. "Helm, heading one-niner-zero— p.g.c. Thirty degrees right rudder."

"One-niner-zero; aye-aye, skipper."

The deck heeled sharply to starboard. A submarine turns like an aircraft, not like a surface ship. It banks into a turn and climbs out of it. And at thirty degrees of rudder any man who doesn't have a good grip on his safety bar may find himself suddenly in flight. The planesmen are strapped in. Everyone else would do well to forget the old saw: "One hand for the ship and one for yourself." In a boat capable of forty knots and forty-five-degree aerial vaults through the surface, things are more simple: two hands for yourself.

"This is sonar. Obstructions ahead and to starboard. Suggest course one-six-five."

*"One-six-five."*

"No . . . no. That's . . . come to one-five-zero . . . fast!"

*"One-five-zero."*

"One-five-zero, aye-aye."

222

Kaseem stood between the two helmsmen. One handled the stern planes; the other, rudders and sailplanes. He watched their compasses, depth gauges, and inclinometers.

"This is sonar. Bottom bearing off all bows! It's a blind canyon. There's no way out of it. Recommend we come to course. . . . No, there's no choice, we'll have to come up."

*"No!"* Kaseem whirled to Murdock. *"Full stop."*

Murdock grinned. The time had come.

He said calmly, "Are you ordering a 'Stop' or a 'Stop Shaft'?"

*"I'm ordering you to stop this boat!"*

Murdock shook his head and lowered his voice, as though he were speaking to a spoiled child on the edge of a temper tantrum. "Do you want us to close throttles and idle the shaft, or apply sufficient steam to stop all rotation of the shaft? Stopping the ship is something else entirely. We'd have to apply back one-third and risk emptying the steam reserves. It's just a little thing, you know, but—"

"This is sonar! We're five hundred yards from impact! Ninety seconds!"

Kaseem started across.

*"Stop this fuckin' boat!"*

Murdock pushed the headset speaker against his lips. "Engineering?"

"Here, skipper."

"Ahead full."

"Repeat that, skipper?"

"You heard me. Ahead full. Do it, goddammit!"

The Trident submarine lurched forward.

Her command center crew had been braced for a loss of power; no one, least of all Kaseem, was prepared for a two-hundred-percent increase in speed. He grabbed for the planesman's seat to keep himself from falling, missed, and wound up flat on his face. His head came up. The black button eyes found Murdock.

"This is sonar! Obstruction dead ahead at two hundred yards! Twenty seconds to impact!"

Kaseem was up and running.

His hands clawed at the air and he growled like a crazed animal.

Murdock snatched off the headset, turned, and smashed it against the bulkhead. By the time he had turned back to face the terrorist, Kaseem was on him. Murdock felt as though a tidal wave had swept through the command center, lifted him high into the air, and then hurled him to the deck.

Suddenly the giant was over him, kneeling on Murdock's chest and driving his great fists into Murdock's face.

Murdock didn't hear the sonarman calling for immediate maneuvers. He didn't feel the deck slanting back as other terrorists knocked the helmsmen from their seats and pulled back their controls. The *Alaska* stood on her cruciform tail and launched herself from the depths. But Murdock didn't feel that either.

He could feel nothing but the blows. They just kept coming. Wave after wave of pain crashed against him, as relentless as the surf.

"Brace for impact! Brace for impact!"

Two crewmen were trying to pull Kaseem off him, but they weren't big enough; with the deck angled at forty-five degrees it was all they could do to stay on their feet.

Murdock was slipping. Each blow took him farther and farther below the surface where an undertow, the eddies and whirlpools of oblivion, tugged at his consciousness.

When the crash came it wasn't what Murdock had expected. There was no shuddering impact. And no rush of seawater filling the forward compartments. A single sharp clang of metal against metal resonated through the

ship. They were inside a mammoth bell, one that someone had just struck with a sledgehammer and then backed
off to observe the effect.

The vibrations stopped.

But the blows had stopped, too.

As Murdock fought back from the depths, he barely
saw Kaseem's face turned up toward the overhead. It
seemed to Murdock that everyone in the command center
was looking up at the overhead, toward the sail. But everyone else was above the surface while Murdock was
below it. All he could see were vague outlines, and shadows reflected and refracted until they were impossible to
identify. Human statues that swirled in confusion, men
startled into immobility, pitched and tossed by the surface of a sea that pulled ever farther away. Murdock was
sinking.

Then the sledgehammer struck again.

This one was even louder than the first and closer, too.
Right over their heads. A hellish peal of colliding metals.

*"What the hell was that?"* Kaseem bellowed.

Murdock stopped struggling to reach the surface. He
let the waves bury his body. The currents sucked him
into the depths.

He drowned in oblivion.

He was carried away, not to another place but to another time.


"What the hell was that?"

A blast of thunder jolted the *Alaska*. She shuddered,
as she would if one of her ballistic missiles were
launched. As she does when a heavy-handed tug operator
nudges her hull too hard or rides up on her bow.

Everyone in the command-and-control center was
watching the overhead. "What the hell was that?" cried
Captain West.

Commander Murdock was looking up, too.

"An explosion, Captain."

But Captain West was already scrambling up the ladder leading to the bridge hatch. Murdock raced forward to the bow escape trunk.

A clatter of small-arms fire erupted from topside.

There was a scream.

Just as Murdock pushed through the hatch into the small air lock, a boot caught the side of his head and kicked him back down the ladder. He grabbed for a rung but lost it; he struck the deck flat and hard. Someone landed on top of him, then dragged him to his feet. Men in orange jumpsuits and orange full-face masks were everywhere. A machine gun muzzle prodded Murdock back into the command center, where more men wearing the same orange outfits and carrying the same kind of weapons were pouring down from the tower. Everyone was shouting. The intruders shouted loudest of all, but with accents that made their orders impossible to understand. Their weapons made everything clear.

They broke up into teams and scattered throughout the command-and-control areas, keeping every member of the *Alaska* crew under guard and aborting any hopes of resistance before they were born.

In Murdock's mind were a buzz of memorized orders, the ship's "repel boarders" and "sneak attack" bills. All worthless. The attack was already successful—the boarders were aboard. Chief Rawleson, the master-at-arms, should be lining his men up at the weapons locker. But the chief himself was locked up in the contaminated section along with most of the men—most probably dead now—and the keys to the locker were in Captain West's pocket. All the drills and the orders meant nothing. Only the chaos of gunfire and shouting was real.

And then the frenzy came to a stop.

"Who are you?" asked Captain West. "What do you want? And where are the medical people?"

One man, bigger than the others by far, stepped right in front of the captain. He pulled off his mask. The stump of a head thatched with steel wool was physically arresting. The two black button eyes glared at West with something that resembled loathing but was much more primeval.

*"Are you in a rig for dive?"* boomed a bullhorn of a voice.

West glared at the man without blinking. When he spoke his voice never faltered. This was the way West would speak if he were dressing down one of his junior officers in the privacy of the captain's cabin, presenting a medal to one of the crew, giving directions in elementary shiphandling—or replying to a terrorist's demands.

"I asked what you wanted."

The big man thrust a Luger semiautomatic pistol against West's forehead.

"I want you to give the order to button up this boat and dive! You've got five seconds."

West spoke without turning his head away from the gun barrel. "No one," he said in the same calm, steady tone, "is to cooperate with these men in any way. That's an order!"

In that confined space the pistol report sounded more like a stick of dynamite.

West flew back off his feet.

"You son of a bitch!" shouted Murdock. He threw himself at the big man in a blind rage. But his attack was stillborn. Two others grabbed his arms and pinned them behind his back with such force they virtually lifted him clear of the deck.

The big man smiled. "Looks like we're going to need a new captain." He turned on Murdock. "Is that you, sonny?"

# Chapter Fourteen

Turning over command of a ballistic missile submarine is a time-consuming process.

The ingoing and outgoing commanders inspect the vessel from the packing on her propeller shaft to her torpedo tube fairings. There are logs to be filled out and signed. The new commander must determine that the submarine has proper charts, personnel, and equipment to navigate safely; that fire and pressure hulls meet current bills; that nuclear fuel and munitions are properly stored, and that classified files are safely secured. Last, and most important, the targeting and war readiness of the twenty-four SLBMs must be verified beyond any shadow of doubt.

Normally a transfer of submarine command requires up to a month.

Not so in Commander Drew Murdock's case.

It had occurred for Murdock in an instant, a single deafening, infinitesimal increment of time.

He looked down at the captain's spread-eagled body, at the bulbous wound on his forehead swollen by gases from the gun barrel and slashed when the skin could stretch no more, at the gathering pool of fluid pouring onto the deck from under bold, block letters on the cap which identified West as CAPTAIN from across the room or the length of the ship.

He wasn't captain any longer.

Drew Murdock had been given his first command.

He struggled in the grip of the two terrorists but they only twisted his arms higher behind his back.

Musa al-Kaseem faced him. His black button eyes were gleaming with satisfaction. Murdock could see he'd enjoyed killing West. If he killed every member of the *Alaska* crew he would enjoy that as well. Two steps took the big man in front of Murdock. He towered over the Navy commander.

*"Are you the exec or not?"*

There was no denying it. Across Murdock's ball cap was XO in the same bold lettering.

Murdock ground out the words with a snarl, "You're damn right I am."

"Well, sonny, you're in charge now. And you've got five seconds to get this sub under water."

The luger's hot barrel pressed against the bridge of Murdock's nose. A moment ago the control deck had been cool. Now his forehead was throwing off sweat.

"Four seconds."

It wasn't supposed to be like this, Murdock thought. He had longed for his own command for so many years he could recite the Navy procedure by heart. It was a time for pomp, not for blood. His shipmates, in their caps and dungarees, should be wearing dress whites. His father should be here and his brother, too, if he could talk Coy into coming. There should be at least one flag officer present, maybe two. Where were they?

"Three seconds."

Everything Murdock needed to say was spelled out. After the invocation and Captain West's farewell address, Murdock would turn to West and say, "I relieve you, sir." Then he would salute the flag commander and tell him: "Sir, I report for duty."

"Two seconds."

For the sake of a smooth transfer of authority and in keeping with tradition, Murdock's first act as the ship's new commander should be to face his crew and announce, "All the orders of my predecessor remain in effect."

"One second!"

It wasn't supposed to be like this at all. The manual offered no speeches for this kind of transfer.

"Time's up, sonny!"

Murdock tried to keep his voice steady, as Captain West had. "All the orders of my predecessor," he said, "remain in effect."

He didn't hear the explosion.

Something slammed against his head and the world went black in that same infinitesimal increment of time. Another increment followed. Longer perhaps, but not to Drew Murdock. Time, for him, had ceased to exist as a measurable quantity. He didn't know that his mind had stopped counting; he didn't know when it started again. It could have been when he found himself hovering in darkness between agony and eternity and fought his way to one side. Either side. Which one didn't matter. Maybe it was later, when the first faint sensations of light and sound blared at his numbed perception—blasts, brilliant bursts of light and sound that merely winked and whispered to him from across the universe. Or later still, when his jumbled impressions managed to rob him of every realization except one—he hadn't died.

"Are you all right, sir?"

Murdock looked groggily around. His head ached. The back of his head was especially bad. It felt as though he'd lain face down under a pile driver. As much as he wanted to know, he dared not explore the damage with his hands, for fear he would find it caved in.

He was now half lying, half sitting in a room that was oddly familiar. The soft overhead lighting he'd seen many times before. The Oriental rugs, too. Even the wainscoted walls covered with photographs of ships of the Third Fleet. He knew them all. It was the officers' study, one deck below the command-and-control center.

When he twisted his head to look around, a bolt of pain shot down his spine and stiffened his body. For a few seconds he couldn't move or even breathe. Then the pain and shock drained away and his muscles relaxed. He took in air. A bit slower this time, and a lot more carefully, he surveyed the room.

"Sir?"

The desks and chairs had been piled atop one another so as to barricade the door leading to the ship's office. Only the joiner door to the main corridor remained clear.

Sitting on the floor at the other end of the room, with their backs to the walls, were the five surviving officers of Murdock's command.

"Can you hear me, sir? Are you all right?"

It was Lieutenant William Fletcher who knelt beside Murdock.

"I'm okay, Navigator," Murdock said, squinting his eyes and searching the room. It didn't sound like his voice, even to him. He stopped. Something was wrong. Too many officers were missing. "Where are the others?" he asked.

"We're all here, sir."

"Captain West. . . ?"

"Sir, he's dead. Don't you remember?"

Murdock remembered. Everything.

He remembered the epidemic that had swept through the submarine, striking down thirty-six crewmen in less than an hour. Twelve of them had died before the medical staff even decided the cause was a highly contagious disease and not some kind of food poisoning. When the medical staff had succumbed to the disease, Captain West had ordered all the watertight doors closed and latched. The dead and the dying were sealed in their contaminated compartments. Forty-two fit but possibly infected crewmen were condemned to die along with them. Murdock remembered that officers and men from the uncontaminated areas were brought into the forward compartments.

The captain had shut down the ventilators to prevent the spread of the disease through the submarine's fresh-air system and then flooded the whole ship with oxygen to keep the sick and the healthy alike from suffocating. Murdock remembered surfacing, radioing to Pearl Harbor for help, waiting for the emergency medical team to arrive, sending up a deck crew when the helicopter was first spotted by the lookout. And every crazy thing that had happened after the "medical" team boarded, Murdock remembered.

"He's gonna be all right," Fletcher announced.

By this time the other officers were forming a half circle around their exec, a couple of them standing and the rest dropping to a knee.

Murdock studied their faces while making a mental list of the absent. Their expressions were strange. He'd never seen them look at him like this before. Then he realized they were looking at him not as the executive officer, not as their link to the captain or even as the captain's designated SOB, but as their new CO.

The epidemic had claimed the lives of their medical and dental officer, a reactor control assistant, and two reactor watch officers, as well as four other junior officers. But even considering these, Murdock counted two officers missing. Wait! Now he remembered that, too. It had been the officer of the deck and first lieutenant who'd climbed to the bridge to assist in boarding the medical team.

Where's Bradley?" he asked. "And Epstein?"

"Both dead," said Lieutenant Commander Benjamin Buchanan.

"Shot," added Fletcher. "Along with six of the men. The members of the deck party. Collins, Echols, Smyth and Barbera . . ."

"And Dillon and Cunningham," said Buchanan.

Murdock took a deep breath. He'd known all those men well and liked them. Officers and enlisted men on

the sub shared close quarters. Discipline was more relaxed than on most surface ships; morale was generally
higher. When the epidemic had struck one compartment
after another and his shipmates had died all around him,
Murdock had grieved right along with the other survivors. Seventy-eight people had surely died from the epidemic. And now nine more had been shot. Eighty-seven
deaths. Three out of four of the sub's complement. Murdock didn't know what to say to his officers. Should he
react to this news with sorrow? That would assure them
he cared. But did he dare show any emotion? Captain
West would have maintained his demeanor regardless of
how many crewmen were lost. This at least gave his staff
a feeling of strength at the top. But Murdock was not
Captain West. And it was too late to decide: The moment
had already passed, and the lines of suffering that had
etched themselves across Murdock's face were too real
and too deep to erase.

"Tell me what happened, after they knocked me out,"
Murdock said. "What was that explosion? Is the ship in
one piece?"

"The ship is okay," offered Fletcher.

"Yes, sir," said Buchanan. "We think the helicopter
blew up right over the bow."

Fletcher rushed on: "After they knocked you out, they
put a gun to your head and said that if one of the officers
didn't give the order—"

Commander Scott Longfellow interrupted. "I did what
I did and I don't apologize for it. . . ."

Thomas and Buchanan were both speaking now.

Murdock raised a hand.

"I'll tell him," said Commander Eugene Shorter. The
ship's reactor officer ranked just below Murdock himself,
and the others quieted at once. "It's like Billy said, sir,
they'd knocked you out and put a pistol to your head and
announced that if someone didn't pass the order to en-

gineering to get under way they would kill you like they did the captain. So Scotty gave the order.''

''I did what I did and I don't apologize for it,'' said Longfellow.

''Then don't,'' snapped Murdock. ''We're submerged now?''

''Submerged and making way,'' said Shorter.

Murdock placed his hands on the floor. Yes, he could feel it now, the faintest vibration from the steam turbines and the single massive screw. By God they *were* making way! But where were they going?

''They marched all the men out of the control room, except a skeleton crew,'' said Shorter.

''Where'd they take them?''

''One deck down to their mess. They're all down there now, under guard.''

Murdock was aghast. ''You mean in the contaminated section?''

Shorter seemed unconcerned. He tossed his shoulders. ''They had a man check it out. A Navy captain who came with them on the helicopter.''

''What captain?''

''He was wearing one of those quarantine suits just like the rest of them. But when he took it off he had on an officer's uniform and captain's bars.''

''Who is he?''

''I don't know. Kostner, Kestler, something like that. They treated him like a prisoner. Ordered him to check you over and then they sent him down to the lower compartments. He came back a few minutes later and pronounced them safe. By then he had taken off the suit. I didn't get a good look at his name tag.''

''But you've no idea who this guy is?''

''No, sir, I don't. Apparently he's from the biological research center at Pearl Harbor. At least that's my guess.'' Shorter went on to explain how he and Buchanan had carried Murdock into the officers' study while

Thomas and Fletcher had cleared aside the desks and chairs at the instructions of the terrorists. "They brought Scotty down pretty quickly when they found out he wasn't going to give them any more help," Shorter reported. "One of the terrorists has been posted just outside the door."

"Do we have any idea who they are or what they want?"

The five shook their heads in unison.

Murdock studied them carefully. Here was his staff until this madness ended. They were all first-rate in their fields—no officer less than first-rate gets assigned to an SSBN. But combat experience was something else altogether.

Ensign Orin "Tommy" Thomas was the greenest among them. This was only his second patrol. Two complete crews rotated assignment on the *Alaska* for seventy-day patrols followed by twenty-five-day overhaul periods. So Thomas had very little experience. Against this he had loads of enthusiasm. As communications officer, the ensign was assigned to the sonar and integrated radio sections just forward of the sub's command-and-control center. Within those steel walls no doubts existed as to whether Ensign Thomas knew his stuff.

Lieutenant Fletcher was next. Early twenties, bright, but a little high-strung. He didn't like people to call him "William" or "Bill," and somehow it had got round the ship that "Billiam" was all right, so this had stuck with the men. In any case, he was a fine navigator. His navigation center was located on Deck One, just forward of the launch tubes in the missile compartment and aft of command and control.

Lieutenant Commander Benjamin Buchanan was both the second youngest officer and second highest in rank next to Murdock. This was easily explained. Buchanan had been a child prodigy, finishing college at nineteen and immediately joining the Navy. The weapons officer was a programming wizard. His real responsibility was the twenty-four SLBMs that occupied the central third of the submarine, a forest of eight-foot-diameter tubes that breached all decks aft of the tower; his station was the missile control center located on Deck Two just below navigation. But in fact, circumstances often conspired to send Commander Buchanan anywhere on the ship that had computers. Which was everywhere on the ship.

The propulsion team of Comm. Eugene Shorter and Lieutenant Commander Scott Longfellow should be Murdock's right and left flank commanders. Longfellow was still an unknown quantity. He'd only been with the ship since they'd left Pearl Harbor the previous week—the *Alaska*'s regular Blue Team engineer had taken seriously ill. The man was an enigma: a friendly enough fellow who kept to himself, a tall, robust man whose hobby was collecting fragile glass jars filled with waters from all the seas of the world. He didn't drink or smoke, and spent all of his free time in the weight room of the recreation compartment, and yet his medical file indicated he was constitutionally frail and could tolerate no drugs of any kind whatsoever. That, plus the fact that Longfellow's duties sent him throughout the ship from his engine room aft to the auxiliary machinery rooms forward and amidships, should have made him a sure candidate to contract the disease. But he'd never gotten sick.

Commander Shorter, as reactor officer, was the engineering officer's immediate superior. Though not as tall, Shorter was built like a bull and had been the *Alaska*'s resident physical fitness freak until the other man joined him in the weight room at least once a day. In fact they seemed to mesh so completely that the term "Long and Short" was already used throughout the ship to refer to the two men's domain—the after-third of the *Alaska* that made up the propulsion spaces. Shorter had served aboard the *Alaska* longer than anyone except for Captain West himself. He had guts, and Murdock knew he could rely on Shorter when things got bad. They were very bad now.

And what about the new CO? thought Murdock. Let's not forget him.

He'd been the ship's number two man for a long time. If his voice had had the force of command it was only because number one was always standing behind him. More often than not the orders he gave had just been handed down from Captain West. When department heads came to him with their troubles, nine times out of ten he could do little but pass them through to the skipper. "You make the decision, Drew," West had so often told him. "But suppose I make a mistake?" "Then you'll have learned something, won't you?" Murdock had tried. As much as he tired of being a middleman, as much as he wanted his own command, he wasn't sure he deserved it. Now it had come. He was the CO. A middleman suddenly thrust to the front. The orders he issued now were of his own choosing, and they would be obeyed. That was the authority. The responsibility that accompanied it was just as absolute—any mistakes were now on his head.

He would miss Captain West very much.

"We have to assume the worst," Murdock told them. "That these terrorists have taken over the *Alaska* in order to get control of her missiles. We have to figure that they will try to fire the missiles, or threaten to do so. The six of us can't have any misunderstanding about what cooperation we'll give these guys the next time they need it. When I say no one cooperates, I mean what I say." Murdock was looking directly at Longfellow. "Is that understood?"

They all nodded.

"Our first duty is to resist these people in every way we can and to regain control of the ship if possible; if we can't do that, we will try to destroy her."

"How?" asked Longfellow.

"I don't know. It would be a last resort. Let's hope it

doesn't come to that. Before we even consider what to do we have to know what we're up against. Who these people are and what they're after.''

Buchanan broke in, ''They looked like Arabs to me.''

Several were now speaking at once:

''Do you think they're Libyans?'' asked Ensign Thomas.

''More likely Shiite Muslims,'' said Fletcher.

''Wait a minute, wait a minute.'' Murdock was alternately eyeing the door and the officers' faces, while waving them to silence with both hands. Doing this made his head ache badly. When they had all quieted down he took several deep breaths before going on. ''I saw only the leader without his quarantine mask,'' he said. ''The big guy that shot West. He looked Mediterranean but not necessarily Arab, and he talked like an American.''

''They all took their masks off after you'd been knocked out,'' offered Shorter. ''They're Arabs, all right.''

''They took their masks off before they marched the men down to the contaminated decks?''

''That's right.''

''Weren't they worried about getting the disease themselves?''

''They didn't look worried about anything as far as I could see, other than the possibility that the disease would wipe out the rest of us and deprive them of the pleasure of doing it personally. But the captain assured them it was perfectly safe.''

''Okay, about this captain. Apparently he's the senior officer present. But he's not a line officer. Accord him all the respect his rank is due, but let's watch what we say or do when he's around until we know more about him. After all, he came with them. But even if he is on their side he may be sympathetic to us. He may even be a prisoner like we are. Is that clear?''

Again the five heads nodded and there were murmurs of "Yes, sir."

"And one more thing . . ."

"Hold it, sir!" Something had alerted Buchanan; he got to his feet, padded to the door, and put his ear to the wood panel. "I can hear them talking. I think they're coming."

The steady drumbeat of footsteps grew louder. They halted outside the ship's study.

Buchanan had backed up to stand beside the others when a booming voice sounded through the door. "I told you to put them somewhere secure. Do you call this secure. . . ?" The crescendo of words reached a climax. There followed a moment of silence and then a crash. The door buckled and a huge fist plowed right through the wooden panel. Slowly it withdrew.

Now another voice came clearly through the hole:

"I'm sorry, Kaseem. I'll have them moved."

The damaged door swung open.

There were four of them. Out of their quarantine suits they bore the unmistakable stamp of self-employed soldiers. Their uniforms were a hodgepodge of military surplus from no particular service or nation. They wore camouflage pants and combat boots of American manufacture. One of the men had a beret and two had gun belts slung bandolier-style over their shoulders. Their multicolored sweatshirts were without any conceivable uniformity, other than the distant date of their last laundering and the fact that each had been subjected to the personalized tailoring of a knife-wielding sloven.

The three hanging back near the door were only smaller, swarthier versions of the first. Impossibly, that one looked even bigger out of his suit. His ogreish black stump of a head rested atop three-foot shoulders that began sloping outward from just below his ears. The rest of his body was designed on the same gargantuan scale, right down to his hands, which were the size of catcher's mitts. The other men were armed with automatic weapons. This man carried no weapons at all, not even the Luger he had used to kill Captain West. It never occurred to any of the officers that the lack of a weapon made him any less dangerous.

*"Back up!"*

Murdock and his officers backed up.

"My name is Kaseem." The big man's eyes roved from one face to another like two pistol barrels in search of a target. "And you . . . officers and gentlemen . . . are prisoners of the People's Islamic Revolutionary Army."

He stopped, almost as though he were waiting for one of them to say something.

"We've never heard of you."

Kaseem's eyes stopped at Commander Murdock. "Too bad for you."

"Right."

"In a few days the whole world will know of us."

Murdock swallowed his fear. The man had an animalistic appearance and manner that left one amazed he was capable of human speech. "What is it you want?"

Kaseem blew a burst of air from his mouth. "I've already got it. I've got you, I've got your boat, and I've got your missiles. What more could I want?"

"It won't do you any good. Without the keys—"

Kaseem held out his big fist. Two gold neck-chains were entangled in his fingers; from each chain hung a slim golden key, a flat strip of metal with square keyways and notches. "Yours . . . and the captain's," he growled.

Murdock's hand went automatically to his shirt front, which suddenly felt bare.

"But you don't have—" Murdock stopped. He had been about to say "missile firing codes" but decided he wouldn't even tell them that much. "You don't have us to show you how to use them. It's not as simple as opening a couple of padlocks."

"You'll tell me what I want to know."

"Don't bank on it!"

He blew air again. The gesture showed more contempt than spitting in their faces.

"You don't think so?" Kaseem's eyes began moving. At Longfellow they stopped. The two men faced one another. "Stand up."

Longfellow stood.

"Come here."

Longfellow took the two steps required.

"You were the one who thought cooperation made more sense than dying."

"Well, I . . . I d-did before," he stammered, "but I w-won't help you . . . not anymore, that is."

"Say that again."

Murdock rose to his feet. "He's only saying what we'll all say. We're not going to help you anymore."

Kaseem glared down at Longfellow. "Is that right?"

"Yes—yes, that's right."

With a swiftness that belied his great size, Kaseem reached out and scooped Commander Longfellow's head into the crook of his elbow. Longfellow was tall and strong, too, but he was no match for Kaseem. He was lifted into the air. His legs flailed helplessly and his fists beat against the bole of an arm that completely encircled his neck.

Murdock started forward along with Buchanan and Shorter, until the three terrorists beside Kaseem slammed back the actions on their weapons.

Longfellow was coughing, gasping for air.

"Let him go!" shouted Commander Shorter.

"All right, you've made your point!" Murdock insisted.

Slowly, Kaseem's huge hand came down upon Longfellow's face, squeezed the commander's skull with his outspread fingers, and then in a single snapping movement jerked the head at a severe angle.

Longfellow stopped kicking. He hung limp from Kaseem's elbow. When the big man loosened his grip, the officer fell to the floor in a broken heap.

Murdock stared at the body.

"Get this filth out of here," Kaseem told one of his men, and Longfellow was dragged out by his heels.

Murdock lost all control. "Dammit, what good did that do? You can kill us all, but that won't get you what you want!"

Kaseem spat. "Maybe not," he said. "And then again, maybe that is what I want." Musa al-Kaseem turned to one of his soldiers and barked: "Put them in the fish tank." Then he stalked out of the compartment, ducking his head and twisting his vast shoulders through the doorway.

# Chapter Fifteen

Kaseem's men led Commander Murdock and his officers down into the torpedo room. The watertight door was closed behind them, the latching dogs hammered tight.

Murdock fell onto one of the bunks, planted his elbows on his knees, and buried his face in his hands.

"I'll tell you something," said Buchanan to no one in particular. "This Kaseem bastard may or may not be an Arab, I don't know, and he may be a terrorist now, but at one time he served on a Navy submarine. I'd bet mammy's garters on that."

"He's crazy!" cried Thomas.

"He's dead," replied Shorter. "What he did to the captain was bad enough. But killing Scotty for no reason—for that, the man's going to die."

Lieutenant Fletcher, the navigator, was nodding. "I noticed it, too." he said. "He knows his way around this sub. And the lingo. Did you hear what he said on the command deck? He didn't ask if we were rigged for dive, but whether we had 'a rig for dive.' And the way he calls her a 'boat' instead of a 'ship.' You're right, Ben. He's a former submariner."

Shorter glared at the two men. "I don't care if he's a former Chief of Naval Operations, I'm still gonna kill him."

Someone laughed.

It had been a nervous burst that erupted involuntarily and ended quickly. Eyes turned to the communications officer. "You mean he's going to kill you," said Thomas. "Let's face it, he's going to kill all of us."

Drew Murdock slowly lifted his head from the cradle of his hands. As he did so, their argument ground to a halt.

"Nobody kills or gets killed until we figure this thing out," Murdock told them.

"But he killed Captain West and Scotty," said Shorter. "You can't order us not to try to—"

"I am ordering you not to try anything without my go-ahead. What you try could get a lot of people killed."

Gradually the four men dispersed themselves onto bunks. This had been home as well as shop to the men of the torpedo crew, but the epidemic had struck here early on. The doctor had moved the first casualties out. The others, survivors but still infected, had simply walked out, trying to isolate themselves from the dying within the contaminated areas.

"What can we do?" Thomas asked, adding tardily, "sir."

Murdock looked around. "I don't know. I don't even know why they brought us in here. Locking us up with these torpedoes makes about as much sense as turning an arsonist loose in a fireworks factory. There's enough high explosive in here to blow the *Alaska* to kingdom come."

"Sir? You wouldn't do that, would you?"

"We wouldn't have to, Ensign."

Ensign Thomas stared at the glossy black cylinders that hung from the overhead. They were two feet in diameter and twenty feet long, nearly the length of the room. They also filled racks bolted to the outer bulkheads, where the torpedo tube nests were mounted. Torpedoes themselves were stored under the bunks in pairs and above them, too. Thomas forced himself to look away.

"That's something else," said Buchanan. Their weapons officer wasn't to be sidetracked. "He calls these torpedoes 'fish.' He's ex-Navy, all right."

"An enlisted man," Fletcher agreed, "judging by the way he feels about us."

"Could you do it, Ben?" Murdock asked suddenly.

Buchanan glared at him. "What? You mean detonate one of these Mark 48s inside the sub?"

"Yes."

"Well, I . . ." Commander Buchanan looked over the room. Hydraulic dollies, benches, and tackle left little space for nonessentials. There was plenty in the way of tools. "I suppose I could," he said. "But, sir, is that the only way? To blow us all up?"

Murdock shook his head. "I don't know. I don't want to any more than you. I don't even know if it would work."

"Just one explosion will kill us, all right," Buchanan said. "Probably the guy sitting outside of that door, too. But not anyone else."

"It wouldn't have to. Not if it punched a hole through the pressure hull."

"What would happen then?" asked Thomas.

It was sad in a way. Murdock didn't know whether to put it gently or straight from the shoulder.

"This isn't a Boston whaler," he said. "You can't saw it in half and expect both halves to head for the surface. When this compartment fills with seawater it'll throw off our trim so fast she'll go down like a brick. Lose maybe four, five hundred feet before Kaseem takes proper action. By that time she'll have reached maximum depth. The farther she sinks the more pressure she finds. At a thousand feet or so the pressure hull will start to buckle. More water will come in, increasing our negative buoyancy and making her sink all the faster. When we hit crush depth, somewhere around fifteen hundred feet, the hull might as well be made out of tin foil."

For a few moments the torpedo room was silent as the

five men weighed the respective advantages of death by drowning as opposed to being blown into small bits and pieces.

Lieutenant Fletcher was the first to speak. "Couldn't you just open up the torpedo tubes?"

"Wouldn't work," said Buchanan. "There's a mechanical interlock that prevents the outer muzzle doors of each tube from being open at the same time the inner breech doors are open. The safety feature can't be overridden. For obvious reasons."

Murdock could hardly believe that five men were calmly discussing the ways and means of suicide and mass murder, but that was exactly what they were doing.

"A Mark 48 torpedo can do a lot of overriding," said Fletcher.

Shorter was nodding his head. "That might work," he allowed. "You could detonate it right in the torpedo tube. Blowing through the two doors would be easier than blasting a hole in the hull." The reactor officer looked to Murdock for approval and both then turned to Buchanan, the only one among them capable of performing the work.

He pursed his lips. "It's a thought," he agreed. "Of course, it's not quite that simple. The torpedo is actually launched, as you may know, by an impulse of air; its charge isn't armed until it's well clear of the sub. But it would be easier to override that safety feature than the interlock on the tubes, and it also means I wouldn't have to remove any of the explosive material from the torpedo." Buchanan did a slow take of his fellow officers and ended up regarding the new CO. "Do you want me to open one up and take a look-see, skipper?"

"I don't . . . Okay, go ahead. But be careful. Navigator, keep an ear against that door. And you, Ensign, watch that access." Murdock pointed to the hatchlike passing scuttle in the center of the overhead. Four levels straight up was the escape logistics trunk on the main deck. The "fish" were lowered to the torpedo room through a ladderway that breached all levels.

Buchanan rigged the block and tackle and lowered one of the torpedoes, with Murdock and Shorter lending a hand. When it was safely on the dolly he strapped it down.

But suddenly Fletcher was flagging both hands. "Heads up. Here they come."

They heard a hammering on the dogs. The wheel rotated completely, and the door swung open before the torpedo could be raised back to its overhead position.

Kaseem's head poked through. His massive trunk filled the opening. No watertight door on the *Alaska* had been designed with his dimensions in mind. Just watching him worm his way through by twisting his bulk should have been funny, but it wasn't. It was frightening, like seeing an ogre emerging from his cave.

Once inside he stretched himself out and looked around the room. Murdock could hear a crunching sound coming from Kaseem's feet, as though he were crushing the iron grating of the walking deck with his weight.

"Look sharp!" snapped Kaseem. "Smartness is next to godliness and all that shit." He looked down at Lieutenant Fletcher. "You're the picket, huh?"

"I don't know what you mean."

"Did you tell them I was coming?"

Fletcher drew himself up. "I sure did," he said.

Instantly Kaseem lashed out with both hands, scooped up two handfuls of Fletcher's shirt, and lifted him into the air until they were eye to eye.

"Well, that's what I meant," he growled. "If I catch you over here when I come in the next time, I'll break your damn neck."

Then he turned and tossed the lieutenant into the room. Buchanan and Murdock helped him to his feet while Commander Shorter braced himself in Kaseem's path.

*"Move it!"*

Shorter stepped to one side.

Kaseem smiled and pushed ahead. "I love a big tank," he boomed, instantly and inexplicably pleased.

He was wandering around the room surveying the facility with an inspector's eye. He looked in the sight glass on the number two torpedo tube's breech door and satisfied himself that it was flooded. He checked the vent/blow valves on the port tube nest. Then he ran his palm down the length of Buchanan's torpedo all the way to the tail, where he spun the shrouded propeller idly and showed his teeth.

"Pump-jet piston engine and monopropellant fuel," he said. "Good for twenty miles at fifty-five knots. Six hundred and fifty pounds of PBXN plastic." Kaseem fingered the guide for the wire that spins out from the torpedo and permits the submarine to control it during its initial stages. "I hear these latest models have two-way data transmission," he went on. "That the fish send you acoustical data for your computers to process while they're making a run. Is that true?"

No one spoke.

Suddenly Kaseem whirled. *"Goddammit, is that true or not?"*

"It's no secret," said Murdock.

Kaseem's rage evaporated as quickly as it had flared. His teeth flashed again in a cruel smile. "Commander," he said, "you ain't got no secrets from me. Now stow this damn fish. If I come back down here and find it unracked again, I will personally shoot every one of you." He turned to the door, "Firuz, gather these tool boxes."

Murdock was surprised to find that three other men had entered behind Kaseem. They hadn't sneaked in—when Kaseem was around one didn't notice anything else. Two of the three were Kaseem's soldiers, but the third was dressed in Navy tans. He was standing off to one side, as though to disassociate himself from the others.

Having issued his orders, Kaseem gathered his volatile passions about him and stormed from the torpedo room. His men, lugging toolboxes with both hands, followed behind him, and soon came the turning of the wheel and the hammering.

Only the newcomer remained.

He was tall and thin and looked every inch the officer. His uniform seemed genuine enough, and so did the expression of concern as he looked across at Murdock.

"You're the executive officer?"

Murdock stood. "Yes, sir. Commander Drew Murdock. You're . . ."

"Captain Laurence Kester. I'm sorry to hear about your captain. I couldn't help him. However, I would like to take another look at you. Two dead commanding officers we don't need."

"Thank you, sir. But we don't understand how you came to be with these people."

"Surely that can wait, Commander. If you wouldn't mind turning around. . . ?"

Murdock did so, lowering his head and exposing the gash on the back of his neck.

Captain Kester pulled some of the blood-soaked hairs to the side and poked at the wound with his fingers. "I suspect you've got one whale of a headache, haven't you? They koshed you good. But you're lucky. Turn back around, please." He examined Murdock's eyes. "Probably concussed. But we're out of my area of expertise."

"What can you tell me, Doctor?"

"Nothing much. Take two aspirins and see me in the—"

Kester stopped and looked around.

Lieutenant Fletcher and Ensign Thomas were closing in on one side of him, Commanders Shorter and Buchanan on the other. Murdock still faced him squarely. Their faces were uniformly grave.

"Just what is your area of expertise, Doctor?"

"I'm a . . ." Kester cleared his throat. "I suppose my attempts at humor are out of place. If you understood what I've been through you might—but never mind. I'm a microbiologist. That's what you want to know."

"We've all been through a great deal, Doctor. You're from the research center at Pearl Harbor?"

"That's right."

"No offense, sir, but do you have any identification? Your military ID?"

For a moment Kester considered pulling rank. He took in enough air for a real harangue. His mouth compressed and his color deepened by two shades. But then something changed his mind. His bluster and his lungs deflated. He nearly laughed. "Of course," he said, "I can't really blame you."

He produced the document.

Murdock looked it over and then handed it back. "Doctor, I'd like you to explain how you came here with those terrorists."

"You want me to convince you I'm not on their side, is that it, *Commander?*" The rank was emphasized. Kester smiled, as he would not at a fellow officer but at a subordinate.

Murdock nodded without smiling back. "Yes, sir. I'd like you to try."

Kester allowed himself another deep breath. When he let it out this time, the last of his fortitude expired with it. Then he dropped down on the bunk Murdock had left, as though his legs could no longer support him.

His face was grave now, too. "You're right, Commander, I have to tell you everything I know, though my part in it is nothing to brag about. I was assigned a team of medical technicians to come here and deal with this situation. We dressed in the quarantine suits and took a small launch across the harbor to Ford Island, where a helicopter was waiting. A Navy patrol boat intercepted us—Kaseem and ten of his cutthroats dressed up like SPs.

They diverted us to the *Arizona* memorial dock. They ordered us out of the launch, lined us up on the *Arizona*'s deck, and shot all of my men in cold blood. It was the most atrocious thing I ever witnessed. Ever heard of. There was nothing I could have done and yet . . ."

"Why didn't they shoot you?"

"I don't know. Dammit, I wish they had. But I suppose they needed someone to communicate with the pilot. Or with the research center, if one of my people tried to reach us by radio."

"You didn't know what they were planning?"

"It was easy enough to guess once we were in the air heading for your submarine, but with a gun against my head the whole flight there wasn't much I could do to stop them."

"Who are they?"

"As far as I know they're exactly who they claim to be, the Islamic Revolutionary Army. But of course that's just a nice way of saying 'terrorist,' isn't it? I'm convinced they're Iranians; at least I overheard a few of them speaking in Farsi."

"You speak Farsi?"

"A few phrases—I was once stationed in the Persian Gulf. Of course, that was before Khomeini and his nuts took over."

"What do they want?"

"I don't know any more than you do. Their leader seems to be quite insane. I wouldn't push him very far if I were you, Commander."

"What choice do I have? I can't cooperate with them."

"No, I suppose you can't. But you can go along until a better chance presents itself."

"Is than an order, sir?"

"What?"

"Are you ordering us to avoid confrontation with these terrorists?"

Kester glanced across the row of hard faces. "I'm certainly recommending it."

"That much I can see."

"Yes, but as to ordering . . . I'm in no position to order anyone to do anything."

"Then you don't intend to assume command of me and my men?"

"Good heavens, no. I'm a doctor, not a line officer. I couldn't navigate across Pearl Harbor in a rowboat. In this behemoth, under these conditions, I'd be nothing but a damn fool to do more than give you my advice. No, Commander, you're in charge here. And I wish you luck."

"Thanks, I'll need it."

"I'll content myself with looking after your men."

Murdock pressed toward him. "Have you been through the other compartments? Are there any survivors?"

"Yes. But it's bad, I'm afraid. You've lost twenty-two of your people."

"You mean twenty-two more? That's practically all of the men. . . ."

"No, I mean twenty-two. The rest of your men will be out of danger before too much longer."

Murdock couldn't believe it. "But we thought that the virus would kill them all. . . . I mean, they were dying so fast and the other men . . . all eighty-nine of them."

"They could have died. Should have, in fact. I don't understand why they didn't."

"This is wonderful news!"

"What treatment did you give them, Commander?"

"Very little. Our medical officer tried but he was one of the first to succumb, and after that Captain West ordered the watertight doors closed." Murdock went on to tell him everything that had happened in those horrible hours of waiting for the medical helicopter to arrive.

At the end Kester nodded understandingly. "Well that was it, then. Your captain is responsible for saving their lives. You see, many viruses, particularly man-made viruses that the human immune system can't fight off, oxidize quickly once they're exposed to the air. This is the only thing that prevents a single outbreak of deadly disease from wiping out the planet. The question is, how long can a virus survive before infecting living tissue? By sealing off the forward and lower decks, West stopped the disease from spreading. By flooding the areas with oxygen, he hastened its destruction. He not only saved all of your lives, but those of the men in the contaminated areas as well.''

"Then you think this was a man-made virus?''

Captain Kester shrugged. "Most likely,'' he said. "Don't you believe the epidemic and the assault were coordinated?''

"Yes. That's clear enough in hindsight. But we don't know how the virus got on the sub or how it was spread from one compartment to another. We don't understand why some of us never even got sick, while others who were working just a few feet away died screaming in a matter of minutes. Nor do we understand how those Islamic holy warriors knew that they wouldn't get sick when they opened up the contaminated sections.''

The captain was nodding, as another doctor might on hearing a man describe the symptoms of his affliction. He waited patiently for Murdock to finish. And then he replied matter-of-factly, as any doctor will, with what he'd intended to say before the patient had so much as opened his mouth.

"Well, assuming Kaseem's men had some way to introduce the virus onto the *Alaska,* there are really only a couple of ways they could have protected themselves and those members of the crew they needed to man the stations. One way would be to inoculate themselves and some of the crew in advance of the epidemic. But that might be tricky. Inoculations don't always work and their people might still get sick, too sick to do their jobs even if they didn't die. The other way was to use a virus with a very quick period of oxidation. And to make sure it only strikes within those compartments where everyone is expendable. Apparently this is what they did.''

"But where'd they get a virus like that?''

"I have no idea.''

"From your research center?''

"I'm sure the Navy investigators will want to consider that possibility very carefully.'' Captain Kester stood up. "Kaseem sent me in here to check you out, Commander. He's convinced he'll need you before this is over. But I have to get back to the CPO quarters. They've moved all the sick in there.''

"Where are the other men?''

"In their mess. Except for the few at their stations.'' Kester pointed to the overhead. "There's a guard positioned to keep an eye on the mess, my patients, and that passing scuttle at the same time. Kaseem feels it will be easier to control the whitehats if he isolates the officers.''

"But they're all right?''

"Don't worry about them, Commander. Just figure out a way to get us all out of this in one piece.''

Kester passed between Shorter and Buchanan and made for the door.

A sense of relief staggered Murdock. He felt as though a great burden had been lifted from his back. Captain West's decision to seal off the contaminated compartments had been vindicated. So far Murdock had made only one decision, and that—

"One more thing, Doctor. Have you seen a lieutenant commander? His name is Scott Longfellow.''

Kester turned. "Yes, I saw him. A few minutes ago. Just before I came in here.''

"Is he dead?''

"Yes. His neck was broken.''

Murdock's mouth formed a thin line.

"I told you that all of my technicians had been shot,''

Kester continued, "but that's not exactly how it happened. Four of my people died the same way as your lieutenant commander. Their necks were broken. I watched Kaseem do it. You can believe I'll be seeing that in my dreams for a long time to come." He shook off his reflections. "Meanwhile, I've got a job to do here."

Kester's speech had been punctuated by the faint crunching of broken glass—the same sound Murdock had heard before—but it ended after the doctor rapped twice on the door. When the door opened he passed through, giving a half smile and a wave to the five officers.

Murdock didn't know what to think about Kester. The man showed every evidence of being just what he claimed, and yet Murdock couldn't help doubting. In the back of his mind he knew that it was the doctor and Captain West together who had succeeded in saving nearly a hundred of his men. Murdock put this success at Kester's doorstep. At his own doorstep was the responsibility for Scott Longfellow's death. Murdock had decided that none of them should cooperate with Kaseem. Nothing yet had vindicated that decision.

Just maybe, thought Murdock, Kester had a better right to command than Murdock himself.

"What do we do, skipper?" asked Buchanan. Shorter was standing beside him.

Murdock shrugged. "Stow that torpedo, Ben."

"And then?"

"What do you mean?"

"We could go to work on one of the torpedoes hanging over the bunks. It'd be slower going. But if anyone came in we could just lay back and pretend to be dozing. Commander Shorter and I—"

"You haven't got any tools."

Buchanan smiled and pulled his hands from his pockets. In one was a pair of screwdrivers and in the other a small set of wrenches. But his pockets were still bulging. "I grabbed everything I could while the commander here blocked Kaseem's way," he said. "He took more of a chance than I did.".

Murdock smiled. "Okay. Stow that torpedo and then go to work on one of the others. But be careful. We thought there were only a handful of us left; now we know there're at least a hundred or more. If you make a mistake they'll all pay the price, too." It didn't occur to Murdock until after the two officers had turned away how absurd this must have sounded. If things went according to plan the forward spaces would flood and the *Alaska* be sent to the bottom, where she would inevitably implode.

It was merely an option, Murdock tried to convince himself.

He walked to the door, knelt, and examined the grating of the deck. There were dozens of glass fragments, most of them slivers no larger than pencil points. Foot traffic had ground the rest into powder. But several fragments were big enough to identify—they were very thin, and curved like the base of a small jar.

Murdock didn't need to pick them up and inspect them to know what they were. But where had they come from? He couldn't begin to guess. He stood up. He worked the pieces into a pile with the toe of his shoe and then stepped on the pile until he had ground it to bits.

"Skipper?"

Murdock came slowly around. "What is it, Thomas?"

"Are you really gonna do it, sir? Blow up that torpedo in the tube and kill us and everybody else?"

Murdock placed a gentle hand against the young ensign's mouth and eased him away from the door. "Maybe it won't come to that."

"But you will do it if you think that. . . ?"

"Yes. Unless I'm dead. In that case Commander Shorter will do it. If he's dead, Commander Buchanan will do it." Murdock waved a hand toward the navigator.

"If not him, then Lieutenant Fletcher. And if not the lieutenant, then you'll do it."

"I'm not sure I could, sir."

"I'm sure."

"Yes, sir, but you're—"

"No, Ensign, I'm sure that you'll do it. Because if it comes to that there won't be an option. You know why we're out here; you know what those missiles can do. Now try to imagine how you'd feel if this submarine surfaced just after a series of nuclear explosions had devastated the United States. If every city of any size had been reduced to blackened radioactive rubble—not just New York or Chicago or Los Angeles, but two hundred cities—a thermonuclear furnace from one coast to the other." Murdock smiled grimly. "The dead would be the lucky ones. For you and me it would be worst of all. We could only watch them all die and know that it was our job to stop it."

Thomas was shaking his head.

"When that happens, skipper, there'll be nothing to go back for—nothing to live for. I'll do what has to be done, the same as the other guys, and when I have, I'll . . . well, I'll kill myself."

"It'll be too late for that, Ensign. I'm not talking about a war with the Soviet Union. I'm talking about the *Alaska*. All that is what this Trident submarine is capable of doing if Kaseem figures out how to retarget those missiles. If he doesn't, but starts a war with the Russians by launching the missiles at them, the end result would be the same. You'll kill yourself. So will I if it comes to that. But we won't do it because we failed in our duty; We'll kill ourselves sending this boat to the bottom, because that's the one way to make sure that those missiles don't launch."

# Chapter Sixteen

Drew Murdock was standing in front of the starboard torpedo tube nest when it blew. A wall of heat and pressure slammed into his face. The blast should have ripped him to pieces. It should have hurled him against the bulkhead with enough force to break every bone in his body.

But it didn't.

Murdock was still on his feet. He saw and heard the torpedo tube door whiz by his head like a ballistic frisbee. A horizontal column of seawater two feet in diameter—with one hundred tons of pressure behind it—caught him full on the chest. It picked him up and blasted him into the watertight door. That should have finished him, too.

But it didn't.

He was swept down a raging river with banks too hard to hold on to and too sheer to climb. The passageway! Somehow he'd crashed through the torpedo room door. The lower deck would flood now; nothing could keep the *Alaska* from plunging to the bottom. To know that he'd stopped Kaseem from firing the missiles ought to have given Murdock one last measure of satisfaction along with his grief.

But it didn't.

Kaseem was waiting for him. Waiting at the end of the passageway. While Murdock was fighting for every breath Kaseem waded toward him, grinning with wolfish delight. The same current that pushed Murdock inescapably into those huge hands barely reached to Kaseem's waist. No matter how hard Murdock struggled he couldn't slow down. The river carried him into the missile compartment. Between the launch tubes. Kaseem clawed at the water as though to speed Murdock toward him. He folded his fists and pounded on the surface, sending plumes of spray high into the air.

"It's too late!" Kaseem was shouting. "The missiles are on their way!"

God, it was true! Murdock could see right through the launch tubes. Empty. Every last one was empty. He looked up through the submarine's double hull and the sea. Twenty-four missiles were streaking into the sky. His vision ended when a giant pair of hands closed over his face and slowly began to squeeze.

Murdock bolted upright.

He sat up so fast that he banged his head on a torpedo hanging over his bunk. He looked warily around—the torpedo had not exploded, the *Alaska* had not been flooded, and Kaseem had not fired the missiles . . . not yet.

On the other side of the room, Dr. Kester and Ensign Thomas were sleeping. Lieutenant Fletcher, sitting near the door, was gawking at Murdock.

"Are you okay, skipper?" asked Shorter.

"I'm all right—just a bad dream. I feel like a damn fool. Haven't had one of those in years."

"If you've slept at all you're a better man than I am; I haven't been able to sleep in two days. Not since those bastards came aboard. And I get nightmares without closing my eyes."

"Your timing is good, sir." That was Buchanan's voice. Murdock cranked his head under the bunk to find the weapons officer putting the last two screws on the torpedo warhead's inspection cover plate. "Can you give us a hand loading 'er into the tube?"

"You've done it?"

"Yes, sir."

They had been working off and on for nearly forty hours to rewire the warhead. Kaseem or his soldiers had made four more appearances altogether, but they hadn't discovered what Murdock's men were up to. In those two days Captain Kester had been in and out—but mostly out—coming here to eat and to rest and then returning to his patients.

By the time Buchanan had vented the number two tube of water and disconnected the ready light on the firing panel, Shorter and Murdock had slung a chain around the torpedo and lowered it onto the dolly. They rolled it to the starboard tube nest, slid it into the waiting tube, closed the breech door, and flooded the chamber. Kaseem could look through the sight glass, he could check the firing panel, but no casual inspection would betray the fact that the tube was loaded.

"When the time comes, all you'll have to do is hit the firing key," said Buchanan. "That will detonate the torpedo warhead instead of starting the engine. You won't even have to open the muzzle door. Both doors will blow together."

"Did you put a delay on it?" asked Murdock.

"I didn't bother to, skipper. If we have to fire this damn thing, everyone on the boat is gonna die. Myself, I'd rather get blown to pieces than drown."

The three men checked Captain Kester and verified that he was still asleep.

"Now what?" the reactor officer wanted to know.

"I've been thinking about that, Shorty."

In fact, Murdock had been thinking about nothing else for the past twenty-four hours. It was easy enough to say that the *Alaska* should be destroyed if it became necessary, and they had figured out a way to do it when the time came. But how were they to know if or when? Moreover, Murdock had decided that it wasn't his job to destroy a one-and-a-half-billion-dollar submarine. It was his job to save her, if it could be done. But they wouldn't know this, either, unless they found out what was happening. Where was the *Alaska* going? What were Kaseem's plans? What could be done to stop him? And how could they find out?

The answer was obvious. Captain Kester had given the answer to him. And the more Murdock thought about it, the more he decided that Kester was right. They would have to go back to their jobs.

"You mean cooperate with the terrorists?" an astonished Shorter had asked him.

"Not cooperate. Just go along with them until a better chance presents itself."

Shorter, Fletcher, and Buchanan exchanged glances. This, almost word for word, had been Kester's advice to them two days before.

When Kaseem came down the next morning and took Thomas away, the communications officer already had his instructions from Murdock. He was to resist their coercions for a little while, but only halfheartedly. "Don't risk getting hurt," Murdock warned him. "We need you to find out what you can." After the bullying reached a certain point, Thomas was to go to his station and do as Kaseem ordered.

He didn't report until nearly ten hours later, when he returned to the torpedo room hungry and exhausted. "What've they got you doing, Thomas, rearranging the furniture?" said Shorter, making a joking reference to the essential fittings on a ship such as masts, davits, derricks, and capstans that are not even found on a submarine.

"I wish that was all," he replied. "It's Kaseem. He tramps about the control room all day long stinking of alcohol and strong-arming the crew; he practically beat a couple of the men to death. Everyone is on tenterhooks. That's okay for a little while, but not for full shifts day after day."

Shorter heaved a deep breath. "One day, when we've had all of that guy we can take, somebody needs to give him some of his own medicine. If he calls me up tomorrow—"

"You'll wait for my go-ahead, Shorty. Just like we agreed." The reactor officer clamped his jaw and nodded acquiescence, but he couldn't quite force a "Yes, sir" from between his clenched teeth. Murdock turned to the ensign. "What'd he want with you, mister?" he asked.

"Checking up on my SOs. Kaseem ran them out before I came in and had me on the phones listening to the traffic. If I didn't give him the same answers they did, he promised to kill us all. I tried to tell him that Fencil and the two other sonar operators had more experience interpreting than I did, and if one of us was wrong it would probably be me, but that doesn't mean anything to Kaseem. He'd sooner kill all four of us than wonder."

"Did you hear anything? What did you tell him?"

"I told him the truth."

"Let's have it."

"We're being shadowed, skipper."

"By what?"

"Another submarine. It's hanging a hundred yards off our port quarter, matching our course and speed."

Murdock was suddenly hopeful. "One of ours?"

Thomas shook his head. "No, a Soviet sub. I think it's a Kilo-class SSK, but I can't be sure. Fencil would know."

"What did Kaseem say to that?"

"He didn't say anything at all. But I didn't believe it surprised him any. Certainly it didn't upset him."

"What do you mean?"

"I'm still alive, aren't I?"

The next day they came for Lieutenant Fletcher as well as Ensign Thomas. And that evening the navigator was able to confirm the stories of harassment and brutality on the command center deck.

"The men can't take much more," said Fletcher. "They'd like to see you on the bridge, skipper. It would make them feel a lot better."

"Kaseem is saving me for something special, Navigator. What about our position?"

"He's doublechecking my quartermaster, just like he did Thomas's SOs," Fletcher said. Every three hours Kaseem sent the QM down to the enlisted men's mess and brought Fletcher in to interpret the SINS readout. The two men never saw one another. They had no opportunity to concoct a false position report. And if their reports didn't match, neither had any doubts about what would happen.

"So where are we?" Murdock asked again.

"Skirting the Marshall Islands. It looks like we're headed for the Indian Ocean."

"Why?"

"Isn't it obvious? Once he gets to the Indian Ocean he can threaten the whole Middle East. Who's number one on the Iranians' hate list—besides the Great Satan in Washington, that is? The Iraqis? The Israelis? It wouldn't take more than a missile or two to eliminate either of those countries."

Murdock seemed lost in concentration. "If he passes anywhere near the Marshalls, he's going to get picked up by OSIS. They've got hydrophones on the shelf all around the islands."

"I wouldn't count on it," said Fletcher. "Do you know what I saw up there? He's got a map. A map that pinpoints every hydrophone in the OSIS system. He knows just where to sail to avoid them."

"Where in God's name did he get that?"

"I don't know, but he's got it. Our only hope of being picked up is if the Navy gets lucky. They must have every

ASW surface ship and aircraft in the fleet out looking for us. They're dropping sonobuoys all over the ocean.''

"It's a big ocean, Navigator.''

Thomas broke in with more bad news. "That rattletrap Soviet sub is still hanging with us,'' he said. "As long as it is, no hydrophone or sonobuoy is going to hear anything else, unless it's sitting right on top of our fair-weather.''

They discussed the terrorists in general and Kaseem in particular well into the night. The news that Fletcher and Thomas brought down from the control deck reinforced their suspicions that Kaseem knew his way about a submarine. "He has been around,'' said the lieutenant, "but I don't think he knows as much as he wants us to believe. If he knew how to read the SINS he wouldn't need to play games with me and my QM. The same goes for sonar. He knows the big things, most of them, but he makes little mistakes. He'll say or do something that doesn't come off quite right. I doubt he has any command center experience. If you ask me, it'll be a little thing that gets him in trouble.''

The following day their weapons officer pulled duty on the command center staff, and the day after that Shorter joined him, supervising the reactor spaces and doubling as engineering officer in Scott Longfellow's absence. Murdock had the torpedo room to himself—except for an occasional visit by Dr. Kester. It was pretty clear Kaseem wanted to undermine Murdock's resistance to cooperation by getting all of his officers to cave in first.

"Something's up,'' Fletcher announced when he returned to the torpedo room to eat and sleep. The others had come down with him. For some reason he hadn't explained, Kaseem was working the four officers together instead of rotating them in shifts. Presumably it had to do with the way they were guarded, but no one knew for sure.

"Yeah, I know,'' replied Shorter.

"What do we know, gentlemen?"

Fletcher answered. "We've turned around. We're now heading back toward the Hawaiian Islands."

"What? Are you sure?"

"Jesus, skipper, how could I be wrong about something like that? Kaseem asked for the headings and I gave them to him. The QM and I verified our position at regular intervals throughout the day."

"What's going on?"

"I don't know, sir."

"What about you, Ensign? Has Kaseem gotten any word from outside? Any radio messages?"

"No, sir. But I can tell you one thing? That Soviet sub has turned around, too. It's still hanging out there like a ghost."

"What do you know, Shorty?"

"They've changed their tactics. Before it was go, go, go. Nothing mattered but speed. We'd been running flank speed for days. Now Kaseem wants to cool it. First thing this morning he ordered the machinist mate to reduce speed to two-thirds." Shorter finished his peaches and set down the can—Kaseem's men had distributed nothing but canned goods since the takeover began. "With reduced power output," Shorter continued, "Kaseem was able to shut down the pumps in the primary loop. This means we're using natural convection rather than the pumps for the circulation of pressurized water. What little noise we were turning out before has just been slashed by half. The man is no fool. He knows what he's doing, and he's gotten hold of some mighty sensitive stuff."

"That's when we changed directions," offered Fletcher. "First thing this morning."

Before Murdock's men could tell him any more, a hammering on the door warned them to silence. When Captain Kester came in and the door closed again, they invited him to join them for dinner. Conversation after that was polite but spotty. For the most part it dealt with the disappointing fare and the health of the *Alaska*'s recuperating crew. No one spoke of these other matters.

It was just as well. Murdock wanted time to consider. He was convinced that Kaseem, initially at least, had needed to get clear of the Navy search teams. This had meant speed at any cost. Maximum speed. And the cost was maximum noise. Maybe Kaseem hadn't cared so much if the Navy got a whiff of his trail so long as it believed his trail led west into the Indian Ocean, where he could threaten the whole Middle East. Now everything had changed. The second phase of their plan had begun. They were sneaking back to the east, toward the United States. The most important thing to Kaseem and his men now was not how long it took them to get where they were going but that they not be heard coming back.

For the fifth night in a row Commander Murdock dreamed his nightmare of the *Alaska*'s destruction. Every night had been the same. Every nightmare had been the same, too. The *Alaska* was always destroyed; his shipmates always died; and always it was too late to stop the missiles from launching. The only difference this time was that when he woke, Murdock was ordered back to work along with his officers.

Kaseem took him to the captain's cabin.

"Okay, sonny. It's your turn to play."

"I've told you, Kaseem, I won't help you."

"You're all alone, Commander. Your men, your officers, they've all done as I've told them. I've got enough crew to get along without you. But if that's the way you want it, you won't leave this cabin alive."

"Is that the way *you* want it?"

Kaseem bared his teeth. "Maybe it is."

"I'll go where you order me to go. I'll say what you order me to say. But I'm going to do everything in my power to save this submarine."

"That's just fine with me, sonny boy. That's what I want you to do, keep this boat in one piece."

"But if you try to launch any missiles I'll stop you. Somehow I'll stop you."

A stream of air shot from Kaseem's lips; Murdock now understood that this was the only kind of laughter the man permitted himself. "Sure you will, sonny. Okay, let's go!"

In the navigation center Kaseem laid out a nautical chart on the table in front of Murdock and Fletcher.

"The Johnston Islands?" asked Murdock.

"You know them?"

"I know of them. There isn't much there. Three small islands and a lagoon surrounded by coral reefs."

"That's right. We'll get there sometime late tomorrow afternoon. That will give us two or three hours at most to navigate this channel to the north and get into the lagoon before nightfall."

"It shouldn't be a problem. The channel is certainly deep enough, according to these charts."

"Very funny. You'd love to see me break the surface, wouldn't you? Well, I will surface. But not until after dark when we can't be spotted by satellites and I've made damn sure there are no Navy ships in the vicinity."

"There won't be. That whole area has been placed off limits until further notice."

"Don't you think I know that? But I'm still taking no chances. We'll go in along the bottom—just as deep as the channel will allow—to avoid setting off hydrophones on the shelf here and here." Kaseem pointed to the east and west sides of the reefs. "Can you do it?"

"Yeah, I can do it."

Murdock's job, briefly put, was to be telephone talker. He was to wear the headphones connecting the command center to the engine room and reactor section, so that Kaseem himself would be free to stalk from navigation all the way forward to radio and sonar. It was up to Murdock to see that they didn't crash into the bottom. But he had to do it the way Kaseem wanted it done.

That night, Murdock mulled matters over.

There was nothing in the Johnstons of any importance; the chain had no value except for its guaranteed isolation. No one was supposed to go anywhere near those reefs, and no one would ever suspect the *Alaska* would sail there. It was the perfect site for a rendezvous. But a rendezvous with whom, and why? Would Kaseem's men debark? Would they take on even more terrorists? Offload one or all of the Trident missiles? Whatever their scheme, the *Alaska* would never be allowed to sail away. All of the officers and enlisted men would be killed, if not at the Johnstons then at the next rendezvous point or the one after that.

As commander, Murdock couldn't allow this to happen.

The next afternoon, while Kaseem prowled from station to station, shook his balled fists in the air, and vented his rage against the crew, Murdock made up his mind.

The waters had grown rapidly shallow, from five thousand feet to five hundred in a matter of miles. No one spoke unnecessarily. They waited for the reports from sonar to come over the squawk box. But more than this, they waited for the staggering crunch of the sub running aground; for the rupturing of steel, the surge of seawater flooding the forward compartments, and the cries of men trapped behind watertight doors that no one dared open.

Only the sound of Kaseem's heavy footfalls making his endless circuit broke the nerve-shattering silence.

"Conn, this is sonar; bottom seventy feet below our keel and still coming up."

With the same single-mindedness with which the crew watched their instruments and Kaseem and his men watched the crew, Murdock was watching Kaseem. He knows, Murdock said to himself. He's a predator who can sense the hunter on his trail. But it's your turn to sweat, thought Murdock, and my turn to prey.

Blowing up the torpedo room in deep water would

surely finish the sub. That had to remain a final option. But now there was a better way—Captain Kester's better chance presenting itself. When the *Alaska* rammed the coral reefs at full speed the bow would collapse, the pressure hull would rupture, and the forward compartments would fill with seawater. Perhaps the lower decks, too. The submarine would lie like a stone on the bottom.

*"Sonar!"* screamed Kaseem.

"Sonar."

*"No contacts? Nothing at all?"*

"I'm reading bottom three hundred feet and rising fast. Fifty feet under our keel. We have to slow down or surface."

Kaseem began raving, but Murdock hardly heard him.

If they sank in water this shallow many of the crew would survive. Not all, maybe, but many of them. They would be trapped together, seamen and terrorists alike, in the compartments that remained watertight.

Kaseem shouted.

*"Bring power to two-thirds."*

Murdock passed the orders on to engineering.

But three hundred feet, even two hundred feet, is too deep to launch missiles. Like the torpedos the rocket engines don't engage until they are well clear of the sub, but in the case of the missiles they engage automatically upon breaking the surface. The sixty-ton projectiles are thrown from their launching tubes by pools of cooling water under the missile canisters that are instantaneously boiled into steam. Below one hundred feet the pressure is too great for the missiles to reach the surface.

Very soon Kaseem ordered power reduced to one-third and Murdock passed this on to engineering, too.

And one more thing, thought Murdock. Navy hydrophones would pick up the sound of their crash. It would be flashed to OSIS command headquarters via satellite. Within hours, rescue vessels would be steaming to the Johnston Islands.

Murdock had made up his mind.

"Conn, sonar; it's a blind canyon. There's no way out of it. Recommend . . . No, there's no choice, we'll have to come up."

*"No!"* shouted Kaseem. Then he whirled and faced Murdock. *"Full stop."*

Murdock grinned. Stall him along until it's too late, he thought. Then he said calmly, "Are you ordering a 'Stop' or a 'Stop Shaft'?"

Kaseem began screaming.

While sonar warned them of obstructions at five hundred yards and called off the seconds to impact, Murdock casually explained the various stop orders and their interpretations by the engineering staff. Kaseem threw himself into a fury. He was on the point of charging across the command center when Murdock spoke into his headset, "Engineering."

"Here, skipper."

"Ahead full."

"What was that, skipper?"

"You heard me. Ahead full. Do it, goddammit!" Then Murdock turned and smashed the headset against the bulkhead. Before he could turn back around, Kaseem had lifted him into the air and thrown him to the deck. Then he was kneeling on Murdock's chest, driving his great fists into Murdock's face.

The last thing Murdock heard was a hellish clanging of metals. Once, and then once again. Right over their heads. Everyone stared at the overhead and Murdock heard Kaseem bellow: *"What the hell was that?"*

He didn't hear or see any more.

Not for a long time.

The undertow dragged him down. Currents carried him far out to sea. Once again time lost its meaning to him, but on this occasion he did not hover in darkness between agony and eternity, free to choose the way that he moved. He hovered in darkness, balancing on a layer between the surface and the ultimate depths from which nothing arises. He couldn't move. Finally, however, the sea carried him back and tossed his body up on the land. A castaway of his own consciousness. How long he'd been adrift or to what foreign shore he had washed, Murdock had no way of knowing.

This wasn't the command center. That much he knew. Neither was it the ship's study or the torpedo room. He could barely make out the banks of control stations and computer terminals, which looked more than vaguely familiar, but his mind couldn't summon the name of this compartment.

He saw faces around him that also struck him with a vague familiarity, but these too remained just outside his complete comprehension. He could recognize, but he could not identify. It was to the nearest of these faces that he posed the classic question: "Where am I?"

"We're in the missile control center, sir."

"Thomas?"

"Yes, sir."

"What are we doing in here? I—I remember getting my brains beat in on the command center. . . ."

"That was yesterday, skipper. You've been unconscious for almost eighteen hours."

Thomas spoke in hushed tones until the whole story was out. As soon as the *Alaska* was sailing straight and level Murdock and his four officers had been hustled back to the torpedo room, where they'd remained through the night. A half hour before, the guards had escorted them here. Murdock had been carried in by Shorter and Buchanan. Thomas ended his story by saying: "I think they've brought us all here to be shot."

"What's . . . ?" Murdock struggled to rise.

"Don't get up, skipper. The doctor says you've got internal bleeding. Some cracked ribs. He doesn't want—"

271

"What's going on?" Murdock's voice was a blend of fear and pain.

"Kaseem's mad as hell, skipper. The Navy's found us. They're coming after us. An attack sub and a sub-chaser, too. Everybody thought they'd dropped an ash can on us, a depth charge that just failed to explode, but now Kaseem says his men found some kind of transmitter, a screamer they think, and put it over the side. He's taken us back out to sea."

"That's crazy. The Navy hasn't—"

"He is crazy, skipper. He plans to fire one of the Trident missiles to show the Navy he means business."

"God . . . !"

Murdock groped for a wall, pulled himself against it, and propped up his back. He surveyed the room through eyes that still viewed the world from the murky obscurity of the depths. Fletcher and Shorter and Buchanan were across the room, being guarded by Kaseem's gunmen. Kaseem himself was nowhere to be seen.

"We've got to stop him!" said Murdock.

Thomas put a restraining hand on Murdock's shoulder and for the first time Murdock saw the gunman, standing over them but off to one side.

They sensed as much as heard Kaseem's entrance. He passed Murdock and Thomas without so much as a downward glance and advanced right toward the other small body of men on the opposite side of the room. Commander Buchanan made as if to rise from his chair at one of the control stations but he was shoved back into his seat.

*"Get started!"*

Buchanan shook his head. "I refuse to take part in this. You can kill me if you want to, but I refuse to help you."

"I'll kill you, all right, but you won't die first." Kaseem turned, grabbed Fletcher with a sudden movement, and dragged him over to where Buchanan could see. Then he shoved a pistol against the navigator's head.

"It won't work, Kaseem!" cried Buchanan. "One life for two million lives. I can't make that trade."

"Not one life. One hundred lives. I'll drag your men in here one at a time and keep blowing out brains until you do what I tell you. This man is first. Then the commander, and after him your communications officer and exec. After they're dead we'll start shooting bluejackets."

Everyone believed him. There wasn't any reason to doubt he would do exactly as he threatened to do.

But Buchanan only shook his head in despair.

*"Well?"*

"I can't."

The pistol exploded. Fletcher didn't fall back because Kaseem still had a hold on his shirt, but his head was rocked viciously to the side. When Kaseem did release his grip, the body dropped in a lifeless mound.

Shorter was roaring with anger. Two of the gunmen were holding him back, but only just barely.

Buchanan, staring at the body in dumb horror, uttered not a sound.

When Murdock made a futile attempt to get up, a rifle muzzle pushed him back down, and for a moment he again felt the waves of delirium lapping at his mind.

"What do you say now, Commander?"

"Goddammit, I can't. I just can't." Buchanan was almost in tears.

Kaseem spun. With one hand he snatched Commander Shorter from the clasp of his gunmen and pulled him in front of Buchanan. He pressed the pistol against Shorter's head.

*"Last chance!"*

Buchanan appealed to Murdock without words.

For an instant Shorter was watching Murdock, too. He

also was wordlessly appealing, but his was a different kind of appeal.

"Okay!" Murdock called. "I told you not to do it unless I gave the word. Go ahead."

Kaseem showed his teeth. And, not realizing to whom Murdock spoke, his grip on the reactor officer eased just a bit.

Kaseem's men seemed to relax at the same time.

They had been prepared for resistance of a kind, for defiance and refusal. But they were not prepared for the sort of assault that Shorter launched. After all, the reactor officer was shorter than Kaseem by nearly a foot and lighter by at least fifty pounds. But Shorter was also exceptionally strong. When he knocked the gun from Kaseem's hand, it went clattering across the room. In that one moment of surprise Shorter was on him. He landed two body punches with all of his weight behind them, and when Kaseem bent over and covered up his stomach Shorter's uppercut was the stuff of which knockouts are made.

Kaseem didn't go out. But he staggered back wounded and confused. His men stared in dull wonder at seeing their leader hurt, their expressions those of disciples watching a god suddenly revealed as a mortal.

In the confusion, Murdock called for Thomas to get to the torpedo room.

The communications officer leapt for the door, but the gunman beside them moved faster yet. His weapon hammered out a fusillade into the corridor.

Murdock managed to sweep the gunman's legs from under him, then clambered to his feet and staggered out behind Thomas. The body lay there near the ladder. There was no time to stop. More shooting erupted behind him, but he didn't stop for this either. He heard shouting, men coming to action. And above it all came the crazed cries of Musa al-Kaseem.

Murdock's first step on the ladder failed him. He grabbed at the rails and missed.

He struck the landing of Deck Three with a shocking concussion of flesh against steel. A grunt of agony, and all of his wind burst from his lungs. His head was spinning. "Ten seconds," he grunted. All he needed of life was ten more seconds. But when Murdock looked up, he knew he wouldn't get them. The mess guard was only yards away, reaching for his weapon and getting to his feet; the ladderway to Deck Four was only a few yards beyond, but it might just as well have been back at Pearl Harbor for any hope Murdock had of reaching it in time. But the torpedo passing scuttle? Murdock swiveled the closure, pulled open the hatch, and dove through the hole headfirst. He fell headlong to the torpedo room grating.

Footsteps banged a barrage on the ladder above him. There was hammering on the dogs of the torpedo room door and the wheel was already turning.

Murdock dragged himself to the starboard torpedo nest. He used the valve handles to pull himself to his feet.

The number two firing key was barely within reach.

No reason to stand to one side.

Only in dreams did a man walk away from an explosion like this one.

He heard voices behind him.

An action thrown back on a machine pistol.

"Fuck 'em all," he thought.

He turned the key, folded his fist, and pounded the firing button home with his last ounce of strength. By any rational calculation this single, simple exercise should have brought the Murdock lineage to a finish, an expeditious and explosive end of the line.

But it didn't.

# Chapter Seventeen

NEPTUNE'S RACE

and just seemed able to suck the blood from his veins.
It left his body numb and his mind . . . cold . . . . . . .
with terror . . . . he could not

Twelve hours and four hundred miles had worked a remarkable transformation in the sea. In the turbid,
plankton-rich, and virescent shallows of the Johnston
reefs it had been a green of emeralds and jade. Now, a
hundred feet below the surface of the virtually bottom-
less tropical Pacific, the water was startlingly clear and
blue.

If Coy Murdock was even aware of this change he did
not give a damn.

He was oblivious to everything except his own survival. Twelve hours and four hundred miles had worked
an even more remarkable transformation in Murdock
himself.

For twelve hours and four hundred miles he had clung
to the *Alaska*'s rudder, an inch and an instant from doom.
Two of the hydrophone's three grapnel-like legs had
snagged the leading edge of the soaring vertical fin. Murdock had held onto the third with both pincers; he'd
squeezed the handles so tight and so long that his fists
shook and blood oozed from beneath his fingernails.
Blood beaded the backs of his hands like sweat. In the
tremendous race of water Murdock's armored body waved
like an ensign; his feet flailed right in front of the propeller. That in itself was enough to unnerve any man. Its
enormous suction tugged at his suit, and the throb of its
nine-foot blades pounded right into his skull. It never
stopped. Even through his armor this maelstrom of froth

and fury seemed able to suck the blood from his veins. It left him cringing with terror, trembling with cold. His arms ached horribly. He was physically and mentally spent. And yet he knew if he relaxed his hold even for a moment, he would be sucked into the vortex before he could draw his next breath or hurl his last shriek of terror.

After twelve hours and four hundred miles of this horror Murdock was no better than a maniac.

He screamed at the top of his lungs. He cursed himself with every profanity in the language. There were times when tears ran down his face. And there were other times when he whistled and hummed little tunes. He laughed out loud.

For hours on end he would be back on Glen Murdock's old salvor, clinging to the lifeline with both hands while the ship rose and fell above the sea, his father shouting for him to dive in and swim to the bottom and his big brother Drew pleading with Murdock to stop.

This didn't matter either.

The screams and the profanities, the tunes and the laughter, the shouts and the pleas were lost the same second he made them, devoured by the propeller and thrown into the backwash.

The end was a long time coming, and even then it was only a respite.

The *Alaska* had turned back out to sea. She had dived at such an angle Murdock almost slid forward off the rudder. Finally she had leveled off and raced for the safety of the vast Pacific void.

A darkness had descended of the kind that exists in the greatest of depths. The *Alaska* was not capable of diving to these depths, but even shallower waters at night are a study in totality. It was night now. And the sub sped onward.

Murdock could see nothing. He was alone with a roaring and thrashing of the sea. An incredible din. He believed no other sound could ever surpass it for pure horror. But when the roar died, something even more horrifying remained. He was engulfed by nothingness—absolute silence and darkness surrounded him. He still gripped the handles, but for the first time he could feel his arms banging the insides of the armor. Outside the armor there was nothing. His head lay against the face-plate and his eyes closed. Maybe he was mad. Maybe the propeller thrashed on but his subconscious, choosing no longer to endure the horrors, had blanked it all out.

There was only one way to find out.

He let go his grip. Nothing happened—the propeller blades didn't hack their way through his armor.

He tried to retract his arms from the tubes, but they wouldn't come. He tried to feel what had caught them but couldn't. For the first time he realized he had no feeling at all in his hands. Everything beyond his elbows was numb. His fingers were still locked around the handles, frozen on the pincer controls.

There was nothing to do but wait.

Slowly a sense of feeling returned. His muscles relaxed. He heard two sharp clicks of the pincers being released, and then he drew his bleeding hands into the trunk of his suit.

Still, nothing happened.

Minutes elapsed while he wrung his hands. He rubbed them together and massaged his fingers.

He wiped the tears and sweat from his face. Then he pushed his hands back down the arm tubes, levered himself to a standing position, and turned on his helmet light. He was in a snowstorm. Tiny flakes of organic particles were falling all about him. With this exception the water was incredibly clear. He pointed the light at the rudder, the deck, and the darkness. Finally he played the beam astern. There it was. A nine-foot bronze blade staring him right in the face. No doubt about it, the propeller had stopped.

The hull to each side of the rudder was barely as wide as a sidewalk, and it began sloping downward almost at once. His legs were shaking so violently it was all he could do to stay on his feet without teetering over the edge.

He staggered up the slope of the *Alaska*'s main deck. The first thing he found was another bull's-eye and cross hairs of an emergency escape hatch, just like the one he had seen forward of the sail.

He stood for a while looking down at the round slab of steel no larger than a manhole cover. Light and warmth were just within. That much he knew. But could he ever get in? The escape hatches are twenty-six inches wide. His A1A suit was half again that in width, and he couldn't climb out of it while submerged. The water pressure wouldn't permit him to. He was trapped in his suit. And the suit was trapped outside the sub.

Once atop the slope he came to the launch deck. At his feet was yet another escape hatch. Beyond that lay a steel deck as wide and as long as a boulevard. Eight-foot circular cutouts in the surface ran two abreast down the length of the deck. These were the Trident missile tubes. The circles were fitted so flush to the metal, the edges and even the hinges, that they might have been chalk lines on the pavement.

A single rough stripe snaked between the tube pairs and ran the launch deck's length to the sail, a safety track for seamen working topside in heavy weather. Murdock used this track as a path and stumbled off down the missile tubes, like a wino down the centerline of a dark city street. When he'd counted off twenty-four of the doomsday doors he stopped.

The three-story sail blocked his path.

It rose thirty feet over his head, and when he turned his light upward he observed a cylindrical casing that was even then rising above the sail. After it had extended to its limit, another narrower cylinder with a curiously shaped masthead began rising from this. Before long this head disappeared through a sheet of bright water that shone through the darkness and reflected his light back down at him like a mirror. The surface!

What were they doing? Taking a sighting? Receiving or transmitting a radio message? If this was why the *Alaska* had stopped, she might begin moving again very soon.

Murdock had just started down the port side of the sail when a brief flame of light caught his eye. It appeared to be moving through the water off the sub's starboard beam. Reflection, or another light? He switched off his helmet light. Yes. Someone was swimming out there. Coming this way, and swinging his beam back and forth in Murdock's direction.

Keeping the sail between himself and the diver, Murdock moved forward until he could peer around the leading edge of the sail. There he was. No, Murdock suddenly realized, this was a second diver. The forward escape hatch was open and a man in scuba was waving a flashlight out into the darkness. Were they looking for him? Had they heard his feet on the deck? Damn him for making so much noise. Now he was trapped. There was no way to escape them: One would come down the right side of the sail and the other down the left. He couldn't leave the top of the sub and, big as it was, there were few places to hide. He couldn't run. He couldn't begin to fight them. These men might not even be armed, but all they would have to do was give him one little push off the main deck.

He found the rungs of a ladder welded right into the sail, which seemed to him to lead up to the sailplane and from there to the bridge. In his bulky armor and with only the pincers to hold on to the rungs, he started climbing.

One wrong move meant worse than discovery. If he fell, he wouldn't stop falling until he'd gone over the side. He took each step as quietly as possible, but with his own light off he was feeling his way from one rung to the next with the pincers and finding his foothold by dragging his iron boots up the side of the sail. Neither procedure was quiet. When he'd reached the port plane he stepped across. The bridge was ten or twelve feet higher up and the climbing now would be much more difficult. Up here the darkness was complete.

He moved to the front of the plane and looked down.

Just as he'd feared, they were working down both sides of the sail. But had this been their plan all along, or had they heard him climbing the ladder and come to investigate? Had they spotted his light?

It now occurred to Murdock that the first swimmer hadn't been searching, he'd been returning from somewhere out in the darkness. The second diver had merely been waiting with a signal light. It was probably Murdock's helmet light that had alerted them. Either that or his raucous ascent up the sail.

He remained frozen as one diver passed beneath him, his beam exploring the darkness by slashing back and forth over the hull. His buddy joined him behind the sail. They faced each other mask to mask, and in the glare of both flashlights amid clouds of air bubbles, the two divers exchanged frantic signals. When they parted, one began swimming clumsily down the launch deck toward the stern while the other aimed his light upward. At the sail.

This second diver wound his way up toward the top, circling the sail and throwing his light about helter-skelter, sometimes even whirling around and illuminating the emptiness of the sea as though he meant to impale one of its denizens on his beam. Watching him move clumsily through the darkness, Murdock decided the man was no more an expert than he himself. The way he kicked, the constant rush of bubbles exhausted from his mouthpiece. An amateur, thought Murdock, like me. He had to be nervous. Night-diving can unravel the nerves even of an experienced diver; this guy must be scared to death. Like Murdock.

He came over the trailing edge of the starboard plane first. His light swept the plane's upper surface all the way out to the end. But he came back hurriedly. Then he started around the sail to the other side.

There was only one way for Murdock to go.

He turned and walked out toward the tip of the plane. It was a nightmare gangplank. He wasn't blindfolded, but he might just as well have been. Certainly it was too dark for him to see the black, winglike surface of the plane, or where it ended in the black of the night. He could just keep going until he walked off the end, or he could risk the light stabbing into his back. He'd seen the planes from above that one time twelve hours ago. How long were they? Ten feet? No, longer than that. Twenty? Surely not. There was nothing to do but keep going and pray that the diver had an attack of nerves and turned back before he got all the way out.

Murdock took twelve small steps. Then he turned carefully around and remained still.

The diver was coming around the sail. He paddled up to the top and shone his light into the bridge. Finding nothing, he started down to the port plane.

Murdock backed up another step.

The beam's circle of light started moving out along the plane, switching from side to side.

Murdock took two more steps back and then two more yet. He had to be near the end.

His left boot went back and down.

And down.

At the same time as he threw his weight forward, another beam of light lanced over the plane and struck the diver on the face. The man turned and crossed beams with the second diver.

Then he dove over the edge to his buddy.

Murdock didn't move.

Both divers swam under the plane toward the forward air lock. One opened the hatch while the second dragged a heavy object right next to the opening. When the two flashlights played over the object, Murdock recognized it even from high above: the hydrophone. This wasn't what they'd expected to find but they'd found something, and they wasted no time calling off the search.

They tried lowering the hydrophone into the hatch, but it wouldn't go. One diver entered the air lock. Then his buddy handed it down to him. That didn't work any better. It was just too big. Murdock watched them signaling each other, and guessed that their debate was whether to throw it over the side now or let someone else make that decision. Apparently they dared not take it on themselves. They set the hydrophone down in front of the sail, entered the air lock together, and lowered the hatch.

It hit Murdock all at once. Maybe he was trapped out here and couldn't save himself, but there was still one thing he could do before his oxygen ran out or he was swept over the side. He could save that hydrophone.

Were its transmitters still working?

Was any craft close enough to receive a signal from it? Murdock had no way of knowing. But he had to assume that there was. He moved to the sail and started down. Now, even more than before, he must make no sound. There was a little time, but only a little. The air lock would have to be vented. Then it would be flooded again when someone else came up to take a look at the object and decide what to do.

His light was on now, but the process of climbing backward down the ladder was maddeningly slow. When at last he reached the deck Murdock trod carefully to the air lock, picked up the hydrophone with a pincer, and lugged it around to the back side of the sail.

He extinguished his light.

He didn't have long to wait. After only a few minutes he heard the hatch come open and saw a beam of light reach out of the hole. Then a head poked through. It was a huge head, with a mask covering a small oblong of eyes and nose. Instead of just swimming up, this diver stretched out first one arm and then the other and pried himself through the hole. And no wonder. His shoulders had to be three feet across. When he'd gotten as far as his waist the big man waved the light to the back, out onto the bow, and finally, over the sides.

If this guy felt the same way about walking the deck of the *Alaska* in pitch darkness as Murdock did, the hydrophone just might be written off as a casualty of currents, and the diver who had set it down would have the riot act read to him for not securing it better.

For once Murdock was lucky.

The light arced upward as the man squirmed back into the hatch. A moment later the light vanished.

The hatch closed.

And Murdock was alone again in the dark silence. He slew the darkness—or at least kept it at bay—by switching on his own helmet light once again. Then the silence died, too. A piercing whine came from above him. He directed his light at the sail. The masthead and casing were retracting into the bridge housing.

Almost at once he heard another sound: a slowly building roar. This sound he knew only too well. He turned toward the stern.

His light didn't even reach to the end of the launch deck, halfway to the stern. Marine snow clouded the water and the propeller was four hundred feet off. He couldn't see it turning. Yet he knew it was turning.

As he stood looking, these organic snowflakes drifted past his faceplate and streaked aft. The *Alaska* was moving again. Slowly at first, but soon too fast for him to hold on.

Even now he was leaning back into the flow, fighting to hold himself upright.

He'd never reach the stern in time. If he did, he'd never survive another twelve hours hanging on to the rudder.

Maybe he wouldn't have to.

The forward edge of the sail, wider and more rounded than the trailing edge, was just a few yards away. Still lugging the hydrophone he circled to the front, verified that the hatch was closed, backed up against the sail, and slid down until he was half sitting, half squatting, with his robot legs planted out in front of him and the hydrophone cradled in his lap.

Marine snow now swept right into his faceplate. His light bore through the blizzard like a fog lamp. Tons of water each second blasted against his armor. In a way, this was worse than hanging from the rudder.

When he turned off the light, the snow and the sea disappeared. He closed his eyes. Under conditions like these it was inconceivable that any sane man could sleep.

Murdock slept.


The transformation of the sea from green to blue that occurs as a result of deepening water, a loss of turbidity, and a change of microscopic life, can be subtle enough when viewed mile by mile through the course of the day. Murdock awoke to find the miraculous alchemy complete. And it was glaring.

The snowstorm had ended.

With the first hint of sunlight the emerald waters had been replaced by turquoise for as far as he could see in every direction except down, where the black jade of the depths was now sapphire. Darkness was spilling over the sides of the sub, deepening the sapphire and brightening the surface gems to pure water. But the only thing Murdock took notice of was the miracle that he could, in fact, see. He had somehow lived through the night.

What's more, the *Alaska* had stopped again. She was surfacing. Someone could come through the escape hatch at any moment.

With maddening awkwardness he struggled to his feet and then straightened up. No need for his helmet light now. He could see clearly. So would any divers that came out to get him. Hide-and-seek time was over.

He moved to the back of the sail.

A whine turned his attention upward. High above, one of the masts was reaching for the surface.

Everything that had happened the previous night was repeating itself.

There was no place to hide. All he could do was go to the rudder and hope they wouldn't search there again. But he'd only taken a dozen steps across the launch deck when he remembered the hydrophone. He couldn't leave it behind. He'd have to go back and get it.

Three things happened at once.

Murdock turned. That was the first.

His heart stopped. That was second.

His blood ceased to flow in his veins and his body shivered with cold. Instinctively he'd inhaled. And then his lungs froze. But all of these were not separate events. They were the effect of Event Number Three:

One of the missiles tubes had come open.

He should have stepped back a few paces. But he didn't. He should have turned and run. But he couldn't. When your heart has stopped beating and your lungs no longer draw air, you don't get very far. You stand where you are with your mouth hanging open and your eyes refusing to blink and you pray that somehow what you see isn't real.

But Murdock knew this was real.

They were getting ready to launch.

The eight-foot hatch fell back on its outboard hinges, exposing not an open hole but a white, cone-shaped closure seal immediately below, which prevented seawater from coming into the launcher. Murdock could hear and see nothing more, but he knew what was happening. Not the details, of course. He knew nothing of the launch sequence, how the individual warheads were armed or what were their targets, not even how the ship's computers gave them their guidance instructions. But he knew that someone, someone so sick and so low that if God were in His heaven such a man would never find himself in possession of any weapon more dangerous than an unloaded cap pistol, this someone was about to launch a two-megaton Trident missile.

Seconds must have elapsed, perhaps minutes, but Murdock had no awareness of time. He should have backed away as far and as fast as he could, but the mere sight of the thing was so unimaginably spellbinding that he could do nothing but stand there looking down.

An explosion of boiling gases in the bowels of the tube shook the deck at his feet, snapping him free of his spell. By then it was too late to move.

The closure seal ruptured. A blunt red nose cone burst through the fragments. A wave of pressure literally picked Murdock up and blew him away.

He landed hard on his back ten yards toward the stern, with a resounding crash of tortured metal that drowned out his cries of pained flesh. The missile's eruption drowned out the crash. It was still coming up, almost reaching the surface of the sea before it was clear of the launch tube. Its immense white body was cloaked in a sheer veil of air, a billion bubbles racing the missile skyward. In losing the race the veil slipped away. He had his last clear sight of the Trident as it broke through the surface. There was an explosion. Swells rocked the *Alaska* even at depth. And then the missile was gone.

Murdock rolled to his feet. He lumbered to the open tube now filling with water and reached it just as the mammoth hatch started down.

There was no time to consider. The black hole was waiting, a seven-foot caliber bore of a gun that had fired its one shot. He stepped off the edge and dropped out of sight.

He thought the bottom would never come. When it did, his impact would alert every man on the *Alaska*.

And it would have, if the tube hatch hadn't come shut at the same time as his feet struck the base of the launcher.

It damn near broke his legs. For a while he felt they *had* been broken.

The suit should have broken, too. Its metal legs should have telescoped into the trunk. Water should be spraying in through a dozen or more cracks. Marie Delamer had explained what would happen once the suit started to leak: It would fill with water until the air trapped inside was compressed to the same pressure as the water around him. He could continue to breathe until the pressures equalized. At that point he could open his helmet, pull the emergency cord at his life vest, and swim to the surface. That would have been good advice ten seconds ago. Now he wasn't so sure. It would take more than a full vest of air to break through the eight-foot steel hatch over his head. Fortunately, the suit had survived the fall.

He got to his feet.

His legs had survived the fall, too.

He was back in pitch darkness. He was still trapped. Would they empty the launch tube of water or not? And if so, how long would they wait? He couldn't have more than an hour of oxygen left in his system.

The answer came almost at once.

It came in the form of a second eruption, smaller than the first and composed entirely of air under high pressure. He could hear and feel it stirring the water. It lasted for some time, but before too long the water level had sunk to the point that small waves lapped at his faceplate. Soon afterward his suit was too heavy for him to stand up, and he knew the tube was dry. Murdock released the pins on the inside of his helmet, threw it back off his head, and crawled out.

Another man might have dropped to his knees at the very thought that he had reached the inside of the submarine and lived to see the outside of an iron shell that could easily end up serving as his tomb on the bottom of the sea. But Murdock was working purely by instinct. His thoughts, his reason, and his judgments were still clinging to the rudder a matter of inches in front of the propeller, listening to his screams and trying to make sense of his little tunes.

He returned to his empty suit and switched on the helmet light so that it illuminated the launch tube. Then he surveyed the surroundings. The walls looked and felt like aluminum, but they probably weren't. They were cold. If the launch had heated them any, the seawater had cooled them off.

A network of thick rubber ridges crisscrossed the walls from top to bottom. And a portal was set flush with the floor. He went right to it.

There was no inside handle. No way to open it from the inside at all. He put his ear up against it, but no sounds came through.

Should he call out? Did he dare to let anyone know he was here?

He tried knocking on the portal but nothing happened. He waited a while, knocked again, and waited some more. In desperation he tried shouting, but that didn't work either. Twelve hours of screaming had taken its toll on his voice; he was completely hoarse. Patience and poise were other casualties. Before long he was kicking at the portal and pounding on the walls with his fists.

Still no one came.

High above, near the top, were two more portals which were used for arming or maintaining the warheads themselves. One of them might yield, Murdock hoped. Or there might be someone on the upper launch decks.

He found himself studying one of the ridges. These had to be fenders of some sort. They stuck out from the walls two inches or so, and ran in vertical and horizontal rows marking off squares of roughly a foot. The tough elastomer padding protected the missile by absorbing shocks and stabilized the missile's trajectory during launch.

Murdock started climbing.

He was halfway to the top, twenty feet from the base, when the small portal just above him swung open and a shaft of light broke into the tube.

"What is it? What's down there?"

Another light, a flashlight beam, explored the depths of the tube, found the empty A1A suit, and then moved over the walls. The beam crossed Murdock's upturned face and stopped.

A different voice spoke.

"It's nothing . . . There's nothing here."

Good God! Murdock thought, they *must* have seen him. He saw the portal begin to close and climbed faster than ever; he tried to call out. But the only sound he heard was the metal door banging shut.

Suddenly it opened again.

"Get back. I'll look for myself."

A head thrust inside. It turned side to side and then down. The dark face was silhouetted by bright fluorescents from outside the tube. Friend or foe, it was impossible to say. Murdock continued to climb.

"Hey!"

A short-barreled weapon pointed straight down.

"Hold it right there!"

Murdock reacted not to the man or the gun but instead to the light, which told him there was yet a way out of his horror. He reached out his hand for the next rubber fender and pulled himself up.

He heard a cry of surprise, then a scream. Something swept over his head, dropped past him, and struck the steel floor twenty feet below with a sickening thump. Murdock didn't even look down. The next thing he knew hands were reaching down through the portal and helping him up, helping him through. He'd come to the end. When the hands released him he slumped against the outside of the launch tube, squinting his eyes at the brightness of the room and letting the warmth fill his body. He wanted to stand, but his legs wouldn't hold him. He wanted to speak, but he couldn't think of anything to say that was worth the effort.

A man wearing tan dungarees, the rank of chief petty officer, and a beatific smile, looked down at Coy Murdock.

"I've been wanting to do that for a week now," he said. "Give one of those mothers a good, swift kick in the butt. And I've got you to thank for the opportunity. We've been listening to you march up and down the deck for eight hours. I take it you're the cavalry?"

Murdock tried to answer. No words came. He cleared his throat and tried again but it was no use. He looked up at the chief and merely nodded.

"Where's the rest of your men?"

Murdock shook his head side to side.

"Who the hell *are* you?"

Murdock pulled out his ID and handed it across.

The chief looked it over. He started to say something to Murdock and then did a quick double take on the card.

"Jesus Kee-rist," he said. "I'd figgered they'd called in the Marines on this thing. The Air Force, too, and maybe even the Army. Wouldn't surprise me to hear the FBI and the CIA was runnin' around crackin' heads." The chief shook his head in disbelief. "But the Wichita Police Department! You just know they've pulled out all the stops!"

# Chapter Eighteen

Drew Murdock stood arm in arm with his father—a picture of happiness. Both men were smiling. The grounds of the U.S. Naval Academy at Annapolis formed the background of the picture. The graduation ceremony had just ended, and a proud Glen Murdock was holding up his son's commission papers for the camera. The photo was so sharp Drew could almost make out the words.

"Over here, Commander."

Murdock turned.

A stranger was sitting in Drew Murdock's chair. Murdock was lying in his own bunk, in his own stateroom. The bunk, the stateroom, the chair, even the stranger were veiled in haze, soft dabs of color smeared in front of his eyes like a watercolor room where an eight-by-ten black-and-white hung on the wall. But which was real, the painting or the photograph?

"Are you awake, Commander?"

Murdock didn't have an answer to that. For some reason he hadn't died. The torpedo hadn't exploded. The *Alaska* hadn't sunk. He didn't have an answer to that, either, unless he'd dreamed the whole thing. Running out of the missile control center, falling into the torpedo room, and activating the firing key just before he collapsed . . . had it all been a new version of his nightmare? Maybe he was still dreaming.

"Commander! Snap out of it. I'm sorry we haven't

more time for you to recover. I know you've been knocked around a bit.''

"Who are you?"

"I am Captain Ivan Yankov."

Murdock grabbed the edge of the bunk with both hands and levered himself to a sitting position. He narrowed his eyes until the veil gently parted and the stranger resolved. He was in his middle fifties, short and heavy. He had blue eyes and pale skin and a poor crop of gray hair.

"You don't look Iranian to me," Murdock said. "Yankov doesn't sound Iranian."

"No."

"Russian?"

"I am here to advise, Commander."

Yes, Murdock decided, he was Russian. A small, muscular man, whose weight had long ago turned to fat and whose bullying ways had turned to bluster.

"Russian adviser to a terrorist organization?" Murdock tried to smile but doubted the results were worth the effort or the pain involved. "Now I've heard it all. We knew you guys trained 'em. We didn't know you actually went along on their jobs and advised 'em."

"Oddly enough, these men were trained by your people, not mine; we never had a presence in Iran. America did. As far as this particular operation is concerned, I think of my role as a mediator. I try to see that their frustrations don't get out of control."

"You're not doing a helluva job, Yankov."

"My influence is limited. And I cannot afford to step in at every incident. I try to restrict my efforts to those occasions when it's necessary that reason prevail over rage. In this case, Commander, I have intervened too late to save your navigator, but I hope to save the lives of you and your crew. Kaseem, as usual, is enraged. If reason is to prevail, then someone will have to be reasonable."

"Talk to Kaseem."

"I have. That is why you're still alive. Your reactor

and communications officers are being treated and will live. I want to keep them alive, them and the rest of your men, as well as yourself.''

"Talk to Kaseem.''

"I'm only an adviser.''

"Then advise him he's gone too far.''

"My advice is for you.''

"I see. And what advice do you have for me, Captain?''

"Tell your weapons officer—Commander Buchanan, is that his name?—to launch the missile.''

Murdock tried to laugh. It was a doomed attempt to fool Yankov and perhaps even himself into thinking he was tough. Unfortunately, the laughter only degenerated into a fit of coughing.

The other officer waited patiently. "I ask you to be reasonable,'' he said at last. "Kaseem will kill every one of you if he has to.''

"He *is* going to kill every one of us. Because he *wants* to. He'll do it as soon as he gets what he's come for.''

Yankov turned up his palms. "We've got what we came for, Commander. All we want to do now is withdraw. But we can't do it as long as your Navy is standing over us. We have to let them know we're willing and able to launch missiles if necessary. When they realize this they will give us the time and the distance we need.''

It was true, then, thought Murdock, what Ensign Thomas had told him. He hadn't dreamed that part. The Navy was out there. And Kaseem hadn't lost them by heading to sea.

Murdock felt the warmth of fresh blood surging through his body. An attack sub and a sub-chaser, according to his ensign. A *Los Angelos*-class SSN maybe. A third the size of the Tridents but fast and highly maneuverable. Her SUBROC, anti-submarine rocket-propelled torpedoes could home in on a codfish at two thousand yards. And the sub-chaser? Not a patrol boat, out here. More likely a small guided-missile cruiser or a frigate, bristling with antisubmarine rockets (ASROC) and Sea Lance missiles. A scent was all the Navy had needed. Now, low-flying planes using magnetic anomaly detectors would locate the magnetic field of the *Alaska*'s submerged mass. Clinker systems in the sub-chasers would sense the minute traces of heat in the *Alaska*'s water trail. Sonar-dipping ASW helicopters would pin-point her location. An amateur like Musa al-Kaseem didn't stand a chance when the Navy moved in for the kill. Murdock's warmth ebbed. None of them stood a chance. He shivered.

"Will you do it?"

Murdock shook his head. "You're forgetting whose side I'm on. I want them to stop you, Captain."

"You're forgetting something too, Commander. There's only one way they can stop us. They'll have to sink us or blow us apart. Is that what you want?"

"It beats global war."

"Nonsense!"

"If you launch one of those missiles, you know where it's going. Not Kaseem's homeland, Captain. Yours. And you know what your people will do in retaliation."

"Of course I do." Yankov remained unaroused. "That's your guarantee none of the Trident II missiles will ever be launched. I wouldn't allow that to happen. That's what you know and your Navy doesn't. When they realize we have the capability to launch, they'll pull back. They'll never take the chance we'd launch a second missile."

"But—"

"We want to launch the Trident III. It's targeted for the Johnston Islands. Which are deserted. No one will be harmed. The Navy will have no further doubt of our resolve. They'll clear enough sea space to give us the time we need."

Murdock was shocked by the Russian's knowledge of

this highly classified information. But he tried not to show it. He couldn't allow himself to be moved.

"I don't know what you're talking about."

"Come, come, Commander. These facts are known to you; they are known to me. Let's be sensible."

"I won't help you."

"But why? Would you prefer that all of your men die rather than allow us to escape?"

"If we go through the launch sequence with the Trident III, Kaseem will be able to launch the twenty-two Trident II missiles any time he wants to. He may even be able to retarget them toward the Middle East or the United States. I can't allow that to happen."

"It will not happen, Commander."

"You can guarantee that?"

"I do guarantee it."

Murdock turned his head and closed his eyes to Yankov's quietly forceful arguments. The Russian's voice, his tenor, reminded him of Captain West more than he dared to admit. In fact the two captains were not all that different. Yankov urged Murdock to put himself in the Russian's place. What would he do if their situations were reversed? How would he convince Yankov to do the reasonable thing? Too many people already have died, he told Murdock. Enough is enough.

It could have been Captain West talking.

Murdock tried to call upon West's strength, experience, and judgment to help him decide what to do. But it didn't help. All he could summon was a mental image of West with a gun at his head saying, "No one is to cooperate with these men in any way. That's an order." What would he have said now?

"I just don't know," Murdock said, shaking his head.

All at once Yankov shouted for his man Abbas.

"I regret that I cannot resurrect your captain from the grave, Commander. Nor your lieutenant, who was shot without my knowledge by Kaseem. However, I guarantee there will be no more killings. And to demonstrate my good faith, I will resurrect someone—your engineering officer.''

The door opened again.

Scott Longfellow entered, escorted by one of the armed Libyans. Amazement brought Drew Murdock to his feet. Here was one man he'd never thought to lay eyes on again.

"Scotty!"

Commander Scott Longfellow smiled bravely. "Hello, skipper."

"We thought you were dead! By god, that damn doctor told us—" And there was the answer.

Yankov put it into words: "Captain Kester is working with us, Commander. He has been from the beginning. I'm being perfectly frank with you now, I hope you appreciate that."

"I should have guessed it," he muttered; "I should have . . . but I didn't." Murdock shook his head at the engineering officer and produced a smile. "Are you okay, Scotty?"

He sensed something about Scott Longfellow that was not in the least bit okay. An aura of sickness . . . of death. Not an aura, an odor.

The engineer smiled again and indicated the pad wrapped around his neck without really touching it.

"My neck hurts like hell but I guess it's not broken. Whatever that Kaseem guy did, it put me out like a light."

"He's unharmed," said the Russian.

"I'm okay. They've been keeping me in the dispensary I don't know how long. Days . . . a week . . . I don't know. They shot me full of drugs and asked me questions. I guess I must have told them a lot of things, skipper, but I just don't remember. If I've let anything slip . . ."

"He told us very little, as a matter of fact," Yankov

offered. "We felt that of all your officers his resistance to interrogation would be weakest. As it turned out, he gave us a great deal of trouble. We didn't even begin learning basic procedures about silent operations of the ship until we'd turned around and headed back to the Johnston Islands. There is much more we never did get. However, I think he's been through enough, and I'm turning him back over to you. There will be no more interrogations."

"I'm damn glad to have you back, Scotty!"

"Same here, skipper."

Murdock wheeled on Yankov. "As long as you're being so frank, Captain, let's hear what happened in the torpedo room. I suppose Captain Kester informed you all about it?"

"About your self-destructing torpedo? Yes. That's why we put him in there, to keep us informed of your plans. We felt certain you'd try something—that's why we put the five of you in there. The torpedo room was the obvious place for your men to construct some kind of defense. And I congratulate you on a masterful stroke. But you couldn't know Kaseem was once a torpedoman. One of the best. Captain Kester informed us about your plan, and Kaseem simply went in when the five of you were on duty and defused the torpedo."

"Very clever."

"So were you. We thought that once you had your plans made you'd pretend to go along with us. Your attempt to run the *Alaska* on the reefs took us completely by surprise. You nearly pulled it off. Fortunately for all of us, it didn't happen."

"Why the honesty?"

"It's time for this to be finished, Commander Murdock. By returning this officer to you I've tried to establish a basis for mutual cooperation between us. If you play fair with me, you'll find me fair with you in return. Order your man Buchanan to launch the Trident III missile, for all of our sakes. Let's be done with this thing so we can all go home.''

Commander Buchanan met Murdock in the exec's cabin. Captain Yankov and the two Iranian escorts remained outside.

"I don't believe it! You want me to launch?"

Murdock nodded. "Yes, I'm ordering you to launch."

"But, skipper . . . you can't mean that!"

"It's the only reasonable thing to do. I have the word of the man who's in charge of this operation that there will be no more launches after the Trident III. There will be no more killings. They just need the time this warning will give them to get away. I've decided to do it. Hell, a week ago we were all set to launch. We'll just do it a week late, that's all."

"This means Fletcher got killed for nothing."

"He got killed—that's the thing to remember, Ben. Too many people have already been killed. If reason is going to prevail, then someone will have to be reasonable. Enough is enough. We got Scotty back again, and I don't want anyone else to die."

The *Alaska* rose to a hundred feet. The navigation masthead was raised to the surface.

By the time Murdock had joined Buchanan and Kaseem in the missile control room, the launch sequence was well under way. The SINS computer automatically fed the ship's coordinates to all twenty-four missiles and three hundred and sixty warheads, adjusting the guidance instructions to each several times every minute even while they dozed in their launch tubes. For tube number one these instructions were updated to the second and verified. One of Kaseem's men went with two missile technicians to the launch deck, where the fire-control systems would be monitored first hand. In the missile room, Buchanan inserted the two keys into the firing panel. He began reciting a prelaunch checklist to his GMM special gunner's mate, while two more fire control men on the guidance control team waited their turn.

Kaseem and Captain Yankov watched with ravenous eyes, not willing even to blink for fear of missing a morsel of the feast that was being laid out before them.

"Enter those preassigned target coordinates," ordered the weapons officer.

Degrees, minutes, seconds, and centiseconds of latitude and longitude were punched into the computer for each of the twenty-six warheads on the one Trident III missile.

"So simple," said Yankov. "The computers do it all."

Buchanan spoke to an MT on the launch deck. "Verify that number one hatch is open."

"Number one hatch is open, sir."

"You have a green board, chief?"

"All green, sir."

He rotated one of the two launch keys a hundred and eighty degrees, while across the room and at the same moment, Murdock rotated the second key. Buchanan threw a number of rocker switches, and then flipped up the "fire" cover cap marked with a numerical one.

"On five."

The gunner's mate did the countdown.

"Five . . . four . . ."

Murdock reached for a stanchion. Yankov, seeing him do this, moved nearer another.

"Three . . . two . . . one . . . fire."

Buchanan pressed the button with a thumb, while holding on to the panel security bar with his other hand. Those few men, Kaseem and his soldiers mostly, who were not steadying themselves, grabbed at anything within reach that was bolted down tight. The recoil from a sixty-ton projectile, even on an eighteen-thousand-ton launching pad, is literally staggering. The deck fell away from their feet, stabilized several inches below them, and waited for them to arrive.

Yankov almost laughed. "Astounding!"

"She's on the surface," announced the GMM. "Ignition verified."

Already Buchanan was speaking to the launch deck. "Close hatch and blow water."

"Closing hatch, aye-aye."

The guidance-control FCs pressed against the television monitors, their hands poised at the keyboards. Ten-digit numbers scrolled past their screens too fast to read. Line graphs to the sides of the numbers broke down the trajectory parameters. Speed and altitude were displayed on one FC's monitor; azimuth and distance, on the other.

"Stage one completion."

From the launch deck came: "Missile control, number one hatch is down and sealed. Blowing water."

Buchanan acknowledged this and then turned to face his audience. "It's just over four hundred miles," he explained. "We're dumping ninety-five percent of its solid propellant into the ocean. Another thirty seconds and it'll be there."

The gunner's mate spoke again without turning away from his readouts. "Stage two completion."

"These days," Buchanan continued, "ballistic missiles are ballistic only under the most liberal interpretation of the word. 'Ballistics' describes a projectile, like a bullet, that is given a certain momentum, a certain direction and speed, and then left to gravity to find its target. Rockets will carry these missiles ninety percent of their flight. After that, the twenty-six warheads are individually guided to their targets by smaller maneuvering jets. Only in the last few seconds of their journey do they actually free-fall, and sometimes not even then."

"Warhead separation, sir."

"Automatic guidance is initiated," said the second FC.

The 32MC box squawked a message from the control room.

"We've climbed to eighty feet, skipper, and we're still coming up. Our sail is gonna be exposed in a minute."

Kaseem whirled to Murdock. *"What's going on?"*

"Not my doing," said Murdock. "Yours. We just lost sixty-two tons of ballast." He picked up the conn telephone from the control panel. "This is the exec. Compensate with your trim to hold our position. When the WO reports number one launch tube is dry, we'll descend to two hundred feet."

"Aye-aye, skipper."

All at once the television monitors stopped scrolling figures. The graphs flattened. And a final set of numbers ran across the bases of the screens.

"That's it," said Buchanan.

"Missile control, this is the launch deck. Tube clear of water."

"Shut 'er down, Gus, and come on in."

"Sir, I'm going to inspect this tube when the pressure backs off. I heard some thumping on the bottom. Something must be a bit loose down there, and our Arab friend here is about to have kittens."

"Do you need any help?"

"No, sir. Buck an' me can handle it."

"What's that all about?" Kaseem demanded.

The weapons officer stood his ground. "Nothing to get in an uproar about. Probably just a loose strip of padding. Or a fish. I once served on a Poseidon that sucked a seven-hundred-pound sea turtle into the launcher. These things happen." Turning away, Buchanan picked up the telephone to inform the manifold operator in the control room that the launch tube was secure. The operator aye-aye'd a descent to two hundred feet. Buchanan turned back to Yankov and Kaseem. "Have you got what you wanted?"

Kaseem's eyes were still gleaming. "Yeah," he allowed, "we got it, all right."

"How'd your missile do?" asked Yankov. "When will you know?"

"The test was scheduled to be monitored by satellite and by Navy tracking ships lying outside the designated standoff boundaries. There are also recording sensors on the islands themselves."

The Russian nodded in understanding. "Very instructive, gentlemen. Thank you for your cooperation." He turned to Murdock. "All right, Commander, shall we get going?"

"Where are we headed?"

"We've delivered our message to the United States Navy. Let's see if they got it. Move us a discreet distance away at a discreet rate of speed, and we'll see if our bothersome shadow continues to follow."

With that, Captain Yankov dismissed himself.

Kaseem led Commanders Murdock and Longfellow up to the command-and-control center, but to the relief of the control crew he didn't stick around. Instead he stalked into the radio/sonar section, and there he remained for the next two hours. Murdock could hear him shouting at the STs. He demanded to know what or who was giving away their position. He used several million dollars worth of communication equipment for a punching bag. He paced relentlessly. And the thunderous reverberations of his heavy footfalls echoed through the ship. When Yankov came to the control room to get a report on the results of their withdrawal, any crewman could have given it to him. Discreet speed and distance notwithstanding, the *Alaska* had failed to lose her pursuers and everyone knew it for there was nothing discreet about Kaseem.

*"They're getting a signal!"* Kaseem bellowed. *"Somebody is sending them a signal!"*

"But why would they dare follow?" asked Yankov.

"Why, hell! I want to know *how!*"

A desperate sonarman tried to suggest that the Russian sub paralleling their course might be a source of the noise, but Kaseem wasn't having it. "How do they know we're with her?" he demanded. The ST had no answer for this—none that is, he felt safe to voice. No doubt he was thinking what Murdock and all the other control and sonar room crew were thinking, namely that if loose lips can sink ships, then Kaseem's mouth, his fists, and his feet were capable of sending an entire class of nuclear submarines to the bottom.

After two hours of this Kaseem burst into the control room and ordered the engines stopped, the turbogenerators shut down, and all auxiliary machinery disconnected or placed on standby. He was pulling the plug. With a sigh the ventilators expired their last breath; the pumps for coolant and trim stopped beating. And when the fluorescents winked out, every last one of them, the ship closed her eyes. She lay dead in the water. Red standing lights burned in every compartment and passageway but this did not keep her alive; this was the death token, the thousand wounds that spurted their luminous blood through the black bowels of her corpse.

"Take the brass hats below!" Kaseem snarled.

Murdock, Buchanan, and Longfellow were prodded belowdecks to the torpedo room. No sooner had the door closed at their backs than it came open again to admit Shorter and Thomas. These two men were hardly ambulatory. They needed help just to get to their bunks, but even this didn't happen until they had recovered from the sudden appearance of Scott Longfellow's ghost.

They were still enjoying this surprise, and the required explanations were still being made, when a second apparition materialized.

The breech door to torpedo tube number two flew open with a bang.

Every eye turned as one to the starboard tube nest.

A man's head poked out of the hole. Out came a pair of arms and a trunk. A wild face looked around. The red glow of the standing lights had turned the iron gray of his eyes to rust. A tangle of brown hair, rather too long by Navy standards, fell over his forehead.

"A little help would be nice!" he barked, in a voice so hoarse it barely rose above a whisper.

Drew Murdock was the first to recover: "Who the hell are you?"

"My name's Murdock. I'm looking for the executive—"

*"Murdock?* I'm Murdock."

"Hello, big brother."

Two silver discs had slipped out from inside his life vest; they swung back and forth from a chain round his neck, sending darts of red light over the room. Dog tags are not worn in peacetime, though Drew had worn tags just like them for twenty-five years.

"Coy? Coy, my god! Can it be you?"

Drew leapt to the tube, dragged his brother out, and held him with both arms until the young man found his feet. By this time Longfellow and Buchanan were moving in, too, while Thomas and Shorter twisted their heads for a look.

"This is my brother!" Drew exclaimed. But no one heard him. Everyone was talking at once. Surprise didn't begin to describe what these men were going through now.

Drew had grabbed Coy by both shoulders and was shaking his teeth loose from the gums.

"Damn, it's good to see you, but what the hell are you doing here? How did you get here? And why you? Are there others here, too?" Without waiting for an answer he turned to Buchanan. "I haven't seen this guy in . . . in twenty years. Can you believe it?" He turned back. "I would never have recognized you. I didn't recognize you."

"I'm thirty years older."

"No, no, you were twelve when—"

"I aged ten years last night. I'll tell you about it some other time. We've got to get going."

"Coy, you're the last person I expected to see. What about the Navy? I hoped they might try to get a SEAL team in here, or some divers, but . . . you? Where are the rest of—"

"I came alone, Drew. Admiral Reinholt sent me. That is, he made it possible for me to get here. We don't have time to go into details. You have to fill me in on what's going on and then we have work to do. But before we go any further I've got some bad news."

"What could be worse than—"

"Dad's dead."

Drew's exhilaration evaporated. "What? How did. . . ?"

"He was killed. These hijackers did it when he tried to help find your sub. There's no time to explain. Other things are more important right now. Do you know that one of your missiles has been fired? Are we at war. . . ?"

Drew's arms had fallen to his sides. He blinked. Something about the red lighting made it hard for him to focus his eyes.

He tried to throw off his feelings of loss. It would have to wait, he told himself. But it didn't wait. It overwhelmed him. "That part's okay," he said. His voice was more listless than calm. "It was carrying conventional warheads and it only struck a deserted island chain."

"The Johnstons?"

Drew raised his brows. "Yeah. You seem to know quite a bit. More than we do, huh? Maybe you'd better start from the beginning."

"I'll talk to you, but that's all. You've got a traitor right here among your men. A conspirator. Until we find—"

"We know all about it," Drew said. "I've just told my officers. It was the doctor. Captain Kester."

"No, not Kester. Kester's in it, all right—he supplied the virus and the quarantine suits and transportation out to the sub, but he's not the one I'm talking about. They put somebody out here before the helicopter arrived. Who do you think spread the virus around in the first place?"

Drew wagged his head back and forth. "Wait, wait." Things were coming too fast. "Who?"

"I don't know. It could be any one of your men."

"The men are being held in the mess. About thirty of them are dead. A lot of the rest are still recovering."

Coy was looking around, studying the faces of the other officers for the first time.

Drew introduced them one by one. "You can't suspect any of these guys. Look at them! We've gone through hell this past week, and we've done it together."

It was true that they looked pretty bad. And Drew was the worst of the lot. His face was a montage of red shades from pink to magenta, but in daylight he'd sport every color of the rainbow. Both eyes were swollen shut. His nose was broken, and his lips were torn strips of flesh held together by scabs. The way he walked, the way he moved, Coy guessed he had some cracked ribs and some internal bleeding.

Shorter wasn't much better off, but he had one arm in a sling to boot. Thomas's right trouser leg had been slit to the waist. It was stained in blood from a couple of bullet wounds on his thigh and calf, the dressings of which were already in need of a change. Longfellow's neck was wrapped in a cloth pad that served as a make-shift brace, and Buchanan had a badly bleeding nose and lip that had made a Rorschach test of his shirt front before being stanched.

"Okay," said Coy, yielding reluctantly. "You ought to know your own people." He gave them an abbreviated account of his activities the previous day and night. Chasing the *Seawind* to the Johnstons, finding the *Alaska* by chance and dropping onto her main deck. He watched their expressions. At first they didn't believe him. They wanted to believe him but they couldn't. But after he had finished, they did. There was no other way to explain his presence.

"Mister," said Buchanan, "you're either the luckiest man that ever lived . . . or the craziest."

"Or both," said Shorter.

Coy let it go without argument. "Your missile man Gus took the M-16 rifle from that dead Iranian. Gus and his pal were going back into the engine room to try to get a couple more weapons, and I came here to free you." Coy displayed a small silenced pistol he'd taken from the body in the launch tube. "Gus told me they were keeping you officers in here, so I came looking. I found the place empty. That torpedo tube door was open and the torpedo had been taken out. When I heard someone coming down the hall I crawled inside. And that's the whole story."

"If what you say is true," asked Buchanan, "why hasn't an alarm been raised?"

Coy indicated the standing lamp over their heads. "An alarm! What do you call all this red-alert jazz?"

"Routine for silent operations," said Drew. "They think there's a screamer on the hull and they're shutting down all the machinery trying to listen for it and hide from the Navy at the same time."

" 'Screamer'?"

"A magnetic device attached to the hull of a target submarine. It sends out a signal to our ASW forces."

"There is a device," said Coy.

"Yours?"

"No, it's yours, but I borrowed it. It's a hydrophone. They'll never hear it, though, because it doesn't send out an audible tone. Your sonar won't pick it up. It sends a weak signal only a few hundred feet through the water. A booster device on the surface has to transmit the signal to an OSIS satellite."

"He's right about that," said Thomas.

"If there's no alert now there soon will be. That Arab we killed will be missed before long and your guys will, too. We've got to move and move fast."

"What are you planning to do?" asked Drew.

"Get you and as many of your men as I can and get out of this damn sub before it blows up."

Drew shook his head. "We can't do that."

"Why not?"

"Leave Kaseem and Yankov and their men to do as they please with the *Alaska?* We'd do better to wait until the Navy moves in."

"Big brother, the Navy ain't here."

"Oh, yes it is. Tell him, Ensign."

"It is," Ensign Thomas confirmed. He had crawled off his bunk and thrown a torpedo swabbing rod under his arm as a jury-rigged crutch. "Ever since we left the Johnstons. Nearly a day now."

"But I was there. I didn't see any Navy vessels. The Johnstons were still off-limits."

Thomas smiled. "You don't see an attack sub."

"Sub!"

"That's right. Probably one of the Sturgeon class. Broad off our starboard bow about two hundred yards. And there's a Russian sub still holding off the port quarter. Between the two of them they've got us bracketed good."

Drew showed more surprise than his little brother. "You didn't tell me the sub was that close, Ensign. And it's off our bow?"

Coy broke in: "It's an American sub all right," he said, "but it's not Navy."

"*What?*"

"It's the *Seawind.*"

Without wasting time on detils, Murdock explained the tragedy of the *Seawind,* his father's efforts to find it, and how it had disappeared just two days before. "It sailed to the Johnstons," he said, "to rendezvous with the *Alaska* and probably to shift cargo and crew. My guess is that Kaseem and his men will take off in the *Seawind;* this Russian guy Yankov will bring over some of his people from the Russian sub to crew the *Alaska.* They needed some privacy to do it. The Johnstons were the agreed-upon site—it was supposed to be off-limits. Now they're looking for another quiet little corner of the ocean. If they only realized the Navy hasn't a single vessel anywhere nearby, they'd surface and finish their business right here and now."

"How can you know all this, Coy?"

"Last night I saw a diver come out of nowhere. At the time I thought he'd swum away from this sub and then back. Now I don't think so. It's a good bet he was coming over from another submarine altogether; he came from the right—you're telling me the American submarine is off that way?"

"What about the surface ship?"

"My guess is that's the *Nomad,* Dad's salvor. Or maybe the *Enchantress,* another salvage ship, a faster one, that I took to the Johnstons. There's no booster sending a signal from the hydrophone on into space; it's being picked up by the marine receivers in the salvor. As long as they stay close they can follow us anywhere we go."

"So the Navy hasn't found us."

"Not yet they haven't, thank god. When they do, brother, they'll blow us so high out of the water it'll take Star Wars technology to find all the pieces. We've got two choices. We can fight our way to the back end of the ship with as many of your men as we can free, pop out the escape hatch, and hope that the *Enchantress* picks us up. That's one. If you're right about the *Alaska* just sitting here and not moving, we may have a second option. We could swim over to the *Seawind* and take her by force."

This elicited a storm of dissent.

"You're crazy!" cried Buchanan; his was the kindest observation.

But Drew had the last word. "I won't leave Kaseem with the *Alaska,*" he said. "We've got to take care of him before we do anything else. You're not crazy, Coy, but you're scared like the rest of us into doing crazy things." He thrust a finger at the overhead. "Kaseem? *He's* crazy. And if he gets wind of what you've been up to, he'll go into that missile room and push every button in sight."

"I didn't come here to fight with you, Drew. I'm just telling you we have to get out of here."

"But I'm still in command."

"Yes, but—"

"And I say we take care of Kaseem before we do anything else. His men will be lost without him, all except Yankov, and I can negotiate with Yankov."

Coy didn't want to give in. He argued, he implored, he did everything but beg. It was no use. Drew had made up his mind. And he made it clear that while Coy wasn't in the Navy and couldn't be expected to take orders, neither could Coy expect others to take orders from him. "You can stay here if you want to," he said in the end. "We'll go without you, but we'll still need your gun."

"A pistol against automatic rifles?"

"It's all we've got."

Scott Longfellow cleared his throat. "I hate to break in on your reunion, skipper, but maybe there's a better way to do it."

"Like what, Scotty?"

"If Kaseem's the man you want, why not lure him down here and let your brother kill him?"

"He wouldn't stand a chance."

"Hold it, hold it," said Coy. "Who is this Kaseem?" Drew obliged him. "He's the leader of the Iranians, a three-hundred-pound brute with his brains in his fists. He's killed at least—''

''Never mind. I know him. The description requires no elaboration—I've seen his handiwork at Pearl Harbor. Even though I don't care much for the idea of shooting anyone in cold blood, I have to agree his blood would be the cold stuff to start with.''

''You'd never get the chance.''

But then Longfellow had another idea. ''He might. Have your brother get back in that torpedo tube and wait. We'll get Kaseem to come in alone. Coy opens up the breech door and shoots him. Kaseem would never suspect a thing.''

''Sounds all right, Scotty. But how do we get Kaseem to come in here?''

''Leave that to me,'' said Longfellow. ''I could tell him you're ready to show him where the transmitter is if he'll give you a guarantee of safety for your men.'' The engineer turned to Coy. ''Where is the hydrophone?''

''On top. Just in front of the tower.''

''All right,'' said Longfellow, smiling. ''Give me five minutes.''

Before anyone could say more, he had crossed to the door and knocked. The door opened. He spoke quietly to the gunman who filled the opening. The man stepped aside and allowed the engineer to pass. The door closed.

''That was easy,'' muttered Thomas.

It took two of them, both Drew and Buchanan, to wrestle Coy into the tube, for he now displayed none of the dexterity that would have been needed to find his way in there alone just minutes before. The tube's twenty-one-inch diameter made it more cramped than the A1A suit. Coy lay on his chest with both arms out in front of his head, looking out through the sight glass and holding the pistol ready with one hand while saving the other to throw open the breech door. Drew closed the breech but left it unlatched.

Then Drew arranged his men into the positions that would allow Coy his best shot.

They waited.

"You gotta admit it took guts," said Buchanan, "After what Kaseem did to Scotty before, for him to go right up and face him like that. He didn't even look scared."

"You know, it's funny," replied Shorter from his bunk.

"Who's laughing?" muttered Thomas.

But Buchanan was more obliging, and asked the reactor officer what was so funny.

"Scotty never said a thing when the skipper's brother was talking about the *Seawind.*"

"What should he say?"

"We bunk together. You know how guys talk. He told me he'd served on a submarine that went down several years ago. I was thinking it was the *Seawind.*"

Drew Murdock turned to them. "Let's keep down the chitchat; we don't want to be overheard before Kaseem comes in."

They continued to wait.

Murdock shifted his position; he looked nervously over his officers but wound up looking at Shorter. "You're sure he said the *Seawind?*"

"I thought he had."

"How long before she sank did he serve?"

"I don't know, skipper."

"He was assigned as engineering officer?"

"I guess so. Junior EO maybe. I just thought it was strange he didn't mention it."

Murdock nodded.

Still they waited.

"When he comes back," said Buchanan, "you can ask him how a ship that sank twelve years ago could be chasing us across the Pacific today. Its nuclear core wouldn't last more than nine or ten years, would it, Shorty?"

"Not normally, no. If it were put on safe shutdown, using just enough power to keep her machinery, her pumps, and her systems from seizing, she could last two, three times as long. Of course, it'd be a job starting her up again. Someone would have to know what they were doing.''

"That's enough talking, fellas; it's been almost five minutes.''

"But, skipper . . .''

"I said that's enough, Ensign. Just think about what we're going to do. Now you're all going to keep out of the line of fire between Kaseem and that tube, okay? And, Ben, as soon as it's done, you close that door to the passageway. I don't care to have a bunch of his men come bursting in till we're ready. Shorty, if he's got any weapons, it'll be up to you and me to get our hands on them fast.''

They nodded, and Murdock turned away. He didn't want to see them right now, to know what they were thinking. "Of course it would be a job starting the *Seawind* up again. Someone would have to know what they were doing.'' Someone, they thought, like Scott Longfellow. But Murdock knew better. It couldn't have been Scotty who'd gotten the *Seawind* under way. He'd been here on the *Alaska,* undergoing interrogation for days and eventually telling Captain Yankov everything he needed to know to evade detection by the Navy. But Thomas and Buchanan and Shorter wouldn't learn that from Murdock.

"It's been more than eight minutes,'' said Thomas.

"We'll wait, Ensign.''

It was true someone could have been slipped off the ship and taken by fast motor launch to the site where the *Seawind* had sunk. Certainly Coy had seen someone swimming back over from the *Seawind* to rejoin the *Alaska* crew. That would have been just hours before the Trident was launched. Just before Commander Longfellow made his startling reappearance.

Scott Longfellow. The enigmatic engineer whose duties took him everywhere on the ship. The man who collected sea samples and put them in little glass jars. The soldier who had heroically resisted Dr. Kester's truth serum for days, but whose medical file said he could tolerate no drugs of any kind whatsoever . . .

Kaseem had almost broken his neck. Or had he?

They'd interrogated him for days. Or had they?

After the self-destructing torpedo failed to explode, Kester was finished as an informer. Yankov and Kaseem had no one to tell them what Murdock and his officers were up to.

"Or did they?"

Murdock whirled back around.

"Ben, quick! Let's get my bro—"

The hand wheel spun on the watertight door. It swung open. Four gunmen barged in.

They aimed their weapons at each of the four officers. Everyone stood stock-still. And then Musa al-Kaseem appeared in the doorway. "If you so much as breathe," he announced in an uncharacteristic undertone, "my men will open fire."

Kaseem circled the room and approached the starboard torpedo tube nest from the side.

Drew Murdock reared forward. "No! Look out, Coy!"

The breech door swung open, but not soon enough or wide enough for a shot to be fired. Kaseem checked the door with his huge hand and then used his superior weight and leverage to close it again. He turned the locking wheel.

*"Load torpedo tube number two. Number two torpedo tube loaded, aye-aye."*

He peeked slyly around to see if his captive audience was enjoying his humor. He gripped the vent and the water-around-tube controls with both hands.

*"Flood number two. Number two flooding, aye-aye."*

"Noooooo!"

The sound of seawater filling the tube seemed to flood

the torpedo room at the same time. Behind Kaseem came a scream of anger and a scuffle of feet as Drew Murdock launched himself forward. There was the thump of a gun butt against the back of a man's neck, and the dull thud of a hundred and seventy pounds striking the walking deck.

Kaseem hadn't bothered to turn around.

*"Open muzzle door"* He spun a wheel. *"Muzzle door open, aye-aye."*

He rotated the firing key.

*"Fire two."*

He pressed his thumb against the button.

*"Firing two."*

A blast of air near the breech propelled both water and Coy Murdock into the ocean. Kaseem spied through the sight glass to verify that the tube was empty before closing the outer muzzle door.

*"The fish is away, sir."*

Kaseem turned to his audience.

He bowed.

# PART IV

# SUBSMASH

Despite a festering seaway, Admiral Reinholt maneuvered the salvor *Enchantress* smartly alongside the *New Jersey*'s accommodation ladder with the precision of a master harbor pilot. In spite of his seventy-two years he scaled the battleship's freeboard with ease. Once at the quarterdeck he saluted the colors flying from the gaff, turned, saluted the officer of the deck, and requested permission to come aboard.

That's when his troubles began.

The OOD was respectful about it. He said he was sorry. But he had orders not to allow it. The best he could do was to notify Captain Krosmeyer at once, and he would have to do this in any case. He was still looking sorry when Captain Krosmeyer appeared.

The captain, on the other hand, looked amazed and rather put out.

Amazed, because he'd never seen Reinholt hatless in the wind, his wispish white hair blowing madly. Reinholt was wearing a rollneck sweater and thick cord pants with sneakers, and he could have passed for an old sailor instead of the old Navy gentleman Krosmeyer knew him to be.

Put out, because Reinholt had no business being here. It was Krosmeyer's business to see that he left.

"Dammit, Admiral," he said, "you couldn't have picked a worse time to come." With a nod to the young OOD, he steered Reinholt behind one of the five-inch gun mounts. "I hope you know those weren't my orders to keep you off the ship. They came from D.o.D. through CinCPacFlt."

"That's not important now."

"The hell it's not, Admiral. Your man is aboard."

"Captain Cassidy?"

"It's Admiral Cassidy now. And if he finds out you're here, he'll have a fit."

"Let him."

"And he'll have my command."

"I don't think so, Louis. Anyway, that's not important now either. I've found the *Alaska.*"

"The hell you have!"

"Yesterday afternoon."

"Jesus, Admiral, the whole Navy's looking for her!"

"Well, I not only found her, I put a man on her."

"How in the world did you manage that?"

"I don't know. He hasn't told me yet. But he's there and he'll do what needs to be done, I'm banking on that."

Krosmeyer shook a grim face. "What needs to be done is for your man to get the hell off the *Alaska.* They're going to blow her to bits. That's what Cassidy's here for."

"How can they do that if they don't even know where she is?"

"Cassidy says he'll find out. He's playing them close to the vest, but he implies that his investigators expect to get word of her location before noon today."

"Noon? That's barely three hours."

"That's right. SubSmash is scheduled for 2400 Zulu. High noon in this time zone."

"Did you say . . . SubSmash?"

"Correct."

"I hadn't . . . By God, that's monstrous. I didn't figure on that." Reinholt was badly shaken.

"Where is the *Alaska,* Admiral?"

"About twenty-eight miles to the south."

"That close?"

"Yes. Another salvor, the *Nomad*, is keeping watch."

Neither man spoke for a moment.

"We've got to do something," said Reinholt at last.

"I've got to inform Admiral Cassidy," said Krosmeyer. "I don't have any choice."

"No, no! We have to stop 'em!"

"Stop them? You mean Cassidy? Why?"

With a darting glance around, Reinholt told him. "Why? Because that's part of the plan. They *want* the *Alaska* to be destroyed. I figured they'd try something—that's why I came to you—but I never in my wildest imagination thought they'd try that."

Captain Krosmeyer thought he detected undertones of paranoia in Reinholt's fears. If so, he'd already told the old man too much. "It's surefire," he said. "They can't afford to miss, not with those missiles on board. And with Subsmash, they won't miss. You can't stop it, Admiral. It's going to happen."

"What *can* you do?"

"I can approach within ten miles of the *Alaska*, but no closer than that—I don't dare to. Any closer and the *New Jersey*'d go down with your sub. I'm sorry, Admiral, but as for your information, well, I have to tell Admiral Cassidy. You know I do."

"You can't!"

"I've got to."

"I tell you we can't let it happen!" Reinholt shook a clenched fist in front of Krosmeyer's face for emphasis, but he saw by the look in the *New Jersey* captain's eye that he'd made a mistake in doing so. By now a lot of people probably thought he was crazy. Krosmeyer was still trying to make up his mind. Threatening the man wouldn't help—what he needed was a persuasive argument.

"Does one submarine mean that much to you, Admiral?"

"Yes. If the submarine has a hundred hands on board it means that much to me."

Krosmeyer waved that away. "They're probably all dead by now. Most were dying of that virus before the hijackers even flew out."

"Then why are they so anxious to blow her up?"

"They're not, we are." The captain pursed his lips in resignation. "Admiral, can you give me one good reason why I shouldn't pass your information on to Cassidy?"

"Yes."

"Make it a very good reason."

"Because Cassidy wants to blow up the sub. And Cassidy isn't with us. He's with them."

"Them?"

"The hijackers."

"I don't believe it." Here it was again, classic paranoia. The man who took over Reinholt's investigation, who cost him his job—he was the villain, not Reinholt himself. The references to a "plan," conspiracies, and to Reinholt's "wildest imagination," cried out "persecution."

"Do you think I'd make up something like that?"

"No, Dan, you're not vindictive enough to do that, but you're—"

"Senile."

"Hell, you're sharp as a fid."

"Well, I haven't been drinking, so that leaves crazy. Do you think I'm a Section Eight?"

"I think you've been up against it for a very long time. Banging your brains against a brick wall twelve and sixteen hours every day year after year can give any man a headache. You're tired. And you need rest."

"Now you sound like that sonuvabitch Packman."

"Is he in on it, too?"

Krosmeyer instantly regretted having asked. It was so patronizing, the kind of a question a therapist might have asked to try to trick the old man into revealing the extent of his complex.

"I don't know," replied Reinholt. "But I doubt it. God knows, if I were behind this thing I wouldn't let him in. But Cassidy is in. He's masterminding the whole show. He framed me for incompetence by having the DSRVs and rescue ships transferred. And he finagled my signature on orders relocating the *Mako* wreckage from San Diego to Seattle."

"I don't know anything about those matters, Admiral. Can you tell me one thing he's done since taking over the investigation which—"

"I don't know that he's done anything at all since he took over. Ten to one you don't either."

Krosmeyer shrugged. "I told you, he's playing them close to the vest."

"I wonder why. You also told me that he's expecting word of the *Alaska*'s location in a matter of hours. I have to wonder where this mysterious word is coming from?"

"Don't you know?"

"I suspect it's going to come from his people on the *Alaska.*"

"Have you got proof of that?"

"Give me fifteen minutes. If I can't convince you, then you can put me off the *Jersey* and no hard feelings. Tell Cassidy where the *Alaska* is and keep your skirts clean."

Krosmeyer folded his arms and thought the matter over in tight-lipped silence. Everything he'd heard in the last several minutes supported the presumption that Reinholt was a neurotic, mentally troubled man. He'd been told this was true by people whose opinion he thought he respected a lot less than Reinholt's. With his windblown hair and his ill-fitting fisherman's attire, Reinholt sure looked the part. But maybe, just maybe, he'd been listening too hard and not hearing enough, looking too far and not seeing what was right in front of his eyes. The *New Jersey* captain made up his mind. He excused himself, crossed to his OOD, and spoke to the young officer decisively.

"Lieutenant."

"Sir?"

"I'm bringing the admiral aboard on my authority."

"Yessir."

The young officer's face was still troubled. "Sir. About my log . . ."

"On my authority, Lieutenant. You're to remember that, in the event of any trouble later on. Until that time, I'd prefer that his name didn't go into your log. Again, on my authority."

At this point the OOD's face virtually beamed. "No problem there, Captain. My memory's even worse than my vigilance."

"Thank you, Lieutenant. And if Admiral Cassidy comes looking for me, you will not remember that Admiral Reinholt and I have gone forward."

"Yessir. I mean, no, sir. I won't."

Krosmeyer moved away. "Admiral? Let's go, sir. You can brief me while we walk. The fo'c'sle will be deserted, and it's as good a place as any if you don't object to the weather."

They followed the lifelines toward the bow, past the five-inch guns and the lifeboats and then past two more five-inch mounts. The semielliptical bridge loomed over them, looking surprisingly modernistic for its half century, thrust forward of the superstructure and walled with glass. When they reached the forward sixteen-inch guns, Reinholt couldn't help glancing up. The barrels, three of them from each of the two mounts—the after superimposed over the other, projected sixty-five feet into space. The largest guns in the world. But size and power aside, Reinholt harbored no illusions that these magnificent cannons were anything but weapons of a simpler war. Sadly, the squat and ugly missile batteries amidships,

**which** could fly farther and hit harder, were weapons of the modern age.

In a modern naval engagement the Cruise missiles would sweep in from over the horizon. Automatic search-and-track radar would pick them up long before the first spotter could turn his glasses in that direction. In less than two seconds unmanned phalanx gun batteries would open fire with uranium-tipped penetrater bullets two and a half times heavier than steel, detonating the missiles' warheads still miles away. High-speed digital computers would calculate coordinates of the attacker, target Tomahawk and Harpoon missiles, and even launch a retaliatory strike unless a human operator aborted. It was frighteningly efficient. Much more so than those guns, with their seventy-nine-man crews that crank the gun turrets around and elevate their weapon by voice command, hand-load hundred-pound bags of powder and projectiles that weigh as much as a compact car. The new way was much more efficient.

But it had no charm.

"It's all too incredible," said Krosmeyer when Reinholt had paused to examine the guns.

The admiral had to pull his eyes away. "Yes, I didn't want to believe it either when Murdock first explained it to me."

"But what you've told me isn't proof."

"No, but there is proof. My aide, Commander Stout, got it, and now so can we."

"He wasn't involved, then?"

"No, I regret my suspicions of him. I always liked Alan Stout. He became curious about a promise Glen Murdock had extracted from the woman diver, Marie Delamer. He suspected that Drew Murdock might have been on the *Alaska* and he radioed for a crew list. Sure enough, Drew was. If Cassidy had only known that, he wouldn't have needed to use the methods he did to get Glen Murdock to help us. Cassidy had convinced Stout that the only way to get Murdock's help was to ask in such a way that Murdock would think Stout didn't really want him to come. Knowing Glen Murdock the way I did, I can't fault that psychology; Glen was that kind. But Cassidy really did want him to come, and he didn't know about Drew. Naturally it looked bad for Stout, going after Murdock like he did, which was just fine with Cassidy.''

"What made Stout suspicious of Cassidy?"

"The *Alaska* crew list, probably. Coy Murdock thinks he spotted a name on it that got him to thinking. He ordered a copy of the *Seawind* crew list right after that, and by the way, I'm going to do the same thing as soon as you can get me in touch with your comm officer. Coy believes that Alan took his suspicions to Cassidy. And disappeared. An infrared signaling device was found in Stout's cabin, planted by Cassidy, according to Coy. Coy also bets that Stout left the *New Jersey* unconscious inside Cassidy's footlocker. He must have been transferred somehow to the Soviet trawler.''

"And that photograph?" asked Krosmeyer. "He didn't look like a man being forced at gunpoint to cross enemy lines.''

"No, he didn't. I could kick myself for that one. Coy spotted it right off. Stout had grudgingly admired the hand signals Glen Murdock had used to thwart his attempt to take over the *Nomad*. So Stout used one like it himself. He gave us the 'okay' sign because he knew we'd be watching, and he hoped we'd be bright enough to make the connection that O.K. Cassidy was our man.''

"So now you're saying that the Russians aren't really involved in taking the *Alaska.*''

"Sure they are. But they didn't take it. Neither did Arab terrorists. Oh, they're Iranians, all right, but they're not holy warriors. They're SAVAK agents left over from the Shah's reign. They've been in on this thing for twelve years, since the beginning. The Russians are a last-minute addition. Cassidy needed a diversion and they were it.

He needed a way to get the *Alaska* out of the picture for a week or so, to move it around without being detected by OSIS, and the Russians helped him with that, too.''

"What's their end?"

"Trouble. They may get to sink a Trident submarine and have the world thank them for doing it. Maybe they thought there'd be a chance for them to get their hands on the sub or one of those missiles, but I doubt that now. Washington says it's a rogue effort by a few hotheaded Russian generals, and maybe they're right. I believe Cassidy approached some people over there about his plan. Offered them the *Alaska*, or a chance at it. Could be the higher-ups turned him down. But somebody bit. Somehow he got in touch with the right general who, for his own reasons, wanted this little venture to come off.''

"Then that's why we couldn't find her?"

"Right. She had a noisy escort every step of the way. A bodyguard, so to speak. But before the show's over, that bodyguard is going to turn. They don't want the *Alaska* to come out of this in one piece. Neither does Cassidy. He doesn't dare let us get it. That's why I want it back—because they don't. Everybody wants it destroyed except me.''

Krosmeyer nodded. "And me. All right, Admiral, I'm in. Tell me what you want me to do.''

With their backs to the six mighty gun barrels, Reinholt and Krosmeyer moved onto the forecastle, the long and narrow nose of the battleship where the anchor chains lay stretched out a hundred feet, from the deck pipes accessing the chain lockers forward to the hawsepipes. Every piece of equipment associated with this ground tackle was enormous in size and strength. The stockless anchors with their shanks thrust right inside the hawsepipes were twenty-five tons of solid iron, and each of their two broad arms was twice the height of a man. The chains were thicker than a man's thigh, and the man could crawl through the holes of a single link. You didn't step over these chains, you climbed over them, and when the anchor was let go and a chain rumbled across the flash plate on the deck, raising a bonfire of sparks, you got out of the way. Even the windlasses, the two drums that raised the anchors, were prodigious-looking, though all the machinery associated with powering them was deep belowdecks.

The two men continued until they had passed the hawse-pipes and stood at the "eyes of the ship." If there had been a fog the lookout would have been posted here, but there was no fog. They were still talking when a sharp lieutenant marched up to them and planted himself crisply at ease.

"This is Lieutenant Allwyn, my communications officer," said Krosmeyer.

Allwyn nodded to the elderly civilian, whose name was not given in return.

"Mister Allwyn," Krosmeyer addressed him, "we want you to arrange a radio patch to the police department in Wichita, Kansas. Can you handle that?"

"Yessir."

"I thought so. That was the simple part. After that we'd like you to rig up a low-frequency transmitter with enough power to reach a submarine ten to fifteen miles away. How about that?"

"No problem. She's surfaced?"

"No. Submerged."

Allwyn appeared to lose his assurance. "That's another matter altogether, sir."

"I know that."

"Water is a bad medium for radio waves. Only extremely low-frequency transmissions propagate underwater, and then it requires a great deal of power. The ELF waves the Navy uses to communicate with its submerged force are the only—"

"Yes, yes, we know about that," said the elderly man.

"But we don't want to transmit ten thousand miles. Ten miles ought to do it."

"I suppose we have the power. I could jury-rig some kind of transmitter. But you'd need a good-sized antenna."

"How big?"

"A lot bigger than anything we've got. The *Jersey*'s only a hundred seventy feet tall, including our tower, and a low-frequency antenna should be ten times that high."

Reinholt walked a few steps away. They couldn't tell if he was looking down the barrels of those huge cannons or off into space.

"You're saying you can't do it?" he asked, with his back to the young lieutenant.

"No, sir. I'm saying it wouldn't do any good. No matter how much power you have, you can't transmit without some kind of an antenna."

"How long would it have to be?"

"You mean how high? It depends on your frequency. To transmit that far underwater you'd want as low a frequency as you could get. Say a hundred kilohertz. That would mean a wavelength of about ten thousand feet. The lower the wavelength, the higher the antenna. A vertical Marconi tower would normally be one-fourth the wavelength. At least two thousand feet high."

"I see."

The lieutenant wondered who this man was. He seemed to know his way around, and yet he looked more like an American Legion local president or VFW bigshot than anything else. He was past any active duty, that much the lieutenant was sure about.

"What would happen if instead of sticking up in the air the antenna were hanging in the water—suspended? Would that work?"

Allwyn considered this. "It ought to. You're transmitting into the water."

"What've you got in mind?" asked Krosmeyer, stepping up beside Reinholt.

The admiral pointed to the long rows of anchor chains, whose half-ton links disappeared down the hawsepipes where they attached to the anchor shackles.

"You could lower your anchor."

Lieutenant Allwyn nodded his head in appreciation while Krosmeyer was thinking it over. "Eleven shots on the one. Ten on the other. Fifteen fathoms per shot. That's only a thousand feet at the most," Krosmeyer observed.

"Together, almost two thousand," said Reinholt. "Walk one all the way down and stop it off. Break the chain on both, shackle them together, and lower the other nine hundred feet."

"God! That's a helluva lot of weight on my windlass," groused Krosmeyer. "Navy regs specify a three-to-one safety factor. I'll have to talk to my ground tackle crew."

"Get 'em up here right now."

"And Lieutenant Allwyn?"

"Have him make the patch to Wichita and I'll meet him in the message center."

Allwyn started off; when he was out of hearing, Captain Krosmeyer muttered to Reinholt, "What do you suggest I tell the ground tackle crew when they ask me about the safety factor?"

"Tell 'em on this one there isn't gonna be any safety factor."

# Chapter Nineteen

Tides change. What ebbs for one, floods another. But never for long. Tide is time, tide is motion, tide is change; the moment it stops coming in, it starts going out, and goes out until the moment it starts coming back in.

When the tide changed for Drew Murdock's men it came in so fast and so hard it inundated the forces of the hijackers like a bore, an unstoppable wall of water that can demolish a coastline or rush for miles up the mouth of the mightiest river.

"What the hell. . . ?" Drew Murdock bolted out of his bunk.

The other officers, Shorter, Buchanan, and Thomas were fighting to their feet, staring toward the torpedo room door with faces that mirrored his startled expression. A clatter in the passageway sounded like Chinese New Year.

"Gunfire," said Murdock.

"Hey, be careful, skipper."

Murdock charged to the door, spun the operating wheel, and pulled it open. A hijacker was kneeling just a few feet away, firing intermittently down the passageway at an unseen target. Whirling, he spotted Murdock coming through the door and started his weapon around. Buchanan tried to push Murdock out of the way, but the commander had already thrown himself into the air.

"Look out!"

Bullets ricocheted off a bulkhead as Murdock landed across the hijacker's chest. Both men went down together and rolled. Then one of them pushed away and bounded to his feet. He lined up his weapon on the other.

A single explosion echoed down the passageway and the hijacker fell back. He crashed to the deck and lay still. Buchanan and Shorter helped Murdock up. "Dammit, Drew, are you trying to get yourself killed, or what?"

"Take it easy, skipper," asked Buchanan.

And then Thomas was hobbling up to them and the four officers watched the sniper approach, a dungareed specimen who was flashing them a smile wider than the three chevrons on his sleeve.

"Gus!"

Buchanan clapped his fire-control petty officer on the back while Shorter and Thomas complimented his marksmanship. Murdock went to the fallen hijacker to recover the dead man's weapon.

"You sure took your time," said the communications officer. "We figured you for a goner."

"Yeah, didn't Kaseem send someone out to get you?"

"No, sirs," said Gus Toole, still grinning. "We been left to . . . what you might call . . . our own devices."

"What's the situation?" asked Murdock, joining them.

"I've got two guys on Deck Three right now," Gus said, sobering, "freeing the rest of the crew."

A burst of automatic fire over their heads interrupted his report. Seconds later the volley was returned.

"Sounds like they're having trouble."

Without waiting for orders, the petty officer raced for the ladder, calling back over his shoulder: "We have to hit fast before they can send down some reinforcements from the upper decks." This possibility had already occurred to the others as well and they hurried after him.

They crept up the ladder together.

"Keep your heads down!" someone shouted, as spent shells whistled over their heads.

The two men, an engine man and missile technician, were pinned down by heavy fire. Lead was ricocheting down the passageway walls. The MT turned when Gus and the others crawled up behind him.

"How many, Buck?"

"Just one, I think. Behind that corner of the mess."

As he spoke, a weapon and two hands (but nothing more) projected into the passageway and loosened half a clip in wild circles. The men melted into the walls and floor platings. "We'd better do something soon," said one. "He's gonna have help in a minute, and they may decide to start using the men for a shield." The gunfire ended for a moment, but this was broken by shouts from the hijacker directed at the upper decks, cries for help were shrieked in an undecipherable gibberish.

"All we done is worry him, and not too much," said Buck.

"What's that over there?"

Beyond the hijacker's position, a part of the deckway was rising. "It's the passing scuttle from the torpedo room," said Buchanan. "But what idiot . . . ?"

Carefully the scuttle cover was laid back and a man's head appeared from below.

"Dammit!" cried Shorter. "That's the skipper!"

"And not a speck of cover."

"Someone go back below and get him out of there."

Instantly Shorter crawled to the ladder and disappeared.

Murdock's head was completely exposed as his weapon came up and out. When his shoulders and arms cleared the scuttle he took aim. And then, just before he could fire from behind the hijacker, he looked up at the 'tween-decks opening atop the ladderway. Reinforcements were on their way down. He jerked the weapon up and hammered lead through the steps of the ladder until the new-comers retreated.

This was all the warning the beseiged hijacker needed.

Bullets pinged off Murdock's scuttle cover and bulkhead, but he didn't even duck. He lowered his automatic and began firing back.

The six men bunched up in the passageway still had no target. They shouted for Murdock to get down.

They say his head fly back as though he'd been socked in the nose. A crimson smear parted his scalp right down the middle. He started to drop back into the torpedo room but caught himself just in time, leaned over the scuttle, found his target with glazed eyes, and resumed firing.

"What the hell's he trying to do," shouted Gus Toole in a fit of insubordination, "commit suicide?"

"Gimme that weapon, Gus."

Ben Buchanan clambered to his feet and dashed down the passageway. Once near the mess he dove to the deck and slid past the corner, firing a continuous spray until his clip had emptied itself and the hijacker stopped moving.

The silence was startling.

He leaped to the scuttle and pulled Murdock through; he didn't stop pulling until they were out from under the upper deck opening.

"Just relax, skipper. Don't you know you've been hit?"

Murdock's wound was bleeding profusely. The bullet had gouged out a six-inch furrow from the crown of his head, but Buchanan couldn't see where the skull had been pierced.

Murdock pushed him away and stood. "It's all right, it just caught the skin." Someone tried to place a compress on Murdock's head but he brushed this away, too. "I'm okay."

The others were closing ranks around them. Shorter climbed through the scuttle. "Get that man's weapon, and someone stand guard under this ladder," ordered Murdock, indicating the one leading to Deck Two. "I don't want any more of them coming down."

Gus and his two cohorts took up positions. "Poke a nose through that hole, let's blow it for 'em," one managed to say before their words were drowned out by excited cries from the mess room. The mess door had come open and men were swelling into the passageway.

The officers tried to keep order.

"Keep those men inside until we decide where to move them," said Shorter.

"No, give that weapon to the chief."

Chief of the Boat Rawlenson strode out of the throng of sailors. Large and powerful, he was the ranking enlisted man and a born sailor. "Chief," said Murdock, "take a couple men and make sure this deck is clear for'ard. Bring any weapons you find back here."

"Yes, sir."

"Skipper?" Buchanan eased Murdock to one side as the chief started off. Two armed men, Murdock's yeoman and the quartermaster, had fallen in behind the chief.

"Make it fast, Ben, we're rushing this ladder in about two minutes." By this time Murdock was losing so much blood Buchanan worried he might not have two minutes left.

"You're going to get your head blown off the way you're going, skipper."

"I'm taking this ship back."

"Fine, but let us help. You can't do it all yourself, and after everything we've been through it'd be a shame if you died now."

"Would it? Get with your missile technician. He seems to have kept his head nicely. Find out how many casualties he's got and how many the other side's lost. If there's any man in the dinette who's just returned from topside duty, I want to talk to him right away."

Gus made his report directly to the skipper. "We hold

the engineering and missile compartments, sir. I stationed armed men at the WT doors leading aft from the command center deck and missile control room. We got them bottled up good.''

"You say no one ever came aft to get you?"

"No, sir. I was just finishing the post-launch check when we heard this banging in the launcher and—"

"Yes, yes I know about the man coming into the tube and your quick work with the hijacker. That was my brother. He said you went aft to secure the engineering— Yes, what is it, Mister Thomas?''

"My sonarman, Fencil here, just came below, skipper. He says Kester and Scotty were in the command center with two of the Iranians when he left.''

"How many of our guys are up there, sonarman?"

"Five . . . no, six, sir."

"What about Kaseem and Captain Yankov?"

"They left the control room before I came below."

"Where?"

Fencil shrugged, though still at attention. "I don't know, sir. But I think they went into the missile center.''

Murdock turned back to Gus. "How many men have they lost?" he snapped.

"Four, sir. Counting this gook here and the one below.''

"That leaves three unaccounted for. They may be with Kaseem and Yankov, or they may be in the officers' staterooms on Deck Two.''

"Yes, sir," said Fencil.

"Okay. That's all. Wait, Mister Thomas . . . here comes the chief with a few more weapons. You take one and give the other to Shorty. Distribute the rest to the men. Okay, Toole, you were saying . . .''

"Buck and me ambushed the second gook in the engine room who was guarding three ETs: Dix, Bayer, and Williams. I gave Williams and Bayer the extra weapons and told them to watch the doors aft of navigation and missile sections. They could maybe use some help if—"

"Okay, that's fine. Good work, Toole. Take your MT and go support those positions. That's all. Yeoman?"

"Sir?"

"Are you up to one more bit of action?"

"Count me in, sir. And all the other men, too. They'll fight with table forks and butter knives if you need 'em."

"It may not come to that. Get your guys ready. How'd it go, Chief?"

"Three weapons. No resistance, sir."

"Okay, then they're all on Decks One and Two. Have you checked the small-arms locker?"

"Empty, sir."

"They've got all the weapons up there. And they'll dig in like ticks if we hit 'em head-on."

"How are you gonna play it, skipper?"

"Hit 'em head-on."

"There'll be problems choosing men."

"We've only got weapons for seven or eight altogether. I know you can find that many—"

"Yes, sir. Seventy or eighty would be no problem. The problem is gonna be the ones we don't take. They won't like being left behind. You might have a mutiny on your hands."

"Tell 'em to get their butter knives ready, because if we don't make it they'll have to follow us up."

Murdock moved to the foot of the ladder.

"Skipper!"

Shorter and Buchanan pulled Murdock aside. Buchanan had enlisted the reactor officer's help in getting Murdock to see reason. "Dammit, sir," said Shorter, "you're the CO. You're not expendable. And you're hurt. Let me or Ben lead the men up while you get your head—"

Murdock's face was stone. "You're wrong, Shorty. I'm no CO. I didn't make the grade."

"Dammit, Drew—"

"And I am expendable. In fact, I'm as good as dead now." Murdock eyed his armed squad. "Let's go," he said. With that he raised his weapon and sprang for the ladder, not bothering to sneak up but instead taking the steps two at a time.

The rest followed on his heels.

If it had been a charge they would have been eight men abreast when they broke through onto Deck Two, but the ladder permitted only one man to ascend at a time. So they fought for a position in line. They pushed and shoved their way to the top.

Had they encountered any resistance Murdock would have been the first of several to die. Their gunfire alone, ricocheting off the steel bulkheads, deck, and overhead, would have torn their own men to pieces.

They met no resistance. The door to the missile room was closed. It was the same for the 'tween-decks hatch leading up to the command center.

They assembled outside these barriers.

"All right, Ben," said Drew Murdock. "Keep the men here. Make sure no one opens these doors or hatches. Shorty? Come with me. Bring the chief and a couple of men. Yeoman, QM, I want to secure these for'ard compartments."

Murdock lurched off toward the bow, with Shorter and the others in hot pursuit. He was the first one to step through every door, daring any unauthorized occupants to riddle him with slugs before he fired at them. They checked the ship's office, the officers' study, the computer room, and then, one by one, the officers' quarters. At the stateroom next to his own Murdock stumbled inside, crouched, rested his hands on his knees, and breathed for two. Blood ran off his head and collected in a small pool in the middle of the room.

"Chief," said Shorter, "check out the other staterooms and the captain's cabin and meet us back here."

The three petty officers moved forward. "Are you gonna make it, skipper?"

"Yes. Aren't these your quarters?" Murdock asked him without looking up.

"Yes, sir."

His head came up. "Which was Scotty's bunk?"

"That one."

"That's his trunk?"

"Yes, sir."

"Where did he keep his sea sample collection?"

Shorter drew back in surprise. "I suppose in his trunk. I caught him looking it over one day. When he saw me that's where he put it, and fast."

"Let's see if we can find it. But be careful."

Shaking his head in confusion, Shorter dropped to his knees at the foot of Longfellow's bunk, and a moment later Murdock was beside him lifting the trunk lid.

Together they dug through the neatly stacked uniforms until they'd exposed a small wooden case on the bottom and pulled it out. Shorter opened it up.

"Well, I'll be damned. They're gone. All but two."

Murdock carefully inspected the miniature jars in their receptacles. One was labeled Arctic Ocean, with latitude and longitude numbers. It was slightly milky. The other was a tea-colored sample from the Black Sea. Murdock could hardly believe a Navy sub had made it into that Soviet sea, but the color of the water lent credence to the claim. It showed a clever attention to detail.

"This doesn't surprise you does it, skipper?"

"That they're missing? No, I'd have been surprised to find them all here."

"What do you make of it?"

"Exhibit A in the murder trial of Scott Longfellow. If, that is, we ever make it back to Pearl Harbor. Here, you keep the case. I just wanted to be damn sure that any extra bottles weren't where Kaseem's men could get their hands on them. For god's sake, be careful with them: Don't let any get broken.''

"But what are they?''

"You might call them throwaway bottles, Shorty.''

"Scotty threw them out?''

"In a manner of speaking. He went from compartment to compartment, opening the watertight doors, throwing bottles inside and then closing the doors quickly before moving on. I found the broken bits of one of these bottles just inside the torpedo room. Any man who was close enough to see him or recognize him didn't stand a chance.'' Murdock stood up and acknowledged Chief Rawlenson's arrival with a nod.

"Secure, sir.''

"Nothing?''

"Any of them peckers on this deck,'' he said, "are in the missile room.''

They were joined in the passageway by sonarman Fencil, who was panting hard from running. "Skipper!''

"What is it?''

"Come quick. There's shooting coming from the command deck.''

They ran back to the ladderway.

Commander Buchanan had braced himself at the foot of the ladderway, with his rifle in hand. Three men had planted themselves behind him, waiting for a signal to move out.

"Gunfire, skipper. We think they may be shooting some of the men.''

"That doesn't make sense. Shoot their hostages?''

"If they're— Listen! There it is again.''

Several bursts of automatic fire sounded quite clearly through the 'tween-decks hatch to Deck One.

"Okay,'' said Murdock. "We can't take a chance. Follow me.''

"I'll take the—''

But it was too late. Murdock had launched himself up

the ladder, thrown open the hatch, and stepped to the command deck. There were sounds off to his left, muffled cries in the control room. And the sound of running footsteps. Off to his right he could hear the crackle of electrical shorts and the flickering of small flames.

The six *Alaska* crewmen were trussed in a neat bundle in the middle of the control room, hands tied behind their backs and gagged but otherwise apparently unharmed.

"Ben, check navigation. Someone ran in there. Chief, follow me."

Murdock found the casualties in the radio room. Every piece of radio equipment in the compartment had been sprayed with bullets. The sonar section had been spared, but not a single radio unit forward of sonar had survived the shambles.

"Damn!" said the chief.

Ensign Thomas came in just as Murdock and the chief had armed themselves with fire extinguishers and begun to spray down the electrical panels. He limped from one station to the next, staring at the destruction in undisguised horror.

Then they raced back to the control room and attacked the ropes binding the six crewmen.

"Talk fast," said Murdock to the first one whose gag had been removed.

"That captain, Dr. Kester, he and Mr. Longfellow put on scuba equipment and climbed up into the escape trunk, sir. Those two gooks shot up the radio room and then ran back past us into navigation with all of their ammunition."

Buchanan hustled in to report. "Gone," he said. "And all the arms from the weapons locker gone, too."

"What happened, Ben?"

"They dropped down through an escape scuttle in the navigation deck into the missile room. I've got a couple of men keeping a watch on the scuttle to make sure none of them come back up. They're trapped. They can't go aft, for'ard, up, or down.''

"So they're all down there together now?"

"Yes, sir.''

"Kaseem and five of his men, and Captain Yankov. And enough weapons and ammunition to hold off a small army.''

"Yes, sir . . . and . . .''

The two men momentarily eyed one another in stone-faced silence.

"And the missile controls,'' said Murdock at last. "The launch buttons to twenty-two Trident missiles are in there, too.''

"Yes, sir.''

"Jesus Christ! How long would it take them to prepare for a launch?''

"We're at launch depth now,'' said Buchanan. "Five minutes. Six at the outside. They've had that already.''

"Couldn't you shut down the launchers from the launch deck?''

"Sure I could, if I had the time. All the launch tubes have manual controls.''

"How much time would you need?''

"Not long. Sixty seconds would do it. But that's per tube. There are twenty-two launch tubes. I'd like half an hour.''

"Well you'd better get going, Ben. Get some men to help you and try to cut down the time.''

"Yes, sir. Suggestion, skipper?''

"Anything.''

"It would only take us a couple minutes to dive below launch depth. Four hundred feet. Five hundred just to play it safe. At that depth it wouldn't matter if they launched or not. The missiles would never reach the surface.''

"That's good, Ben.'' Murdock slapped him across the back. "Okay, leave that to me. On your way to the launch deck." As the weapons officer hurried away, Murdock whirled to his quartermaster. "Higgins."

"Sir!"

"Sound general quarters."

"Aye-aye, Commander."

The QM moved to the internal communications panel and depressed a switch that was isolated from all the others on the 1MC board and clearly marked.

A horn blared its strident alarm in every compartment and section of the ship while the call was repeated over and over: "General quarters! General quarters! All hands man your battle stations." What followed was organized bedlam. A charge of feet sounded in the passageways and on ladderways as the men raced to their battle stations with practiced speed and efficiency. Airtight and watertight doors banged shut. Hatches were secured. The *Alaska* was battened down to ZEBRA condition for maximum flood-and-fire control. She wasn't a dead ship any longer. A flood tide had washed life back into her corpse.

When Commander Shorter reported to the control room as CIC officer, Murdock, quickly briefed him on their situation.

"How about power, Shorty?"

"The reactors are ready when you are, skipper. I assume you want some headway?"

"I don't think so. There are two attack subs out there that would love an excuse to put some holes in our sides."

"What, then?"

"Dive. Drop like a stone for four or five hundred feet, and then get the hell out of here before they decide what to do with us. You're acting exec, Shorty. I want you in the secondary control room. Get your Combat Information Center together and see that a damage control party is formed right away."

"Yes, sir." Shorter turned and sped off.

Murdock placed a telephone headset to his ears. "Engine room, control; how's our steam?"

"Engine room, aye-aye; wait."

"Torpedo room, control; load torpedo tubes one, two, three, and four."

"Torpedo room, aye-aye; loading tubes one, two, three, and four."

"Control, engine room; steam is at sixty percent. I can give you two-thirds power, skipper."

"I want a hundred-percent steam and I want it fast. Ready for maneuvering at flank speed. On my call and not before."

"Engine room, aye-aye."

"Sonar, control; are your ears on?"

"This is sonar, aye-aye."

"There are two other submarines out there, and if either of their captains so much as breaks wind, I want to know about it before the nearest man catches a whiff."

"Aye-aye, skipper."

Murdock swept his eyes over his control room crew. "Rig for dive, gentlemen."

"Helm ready, skipper."

"Dive manifold ready."

"Commander, I've got a light out on my Christmas tree."

"What is it?"

"Outside escape hatch not set . . . forward air lock."

A dozen pairs of eyes looked up to the escape trunk by which Captain Kester and Scotty Longfellow had just left the submarine. Seconds later, the damage control assistant was reporting to Murdock.

"The inside hatch cover is closed but the air lock is still flooded, Commander. Looks like the last man to leave the trunk simply left the outer hatch open."

"What can you do?"

"Nothing from inside. We can't open the inner hatch without bringing in the whole ocean. We could surface. . . ."

"No."

"Then I'll have to send a diver out one of the other escape hatches and close it from outside."

"How long?"

"Ten minutes."

"No."

The DCA shrugged. "What, then, skipper?"

"Will the inside hatch withstand a dive to five hundred feet?" Murdock asked him.

"The book says no. But you might get away with it." Murdock smiled.

"Let's find out." He turned to the manifold operator. "Flood trim tanks."

"Aye—"

"*Commander Murdock!*"

All activity stopped.

All eyes turned to the intercom speaker.

The caller hadn't identified himself. He didn't have to. The crew had listened to that bullhorn of a voice for too long ever to mistake it. The ship's intercom was sensitive enough to transmit a whisper from one end of the vessel to the other, but this was a bellow that shook the very decks at their feet.

"*Murdock, this is Kaseem in the missile center. Answer me!*"

Murdock said nothing.

"*I have a depth gauge in front of me. If the submarine descends below our present depth of one hundred feet I shall begin launching missiles at random.*"

One by one the heads and the eyes turned to Murdock. He said nothing.

"*If you do not reply to me within ten seconds, I shall launch the first missile.*"

Seconds ticked by.

Murdock strode to the intercom and depressed the switch connecting him to the missile room: "This is Murdock."

"*You heard what I said?*"

343

"Yes."

*"I am ordering you to surrender. I want you and all of your officers and all of your weapons turned over to me here in the missile room. Within the next three minutes."*

"Or . . ."

*"Do I have to repeat it? The missiles are now ready to launch."*

"Is Captain Yankov there?"

*"He is."*

"Let me talk to him."

*"That won't be possible."*

Murdock rushed ahead. "Captain Yankov, I know you can hear me. This is one of those times when reason must prevail over rage. If you still have any influence with Kaseem I suggest you use it now, for all of our sakes."

The intercom was strangely silent.

"Captain, you haven't had time to retarget those warheads. You know where the missiles will go. You can't let that happen. None of us want that, do we, Captain?"

Silence resounded throughout the room.

"Well, Captain?"

*"He didn't hear you, Murdock. He was too busy being dead. But he felt much the same way. In fact, his opinions on the matter were even stronger than yours, for the obvious reasons. Unfortunately the man's neck was weak. He's lying here at my feet. And his opinions no longer concern me."*

"Goddammit, Kaseem . . ."

*"You have two minutes, Murdock."*

Murdock exhaled long and hard. He looked slowly around his command center. "Quartermaster."

"Yes, sir?"

"Have Commander Shorter meet me at the forward missile room door as soon as possible. Tell him to bring that box he was safekeeping for me. Then get to the launch deck and ask Commander Buchanan for a progress report. Don't use the intership communications, Kaseem may be listening in. Make it quick.''

"Yes, sir.'' The QM hustled out.

Ensign Thomas appeared from the sonar room. "You want me, too, skipper?''

"No,'' said Murdock, "you'd better stick around. You're in command until Shorter shows up.''

With that Murdock left the command center. He descended the ladder to Deck Two and walked back to the missile room.

The bore tide was still coming in.

Nothing could stop it. Not Kaseem with all of his strength and all of his men. Not even Murdock himself.

Shorter's objections meant nothing. He might have objected to a rising wall of water for all of the good it would do.

Just before the two-minute deadline was up, Drew Murdock opened the missile room door. At a glance he could see there were no members of the *Alaska* crew inside. That would make what he had to do a lot easier.

The five Iranian gunmen were scattered throughout the room, kneeling and pointing their rifles at Murdock. Kaseem hovered eagerly over the launch panel. The twisted body of Captain Yankov lay at Kaseem's feet. He was dead, all right. When a head takes that angle to the shoulders, death is the instantaneous result.

That was even better.

*"Where are the rest of your officers?"*

"They're—''

*"I want them all in here now!"*

"What about Captain Kester and Commander Longfellow? Do you want them?''

It started out as a rumble, like a mine caving in deep down in the big man's stomach, but when he opened his mouth it was not dust and smoke that belched out but laughter.

*"You hope to trade prisoners with me? You fool. Do I*

*care what happens to Kester and Longfellow? Kill them. Do whatever you want with those two . . . officers! It won't mean anything to me.''*

''I don't have them. We control every compartment of the ship except this one, but Kester and Longfellow aren't here.''

Kaseem straightened to his full height and narrowed his eyes. *''You're lying!''*

''No, I'm not. You're the fool. Kester and Longfellow, your comrades-in-arms, have left you holding the bag.''

Kaseem looked nervously around. His position was unassailable. But he was starting to sweat.

*''Get them in here!''*

''You still don't get it, do you?''

With a savage snarl Kaseem closed in. Murdock held his ground, and the bigger man stopped when the distance between them only had been halved. Kaseem wanted to attack, but he didn't. He was like a beast that approaches within springing distance and waits for its prey to show fear, or for its own bloodlust to drive it into a rage that will overcome its hesitation. He glared at Murdock with feral fury.

Murdock kept talking. ''Scotty Longfellow knew that some of my men had overpowered one of yours. He knew they'd gotten their hands on some weapons and were going after some more. Scotty found that out from my brother, the man you blasted into the sea. He told you about my brother because Coy worried him. But he didn't tell you about the rest. What did he do? I can guess if you'd like. He or Dr. Kester arranged for you and the captain there to come down into the missile room.''

Kaseem had gone stiff. His every muscle tensed for the inevitable leap.

''He knew about a transmitting device on the bow, too, but I doubt he mentioned it to you. You see, he and the doctor had no intention of hanging around. They left through the forward escape hatch before we took over the control room. And they left the hatch cover open. Why? So no one else could follow them out. Not your men. And not you."

*"Those dirty back-stabbing sons of bitches!"*

Murdock suppressed a cruel smile. He had to make Kaseem mad. Mad enough to kill. But not crazy enough to launch any missiles.

An almost human self-control turned Kaseem toward the firing panel.

"You're a sacrifice play, you idiot." Murdock swung a hand around the room. "You've been left here to die, you and all of your men. Outsmarted by the likes of Longfellow and Kester." Murdock laughed out loud. "A couple of—"

*"Officers!"*

Kaseem turned back around.

"That's right. A couple of officers like Longfellow and Kester."

*"And you!"*

"Sure, like me. I'm going to outsmart you, too. You're big and you're strong, but you haven't got shit for brains."

Kaseem sprang.

Murdock had known it was coming. He had seen the primeval rage detonate in the big man's eyes a moment before he exploded.

He rushed Murdock, grabbed him with those great hands, and threw him against a bulkhead. Murdock fell to the deck. And then Kaseem was over him, pummeling Murdock's head, his stomach, and chest with blows. Murdock had no way of knowing how long it went on. He didn't have the strength to fight back. He fought unconsciousness instead. He couldn't black out. That was the one thing he couldn't do. He had a dazed impression that some of Kaseem's men had closed in and were shouting and tugging at their leader's clothes. They must have figured this was a diversion, that the doors would open and armed sailors would mow them down. But it didn't happen. Minutes passed. The doors remained closed.

Murdock's tide had reached its height. An angry surf battered the shore, throwing its fury as high and as far as it could reach in its hatred of all things terrestrial before the ebb tide forced its retreat. Waves lifted Murdock up and smashed him into the reefs. Not once, but again and again. Each time he would cling to the rocks until the back-rush again pulled him down. It couldn't go on forever. Murdock couldn't last. At some point the sea would either spew him out on the beach or tow him back out to the greater depths, this time for good.

Finally, abruptly, it ended, and for no apparent reason.

Murdock felt a great weight leave his chest. He tried to roll over and get to his hands and knees. He couldn't find the strength. Twisting his head to one side to follow Kaseem was the best he could do.

Kaseem had stood. He was looking around.

*"What are they doing?"*

Now Murdock heard it, too, a banging outside the doors.

He struggled to keep his head above water. Somehow he had to endure just a little bit longer. After that, let the sea have him. He tried to speak but he couldn't. His mouth was full of blood and his lips were smashed beyond use.

He wanted to tell Kaseem it was over. That his crewmen were locking them inside. Hammering wedges against the dogs to keep the doors from being opened from the inside or out until the *Alaska* arrived at Pearl Harbor. But it wasn't important that Kaseem understand.

Kaseem had moved to the intercom. He called to the control room and shouted a threat that Murdock didn't hear. But it didn't matter. The doors being locked meant that the missiles had been shut down from the launch deck. Nothing you do in here can make any difference now, Murdock thought to himself.

The answer Kaseem got from Shorter must have been very much the same as Murdock was thinking.

Kaseem whirled. He rushed Murdock again. But then he froze.

Murdock had pulled something out of his pocket and raised his hand as high as he could. It was a small glass vial of Black Sea water. How very appropriate, he thought. A toast to Captain Yankov and to the missiles that won't ever fly.

Kaseem's eyes bulged from his head. His mouth gaped and his nostrils flared. He yelled something to his men. He ordered them to stop him, to grab the bottle before it broke.

His words meant nothing to them.

They turned and ran.

But to where?

Kaseem started forward, changed his mind, and threw himself against the door, screaming at the top of his lungs.

But to whom?

Murdock smashed the bottle against the steel deck.

And then he lay still. He let the waves bury his head. He let the sea gather him into its depths. Drew Murdock had never been afraid of the sea. Not at all. He had loved it. Maybe that was his mistake. He had loved it too much. And he'd forgotten what his father had warned him: The sea is an angry god, his father used to say. You can love it, you can even worship it, but more than everything else the sea is a god to be feared. Because it never forgives. And it doesn't love back.

# Chapter Twenty

When the torpedo tube door closed in Coy Murdock's face there wasn't a lot he could do.

He could breathe . . . until the tube started filling with seawater, and then he couldn't even do that for very long. He could beat on the door till his knuckles turned raw, or beg them to let him out. But neither of these would help.

Coy pushed until he heard the locking mechanism engage, and then he stopped. He didn't waste time or energy trying to punch through a door designed to withstand a hundred tons of pressure. When seawater rushed into the tube he didn't utter a sound. It would have been a waste of breath.

He breathed.

He loosened the manual inflation valve on his life vest and blew the thing up as fast as he could. The vest should have been inflated three, four, and then five times over, but the hydrostatic pressure of sea water coming in through the tanks compressed the air as quickly as he could exhale it.

The last cubic inches of air he sucked from the roof of the tube and held in his chest.

He heard the muzzle door open; he saw a circle of blue twenty-one inches across and twenty feet off. Blue light reflected into the shaft.

Cold water sapped the heat from his body. Salt burned into his eyes.

And then an explosion of gas hit him head-on. It was so violent, so unexpected, it emptied his chest like a blow to the solar plexus. Instinctively he inhaled, and was shocked to feel air, not water, filling his lungs. Air, not a powder charge, propelled him through the torpedo tube. His arms clawed at small cracks in the slick metal surface; his feet flailed on the walls. But there was no slowing him down. The last bit of metal slipped out of his grasp and he thrashed in a dense cloud of opalescence, uncultured and unmatched pearls more valuable than any gem for the air they contained. They followed him toward the surface until, by a sleight of submarine design—a poppet valve—with which Coy Murdock was wholly unfamiliar, these bubbles were sucked back into the tube and Murdock was alone with the sea.

He was going up.

Marie's words echoed in his ear: Don't forget to breathe out.

He exhaled while the rounded bulk of the port bow fell past his eyes. When it canted away to the main deck he paddled with all fours just to stay against the hull.

The sail was off to the right, but he'd never reach it. As he rose, his vest was ballooning—the same way his lungs would have ballooned until they finally burst. Now he'd just keep going up faster and faster. To his left was the escape trunk, but he'd never get into this either. The hydrophone was wedged against the sail, right aft of the trunk.

He scrambled frantically, awkwardly through the water, reached the hydrophone just before he rose out of reach, and managed to grab hold of one of its legs. The hydrophone's weight was enough to neutralize his buoyancy. He hovered over the deck.

He had to hide the hydrophone. He had told them where they could find it—now it was up to him to keep them from getting it.

Murdock looked swiftly around. The water was transparent enough—even without a mask he could see a good distance. The surface was less than a hundred feet up. He could make it. But then what? The *Nomad* or the *Enchantress* might never spot him. Meanwhile, the *Alaska* could move on. And the *Seawind*, too. He had two or three minutes of breathable air in his vest. And nowhere to go. At least, nowhere on this vessel . . .

He searched the water ahead and off to the right. He saw nothing. But Drew had said the *Seawind* was there. And that was one place they wouldn't expect him.

What had the young officer said: broad on the starboard bow? Bow he knew. Starboard, too. But broad? Wide. Wide off the right front end? The guy could have just said so. Five seconds wasted.

Murdock kicked off his shoes and started swimming. He swam one-handed, because he couldn't let go of the hydrophone without going up. But then almost immediately he needed air, and he used the free hand for holding the vest inflator valve in his mouth.

He breathed into and then out of the valve. It was worse than tying a plastic bag over his head but there was no other choice. If he just exhaled into the water and inhaled from the vest he'd get maybe six breaths of air. It wasn't enough. His vest would lose all its buoyancy and soon he'd be forced to drop the hydrophone.

His expelled air contained unused oxygen. He'd hang on to it. Reuse it.

This wasn't the kind of theory that sounds good but fails to work well in practice. It didn't even sound good to Murdock. It was dumb. It was fatally flawed. And it was all that he had.

A matter of yards farther on he was starving for air. He'd held his breath for nearly a minute the first time. The second time he couldn't last thirty seconds. Before his six breaths were used, he was holding the valve to his mouth and breathing in and out without stopping. His lungs ached. He had to take another breath. So he took it. But breathing didn't make the aching go away.

He thought about turning around and going back. But when he turned to look, the *Alaska* had disappeared completely.

There was nothing to do except go up. Or go on.

He started kicking again. If he was moving at all, he couldn't sense it. His legs and arms had gone numb. His head pounded. And either he was swimming straight down into darker water or his eyesight was going, too.

The *Seawind* appeared quite literally out of the blue. Black shadows had swum past his eyes, but this was only the onset of blindness, the result of oxygen deprivation and a sign of his consciousness fading. Then some of the shadows formed themselves into vertical and horizontal planes. The propeller had a shape and a shade all its own. Murdock was too desperate to rejoice. By the time it registered that he'd stumbled onto the *Seawind,* his need for oxygen was just that much further advanced.

He drove himself onward harder than before.

The stern of the submarine passed below and behind him inch by maddening inch. His muscles had become so weak his limbs seemed to hang from his body.

There was a void in his lungs. Even when he inhaled to his limit they remained empty. His heart swelled with each beat, growing bigger and bigger, beating harder and harder as if it were trying to fill the vacuum. No quantity of air could satisfy him. His lungs heaved the same air in and out again and again without stopping. Air all but depleted of oxygen.

His brain was going now, too.

He was dizzy, half-blind. From one second to the next he couldn't remember where he was going, what he was looking for. He simply had to keep going and looking.

As Murdock swam over the deck, he saw something move. His obsession was such that he almost didn't turn, but he did. A hatch cover aft of the sail was coming open.

A man's arm levered it up and back on its hinges. It was a diver. His masked head popped from the hatch and he started up.

He saw Murdock. Both men made up their minds at the same time.

The diver started back down. He reached for the hatch cover.

Murdock pulled the pistol from his belt, aimed it point-blank at the diver's chest . . . and fired.

There was no way around it. His only choice was to kill.

Murdock couldn't even claim temporary insanity for this act of ordinary madness; he was desperate beyond measure, but rational in the extreme. He had no strength for a fight and he knew it. He had no time for finesse. He needed air now.

The pistol made an odd popping sound and fizzled when bubbles squired out of the barrel.

Then the diver arched his back and fell over the hatch. Murdock grabbed him, ripped off the mouthpiece, and shoved it between his teeth. The aching of his lungs disappeared with his first inhalation. He blew it out and inhaled again, not savoring the fruits of his crime but gulping them down in huge hunks the way a wild animal swallows its kill. He took a few more breaths too deep and too fast before he'd calmed enough to slow down. Breathing the good stuff like that would put him out just as sure as not breathing at all. By this time the shadows had left his vision. His head still hammered and his limbs still hung heavily, but after a while these symptoms went away, too.

The diver had been nothing.

Murdock had wanted the scuba. Killing had merely been the easiest way to get it. But the body remained while the prize escaped toward the surface in a cloud of bubbles. In ten years as a policeman he'd never shot anyone. He'd never even fired his gun on the streets. Now, after five minutes in the water, he'd killed for a breath of air.

Murdock lifted the diver out of the hatchway, verified that he was dead, took off his tank, mask, and flippers, and then let the weight belt drag him over the side. It was the safest thing to do, but somehow it wasn't the right thing to do. On an impulse Murdock grabbed for the body and pulled the lanyard on the life vest. As it inflated, the body rose toward the surface with Murdock's air bubbles.

When it was gone, Murdock dropped down into the hatch with his equipment, abandoning the hydrophone on the deck rather than trying to force it through the hatchway. He put on the mask and cleared it, closed and locked the hatch with the hand wheel, and looked around.

A light had come on automatically.

He was in a small tank. There was another hatch right below him, and control valves clearly marked on the sides of the tank. A copy of the decompression tables was posted on a plastic board right above a timer and a pressure gauge, but Murdock couldn't believe he'd been deep enough long enough to warrant decompression.

He blew the water from the tank by following the marked instructions, vented the pressure, and then set the breathing equipment to one side and pulled open the lower hatch.

A wave of foul air assaulted his nostrils.

He nearly gagged. He covered his nose and dropped the hatch cover.

What little of the stench had seeped into the air lock was enough to send Murdock scurrying for the scuba tank and mouthpiece.

After a while he opened the cover again and peered out. There was no sign of whatever had caused such a stink, but he saw something else of more immediate value. At the foot of the ladder that descended to the deck someone had laid out a complete set of clothes: trousers, shirt, jacket, even socks and shoes. Undoubtedly these belonged to the man he'd just murdered. Lying beside the clothes was a simple gauze respirator, the kind of mask used by Navy painters.

Murdock removed his life vest, took a last gulp of air from the scuba, and then climbed down the ladder. The first thing he did at the bottom was slip the mask over his mouth and nose. It was hardly up to the task but it was better than nothing, and it would help to hide his face in case he encountered any of the submarine's crew.

He took off his wet things and threw them into the air lock. The other clothes he put on at once, after which he shoved the pistol back down his pants and looked quickly around.

If the warning signs on the airtight door behind him could be believed, he was outside the reactor compartment. Murdock believed the warnings to the extent that he didn't venture through the door. Eventually he found a passageway that led aft around the reactor to the engineering spaces, but he didn't find anyone manning the machinery. Banks of control panels lined both sides of one room, the bulkheads, and overheads, but there was nobody monitoring he equipment. Beyond that were the steam-driven generators. Once again, unmanned. In the after-most section Murdock found a maze of pipes, electrical wiring, motors, and maintenance equipment, and nothing more.

Then, moving forward again, he almost bumped into three men coming back down the passageway. Only by cutting through the reactor compartment did he manage to miss them. It was a close call in more ways than one. Electrical panels were glowing all around him, vermilion lights throbbed overhead, and a narrow gantry encircled a shaft that was sunk in the deck like a hatchway to hell and that radiated an unearthly luminescence. He didn't look down. Nor did he glance at the readouts. He raced along the gantry to the opposite door, closed it behind him, and stood there giving himself the once-over.

Satisfied, he worked his way into the bows. In the living and control spaces he passed cabins with men resting inside. To his surprise they even slept wearing their masks, but after a moment's pause he understood. To be able to sleep *without* masks would have been more surprising.

The crew were a rough lot. He counted two dozen men altogether, excluding those on the command levels which he avoided. All wore breathing devices of some kind or other.

But there were still two things he hadn't found. The first of these he stumbled upon on Deck Two just below the command center.

It was an ordinary sailor's white denim sea bag. The name of the sailor who'd owned it was scrawled in bold black letters on the top near the draw string: KERNS. Another sea bag just like it was lying on its side: DREVECKY.

Murdock looked down the passageway. There must have been a hundred of them. All standing or piled up on the deck, plump full with their drawstrings drawn tight. They filled the passageway until only a narrow traffic-way remained to the side. They were propped against a ladder which breached the overhead to the control room.

Murdock knelt at the first one. He loosened the drawstring and looked in.

He'd known it was here, but he'd expected to find it in crates. That's how the treasure had been described to him. He'd not even considered the difficulties in moving so many awkward containers into and out of the air locks. Difficult? No . . . impossible, given the short time they'd had to complete the job. Most of the crates probably wouldn't even fit through the hatches. So they hadn't done that. They had taken the cargo off the *Batavia*, loaded it into a net suspended from a crane on the *Enchantress*, motored over to the *Seawind,* broke open the crates one by one, and dumped the priceless contents into the open air locks. When a lock was full someone inside would blow out the water, open the lower hatch, and let the *Batavia* treasure pour into these sea bags.

That's what Murdock was looking at now. The *Batavia* treasure: diamonds and rubies. Emeralds, jade, turquoise, and sapphires.

And gold. Gold carvings, golden goblets, gold tiaras and crowns. Necklaces, statuettes, even a courtier's knife and sheath made of solid gold. Gold masks, idols, and coins. In their present form they could furnish a dozen museums. Melted down, they would still represent untold millions.

Murdock, moving past the bags in a trance, started up the ladder to the control room, where he could see even more cargo. Sure enough, when they'd run out of sea bags they used garbage bags, cardboard boxes, and anything else they could find. The whole command deck, radio and navigation rooms, too, was being used as a hold. Only a few men stood at the stations. This was just as well. There was no room for more, cargo or crew.

"Where's my food? I thought Sloane was bringing me something to eat, dammit!"

Murdock ducked. Two men walked by the hatchway.

"I'm sorry, Mr. Wick. I sent him across to the *Alaska* with that signal. I thought someone there might be able to make some sense of it."

"It's still coming in?"

"Like clockwork. Same code. Same message."

The two men paused right at the top of the ladder. The smaller of the two matched Archie Wick's description to a T: a shriveled troll of a man. Even his voice, mask or no mask, was a grating troll's voice.

"We were supposed to have the inside track on all Navy communications."

"We don't even know it is a Navy communication. It's not their frequency and it's not their code."

"Whose code is it?"

The man with him was also an American, like all the other crewmen—probably members of Wick's crew, the ones he'd needed to operate this submarine. The ones he hadn't needed were occupying more permanant positions in the *Batavia*'s prize cargo-hold.

"Who knows? Thirty code? It's a new one on me. And so is a two code. The Navy doesn't designate their codes with numbers like that. And why two codes for one message of only half a dozen numbers? It's not Navy. I'm sure of that. But the MO signal between the message repetitions is Navy—that's the part that bothers me. It's a kind of homing signal. I sent Sloane over to confirm that with the *Alaska*'s radio people. Maybe one of them can make something of it."

"All right, we'll wait for his report. But I won't wait for long. H-hour is less than fifty-five minutes, and I want to be long gone by then. If Kester, Longfellow, and Lupo don't show up in fifteen, we're taking off."

"Whatever you say."

"Where are you going? The radio room's for'ard."

"I'm taking a break, Archie. I been staring at those numbers so long . . ."

"In that case why don't you get me something to eat?"

"Have a heart!"

"I can't stand going near the damn galley."

The second man grumbled that he would go.

Murdock stole back down the ladder and found his way to the galley. It was a compact nightmare in stainless steel, a Navy cook's dream. Two slim men could stand side by side in the middle, and neither would have to take a step to reach whatever they needed. Neither would be *able* to take a step, for the deck space wasn't big enough for that. But the galley was equipped with everything in the way of food preparation: pots and pans by the dozens, and every conceivable appliance for mass production of food. Beyond a short passage lined with dishware and utensils, a swinging door presumably led to the enlisted men's mess. Another door yet was to a "reefer" or frozen foods locker, and Murdock wondered if any of that would still be edible—the refrigeration equipment had been off for more than a decade, but during that time the *Seawind* had been sitting in a thousand feet of ocean, where the water temperature never rose much above freezing. In a cold, confined environment like this one, rotting would take a very long time. But something sure stank. The stench was much worse here than any place else he had been.

Murdock hadn't gotten any farther than that when he heard footsteps in the passageway.

"Now I'm Wick's personal mess boy, can you believe it? That little fairy!"

"Quitcher griping!"

"Anything's better than staring at those damn signals, I says to myself. I've got code thirty and code two coming out my ass, and those numbers, too. I don't think there's any sense to it. Gimme a break, I says to Wick. Okay, he says, go get me some chow. This is a break? Coming down here to this hellhole?"

"You'd better shut up. Unless you can talk and hold your breath at the same time."

Murdock looked hurriedly around. The galley was too small to offer a hiding place. Murdock crossed to the mess decks. For the first time he noticed the masking tape that had sealed the cracks round the door's sides, top, and bottom. Too late. His hand had already pulled the door open. He sensed something terribly foul. But he was already stepping inside, pulling the door closed behind him. He was only half-aware of having done this. It was almost as though the stench had reached out with its fetid fingers and pulled him inside.

Murdock's knees buckled. He felt immediately, physically sick.

He reached up to the light switch and threw it on.

His eyes widened at the sight. His hands leapt to the respirator and pressed it hard against his face. Here was the source of the stench that pervaded the *Seawind*. Death. The ship reeked of death. Nothing Murdock imagined could have prepared him for this. The one hundred and twenty-five enlisted men and officers who had crewed the submarine were piled nearly to the overhead in the center of the room, their bodies in such advanced stages of decomposition that it was not even possible to say where one body ended and another began. The clothes had rotted away years before. The rest was a monstrous pile of human putrefaction. They should have been stored in an airtight compartment. They hadn't been, because no one had known that the *Seawind* would be needed again. And when the killers had returned to this hellhole years later, not a man among them had had the backbone to transfer the remains. So they taped up the cracks around the door. They turned on the ventilators full. They wore masks when they worked and when they slept. And they carried the stench on their bodies wherever they went.

For several moments Murdock was powerless to rise. His head spun in circles and his body swayed. After a seemingly endless interval he summoned his strength ounce by ounce, fought to his feet, and fell back through the door.

When he stumbled into the galley, one man was scooping something out of a can. The other had not hung around. The man turned and stared, his expression behind the respirator a unique mix of surprise and anger.

"What the hell. . . ?"

Murdock was in no mood for subtleties. He pushed his pistol into the man's face.

"The message," he rasped. "Repeat it."

"Who the hell are you, and what message are—"

"The radio message, goddammit!"

Surprise had left the man's expression. He sensed that Murdock could hardly stand up. He knew somehow that Murdock wouldn't shoot unless he had no other choice. Help would come down the passageway any minute: help for him, not for Murdock.

"I don't know what you're talking about, pal."

Murdock spun him around. He pushed him through the swinging door to the mess decks.

"No! No, wait!"

The man's confidence evaporated. His eyes were filled with horror. When they reached the pile of half-consumed corpses his hands clawed at Murdock's front and his legs scrambled for balance. The two men plunged—Murdock on top of the other—into the mass and submerged themselves in once human goo. After tearing off the other man's respirator, Murdock buried his face and then pulled it out. What he saw shocked even him. He had expected panic. But the face he found had a look of wild, mindless hysteria.

"The message. Give it to me."

The voice was hardly recognizable as human. "Oh god! Let me out . . . !"

"Talk!"

"Code thirty, ten, eighty, fifteen . . ." The man winced. He swallowed air through his mouth and gagged. He was trying to talk without breathing. "Double-zero, ten, sixty-two, code two. That's all, I swear that's the whole thing! For god's sake let me out of here!"

"What's 'H-hour'?"

"I don't . . . I can't . . ."

Murdock shook him, then prodded him with the gun. But it was no use, the man was gone. Unconscious, or dead, it didn't matter to Murdock.

He crashed back through the galley to the passageway. Had anyone challenged him he would have shot the man then and there, one man or a dozen men. He would have thrown their bodies onto the pile. They deserved worse than that. But Murdock could think of no worse punishment than for these jackals to spend a few hellish minutes, an eternity, as Murdock had spent, in that room.

He looked for and finally found a head in the officers' country and fell over the basin. He was sick not once, but again and again.

He threw water on his face. He pounced on a bar of soap and scrubbed his hands and arms. He rubbed the bar over his shirt. It didn't do any good. No soap in the world could ever cleanse him of that.

# Chapter Twenty-One

The death-throe screams that sliced through the watertight doors of the missile compartment and rang down passageways and ladderways to every part of the ship were merely echoes. They were replays of the chilling chorus that a week before had filled the *Alaska*. In every section and at every battle station sailors stopped what they were doing and listened.

This time it was not their shipmates who were stricken. Who clawed at their own throats. Who threw themselves on the deck in convulsions. Who vomited blood. Who died. It was Kaseem and his men. None of the sailors would have offered a moment's pause for the souls of that bunch. But to a man they lowered their heads just the same. It was the cries of other men that echoed through their minds. Only those in the command center knew the truth: that one small cry among the screams deserved a farewell.

Commander Shorter stood like a man in a spell as the sounds died away. All of them stood or sat like that.

The dive operator failed to see the red light on the Christmas tree go out. But when he glanced at his board, it was green top to bottom.

"Mr. Shorter!" called the operator. "Sir, the forward escape hatch has closed!"

Shorter didn't turn.

"Mr. Shorter?"

A young sailor near the diving operator whispered, "Call him 'skipper'."

"But . . ."

"He's the CO now."

But then Shorter's spell had ended and he jerked around by reflex. "What was that?"

"Sir, the for'ard hatch . . . it's closed."

"Can you blow the escape trunk?"

"Aye, sir."

Shorter checked the board. He exchanged glances with the operator. He turned slowly around, trading glances with all of the men in their turn. Then he took his position in the control center.

"I want all of you to remember what happened here," he announced. "I want you to take it with you to your graves, whether that comes fifty years from now . . . or five minutes."

Men solemnly nodded their heads and there were murmurs of "Yes, sir."

Shorter activated the intercom. "All hands, now hear this: This is the . . . CO speaking. The *Alaska* is now in our hands. All the boarders have fled or been killed."

The cheer that rose from all decks forced Shorter to pause.

"That's enough, men—it's too early to celebrate. Most of you probably know there are a couple of enemy subs in the vicinity who would love to poke holes in our sides if they found out what I've just told you.

"We're diving now to maximum depth. Once we get there—if we get there—we'll try to slip away. Both of these subs are faster than we are, more maneuverable, and they carry a damn sight more armament. But we've got one thing they don't have. We've got you. So look sharp. The captain and the exec got us this far. Let's show 'em what we can do. Commander Shorter out.

"Are we ready, people?"

Crewmen whirled to their stations, gripped their controls, and regarded their instruments with fixed stares. Behind Shorter the quartermaster donned a sound-powered headset and prepared to relay his commands.

"Switch to red."

The lights winked out; a heartbeat later they returned ruby-red.

"Let's dive, people!"

The trim tanks were flooded. The *Alaska* was buttoned up for depth and battened down for action. Slowly at first, and then more and more quickly, she descended.

"Do we have power?"

The QM passed on Shorter's query to engineering.

"Aye-aye, sir. Just give 'em the word."

"Not yet."

"One hundred fifty feet, Skipper."

"Sonar, control room; talk to me."

"Sonar, nothing to report. Neither sub has done a thing. We seem to have caught them flat-footed."

"Trim, down ten to the eye."

"Aye-aye. Down ten degrees."

The decks pitched forward and, as they did, a bang of metal against metal sounded from the escape trunk. The inner hatch had opened and closed.

Someone was coming back in.

Chief of the Boat Rawlenson, the master-at-arms, drew his service revolver and rushed forward.

Two flippered feet descended the ladder. Then a scuba tank and the back of a diver's masked head. When the diver turned around and the face mask came off, Shorter's bruised face contorted in a sudden display of amazement.

"You!"

Coy Murdock tried to smile but couldn't quite muster the necessary muscles. Then he started to sit down, but the weight of his tank proved too much and he simply collapsed.

They helped him off with his scuba equipment.

He was breathing hard and trying to talk, something about hating the water, but they didn't understand any of this. "I saw . . . that open hatch," he managed to explain between pants, "and I said to myself . . . better to get shot by hijackers than . . . to spend one more damned second out there."

"Shall I take him below?" asked Chief Rawlenson, as he helped Murdock to his feet.

"It's all right, Chief. This man is Commander Murdock's brother. Follow me, Murdock." Shorter led them back to the control station, explaining as he went that the resistance movement Coy had started among the *Alaska*'s crew had proven completely successful.

"We're at three hundred feet, skipper."

"Control room, this is sonar; I'm picking up a general alarm in one of the subs."

Shorter acknowledged this report.

"Where's Drew?" asked Coy suddenly.

"Your brother is dead," replied Shorter.

"What! How. . . ?"

"Drew took the last of the boarders with him. I haven't time to explain more just now. Sit down here, please; don't move around or make any disturbance."

"I want to— Where is he?"

"He's in a contaminated section. You can't see him. Please keep quiet. Sonar, report."

"Yes, sir. I'm getting increased compressor activity on the Russian sub."

"What's our depth, Hicks?"

"Four hundred sixty feet, skipper."

Murdock fell into the chair beside Shorter. He combed his longish wet hair back with his fingers and closed his eyes. There was a bitter taste in his mouth. After twenty years apart from his brother, he had had ten minutes before losing him for good. Any victory after this would smack of defeat.

"Commander," he said, "there's one thing I have to tell you. You've been getting a radio message. . . ."

"Not now, Murdock."

"It's important."

"Later!"

"Five hundred feet, sir."

"Control room, sonar; I've got a propeller—no, I've got two. Both subs are making way."

"Okay, sonar, keep me informed. Ahead full."

"Engineering, control; ahead full," said the QM.

"Helmsman, right standard rudder."

"Aye-aye, right standard rudder."

"Answering ahead full."

The men held onto the safety bars and controls as the submarine lurched ahead and skewed into a sharp right turn at the same time.

It was all Murdock could do to stay in his seat. But when he looked up Commander Buchanan had just walked into the room, and he realized this was old hat to them.

"Thought you might need some help."

"Thanks, Ben. Stay handy." The calm of their voices astonished Coy. "Okay, Helmsman, meet her."

"Aye-aye, skipper; rudder is amidships."

"Control room, sonar here; I'm gonna have trouble with these soundings. I can't get a good sweep over our heads."

"Give me a guess, sonar."

"I think our second ghost, the American sub, is moving off to the south."

"What about the Russian sub?"

"It's diving, sir. Three hundred feet up and closing, bearing two-two-zero. Trailing twenty-five hundred yards behind us and closing."

"Okay, sonar. Helm, left standard rudder. Come to heading zero-five-zero, p.g.c."

"Aye-aye, left standard rudder."

The deck rolled to the left.

"Depth seven hundred feet, skipper."

"Trim her up, Harris. I want all the maneuverability this boat has got."

"Yes, sir. Adjusting variable tanks to neutral buoyancy, skipper."

"Let's have flank speed."

This was relayed. "Answering flank speed, sir."

"Mind your rudder, helm."

"Aye, sir."

"Zero bubble, skipper."

When the steam valves were opened full and the *Alaska*'s turbines red-lined, the vibrations could be felt from one end of the ship to the other.

"Helm, make it thirty down. Hold at nine hundred feet.

"Aye-aye, skipper, increasing dive angle to thirty degrees."

No sooner had the deck leveled its roll than it pitched forward at an impossible angle and the sub rocketed downward at a speed that left Murdock's heart far behind.

Buchanan and Shorter exchanged bland faces; the weapons officer raised crossed fingers.

A minute passed. Then another.

"Control room, sonar; that surprised 'em, skipper. We passed three hundred feet right under her keel."

Some of the men exchanged nervous smiles.

"You can't outrun 'em, skipper," said Buchanan. "You're lugging around fourteen hundred tons of missiles they don't have."

Shorter muffled the QM's mouthpiece in his fist. "Maybe not. They may be faster than we are but we have one advantage. We know what we're going to do and they don't."

"What *are* you going to do?"

"I wish to hell I knew."

"There's this, too. As long as we're running away, we can't fight. If they start launching torpedoes, we can't fire back."

"What has she got, Ben?"

"Wire-guided, like ours. Not so accurate and not so fast, but plenty fast and accurate enough. And at any kind of close range, her maneuverability will more than make up the difference."

"Control room, sonar; the Russian sub has turned around too, skipper. She's coming after us, there's no doubt about it."

"Acknowledged," said Shorter. And then he muffled the QM's mike again. "Any suggestions?"

"Why not try a little dialogue?"

"You mean talk to 'em?"

"Sure, why not?"

"Sir, we've reached nine hundred feet and I'm leveling off."

"Acknowledged, helm. QM, let's have Ensign Thomas come to the control center."

"Radio room, control center; report to the CO at once."

Seconds later the communications officer joined them.

"What are the chances of getting a message through to that Soviet sub?" Shorter asked him.

Thomas shook his head firmly. "No chance at all. Three hundred rounds of ammunition can do quite a job on IC boards. The radio room is nothing but parts, and not many of them are in one piece. My people are trying to patch something together. With luck, we may have a receiver going here soon."

"How long?"

"Ten or fifteen minutes."

"No transmitter?"

"Not for several hours."

"Well," said Buchanan, "now we know why they shot up the radio room."

Behind them Coy Murdock stood up. "Have you guys been getting a coded signal. . . ?"

The intercom squawked an interruption: "Control room! Sonar! I have a contact. They've launched a torpedo!"

"Bearing, range, and speed?"

Thomas raced back into the sonar room.

"Bearing one-seven-zero at sixteen hundred yards. Fifty-five knots!"

Shorter wheeled to his steersmen. "Helm, left full rudder."

"Aye-aye, left full rudder."

"Come to heading zero-four-zero."

"Zero-four-zero. Aye-aye, sir."

Buchanan quickly moved to one of the computer terminals and began rattling off calculations as fast as the computer generated them. "Their torpedo travels at forty-five knots and is closing on us at . . . about eleven knots," he announced. "She's fully guidable to the end of her guide wire, which is, say, twenty-six hundred feet. After that its a sound-seeker with the depth setting fixed."

Shorter acknowledged this with a nod. "If we wait till the fish leaves the guide wire and then make a quick change of depth and shut down the turbines, you think it might. . . ?"

"It might."

"Sonar, control room; give me separation of the fish to the Russian sub and seconds to impact."

"Sonar, aye-aye. Twelve hundred feet separation; one minute, five seconds to impact."

"Keep talking."

"It's gonna be close," said Buchanan.

"Tell engineering to pour it on back there."

"Answering another few RPMs, skipper."

"Fourteen hundred—fifty-seven seconds to impact. It's coming right up our tail. Sixteen hundred . . . now seventeen hundred. Eighteen hundred . . . Forty seconds to impact.''

Shorter ignored the intercom. "How sure are you of those numbers, Ben?''

"Reasonably sure. I'd stake your life on it.''

"Thanks a lot.''

"Twenty-one hundred feet and twenty-eight seconds to impact.''

"Goddammit, Ben, Drew should be here. He ran these drills with Captain West a thousand times. All I know is that damn reactor plant.''

"Twenty-four hundred feet and seventeen seconds to impact.''

"Have engineering get ready to shut everything down. We're going to idle the shaft on my signal.''

"Twenty-six hundred feet and nine seconds to impact.''

"Okay, that's it. Helm, climb! Up thirty degrees!''

"Aye-aye.''

"Idle shaft!''

"Shaft idling, skipper.''

"Twenty-seven hundred feet and five seconds to impact. Four. Three. Looks like she may pass below us.''

The ship turned quiet. Murdock was holding his breath. As he looked around him he knew that a lot of others were doing the same thing.

"Control room, sonar; passed ten feet under our keel.''

A dozen men exhaled.

Murdock was one of them.

Not Shorter: "Ahead full. Fast! Helm, turn to two-two-zero; right full rudder. Let's see what they do if we face 'em and they're lookin' down our torpedo tubes.''

"Aye-aye, skipper; two-two-zero; right full rudder.''

"Answering ahead full, sir.''

"Load torpedo tubes one and two.''

"Torpedo room; control; load tubes—'' The QM

whirled. "Torpedo room reports tubes one, two, three, and four loaded and ready for firing, skipper."

"Good man."

"Skipper! This is sonar! The Russians just launched another fish! Bearing one-two-zero at two thousand feet. We're turning right into it."

"Helm, hard over!"

"Aye-aye, skipper."

Buchanan leapt for one of the stanchions. "You don't have the speed or the distance to dodge it again."

Murdock wrapped both arms around a safety bar as the *Alaska* rolled onto her side and pirouetted on her starboard dive plane in a demonstration of hydrobatics that would have paled the faces of her builders at the Electric Boat division of General Dynamics.

It was a stunning maneuver, especially as experienced from inside the sub. The deck and the overhead had turned into walls and the men were hanging off the backs of their chairs.

It was a magnificent display of ship-handling. But it wasn't enough.

"Sonar, six seconds to impact."

"Fire torpedoes one and two!" shouted Shorter.

"Torpedo room; fire one and two."

"Three seconds to impact!"

Shorter dove for the intercom, threw the switch, and shouted into it: "All hands, brace for impact!"

"One and two away, skipper."

The torpedo struck the *Alaska*'s main deck, aft the sail, with a combination of horrors.

There was a roar like all the surfs of the world rolled into one thunderous crash. Decks lurched out from under men's feet. Safety bars were torn from their grasps and the men themselves tumbled out of their seats.

Everything shook violently. And the shaking continued even after the explosion had ended.

Water sprayed into the control room from half a dozen

sources: cracked pipes, broken valves, even through the access hatch to the sail.

Then came the hellish wrenching of steel as the outer hull ripped open.

If Neptune himself had gripped the submarine with both hands, one on the bow and the other on her tail, and tried his damnedest to break her in half, all the while growling and shaking with fury, the resulting destruction wouldn't have been very much different. Then the shaking stopped.

Murdock picked himself up off the floor.

But there was nowhere for him to go, nothing for him to do. He could only stand there watching in awe as men all around him hurried back to their stations. Shorter, drenched to the skin, moved into the center of the room and began shouting orders to the damage control team, to sonar, and the torpedo guidance crew.

Buchanan was back at his computer.

A repair party of tool-wielding technicians wearing the crossed fire ax and maul of damage control hustled in, split into groups, and attacked the high-pressure leaks with a calm competence that only comes with endless drilling. Hand wheels were tightened, pipes were disconnected or rerouted. Iron wedges were hammered into small cracks and caulked with quick-dry epoxy formulas. Portable pumps began removing water from the deck.

Through the chaos, Shorter's voice rose. "Did we get 'em?" he demanded.

"Negative, sir. Torpedo room reports two misses. They lost guidance control when the fish hit us and the Russian sub was too close for the torpedoes to home. Shall we fire three and four, sir?"

"We're not in position; hold on. Sonar, are you with us?"

"Aye-aye, skipper. This is sonar."

"What's she doing?"

"Just sitting there, skipper. About half a mile out, bearing . . . zero-two-eight."

Shorter turned to his steersman. "Have you got enough way to come around, helm?"

"No, sir."

"Is engineering still with us?"

"Engineering reports water coming in, sir, but the repair parties are working on it. They're also losing steam through a breach in the secondary loop and—"

"Can we get ahead one-third?"

"No, sir, but they'll give us what they can."

"Skipper, this is sonar again. She's moving around on us. Now bearing zero-three-five."

"Is she looking for a broadside, sonar?"

"Don't know, sir. But this close, she can turn a lot faster than we can. We'll never get lined up on her if she doesn't want us to."

Buchanan came over to Shorter. "He's right," said the weapons officer. "At three or four miles our fish would tear them to pieces. But at close quarters like this, it's their game. All the advantages are theirs."

"Control room, sonar! Another torpedo!"

"Bearing?"

"Zero-three-zero at eleven hundred feet."

"Engineering?"

"Still losing steam, sir. They'll need some more time to—"

Shorter cut him off and whirled to the manifold. "Blow negative."

"Aye-aye, Blowing main tanks."

Oh, Christ! thought Murdock, here we go again.

"Skipper, something's wrong! We're not holding air in the main tanks."

The damage control assistant hustled over with a husky hull-maintenance technician. "The outer hull is open, skipper!" shouted the DCA. "That last hit. The pressure hull has held, at least for now, but we can't expel ballast until the outer envelope is sealed.''

"What? You're telling me we've lost the main tanks?''

"Yes, sir, I am.''

"This is sonar. Torpedo at five hundred feet. And closing fast!''

"Ben?''

"You can't go forward or backward, you can't go up. What choice do you have, skipper?''

"Right. Harris, flood trim tanks. Fast.''

"Aye-aye; flooding trim tanks.''

"Torpedo at three hundred feet and closing.''

Shorter activated the intercom again: "All hands, brace for impact.''

The DCA clutched a safety bar with both hands. "We're almost to maximum depth now, Commander,'' he said. "And we're taking on seawater. The pressure hull is holding for the moment, but I wouldn't advise going any deeper than you have to.''

"Torpedo at two hundred feet!''

"Harris?''

"Going down, skipper. Nine hundred fifty feet. Nine hundred sixty. Seventy.''

"Torpedo at one hundred feet and still closing!''

There came a moment of silence.

"Fifty fe—''

Another crash interrupted the sonarman's call. This explosion was different, not a body blow, but a roundhouse that rolled the submarine onto its side. The *Alaska* was badly shaken. Decks listed to port and pitched down by the bow.

More water sprayed down on the control room.

Even before the deck righted, the repair parties had gone back to work.

The intercoms were jammed with reports of damage.

"They hit the sail!'' shouted the DCA to Shorter.

One of the steersmen confirmed this. The dive planes on the sail had seized.

"Sir! We're at one thousand feet and still falling!"

"Blow negative trim."

"Aye-aye."

"Tell engineering we need power and we need it now."

"Engineering's still working on it, sir."

Buchanan moved in close to Shorter. "We can't survive another hit, you know that."

"I'm not sure we've survived that last one. Harris?"

"One thousand fifty feet, skipper. We're slowing a bit. But we're heavy."

The DCA was back and the hull technician was with him. "Sir, we've got a flooded sail. It's probably been holed near the starboard dive plane. You've lost the hydraulics. Nothing can be done about it down here. Can't even get into the tower without flooding the whole control deck."

"Eleven hundred feet, skipper." Harris's voice almost cracked. "A hundred feet into the red."

"Skipper," said the QM, "engineering says we can have two-thirds power."

"Back two-thirds!"

"Aye-aye, engineering answering back two-thirds."

"Sonar, this is Commander Shorter; where's that Russian sub?"

"Sonar. Gone, skipper."

"You've lost her?"

"No, sir. She's just gone. Bearing zero-four-zero at four thousand feet. Making thirty-four knots to the northwest. She's leaving."

"Thank God for that! Harris?"

"Eleven hundred ninety-five feet . . ." he announced. "And . . . twelve hundred!"

Shorter cracked a smile at Buchanan. "Would you like to go in the record books, Ben?"

"We're in it now. No Trident's ever gone below eleven hundred feet. Another three or four hundred feet and we'll make the record books for sure—no Trident's ever imploded before, either."

"Twelve hundred fifteen feet."

Shorter moved close to Buchanan and spoke in an undertone. "Ben, we need to split up. Should have done it long before. Get to the radio compartment and see if you can help Mr. Thomas."

"Right."

"Twelve hundred twenty-five feet. And we've stopped!"

A few cheers burst from the control room crew. High fives were exchanged out of sight of the commander.

"Holding at twelve hundred fifteen. Okay, now we're starting to rise. Twelve, ten. Twelve hundred. Skipper, we're going up!"

"Stay with it, Harris."

Shorter stayed with it until the diving officer called out nine hundred feet. At that point he ordered engineering to give ahead two-thirds and told the helm to climb to four hundred and head to Pearl Harbor.

A swell of triumph surged through the command center crew with the rising tide. Victory had come like a bore, too fast and too hard to believe. It would keep coming in until the moment it started back out. Now the tide had reached its full height. Men traded glances. They were still alive. They were heading home. In that one moment hope, disbelief, doubt, and relief swirled among them as the confused waters swirl just before the tides change.

"Hold it!"

Shorter whirled. Most of the operators whirled around, too. Everyone froze.

Murdock had moved in behind the Chief of the Boat and put a pistol against the small of his back. With the other hand he slipped the chief's own weapon out of its holster, stepped away into the middle of the compartment, and aimed both weapons at Shorter.

"I'm taking command of this ship."

"I don't believe it!" cried Shorter.

Everyone else looked just as astonished.

"Commander, tell the bus driver there to head north as fast as this thing can go."

"You're with them, Murdock?"

"Do as I tell you."

The reactor officer shook his head slowly. "This ship is in no condition to proceed anywhere at top speed. We're in bad shape. We have a flooded sail and water in the lower decks. The main buoyancy tanks are ruptured. With our trim tanks blown we've just barely got neutral bouyancy, and we'll sink as soon as we lose forward speed. But if we move too fast we'll tear ourselves to pieces."

"Give the order now!"

"You bastard, you want us to follow that Russian sub? I won't do it. I'd rather take a chance here with you than with them."

"Okay . . . here." Murdock reversed the gun in his right hand and lobbed it to Shorter. "That was just an attention-grabber. You weren't listening to me. Now you'll have to. I'm still taking command of this sub, but I'm doing it legally." He reached into a pocket and produced a folded piece of paper saturated with seawater. He had to open each fold carefully to keep it from tearing. "Here are my orders, Commander. Signed by Admiral Reinholt. They put me in command of SSBN 732, *Alaska*. Here, Chief." Murdock tossed the chief his own pistol.

Shorter took three steps forward and took a look at the paper while keeping his gun trained.

"What is this, some kind of a joke?"

"No joke."

"They sure look genuine enough," Shorter announced.

Murdock turned to the steersmen. "Go north," he said. "At top speed."

The steersmen looked to Shorter.

"Course three-six-zero, p.g.c., helm. Maintain your depth."

"Aye-aye, sir."

Shorter moved to the intercom. "Engineering, this is the control room. Ahead full."

"Are you sure, skipper?"

"Do it." When the "aye-aye," came back, Shorter turned off the intercom and glared at Murdock. "Would you care to meet with me and the other officers in the navigation room, Murdock?"

"Glad to oblige."

The quartermaster was asked to excuse them, but the two damage control men working in the navigation area remained where they were because their duties superceded all other activities.

Shorter, Buchanan, Thomas, and Murdock squared off around the navigation table.

The reactor officer spoke first. "What is your rank, Murdock?"

"Sergeant."

"You're not Navy!"

"Not exactly."

Shorter's head wagged in dismay. "Sergeant Murdock has orders signed by Admiral Dan Reinholt giving him command of the *Alaska.*" He paused to give Thomas and Buchanan a chance to absorb this extraordinary bit of news. "Rather than make for the safer and shallower waters of the Johnston Islands, which are just to the south, or to Pearl Harbor as I wanted to do, Sergeant Murdock has ordered us north into deep waters in pursuit of the Russian Sub. He is going to—"

"Excuse me for interrupting, Commander, but we

don't have time for all this military bullshit. I don't give a goddamn about the Russian sub. You, Thomas. Aren't you the communications officer?''

Thomas's brusque reply was heavy with contempt. He was standing straight and stiff, as though balancing a saucer of sour milk on the top of his head. "I am," he snapped.

"You've been getting a signal. Code thirty. And then a succession of two-digit numbers."

Thomas stared. After a time he grudged acknowledgement by dipping his head so slightly it would not have spilled a single drop of milk from the saucer. "I never saw it. I was locked below with your brother and these officers. But you're right. My radioman tells me that we did receive such a message for some time. Until the radios were destro—''

"Where did it come from?"

"I don't know. As I said, I wasn't there. Kaseem took the hard copies. He went crazy trying to find what it was and to whom it had been sent. The Russian captain appeared to be mystified by it, too. They certainly weren't any of our Navy codes or communica—''

"Okay, okay, we're still short of time. Can you find out?"

"Of course I can." Thomas went to the intercom and spoke with someone in his radio section. He rejoined the group in seconds. "I'm having the radioman report to us here. As a matter of fact, he informs me that we now have a receiver going and that we're picking up that same message again. He's bringing a copy. But we still don't know who it's for. It's not Russian, it's not for Kaseem, and it's not ours, that much I can guarantee."

"I know who it's for," Murdock announced.

"Who?" Shorter and Thomas spoke together.

"Me."

"You!"

"That's right."

"What's it mean?" asked Shorter.

"I can decode it, but I may need help making any sense out of it. Code thirty, ten, eighty, twelve, double-zero, sixty-two, Code two. Does that sound right, Thomas?"

"The two codes are correct. That was one of the things that threw us, two codes for one short message. As for the numbers they sound correct, but until I have a written copy . . . just a second, that'll be my radio operator." Thomas hurried to the door and returned moments later with a small tear of computer-print paper. "Here it is. You're right: Code thirty, ten, eighty, twelve, double zero, sixty-two, Code two."

"Is it coming from the north?"

"Yes. North by east. Eleven points off true north. At a distance of about ten miles fixed."

"What is this cipher, Murdock?" asked Shorter. "And why a special code to you? Just who are you, and who do you work for?"

"Relax, Commander. I'm not the CIA. That's a simple police ten-code. Any cop in the country could decipher it. Code thirty is an alert—police officer needs help. In this case there's only one policeman around and that's me."

"You!"

"Yeah, I'm a detective sergeant. So I'm in big trouble and all of you here with me are in big trouble, too. The ten-eighty is the explanation. It means explosion."

"So that's it," snarled Shorter. "Well, we just got hit twice by explosions. . . ."

"I don't think that's it. The next two numbers are not ten-code but they are Navy. Twelve and double-zero. That's twelve hundred. Military time for high noon. Right? When I first heard about this message, it was about five minutes after eleven, and the man commanding the *Seawind* was talking about an 'H-hour' in fifty-five minutes."

"'H-hour'?"

"Yeah; I take it you know what that means?"

Shorter shrugged. "Almost anything. It designates the time that something will happen."

"It's twenty to twelve now."

"What about the rest?" asked Buchanan.

"Ten, sixty-two—meet the civilian. That one bothered me for a little while, but not very long. It's Reinholt. He's lost his job and he'll soon lose his commission because of this thing. He's the only person who knows enough about me to have arranged for this code. So we're supposed to go to him wherever he is, and we're supposed to get there just as fast as we can. That's the Code two. Move fast, but no lights and no siren."

Thomas was nodding his head. "Silent running."

"Now, wait a minute!" Commander Shorter was far from convinced. "You're saying that you're a policeman, not a naval officer. You're telling us that Admiral Reinholt has been relieved of his duties. What good are those orders of command? By what right. . . ?"

"Don't give me that crap. I don't believe assignment orders are canceled just because the man who issued them retires."

"You're not Navy!"

"And I don't know starboard from stern without stopping to think."

"Then what is it about you that Reinholt would draw up these orders? Are you some kind of a marvel? Or is he crazy? Is that why they relieved him?"

"Take your pick."

"Well, I'll tell you this. I'd be the crazy one if I turned over command of this submarine to someone like you."

"Then keep it. I don't want command. I want you to follow that signal to the north."

"That's something else. We're going north now. How'd you know it was coming from the north before Ensign Thomas told you about it?"

"The *Seawind* headed south. They didn't want to take

any chance of running into whoever was sending that signal, but they wanted to get away from us as fast as they could. Same with the Russian sub. They must have just gotten word of what kind of trouble we were in and didn't dare take the time to finish us off. They knew we were doomed. And so was anyone who struck around. Suddenly they couldn't get away fast enough.''

Shorter was shaking his head. ''That's what I don't understand, this explosion at twelve hundred hours. What the hell is that all about? Depth charges? SUBROC or ASROC missiles? I say we head for Pearl Harbor and risk it.''

''I agree,'' said Thomas. ''I can try to get one of the transmitters working. Before we get there we can radio in and report that the ship is in our hands.''

''You'll never get there,'' said Murdock. ''Dammit, can't you tell time? It's quarter to twelve!''

This didn't faze Shorter. ''Nevertheless, Murdock,'' he said, his tone sharpening, ''I think we're all agreed that Pearl Harbor is the way for us to go.'' He shot Buchanan a darting glance in hopes of achieving a consensus, because Buchanan had been strangely still.

Now the weapons officer was shaking his head.

''What is it, Ben?''

''Shorty, have you ever heard of SubSmash?''

''Sub smash? No.''

''Me either,'' Thomas admitted.

''What is it?''

''It's a contingency plan, designed to be used against enemy submarines that penetrate our defenses. It's a method of destroying a submarine when OSIS has only a general idea of her location. When her destruction is imperative.''

''How?''

''It involves detonation of an undersea nuclear device at the sub's last known location. A two-and-a-half-megaton nuclear bomb.''

384

Thomas and Shorter exchanged expressions of horror.

"They wouldn't," Shorter declared.

"They will," snapped Murdock.

"How can you—"

"I know what you don't know, Commander. I told you Admiral Reinholt was removed from his position overseeing this investigation. The man who had him removed, the man who probably took his place, is a pal of Dr. Kester and that officer of yours . . . Longfellow. Kaseem is another of their group. If they're gonna get away with what they're doing, the *Alaska* will have to be destroyed. That was the plan from the beginning; I'm sure of it."

The Shorter who confronted Buchanan this time was much less sure of himself. "What do you say, Ben?"

"This isn't a board meeting, Shorty; votes don't count. If you're challenging Murdock's orders it's your decision to make. If you think they're good—and they look good to me—then the decision is Murdock's. He strikes me as a man who can make a decision. Personally, I don't think it matters what we do or who orders it done."

"What are you getting at?"

"If I'm right about this SubSmash thing, we're in deep trouble. Those Russian torpedoes that almost sent us to the bottom carried about five hundred pounds of high explosive. A two-and-a-half-megaton nuclear bomb is equivalent to five *billion* pounds of high explosive."

"Go ahead, Ben. Let's have it."

"A nuclear explosion like that will vaporize a cubic mile of ocean. Turn it to steam. Fish, plants, anything in the immediate area simply ceases to be. The shattering effect would disintegrate this ship from two, maybe three miles away, even though the buffering ability of water is better than air. But that's not the beauty of the plan. If they detonate a nuclear device underwater, they won't even have to come that close."

"Spell it out."

"An underwater explosion that size will set up what's known as a 'mining effect.' A series of compression waves, concentric sub-surface seismic-like waves called 'supernovas,' which flow outward from the blast for many miles. They're called 'supernovas' because they grow like a star that goes supernova, getting bigger and bigger, spreading out farther and farther until it consumes the planets orbiting around it. But these waves don't burn. They break. Maybe you've seen how sound waves of a certain frequency and volume can shatter glass. That's the idea, but these are another kind of sound waves that only propagate underwater: infinitely larger, infinitely more powerful. They can crack the hull of any ordinary submarine like a matchstick. A submarine in our condition wouldn't have a prayer."

Now Shorter was fazed; his voice trembled. "How far away would we have to get?"

"I don't know, this is all just theory; it's never been done. Assuming they're not tracking us, the farther away we got the better chance we would have. But in fifteen minutes . . . that's not much time or distance."

No one spoke for several seconds.

"All right, Murdock," said Shorter at last. "I'll go this far with you. If you're so certain of your reading of this message that you're willing to stake the lives of every man on this ship. . . ?"

"Hell, yes."

"Then we'll go your way. But I'm not turning over the command to you. What do you say to that?"

"We've got ten miles to go and only fifteen minutes to get there. I say let's put the goddamned pedal to the floor and see what this son of a bitch'll do."

Shorter went to the intercom and ordered engineering to advance RPMs to flank speed.

# Chapter Twenty-Two

The *Alaska* didn't tear herself apart running away. But she didn't get away either. The explosion came just as Murdock had warned; its compression waves struck the sub as Buchanan had feared. This is what tore her apart.

They were within half a mile of the signal source, still making maximum speed, when a sudden shrill scream galvanized the command deck crew in a way no bo'sun's pipe ever could. Sonarman Fencil staggered out of his section with both palms ground into his ears. He had stopped screaming but his mouth was still wide open, his face frozen in a death mask of agony. Before Fencil had taken a dozen steps his legs turned to jam and he crumpled.

Shorter and Chief Rawlenson got to him first. Thomas raced into the sonar room and when Murdock followed him, he found the communications officer staring at the sonar screen in a stupor of disbelief.

What they saw deserved that. What they didn't see was even more staggering yet.

Farther south a mountain of water rose off the surface of the sea. It cratered, and vomited a vertical column of steam a mile wide and several miles high. Convoluted masses of superheated vapors eclipsed the noon sun. They heaved and roiled their way across the heavens. Before the mountain had collapsed upon itself, a vomitive black overcast spanned the horizons.

At ground zero minus two thousand feet the devastation was much more dramatic.

The explosion had vaporized ten billion gallons of seawater and created an undersea void the size of Pearl Harbor. Surrounding waters rushed in with such force and volume they became a maelstrom of currents. A single savage whirlpool formed on the surface, a whirlpool so immense it could have sucked a whole fleet of ships to the bottom in a matter of seconds.

Spumes of sizzling spray shot a thousand feet into the air.

Tsunami-sized surface swells two and three hundred feet high gathered momentum and rolled out from the center of the destruction.

But these effects were nothing compared to the forces at work far below. Before the smallest wisp of steam had risen into the sky, before the tiniest ripple had formed on the surface, the first supernova was born. It was a single spherical surge of compressed water. Other smaller waves, continually increasing in size and power, were thrust out in front of it. Still others, continually decreasing in size, came behind.

These slow-building, slow-moving waves had only begun to reach their full force when the skies turned black and the ocean surface became a tumbling nightmare of mountainous swells. By this time the first of the waves had struck the sea floor. Silt and sea dust rose in clouds off the bottom. Igneous rock structures crumbled. Canyons collapsed. And the whole seabed shook with tremors that registered as Richter-six earthquakes as far away as California and Japan.

The supernovas advanced in ever-widening circles like concentric walls, each one harder and heavier than the last. The bases of these walls continually shook the sea bottom. The tops of them propelled the huge surface swells out in front of their paths, like solar winds advancing in front of a relentless red giant star.

But it was the supernovas themselves that appeared on the *Alaska*'s sonar screen and that held Thomas and Murdock entranced.

Arced bands of light, each brighter and wider than the last, moved up from the lower half of the scope. The first band of white moved toward the center of the scope while the second took its place and the third took the place of the second. Bands four, five, and six moved onto the screen.

On the panel in front of them were the headphones Fencil had thrown down. They were still blasting away in decibels far above the levels of pain. These intermittent bursts of acoustic energy had shattered the sonarman's eardrums. The blast itself must have fried a good part of his brain.

Neither Thomas nor Murdock uttered a sound. They didn't breathe. They stood watching the white bands closing in and listening to the thunder of each new supernova that appeared on the screen.

Then a radioman rushed in from the communications room, braked when he saw Thomas, and snapped them out of their trance. "Sir, the source of that message is dead ahead, no more than a thousand meters. They've got an antenna lowered into the water. But now the receiver's gone crazy. It's shaking so bad we can't get anything out of it. What should we do?"

"It doesn't matter," said Thomas.

He was oddly calm, a condemned man resigned to his sentence. More than anyone else on the ship he knew what those signals must mean.

"Do you want me to—"

"Take your battle station, sailor, and hang on."

With a hasty "yessir" the radioman vanished.

Thomas yanked the headphone jack from the panel. The threnodic booms ended abruptly. But as the communications officer turned away and hobbled into the command center to report, another kind of din had taken its place.

Footsteps hammering the decks in a chaos of battle-readiness. Men's voices raised in the most real kind of alarm.

Murdock slumped into the sonarman's chair. He listened to the announcements coming over the intercom. They made no sense to him. He heard orders shouted and "aye-ayes" called back, but he didn't know what they were. He could tell that the sub was slowing down, but how would that help? How could anything help them now? Men raced past him, some going aft and some forward. But try as Murdock did, he couldn't imagine what possible good they could do.

Either the *Alaska* could bear up to a nuclear pounding . . . or it couldn't.

Then the announcements ended. The shouting stopped and so did the running; the ship fell silent.

A single voice floated in from the command center.

Shorter was questioning someone—Buchanan? Should they turn and meet the supernovas head on, or run before them?

Murdock listened intently, but Shorter got no reply.

Someone may have shaken his head, but more likely not. They were probably all doing what Murdock was doing, waiting to die. The sea on a rampage was an enemy they couldn't run away or hide from. How do you escape the sea in a ship?

Murdock exhaled and then inhaled again quickly. Another few seconds of life guaranteed.

As the first band of white moved into the center of the scope, he gripped the panel with both hands.

The first of the waves struck the *Alaska* like a speed bump at sixty miles an hour. There was a bang; everything shook. And then it was over. That wasn't so bad, Murdock said to himself. Three seconds later the second one hit—only a little bit harder. And a little more damaging.

For a moment all the lights went out. But they came right back on.

Murdock couldn't turn away from the scope. The waves were moving in faster than before. They were brighter, and the distance between them was smaller.

The third struck with the resounding crash of one vessel ramming another. Again the lights went out, but this time they stayed out. In a few seconds the red battle-lamps came on, and when they did they revealed several small, blood-red showers spraying down on the room.

Silence died screaming.

Men were shouting. Repair parties scurried from compartment to compartment and deck to deck.

Between crashes four and five Commander Shorter dashed past, heading toward the radio room, but quickly came hurrying back. Murdock called out to him. Was there anything he could do to help? He didn't ask if there was anything anyone could do, but this is what he wanted to know. Shorter didn't bother to answer; he didn't even slow down.

Plug and patch crews began shutting off valves. They drove their iron and wood wedges into cracks and began the long job of sealing chinks in the hull. Dewatering teams set out portable pumps at some of the deeper pools.

The crashes kept coming. Nine and then ten. Murdock had lost count when the worst of them collided into the sub like a concrete wall. A supernova picked them up and hurled them ahead. An ear-splitting wrenching and twisting of steel filled the air, as if every plate and rivet had been simultaneously ripped out of place. Water was coming in through deckheads and from outside bulkheads too. It sprayed in here and there with fine but powerful mists, but from several places it was gushing in with terrifying volume.

Repair parties attacked these bigger leaks first, but

there were too many of them and too few men working damage control, even when their numbers were augmented by men from other specialties. Every other job now took second place to keeping the *Alaska* afloat.

One after another of the compartments was sealed off and abandoned.

It couldn't go on forever.

When the pressure hull started to buckle all over the ship, even major leaks were abandoned. Dewatering, plugging, and patching teams gave up their efforts and joined the shoring parties.

Murdock hadn't realized how bad it was until a metallic shriek jerked his head up. A blister on the overhead was already half the width of the room and swelling by the second.

He shouted for help at the top of his lungs but no sound emerged. His heart had lodged in this throat, obstructing even a whisper. He swallowed it down and tried again. Although he didn't much care for the panicked, piercing tone, a return shout assured him help was on the way.

He fell back in the chair to watch the ceiling sink lower and lower.

By the time a repair squad broke into the sonar section with jacks, braces, shores, and strongbacks and went right to work, the overhead was completely concave. Near the center of the room it was barely six feet off the deck.

The pounding continued, and yet it had eased up a little. Now each blow was a bit weaker than the last. Yet these less damaging supernovas worsened the damage the others had caused.

The fact that the decks were still pitching violently even as the blows subsided didn't upset the repairmen, at least not physically. Emotionally they were all pretty far gone. Coy Murdock could see that on their faces. This senseless havoc coming on top of everything else they'd already endured was too much.

They labored like machines. One of them was swinging a twenty-pound sledge against a shore while another man held the beam in place and two others positioned the shores top and bottom. Failure didn't depress them. It was only one more of many. Success didn't cheer them. There were many more failures waiting.

Something drew Murdock back to the sonar. The last of the waves were moving up through the center of the screen. The blows were minor again: speed bumps on the highway. Was it over? Had they really survived?

The mere possibility buoyed Murdock's spirits.

He worked his way over to the repairmen to offer them help, cursing his clumsiness all the way. The sub was down at least thirty degrees by the bows, and his land-legs hardly kept him from falling. He advanced along a safety bar hand-over-hand and crawled the last few feet on hands and knees. Could they use this help? The supervisor told Murdock to clear out of the room.

Murdock didn't argue. He wanted out badly.

No sooner had the last wave nudged the submarine than another thumping began, more raucous even than the buckling of the hull. It was a half banging, half scraping, like a saw blade with six-foot teeth dragging over the hull and up the side of the sail. By the sound of it the *Alaska* was about to be sawn in half.

He moved into the control room. The deck was angled so badly he had to throw himself from stanchion to stanchion and from one safety bar to the next.

Once there he froze.

This overhead was buckling, too, and a dozen shores were already wedged into place. It wasn't enough. Sheets of sea water inundating the few operators still at their posts made it impossible to see across the compartment. Several of the instrument panels were throwing off sparks—a good many more were already black. Commander Shorter was wading around in six inches of water. So were Buchanan and Thomas, going from station to station to see what still functioned. The ship's internal communications were out, and when a messenger opened the hatch to report on flooding conditions belowdecks, water cascaded down the ladderway to Deck Two.

It was hard to believe that only a matter of minutes had passed since Murdock had left this compartment.

"To hell with that!" Shorter said. "What about the stern planes?"

"Nothing we can do, sir. Not from inside. The DCA figures one of the planes must be jammed against the hull. He says it can only be got at from outside."

"Tell the engine room I want full power astern. Fast!"

"It won't be much, sir. One of the steam generators is out and—"

"Move it! Everything he's got!"

"Yessir!"

The hatch clanged shut and the wheel spun.

"That was the last of the pressure waves," called out Murdock. "It looks like we made it."

Shorter gave him a poor substitute for a smile and barked a laugh void of humor. "We didn't make it. We lost."

"What's wrong?"

The reply came not from Shorter, but from the operator in front of the dive station.

"Twelve hundred eighty feet!"

Murdock's heart sank. Two hundred eighty feet below maximum operating depth.

"What's going on?" he yelled.

Shorter was still swinging his head. "We've lost the stern planes now in addition to the sailplanes. Most of our power's gone, too. Our bow is heavy and we're going down."

"Twelve hundred ninety feet!"

Without the dive planes to keep her nose up, the *Alaska* could only plunge to the bottom. Reversing the propeller was a move of desperation. The turbines had only a fraction of their forward power moving astern, and now they had lost most of their steam.

"Thirteen hundred feet!"

They could hear the crunching of the pressure hull all around them. Over their heads, mostly. It sounded like the submarine was being crumpled into a ball. And above everything, they heard the grate and bang of the mysterious saw severing the hull down the middle.

"Thirteen hundred twenty feet!" The operator's voice nearly cracked with fear. "The engines have slowed us down, skipper, but we're still falling."

"Two hundred feet to crush depth!" warned Buchanan. "Somewhere between fifteen hundred and two thousand feet, the sea's gonna wad us up like a ball of tin foil."

"How deep is it here?" Murdock asked.

Buchanan shouted nervously. "Twenty-two thousand feet!"

Murdock whirled to Shorter. All hope had left him, but anger remained. "Do something!" he shouted.

"What do you suggest?"

"There's nothing to do," called Buchanan.

"Our ballast tanks are gone," added Shorter. "We've got all kinds of compressed air, and the Emergency Buoyancy System to pump more, but nowhere to put it."

"Thirteen hundred fifty feet, skipper"

"Goddammit, do something! Anything! Even if it's wrong, you've got to do something!"

"It's over, Murdock."

"Put air pressure into the compartments. Force out the incoming water."

"Wouldn't work! The air would go right out the cracks in the pressure hull. That's how the water's coming in!"

"Then put it somewhere else."

"There is nowhere else." Shorter gripped a stanchion with both hands and swallowed hard. "It's over."

"Thirteen hundred seventy-five feet, sir."

Murdock growled like some species of carnivore.

And he charged.

He slogged up the sloping deck, kicking sprays of water across the room, grabbed Shorter by the front of his shirt and yanked him around.

"This is your ship, not mine!" he screamed. "You're in command! Goddammit, if you don't do something, I will!"

"You?"

"I'm warning you. . . ."

"What can you do? I'm telling you, Murdock, this ship is finished."

Murdock whirled to Buchanan. "Launch the missiles!"

"What?"

"The Tridents! Launch every one of 'em as fast as you can."

"We can't do that," cried Shorter.

Murdock turned on the man with both fists cocked. But he didn't swing.

"Goddammit," he said, "one of these days you guys are gonna come up for air and see that we don't need those damn bombs anymore. Speaking as a guy who lives up there—and who wants to go home—I say the time has come. Launch 'em. And fill the empty tubes with compressed air."

Shorter looked mechanically at Buchanan.

"Will that work?"

The weapons officer was nodding his head in a dumb kind of acknowledgment.

"By God, it just might. We could launch 'em, all right. They'd never reach the surface. It'll take a helluva lot of pressure to blow the tubes dry, but pressure's the one thing we've got." He was looking into the distance. "The sub is eighteen thousand tons submerged, but only a few hundred tons of that is real negative bouyancy. Even in our condition a thousand tons max. The twenty-two missiles weigh fourteen hundred tons." He was throwing the words out as fast as he could. His nervous energy turned suddenly hopeful. "It'd be barely enough."

"Those damn missiles are going to the bottom one way or another," said Murdock. "What difference does it make if we don't go along?"

Shorter was looking at Murdock strangely. "I begin to see . . ." he started, and then let it go. "All right, go, go, Ben," he said, and almost pushed Buchanan toward the ladder to the missile deck.

Suddenly the weapons officer froze.

"What's wrong, Ben?"

"All the missiles have been shut down from the launch tubes," said Buchanan. "To stop Kaseem from . . . That means they'll have to be individually fired from the launch deck. It could take twenty minutes."

"Skipper!"

The three men swung toward the dive station and the wan-faced operator, whose job it was to monitor the big depth gauge. He didn't need to say it—the gauge was of a size to be read from across the compartment—but it was his job to say it: "Sir, we just passed through fifteen hundred feet."

He had to shout to make himself heard.

The hull was shrieking under the torture of millions of tons of pressure. It was collapsing right in front of their eyes. The scraping and banging on the side of the hull was louder than ever, and the crunching of the walls and overhead were not to be believed.

No one among them imagined the *Alaska* could withstand another twenty seconds of this; in twenty minutes she would lie on the bottom in a thousand pieces.

"Someone, somehow, buy me some time!" pleaded Buchanan. He was looking directly at Murdock. Without waiting for an answer he ran toward the launch decks as fast as his legs could carry him.

"Well?" Murdock cried.

"Nothing." Shorter's head was wagging from side to side in a show of utter helplessness. "I tell you there's nothing we can do. He'll either make it in time . . . or he won't."

"You know he won't make it."

"Then none of us make it."

Victory, just within reach and snatched out of their grasp.

Once too often.

Murdock felt himself slipping.

"Sometimes," said Shorter, "you just wait to die."

That was it.

Murdock had a vague notion he knocked Shorter aside. And then the steps of the ladder fell under his feet. The passageway to the launch deck flew past.

He broke into the launch deck like a fiend. Missilemen stared at him wide-eyed and Buchanan stepped forward. Somehow Murdock made himself understood. Before the weapons officer could think of an argument, Murdock dove into the number one launch tube and scrambled inside the A1A suit still propped against the tube wall. Water was already flooding the tube. In seconds, it was filled.

Forty feet over his head the giant hatch lay back on its hinges.

Murdock had only switched on his helmet light when a solid blast of superheated steam lifted him up and launched him out of the tube, up, up through the hatchway, high over the main deck. A riot of air bubbles threw his light back in his eyes. He could see nothing more. There was nothing more. The vaporous cloak was his armor—the steel suit only kept out the pressure, the bubbles held back the night. And then his flight came to an end. He'd stopped climbing. The air bubbles whisked over his head, and infinite darkness moved in.

He was falling back down. His arms and legs thrashed in an awkward, hopeless attempt to turn himself around.

He fell through eternity. But he was falling only a little bit faster than the submarine itself, and when he landed on the deck the crash wasn't nearly as hard as he'd feared.

He rolled onto his chest. He tried to get up but he couldn't. His legs were dangling over an edge. The edge of what? He was in a large hole in the hull. The open launch tube? It must be! He was half in and half out, and he could hear the hatch coming closed.

His pincers raked at the smooth surface of the deck. His legs kicked against the walls.

He couldn't pull himself out.

The hatch came down right in front of his faceplate; it closed with the crunching finality of a bank vault, but it didn't even touch him. He wasn't in the launcher at all. He was forward of the tube, in some kind of rent that stretched completely across the broad deck.

This was the tear in the outer hull. So wide and long Murdock didn't wonder the ballast tanks wouldn't hold air.

He aimed his light at the stern. The launch deck was angled up thirty degrees or steeper, and the tail was a city block away. He couldn't even crawl out of this hole. What hope did he have to reach the tail fin? What had possessed him to think he could straighten a damaged stern plane? If it was even close to the size of the bow planes, it would be as big as an aircraft wing and weigh many tons.

He had only seconds to move aft and repair what would take weeks in a dry dock with special facilities and tools.

Murdock turned away from the steeply sloping deck. He knew it was hopeless to think about scaling that deck, but that's not why he turned. A hellish sound had brought him around.

He was just aft the sail. His light played over the towering slab of black steel; it climbed higher and higher in search of that hellish banging and scraping, the clatter that threatened to saw the *Alaska* in half. It was ten times as loud here as it was inside. And it was right here.

Halfway up, his light found the starboard dive plane. He aimed his light higher.

There was the top of the sail, the bridge. And then he saw something thrust up higher yet.

No, no. It wasn't thrust up, it was going up.

At first he thought it must be one of the masts. A periscope or navigation mast. But it wasn't. It was too big for that.

It looked like a chain.

The links were each longer than his body, and so big he could have swum through the holes if he hadn't been wearing the suit. As the submarine sank, the huge links thumped over the side of the bow, scraping and grating in an infernal racket. The links ran up the side of the sail right in front of the starboard plane. They ran over the leading edge of the plane, too, banging from one link to the next. That was the sound, but what the hell was. . . ?

Suddenly he knew.

They had been thrown right into an anchor chain—by the size of the thing, an aircraft carrier's or a battleship's. The dive plane had caught on the chain and kept them from going on by. But it hadn't kept them from diving.

Murdock started down the right side of the sail. The deck was so steep he'd have slipped straight over the bows if the onrush of water hadn't kept him from falling.

He stood right inboard from the chain and watched it come up link by link. Only it wasn't coming up; the sub was going down, a link every second. Once they came to the end of that chain . . .

The beams were too wide and too canted for him to look over the side or see the end of the chain. He couldn't jump far enough to reach it. Murdock turned to the sail and climbed up the ladder welded onto its plating.

He climbed clumsily from one rung to the next until he

was just under the bridge, and then he stepped across to the plane.

Here's where the Russian torpedo had struck, the side of the sail just on top of the plane. The sail's four-inch-thick plating had been peeled back in a ragged circle, like a can opener cutting through tin. It had left a hole big enough for a man to walk though.

Murdock turned his back on this hole and walked out several feet along the sailplane to the chain.

There it was, inches away. The links banged up in front of his faceplate. His arms weren't long enough to wrap around the bar of one link, but he could push his suit through the eye. He could hold on.

It was his last chance.

But he couldn't make himself do it.

He made himself walk out to the tip of the plane. He aimed his light down. Even as he watched, the anchor materialized, hanging at the end of the chain, hovering in darkness three miles above the bottom of the sea. It started up the side of the bow.

It was the size of a Sherman tank and probably as heavy. The shank was as big around as a tree trunk, and the twin flukes were surfboards of four-inch-thick solid steel.

But the anchor was stockless. The arms didn't stick out, but tucked up parallel to the shank until the anchor dragged on the sea bed and activated the tripping palms, which then rotated out.

When the horror of this struck Murdock, he knew that he'd already made up his mind what he must do.

"Somebody, somehow, buy me some time."

That's what Buchanan had said. Just a few minutes. It was mad, Murdock knew. But he didn't think he was mad. Madmen don't think. They don't hope.

"Dad! Dad, if you're out there. . . !" He said that much out loud before stopping himself. "I could use some help," he added under his breath.

And then he threw himself off the plane. He fell past the sail, past the bow. One of his arms dragged over the links as he dived. And then the anchor shank was right in front of him. He wrapped both arms around it. Still he fell. Then the trunk of his steel suit wedged between the shank and one of the flukes and his fall came to a sudden, screeching halt. He was jammed tight.

He pushed the fluke out. It was ungodly heavy, but it was also perfectly balanced and swiveled down and away when all of his weight came against it.

His light played over the *Alaska*'s hull descending just beside him. He'd no time to waste. The anchor had stopped dragging up the metal plating. The main deck had fallen away.

He looked up. The starboard dive plane loomed just above. He had only the one chance. And it was going to be close.

He pushed harder on the fluke until it swung out about forty-five degrees, and then he put both feet against it to force it the rest of the way. The fluke's pointed bill scraped under the plane with a horrendous crash.

It was such a jolt Murdock almost fell off; he grabbed at the shank just in time.

Then the unforeseen happened.

The submarine shifted her weight. Murdock might have known she wouldn't balance on one side alone, but he hadn't. She rolled to port, and the dive plane slipped off the side of the anchor. The fluke swung upright again.

Murdock didn't even try to stop it.

He had failed.

He watched the submarine roll away. Once free of the anchor she righted herself for her death dive to the bottom. But this righting movement brought the sail back. The ragged hole above the plane swung toward the anchor. Murdock saw one last chance. There would be no others. He threw himself onto the fluke and held on. His weight rocked it down, straight out from the shank.

The anchor and the sail came together—Murdock and the fluke as one plunged into the hole.

The crunching of steel was appalling.

His suit, caught between the anchor and the thick hull of the sail, stood no chance. It crumpled like plastic. It tightened against him.

Untold tons gripped his chest. Razor-thin sheets of seawater tore through his clothes and his skin. His legs grew instantly cold as frigid water sliced up his trunk.

Pressure doubled, redoubled, and doubled again. It was ten and then twenty and finally thirty times surface levels, as the sea, having once breached the crushed remains of his armor, squeezed him in its giant's fist.

He lay like that for many minutes, breathing in gulps and with his heart hammering a hole in his chest, as the *Alaska* and the ocean grew still. The flame in Murdock's consciousness died to a flicker. Just before it puffed out, he felt the sub lurch. It was the first of the missiles fired off into the darkness. One by one the sleek white rockets rose, and one by one they came spiraling back down past the *Alaska* and dived to the bottom of the sea.

# Chapter Twenty-Three

The combat information center of the *New Jersey* hadn't seen such a fuss in years.

A first-time visitor would have taken one look at this war room and reached the inevitable conclusion that the *New Jersey* was at war. Her eighteen stations for radar, sonar, communications, electronic countermeasures, and antisubmarine warfare were bustling. Operators reported to a half-dozen supervisors who milled from station to station. Supervisors in turn made reports to the executive officer, and the exec summarized these for Admiral Cassidy while passing complete reports on to the bridge. Fleet-footed messengers hustled between supervisors, between stations, to the action board where events were being posted, and back and forth from the bridge.

If activity and tension levels were high, then the noise level was right through the roof. That uninitiated visitor, after marveling that in the helter-skelter of traffic no one collided with another, would have concluded that every operator and every supervisor were talking at the same time.

Most vocal of all were the radiomen. They coordinated intra-ship, ship-to-ship, and ship-to-shore communications, as well as communications with a E-2C Hawkeye circling overhead and a Sea King twenty miles to the south that was carrying the SubSmash device.

How could the visitor have surveyed this scene without

being convinced that the battleship was engaged in a nuclear confrontation?

It was.

One radioman's voice rose above the others.

"SubSmash has been launched!"

A sonar supervisor ordered his operators to mute their earphones before the blast. Not coincidentally, the overall noise level dropped by half. This lull was startling. Seconds later one of the sonarmen announced: "Detonation verified, sir!"

Activity suddenly intensified.

By contrast, things were quite calm on the bridge just forward of CIC. Captain Louis Krosmeyer was studying the ocean to the south through powerful binoculars. It was a seaway now. Ten-foot waves came out of their port quarter, but the troughs were hidden beneath a white, foglike spray, spume blown off the crests and whipped along the surface by thirty-knot winds. The *Jersey* could handle a lot more than this. But when the supernovas passed under the battleship's keel there would be a lot more than this. For now activity was centered in the CIC, but in just minutes it would be the other way around. Krosmeyer's place was here on the bridge.

"Captain Krosmeyer."

The *Jersey* captain depressed his intercom. "This is the captain."

"This is Admiral Cassidy in CIC."

"Yes, sir."

"Wait until the compression waves have passed us and then steam into the area. Understood?"

"No, sir."

"What's that, Captain?"

"Sir, I'm not moving until the man upstairs assures me that things have calmed down. There may be some rough water out there that we can't see from down here."

"All right. Have it your way."

Cassidy switched off the intercom and directed his displeasure at the whole CIC. He didn't like Krosmeyer's tone. You don't talk that way to an admiral. *He* certainly never had. Cassidy clasped his hands behind his back and moved out into the station circuit. He didn't bother to look where he was going. It was up to the others to look out for him.

He moved past the comm boards to the radar and finally to the sonar stations. He stopped behind one of the sonarmen and glanced down at the screen. "What's this blip?"

"Submarine, sir," said the operator without turning.

"What submarine?"

"I can't say, sir," he replied.

"Who's your supervisor?"

But a stiff lieutenant had already approached the flag officer. "Yes, Admiral?"

"There's a blip on the screen here reading half a mile out. The CPO says it's a submarine."

"Yes, sir." The young lieutenant beckoned the executive officer with a hand.

"Why wasn't I informed?"

The XO stepped in. "What's the problem here, sir?"

"I want to know why I wasn't informed about this blip. If it's a submarine, I damn well should have been informed."

"Yessir."

"What submarine is it?"

"I can't say, sir."

"Well, what class? Do you even know if it's ours?"

"I can't say more than I have, sir."

"You've said nothing, Commander."

"Captain's orders, sir."

Cassidy's color deepened by several shades of red; he turned and tramped toward the intercom. On the way over he intercepted a messenger heading to the bridge and snatched a paper out of the man's hand. His face flushed even more as he read it. He flipped on the nearest intercom.

"Captain Krosmeyer?"

"This is the captain."

"This is Admiral Cassidy again. Report to the CIC at once."

"Admiral, there is a very heavy sea coming in from the direction of the explosion. I should remain on the bridge."

"Come in here now, Captain. That's an order."

"Yes, sir."

Cassidy pressed another switch. "Master-at-arms? I want two security people in CIC on the double."

Seconds later, Krosmeyer was standing in front of him while Cassidy read from the intercepted paper. "I've just gotten a report from the Hawkeye," he said. "It has sighted a pair of salvors to the north of us about fifteen miles. What do you know about that?"

"I know they're there, Admiral. But they're outside the standoff boundary, and there's nothing we can do about it."

"Is either of those vessels the one Admiral Reinholt took when he left Pearl Harbor?"

"Yes, sir."

Cassidy's jaw was trembling. "Is Admiral Reinholt still aboard her?"

"No, sir."

"What about this submarine on your sonar? Your men say they've got orders from you not to inform me about it."

"That's correct, Admiral."

"Captain, I want to know what's going on here, and I want to know now."

"I'm afraid I can't discuss this with you, Admiral."

"This is rank insubordination! Worse, it's mutiny!"

Krosmeyer remained cool. "No, sir. A captain can't mutiny against his own ship."

"I'm the ranking officer on this ship."

"I beg your pardon, Admiral, but that isn't true. The senior officer present afloat is Admiral Dan Reinholt."

"Reinholt! He's here?"

"Yes, sir."

"What nonsense is this!"

A pair of burly marine guards entered the CIC; they crossed to the two officers and stood off to one side at attention.

"Tell me where Reinholt is and what's going on, or I'll have you placed under arrest here and now."

"I'm sorry, Admiral, I can't do that."

"All right, if that's the way you want it." Cassidy pivoted ninety degrees, to the marine sergeant in charge of the other. "Sergeant, place this man under—"

A voice rose from behind Cassidy: "That won't be necessary, O.K., I'm right here."

As Cassidy turned he saw Admiral Reinholt, in sneakers, corduroy pants, and rollneck sweater, coming up behind him.

"By God! You! What are you doing here?"

"The same as you. Looking for the *Alaska*. Only you've come here to make sure that she's destroyed. I've come here to help her survive."

"Sergeant, I want both of these men arrested."

The marine was unsure but unshaken. "But, Admiral," he said. "This is the captain."

"I know he's the captain. But I'm ordering—don't look at him, look at me! I'm an admiral, I outrank him. And I'm ordering you to arrest both of them."

"But, sir," the marine persisted, "Admiral Reinholt here outranks you."

"Goddammit, I'm giving you an order!"

"Sir, I take my orders from the captain."

Cassidy turned on Krosmeyer in a rage. "This will finish you, Captain."

Before Cassidy could go into detail, the *New Jersey*'s

executive officer intervened: "Captain, you're wanted on the bridge. Some ugly swells approaching from the south."

Excusing himself, Krosmeyer hurried forward.

Admirals Reinholt and Cassidy moved over to the sonar station, which displayed the submarine blip moving underneath the battleship. If having two flag officers standing behind him frayed the operator's nerves, he didn't show it. And in just seconds there was a much greater cause for frayed nerves than that. A series of huge swells began rolling under the *New Jersey*, swells big enough to pitch her up and then down through sixty degrees of arc.

They weren't the two- and three-hundred-foot tidal waves that had rolled out from the center of the explosion; they'd lost much of their size. But even these were more than big enough to swamp any but the most seaworthy of vessels.

The underwater equivalent of those waves was depicted on another sonar screen, as the supernovas marched under her keel.

"The sub's reducing speed," said the sonar operator to Reinholt. "She's about five hundred meters off now, and just barely making way. They know what's coming. They're trying to save the engines."

"Why don't they just surface?"

"I don't know, sir. Maybe they can't."

"Do you know which submarine it is?" Cassidy put in.

"Tell him," said Reinholt.

The operator said without looking around: "It's one of ours. A boomer."

Cassidy glared at the screen in silence.

"It's the *Alaska*, all right," added Reinholt, answering the question Cassidy hadn't the courage to ask.

"That's not possible. The chopper placed her more

than twenty miles to the south just a few minutes ago. How could she get here that fast?''

"She couldn't. She didn't go south.''

"But—''

"The chopper was tracking a hydrophone signal, just as you'd told them to do.''

"How did you know—''

"How did *you* know we'd put a hydrophone on her?''

Cassidy had nothing to say. He was mentally trimming his sails to meet an unexpected and possibly dangerous shift in the wind.

"No matter,'' said Reinholt. "You knew. But you didn't know my man had transferred the hydrophone to the *Seawind.* ''

"What?''

"That's right. At least that's what I assume must have happened. One thing I do know for certain—you blew up your own submarine.''

Cassidy stopped breathing. Even with fair warning given this news took him aback. He closed his eyes and lowered his head. "You could be responsible for a holocaust.''

"I don't think so. I think we've seen the end of the killing. And I think you're responsible for every death up to now.''

Cassidy drew himself up. He had no way left him but to bluster. "Even you can't make a charge like that without evidence.''

"My evidence is there,'' Reinholt said, pointing to the sonar screen. "When she surfaces, we're all going to learn the truth.''

"Sir, here come the compression waves!''

The supernovas appeared on this sonar, too, moving down from the top of the screen. The sonarman turned down his volume control and dashed off a message that went straight to the bridge.

One by one the compression waves passed over the tiny blip in a race for the center of the screen.

Several minutes passed in complete silence.

"Man, they're taking a pounding!" said the operator.

"Are they still making way?" Reinholt asked him.

"Barely. She's only a few hundred meters out now, sir, but her hull's taking such a beating I can't get a good sounding on her propeller or engine. I think the waves are just pushing her ahead now."

The executive officer had been monitoring an adjacent sonar screen, and he announced suddenly, "She's diving!"

Reinholt moved over beside him.

"She slipped from five hundred feet to seven hundred in just a few minutes when her engines slowed down. We picked up increased RPMs after that, as though they were trying to hold onto their depth, but she just kept falling and now— What is it, Lavery? Okay, she just dropped below a thousand feet, and she's going down like a stone."

Cassidy moved in to gloat. He wasn't smiling—he might never smile again—but smugness was written all over his face.

"Eleven hundred feet."

"It looks like your evidence is going to the bottom, Admiral," Cassidy murmured under his breath.

One sonarman called off the depth, while another watched the tiny blip crawl into the center of his scope.

There it remained.

Thirteen hundred feet, fourteen hundred, and fifteen.

The war room grew still. Nobody moved or spoke; they didn't look at one another. They didn't know how to feel. They had done their best to destroy the submarine, but they took no pleasure in watching or hearing her die.

The sonarmen had no choice. They were holding their

headphones to their ears listening for the final crush of steel that would mean the sub had imploded.

"Eighteen hundred feet and she's still in one piece. . . ." said Lavery. If he had anything to add, he didn't get the chance.

The deck dropped from under their feet. The bow of the battleship pitched into the sea. This was no swell. And no tidal wave either. It was as if they had sailed off the end of the world.

Reinholt raced to the bridge and saw Captain Krosmeyer staring down at his bows. And he saw why. The fo'c'sle was completely submerged as far back as her windlass. From the bridge the big gun barrels appeared to be firing right down into the water.

Slowly, agonizingly, the bows lifted, but they remained so low that the hawsepipes were barely clear and every swell rolled over the gunwales.

Krosmeyer was talking into his headset. "Break that damn anchor cable! I don't care where you do it, just break it and trip the Pelican hook before we're dragged under!"

Reinholt saw the ground tackle crew venture onto the fo'c'sle. Water still ran off the deck and out the side scuppers, but every new wave from the south washed it again. The crewmen were wearing life jackets and lifelines, but still he didn't envy their task. Those words were going through Reinholt's mind: "Break the anchor cable . . . before we're dragged under!" Those and Marie's words, too: "Glen had managed to grab hold of a towline with his pincer and hang on. . . . We hadn't found him so much as he had found us. Now I ask you, who but Glen Murdock could have pulled off something like that?"

Reinholt leaped forward and grabbed Krosmeyer's arm. "Belay that, Captain!"

"What!"

"Don't break that cable! It's snagged on the *Alaska.*"

"But how. . . ?"

"I don't know how. I think I know *who,* but you'll have to ask him how he did it. Cancel those orders!"

Krosmeyer spoke into his headset before confronting the admiral. "Dammit, Dan, we've got to do something!"

"Heave her right up!"

"That's crazy. Even if my windlass was powerful enough, which it isn't, the cable would part."

"There's a hundred and fifty men on that sub!" pleaded Reinholt. "Maybe some are dead, but a lot of 'em may be alive. Don't cut 'em loose!"

"He's got no choice," interrupted Cassidy, who'd come in behind Reinholt. "There are ten times as many men as that here on the *New Jersey.* All of them alive. He has to think of them first."

"Louis, I'm telling you. . . ."

"Don't listen to him, Captain Krosmeyer, he's certifiably insane. And I can prove it. If he'd returned to Washington as he'd been ordered to do, he'd be answering to charges of complicity in this mess. He's involved in the hijacking. He dispatched the DSRVs where they wouldn't be available when we needed them. He arranged for the *Mako* debris at San Diego to be transferred and dumped at the downsite. He's responsible for everything."

Reinholt just shook his head. "I'm not going to argue with you, O.K. Not while those men are fighting for their lives." Reinholt showed Cassidy his back. "Louis, you've got to bring them up. Or try to. If that's insane, lock me up and throw away the key."

"Maybe it is, Dan. Maybe it is. But by God, I'll book the padded cell next to yours."

Krosmeyer spoke into his headset.

"You're both going to answer for this!" cried Cassidy. He was losing control. "I'm in command of this operation! You do as I say! If you bring up that sub, whatever happens now will be on your heads, not mine!"

Cassidy kept this going off and on for the better part of ten minutes while the ground tackle crew fought to hoist the anchor. Admiral Reinholt wanted to go forward and help them, but Krosmeyer assured him that his first lieutenant, bo'sun, and ground tackle crew knew their job, and if they couldn't do it it couldn't be done. At the end of those ten interminable minutes they were forced to admit that it couldn't be done. They had raised the cable not a link in that time, and reported to the captain only that the windlass wouldn't take much more trying; if the chain itself didn't part it would soon take the *New Jersey* under.

And then, miraculously, the windlass started to raise her.

Krosmeyer passed this news on to Reinholt.

They pressed against the forward screens and watched the feverish activity at the bows. Sure enough, the windlass was slowly taking in cable. The only observable evidence was in the bow itself, which was now riding higher above the water than just seconds before.

"The cable's parted," said Cassidy, with something like satisfaction.

"No," snapped the captain, "my first lieutenant reports there's reduced weight on the cable, but more than an anchor and scope."

While they waited for an explanation, Cassidy reversed his arguments and began warning that if the *Alaska* came up her missiles could be fired. This, too, would be Krosmeyer's and Reinholt's responsibility.

Not until a messenger rushed in from the CIC did the answer suggest itself.

"Sonar says they're firing missiles," said Krosmeyer. "One right after another."

Reinholt nodded. "Throwing off ballast," he said.

This seemed to make nonsense of Cassidy's arguments, but he didn't realize this and continued to berate the two men for their actions. They, not he, would be responsible.

Not until the *Alaska* rose through a thousand feet of depth did Reinholt reply. He turned on Cassidy.

"I'm responsible, all right. I'm responsible for your actions while you worked for me. But you, O.K., you hijacked that submarine. You killed the members of the crew with some kind of virus, and then you, you personally, took over command. You'll answer for that."

Cassidy managed to produce his superior smile. "You see what I mean, Captain. He's insane. How could I have done that? I've been with him, or in Washington, ever—"

"Not the *Alaska*. I'm talking about twelve years ago. The *Seawind*."

Cassidy just stared. He was still mentally in irons.

"You were executive officer of the *Seawind*," said Reinholt. "Laurence Kester was the medical officer. Scott Longfellow was the ship's engineer. Isn't that right?"

"What's that got to do—"

"It may interest you to know that I've got a list of the *Seawind* crew, and descriptions of the surviving crewmen. You, Kester, and Longfellow are it. Three others lived through the accident, too, three enlisted men: a torpedoman and two divers. Lupo, Ashe, and Meadows. Do those names sound familiar? You spent several days in a life raft with them."

"Sure, I knew 'em. So what?"

"Salvatore Lupo, the torpedoman, matches a description of the hijacker's leader to a T. Don Ashe's description is identical to that of Archibald Wick, who's been looking for the *Batavia* treasure for more than ten years. The third man, a younger diver named Meadows, could be any member of his crew."

"Again I say, so what?"

"So it's all over, O.K. I've got the whole story now. I know what this is all about. It isn't about hijacking—it's about piracy. It has nothing to do with a Trident sub or Middle East politics or East-West relations—it has to do with torpedoing and looting an Iranian freighter.''

Cassidy glowered at Reinholt but let the other man go on talking.

''The six of you used a virus to knock out the *Seawind* crew. You'd found out about the shipment of valuables from Iran in the *Batavia* freighter. We know Kester has ties to Iran and speaks Farsi. He was your source for the virus, too. He could make sure you and your pals didn't get sick. Longfellow could keep the sub going. You could navigate. You also needed a torpedoman to sink the *Batavia* when you found it—examination of the *Batavia* wreckage will confirm that she wasn't rammed, she was torpedoed. And you needed the divers for the scuttling operation of the *Seawind* and later, too, to help raise the *Batavia* cargo. You needed them, but everyone else had to die.''

''This is slanderous speculation, Admiral!''

''I imagine you planned to come back in a year or two and bring up the treasure. What went wrong? Couldn't you find them? Were they buried too well? Maybe the antidotes Kester gave you didn't work very well, and you were too sick to know precisely where she'd gone down. Was that it?''

Cassidy said nothing now.

''So you reported the accident as having occurred miles away from where you knew it took place. You three officers remained in the service for the sake of appearances. But the others got out. Ashe, with sixteen years toward retirement, just failed to reenlist; he changed his name to 'Wick' and started looking for the wreckage. Meadows, the younger diver, got out on a medical discharge. Lupo's enlistment wasn't up for three years and he hadn't been hurt, but he was a troublemaker and it was no problem for him to get himself kicked out on a bad conduct. He didn't turn up until you needed someone to ramrod your SAVAK squad, and at that point he changed his name, too.''

"You can't prove any of this."

"And then the *Batavia* was found. But not by you. Glen Murdock found it. You probably wanted to move in, kill him and his crewmen, and raise the treasure yourselves, but you couldn't. He'd informed the ship's owners as international law requires. He'd informed me, too—through you—but the message didn't reach me for more than a week while you made your plans. You needed time to plan, because Glen had also informed the Navy at Pearl Harbor. He knew they'd want to be involved in the search for the *Seawind*. Those Navy ships lying to at the site made any raid on the *Nomad* unthinkable. So you pulled a diversion. Maybe the biggest diversion in history, but that was all right because the rewards would be the biggest in history. You got in touch with your SAVAK pals, had Longfellow transferred to the *Alaska*, cooked up another batch of virus, and played god of the high seas for a few precious days until Wick transferred the treasure to the *Seawind*, shot the crewmen he no longer needed, scuttled his salvor, and headed out to the Johnstons to meet with Lupo and the others and take them aboard.''

Cassidy dragged his hand across his mouth. "It's a good story, Admiral. But without any evidence, that's all it is. A story. Where's your evidence?''

Reinholt moved toward the forward screen and extended a hand in the direction of the bows. "Right there," he said.

The *Alaska*, her main deck awash, lay tied alongside the *New Jersey* by a short scope of anchor cable and the anchor itself, wedged into the submarine's sail. Four hundred feet aft of the sail her tail fin thrust out of the water like a giant shark's fin, but water still washed across the bow and the launch deck.

Battleship sailors rushed to the lifelines.

The first submariner—it was Commander Eugene Shorter—to climb through the escape hatch let out a whoop and smiled broadly as others came out behind him. These other hands took his cue, and whistled and waved.

Their celebration was short-lived and bitter.

*Alaska* crewmen and a rescue party from the *New Jersey,* armed with crowbars and acetylene torches, ascended to the dive plane to separate the sail and the anchor from the man pinned there. When they finally got Murdock's helmet open they found the A1A suit filled with water up to his chin. The suit itself was so badly crushed they couldn't lift him out.

Thirty minutes later, he lay on a stretcher on the *New Jersey*'s fo'c'sle. He was breathing unaided again. He was semiconscious. And he was in obvious agony. The medical officer was explaining that Murdock was not going to live.

"He's got some cracked ribs. Some internal injuries too, I'm sure, and he's suffering from oxygen poisoning. Any of those could kill him. But they won't. He'll die from decompression sickness—the bends—in a matter of minutes if we don't get him under pressure again. There's no recompression chamber on the ship. None within reach. That's not something I can fix in the sick bay. He either gets under pressure, or he dies."

Admiral Reinholt had been kneeling beside Coy, but now he stood up and spoke with quiet force. "Put some scuba gear on him," he said. "Lash him to that anchor and lower him back down."

No one could believe it.

Even the crewmen who used webbing to tie Murdock onto the anchor could hardly credit their own actions. Coy's uncomprehending eyes followed their movements, and when they stood at the lines and lowered him into the water his mask was turned upward in dazed disbelief.

And then he was gone.

The anchor was let go to two hundred feet.

"He'll never make it," said the MO. "He's suffering from blood loss, pain, and shock. He needs treatment. He needs to be kept warm and watched closely. Instead we're sending him back down to that freezing black hell to die all alone."

Reinholt shook his head firmly. "He won't die."

"How can you know?"

"Because I know him. In a way, I've known him for forty-five years. And I know that from now on, whenever he's down there, he won't be alone."

# Chapter Twenty-Four

"Man overboard!"

The action call raced through the battleship.

Life buoy watchmen threw dye markers and float lights over the side. Prompt CIC posters marked the plot to record bearing and distance on the board. And with the Trident sub trailing behind on a towline, Captain Krosmeyer initiated a sharp Williamson turn that brought the *New Jersey* back past the smoke. It was all in vain.

They lowered the lifeboats, sent spotters aloft and to all sides of the ship, and had the Sea King fly patterns for nearly an hour. They found nothing.

Not until it was positively confirmed that the man was Admiral O.K. Cassidy, that he had broken away from his two marine guards and leapt over the lifeline, did Krosmeyer call off the search.

The man did not wish to be found.

Even from across Pearl Harbor the *Alaska* looked pretty bad. Her pressure hull had taken the brunt of the damage, and though the hydrodynamic outer hull—which retained most of its graceful lines—covered this nicely, the large holes in her sail and on the main deck forward of the launch tubes, as well as a tail fin several degrees port of plumb, made her look like something being towed out to sea as a gunnery target.

Admiral Reinholt drove by in his jeep without slowing down. Coy Murdock didn't ask him to stop.

Coy didn't look too bad, either. He had several broken

ribs, some very sore muscles, and the basis for an unhealthy fear of the sea that could easily last him the rest of his life. But he had an outer hull, too, with only superficial damage, and none of the real injury showed.

"Drew's body, and the bodies of the other *Alaska* crewmen who were killed, are being flown to Washington for ceremonies and burial at Arlington," Reinholt informed him.

"How many men did survive?"

"Counting the officers, Commanders Shorter and Buchanan and Ensign Thomas, there were just over a hundred survivors. They don't have any illusions about who saved their lives. They owe you, Coy, and they know it. So does the Navy. So do I, for that matter."

"Losing Drew is the part that hurts."

Neither man spoke until they had rounded a corner of the harbor. "At least," said Reinholt, "you're free to go on with your life. If you had any ghosts in your past I'd say they've been dealt with."

"What about you, Admiral?"

"Me? I didn't have any ghosts. A devil or two, but no ghosts."

"Speaking of Eliot Packman. . . ?"

"I'll tell you about that," said Reinholt, injecting a bit of humor into their grim conversation. "Packman's trying to pretend he supports me. Is that rich? He pushes me out because I don't work with the Soviets and because my man is responsible for this fiasco. Now we find out that the man responsible, Cassidy, is really Packman's man, and Packman has given sensitive Trident information to the same Soviet generals who helped Cassidy pull the thing off. So as the dust clears, I look around and find Eliot Packman pushing me back into harness."

"So you've got your old job back?"

Reinholt grunted. "I don't know. I don't know if I want to go back after what I've been through. In the meantime," the admiral added with a smirk, "I'm letting them tempt me with offers."

They passed by the battleship *New Jersey*, looking bigger and prouder than ever. The old warrior had saved the younger one, and Coy wondered which of them, the battleship or the nuclear submarine, was really the dinosaur now.

"How about you, Coy, have you decided what you're going to do next?"

"Yeah, I have. But there's a certain someone I have to say good-bye to before I do."

"I can guess who that is."

Then it was Coy's turn to smirk. "You'd be wrong," he said.

Reinholt maneuvered the jeep to the wharfs on the south side of the harbor. He stopped at a familiar dock, where a familiar salvor was tied alongside. A brow—really just a .couple of planks covered by plywood—led down to the *Nomad*'s deck, but Marie Delamer and Captain Pad Duggan ascended to the dock and met Murdock there.

Behind them came the whole crew: the divers Mac, Reed, Sushi, Emmott, Willy, and Findlay; the mechanics Gandy and Babbit; and all of the deckhands too. After Murdock shook hands all around, Reinholt offered to come back later to give him a ride to the airport.

Marie looked startled at this.

"No," said Murdock, "please stay."

"I'd only be in the way," Reinholt replied. "Besides, I've got a million things to do."

"You're not in the way," Marie told him.

"He's welcome to share our celebration," said Duggan expansively. "The party wouldn't be complete without him."

"Well, of course, if you think I should."

"I think you'd damn well better," said Murdock.

They descended in a body to the *Nomad*'s galley, which

was festively decorated, and where food and drinks of such variety awaited them that one question—what Marie and the crew had been doing the last twenty-four hours, while Coy was being pieced back together in a Pearl Harbor hospital—answered itself.

There was a "Welcome Back" banner, hand-fashioned party favors, and other signs that the *Nomad* crew had been confined to the ship again with nothing—not even underwater mischief this time—to do. A makeshift banquet table was already set. Coy was assigned a seat at the head, while a place was laid for Admiral Reinholt at the opposite end.

Duggan had even prepared a speech. A half hour later, when everyone had eaten and drunk his fill, the Irish captain rose to his feet.

"Though it pains me to admit it," he said in his thick brogue, "the man who came to us one week ago was not much to like. I know I didn't like him too much, and I'm the kind what likes and is liked by all." There were some hoots and howls at this, which Duggan quieted with a scowl. "But it's plain to see that we've whipped him into shape and made him the man his father would have wanted him to be. Whether he goes or stays, he'll be the better man for having lived a bit of his life on the sea and having gotten to know us for the grand fellows we are."

Applause followed Duggan's words and didn't stop until he had seated himself on Coy's left. Marie, to his right, stood up. "All I want to know," she said, "is whether he's going or staying. But I won't ask him now. I'm afraid of what he might say. I don't want to leave this ship and all of you, but if he goes I guess I'll have to go, too. So," she said, smiling as only a French girl can smile, "I'll ask him later when we're alone."

This was greeted by whistles and oohs.

But then the cabin grew silent, and one by one the eyes of everyone fell on Coy Murdock. He pushed back his chair and stood up. The hell of it was he had no speech prepared. And what he had to say was not what they wanted to hear.

"As most of you know, I came here for one reason only: to find the man that killed my father. Finding murderers is what I do for a living. You might not believe it from the way I've handled myself out here, but I'm really pretty good at finding murderers. As for the rest of it—stumbling onto the *Alaska,* lucking my way aboard, and managing to stay alive until the admiral fished us all out—well, I can truthfully say I was out of my depth." He waited for the laughter to die down. "In the end, I found more than I bargained for. I found some good friends. I found my brother, and in a way you could say I found my father, too.

"But," he said—and here Murdock paused—"I didn't find the man who killed him."

Murdock's gaze moved down the table, studying one by one the faces of the men. Mac, hard and unsmiling, looked back without turning away or blinking the way Mac always did. Sushi's black, dagger-like eyes and infectious grin revealed everything and nothing about him. Emmott wasn't meeting his eyes. He was reading Murdock's lips, but focused with such intensity one might have thought he was trying to read his mind.

"Whoever sabotaged the minisub," said Murdock, "murdered my father. I didn't know who he was until today. All I knew was that it was one of you here on the *Nomad.*"

The galley turned preternaturally quiet.

Gandy was already half-wired, but this caught his attention. Babbit frowned, opened his mouth, and closed it. Willy, Reed, and Findlay, three quiet divers who remained in the background and did their jobs, remained quiet now. Pad Duggan half rose from his seat—gravity eased him back down. Murdock remembered the first time he'd spoken to these men. It had been right here in this galley one week ago. They hadn't much liked him back then. They hadn't much reason. He was the outsider. In a way he still was. He'd made inroads, but these were fast disappearing.

Murdock continued. "We all settled on Commander Alan Stout when we thought he was a traitor. He'd had the best opportunity. Admiral Reinholt had a chance to do it, too. He was here that day with a number of Navy men just before Marie and my father and Stout went down. But neither Stout nor Reinholt did it."

"Who did it?" snapped Pad Duggan.

"The sixth man."

"Who?" someone asked.

"This was a six-man operation. I'm not counting the SAVAK agents, who were bribed for information and who surely had some kind of cut on the treasure. I don't count the Russians, who had their own reasons for signing up, or Archie Wick's crewmen, who were little more than hired thugs. Six men. All of them dead except one."

"Who?" asked someone else.

"Who?" Duggan demanded.

"Look around, Captain. He's one of these men."

By now, all of them were looking around. When they looked back at Murdock he saw the doubt in their faces. He was the outsider. They were silently closing ranks.

"A lot of this is classified; I may know something I'm not supposed to tell. But all of you know about the *Seawind*. You know that six Navy crewmen survived the accident between that submarine and the freighter *Batavia*. One of these men was later assigned to Admiral Reinholt's staff. From there he arranged for assignments for his friends. He got one put in charge of a Navy medical research facility within a few hundred miles of the accident. When they decided to hijack the *Alaska* as a quick diversion, the *Alaska*'s regular Blue Team engineering officer came down sick—thanks to a potion from the doctor, no doubt—and their engineer took his place. The big hijacker was a former torpedoman, and Archibald Wick was a Navy diver. That's five of the six men who survived the *Seawind* accident.''

"Who's the sixth man?" asked Duggan.

"A diver."

Mac spoke up. "You're saying it's one of us?"

"Uh-huh. Cassidy drowned. My brother Drew killed the torpedoman. The doctor, the engineer, and Archie Wick died when the nuclear device blew up the *Seawind* instead of the *Alaska*. What saved us was the fact that Cassidy knew about the hydrophone we'd planted on the *Alaska*. He'd ordered the Navy helicopter carrying the bomb to home in on that signal. Cassidy knew everything. Everything except the fact that I had moved the hydrophone to the *Seawind*.''

"You knew . . . even back then?" asked Marie.

"No."

"Then why did you move it?"

"I guess I panicked. Why didn't I move it back though, that's the question. When the time came to carry it back I'd seen Archie Wick on the *Seawind*. This whole plan, the hijacking of the *Alaska*, only came about because my father, not Archie Wick, found the *Batavia*. They needed him dead, and they needed to get the Navy ships out of the area for at least a few days. But they knew all along that my father was looking for the *Batavia*. They had to know he might find it first. And when he did find it they knew that, too, even before the Navy found out." Coy held up a fist. "They had a man on the *Alaska*," he said extending his thumb, "a man on Reinholt's staff," a finger, "a man on the medical team that went out to the *Alaska*," another finger, "a man with the hijackers themselves, and finally"—Coy showed an open hand— "a man who had spent ten years in search of the treasure. That's five of the six men. There was only one base left to be covered. The *Nomad*.''

Captain Duggan could stand it no more. *"Who?"* he growled.

Murdock had made his case. Either they believed him or they didn't.

"His name is Donald Meadows. But he's changed his name since he came to work here. He's a diver. At least he was when he left the Navy—it's safe to assume he still is. He probably hired on with the *Nomad* soon after Murdock Salvage showed an interest in recovering the *Batavia* cargo. Does that narrow it down any, boys?"

The six divers, not including Marie, were looking at one another, mentally running down dates and events.

"This ought to help. This sixth man, whoever he is, he got word to Cassidy about the hydrophone we'd planted on the *Alaska*. Sometime after I went down that day, he had to use the radio, either on the *Enchantress* or here on the *Nomad*. Babbit? You're in charge of the transmitter on this ship."

Babbit Cook was nodding his head slowly, looking at none of the others. He knew which one.

But he didn't say.

"And one more thing. Admiral Reinholt?"

"Yes?"

"Donald Meadows got a medical discharge immediately after the *Seawind* sinking. What was the reason?"

Reinholt cleared his throat. "He was the last man out of the *Seawind*, according to the story they told us. He'd come out too fast and too deep. His eardrums ruptured. And never healed. From that day on the man was stone deaf."

Emmott wasn't looking at Reinholt, so he couldn't have caught what the admiral had said. But he must have known. When first Mac and then the others turned to him, one after another, he knew.

He stared off into space for only a moment before his head fell into his hands.

"Well, I'll be damned," said Gandy.

"What'll we do with 'im?"

A number of the hands and divers had formed a circle around Emmott.

Mac growled, "Let's take a sail out into the channel. It'll be dark in a few minutes. We can wrap a chain around his neck and see if it'll float."

"No!"

Murdock crossed to them and pushed his way inside the circle. "Why do you think I brought Admiral Reinholt here? Emmott's in his custody now."

"You'd turn him over to the Navy?"

"It's their investigation. They'll hold him for whatever court has jurisdiction. That's the law."

"But he killed your father!" said Mac.

"I know what he did. But I'm a cop. We're turning him over to Reinholt. You're not questioning me again, are you, Mac?"

For a moment even Mac himself wasn't sure. Then the diver chuckled. "No," he said, "no, I guess I'm not."


As a matter of fact, Mac drove Admiral Reinholt to Security Police headquarters. Emmott was pinched between Sushi and Gandy in the backseat of the jeep. Never was a murderer better guarded.

Now Coy found himself standing in the bows again, watching the incandescent bonfires of the harbor mock the starlit sky—dock lights, buoy lights, running lights of passing ships, and riding lights of ships at anchor.

"What are you thinking about out here, Coy?"

Marie was standing not a yard away, forearms resting on the rail, following his gaze across the harbor. As always, she looked sleek, streamlined, almost like a creature of the sea. Exotic, he thought, but tonight she didn't look quite so unapproachable.

"This harbor," he said, "looks smaller than the last time I stood here."

"Yes. The sea is like that, it shrinks things. People,

too. Of course, sometimes—not very often, but some-times—it makes people bigger." She smiled, and paused to take a breath. "Coy?"

"Yeah?"

"What are you planning to do?"

"Do?"

"Are you going or staying?"

"He's staying."

Murdock whirled around. Pad Duggan was resting his elbows on the rail, not ten yards away on the other side of the bow.

"Why should I stay?" Murdock called back, "I have a job in Wichita."

"You have a job here," said Marie.

"Do I?"

"Of course. The *Seawind.*"

"What's that to me?"

"It's a wreck. Somebody's got to salvage the pieces. Reinholt owes you a favor, doesn't he? You could get the Navy contract like that." She snapped her fingers.

"You don't need me."

"You know where it went down, don't you?"

"Pretty close, yeah."

"And you went aboard her, didn't you? You know where the treasure is located?"

"Sure."

"Well? That information is very valuable on a salvage job. You could be a big help."

"And that's why you want me to stay?"

"She's crazy about you," growled Duggan. "That's why she wants you to stay."

"Pad!"

"You're both a couple of fools. Marie, for the love of Mike, why don't you say what you're thinking."

Marie acted hurt but she wasn't. She leaned in very close to Coy and whispered in his ear. *"Tu peut avaler la mer."*

"What's that—ow! my ribs, careful—what's that mean?"

"You can swallow the sea."

Even in the darkness he could see that she was blushing. For a French girl, Marie made an unaccomplished flirt.

"That's not what I want to hear."

"What then?"

"Any fool can gulp salt water. Why me? Why not somebody else?"

"I don't want somebody else. Not anybody else."

"I'd like to hear you say it."

"All right. I want you, Coy Murdock. You're the only some*body* I care about. You're any*body* and every*body* that I ever want. No*body* but you will do. Is that what you wanted to hear?"

"Yes!" Coy Murdock turned to Duggan and smiled hugely. "Did you hear that, Captain? She called me 'buddy.' Ow! Hey, watch those ribs, darlin'!"

Stephen E. Forbes

## ABOUT THE AUTHOR

Stephen K. Forbes was born in Topeka, Kansas, and educated at Tulsa University and the Defense Information School. He has worked as a private investigator, an oilfield roughneck, a martial arts instructor, a parachute jumpmaster and pilot, as well as a newspaper and magazine editor. He currently lives with his wife, Polly, and three sons in Montana. His previous novel, *False Cross*, is also available in a Signet edition.